# Praise for *Faker*

"A funny, charming, and thoroughly entertaining debut. I couldn't put it down!"

—Samantha Young, *New York Times* bestselling author of *Fight or Flight*

"A fresh, sweet, and funny story about how the people we think we know can surprise us in the sexiest way. Full of swoony kisses and heartfelt honesty, *Faker* is like a warm, reassuring hug."

—Lyssa Kay Adams, author of *The Bromance Book Club*

"I loved every page of Smith's wonderful debut! The romance was sweet and heartwarming, but it was Smith's ability to write a main character who embraces all of her power that had me cheering throughout this book."

—Alexa Martin, author of *Fumbled*

"Written with insight and humor, Sarah Smith's *Faker* is a charming, feminist, and diverse romance that will have you hooked until the very last page."

—Sonya Lalli, author of *The Matchmaker's List*

"A sweet, slow-burn romance between rival coworkers at a power tool company makes for a promising debut."

—*Kirkus Reviews*

"Smith brings the heat in more ways than one in this enemies-to-friends-to-lovers story with a splash of humor. . . . Perfect for fans of Tessa Bailey and Christina Lauren."

—*Booklist*

TITLES BY SARAH SMITH

*Faker*

*Simmer Down*

# Simmer Down

SARAH SMITH

JOVE
NEW YORK

A JOVE BOOK
Published by Berkley
An imprint of Penguin Random House LLC
penguinrandomhouse.com

Library of Congress Cataloging-in-Publication Data

Names: Smith, Sarah, 1985- author.
Title: Simmer down / Sarah Smith.
Description: First edition. | New York: Jove, 2020.
Identifiers: LCCN 2020003766 (print) | LCCN 2020003767 (ebook) |
ISBN 9781984805447 (trade paperback) | ISBN 9781984805454 (ebook)
Subjects: GSAFD: Love stories. | Humorous fiction.
Classification: LCC PS3619.M59298 S56 2020 (print) |
LCC PS3619.M59298 (ebook) | DDC 813/.6—dc23
LC record available at https://lccn.loc.gov/2020003766
LC ebook record available at https://lccn.loc.gov/2020003767

First Edition: October 2020

Printed in the United States of America
1 3 5 7 9 10 8 6 4 2

Cover art and design by Vikki Chu
Book design by Elke Sigal

For Alex.
You are the best book boyfriend
inspiration I could ask for.

And for you, Mom.
You would have liked this.

# Chapter 1

Ocean air has a funny effect on me. Maybe it's the salt.

I inhale while driving along the lone main road in southern Maui. The briny moisture hits my nostrils, coating the back of my throat and lungs. I wince at the slight burn. A handful of breaths and I wonder just how close I am to reaching my daily allotment of sodium. Leave it to a food truck owner to view everything around me—including oxygen—in terms of food.

But that's how all-consuming food truck life is. It's my work, my thoughts, the air I breathe. It seeps into everything. I've only been doing this a year, but that's one of the first things I've learned.

I shove aside the thoughts of saline air. Instead I run through my mental checklist like I do every morning while navigating the slow-moving traffic to my parking spot near Makena Beach, one of the most popular tourist spots on Maui.

Chicken *adobo* wings are chilling in the fridge. Check.

So are the papaya salad and fruit salad. Check.

*Pansit* is freshly made as of this morning and ready to dish up. Check.

A fresh batch of vegetable oil sits in the fryer, ready to heat. Check.

Waiting for the oil to warm should give me just enough time to prep everything for the day. Check.

For a split second I'm smiling, satisfied at the menu I've put together for today with a shoestring budget and limited supplies. Everything's ready to go. The garnishes, the utensils, the napkins, the whiteboard with today's menu written on it. Check, check, check, and . . . damn it.

I groan while gripping the steering wheel. I forgot the menu board at the commercial kitchen where I prep the food every morning. Again. I sigh, my cheeks on fire when I think about what an amateur mistake I just made. That means I'll have to recite the daily specials and prices in addition to the standard menu items to every customer who comes to the window to order, an annoying and unprofessional act.

I shake my head, disappointed that I've tainted the workday before it's even started. It's only marginally worse than my typical mess-up with the menu board. I wince when I remember how I almost always forget to display it until after sliding open the window, which signals that I'm open for business. And when I remember it, I spin around, usually knock over a rogue sauce bottle or metal bowl, scurry out of the truck, prop it up at the front, and run back inside. That's when I typically trip up the stairs while customers gawk. It's like the cherry on top of a hot mess sundae, a dead giveaway that despite all my planning and all my checklists, despite my year of hard work, long hours, and on-the-job learning, I don't belong in this food truck world.

I slouch in the driver's seat as I begin to deflate. No other food truck I've been around seems to struggle with the basics like I do. A whole new checklist slides to the front of my mind. My very own life checklist that I never, ever thought I'd have.

I'm twenty-nine years old and struggling to make a living in the most popular tourist destination in the Pacific Ocean. Check.

I started a food truck business with zero food truck experience. Check.

I mistakenly thought that all my years working in high-end restaurants would be all the prep I needed to run a food truck. Check.

I share a condo in Kihei with my mom—a condo that was meant to be my parents' retirement haven. Check.

A familiar sinking feeling hits, one I haven't felt in weeks. It's a heavy dose of doubt mixed with good old-fashioned insecurity, reminding me just how out of my element I am.

Another lesson I've learned? Life doesn't always care what you have planned. Sometimes it pulls the rug out from under you and takes one of your parents with it, leaving you and your only living parent under a mountain of medical debt, your savings ravaged, and with zero viable options on how to dig your way out. So you and your mom pick up where she and your dad left off. You take the used food truck your dad bought because it was his and your mom's dream to run their own food truck in Maui during their retirement. You put the only professional skills you honed—your cooking and restaurant skills—into fulfilling your dad's last wish. You put your heart and soul into that food truck, cross your fingers, and hope for the best.

I silently recite my other checklist, the one I mentally skim in my head each day, whenever I need a reminder of why I'm here and why all the struggle is worth it. It's the one checklist I'm eternally grateful for.

My mom is alive. Check.

I get to see her every day. Check.

Even when I mess up, I'm fulfilling the promise I made to my dad. Check.

I focus, crossing my fingers around my grip on the steering wheel, hoping for a good day. I hope I sell out during today's lunch service. I hope that weird grinding noise that emanates from this rickety truck is just a fluke, and not a sign that I need to replace the brake pads, something I can't afford. And I hope the gas in the tank is enough to last me until the end of the week, because I can't afford that either.

With every new concern that hits this mental checklist, worry bleeds into my gratitude. I sigh, gazing out my window at endless palm trees and sand, homing in on the soothing crash of the waves. At least I can count on the stunning beauty of Maui to put me in a pleasant mood most days. My heartbeat slows, my jaw relaxes, and my hands loosen around the steering wheel.

Soon the road transitions from smooth pavement to pockmarked concrete. I pull into that perfect semicircle of dirt overlooking the ocean that I just happened to stumble upon back in December. Once again, I'm grateful. For the last three months, this has been Tiva's Filipina Kusina's go-to parking spot. Because of that, we have a steady flow of customers from Big Beach, which means a reliable income most days. Which means we're that much closer to being out of the hole.

As I turn off the engine, I fix my gaze on an unfamiliar silver food truck situated right next to where I normally park. I climb out and walk over, zeroing in on the Union Jack flag decal that rests on the left side of the window. Over the window reads "Hungry Chaps" in bold black letters. On the right side of the window is a cartoon image of a plate of fish-and-chips and some half-moon-shaped pastry.

I sigh. Hungry Chaps must be a new addition to the island food truck circle. They must not be aware of the unofficial policy of not encroaching on another truck's territory. I practice a smile and stroll to the closed window of the truck. It's my turn to offer a friendly welcome and a polite explanation of Maui's unspoken food truck etiquette to this newcomer, just as the established food trucks did for Mom and me when we first started. The rules are simple: no parking in spaces that other trucks have occupied long term, and no parking too close to another truck unless you have their permission.

Living on an island makes competition fiercer—there's only so much space to begin with. When we first started out, we couldn't find regular parking and had to drive all over the island from open spot to open spot. It was impossible to build a customer base that way, never having a consistent location where people could easily find us. It meant months of unsteady income, which meant we were barely breaking even.

I knock on the cloudy glass window. A lightly tanned face pops up from behind the counter. The window is so smeared that I can barely make out the person.

"Hi there! Do you have a sec?" I say.

"Absolutely! Just a moment," an English-accented male voice answers. I smile. His accent sounds a lot like that of my uncle, who lives in London with my auntie Nora. I wonder if this guy's from London too.

A thud sound and the clang of metal dishes crashing to the floor echo from inside the truck. Out of the corner of my eye, I see a man exit from the back.

He strolls up to me, kicking up clouds of dirt with his heavy steps. He's a tall, sun-kissed drink of water with honey-hued hair cropped close to his scalp and a few days' worth of dark blond scruff on his cheeks. I tilt my head back to get a proper look at his face.

That's a new one. I'm nearly five feet ten inches, and my neck is perpetually sore from having to peer down at people. But this guy has to be pushing six feet three inches, maybe even six four.

He looks familiar, even though I know for sure I've never seen him before. Probably because he looks like a hybrid of Michael Fassbender and Zac Efron. In other words, impossibly good-looking.

He flashes a smile at me, and I promptly forget what I was going to say. Instead I respond with what I assume is one of the dopiest grins I've ever beamed at another human being.

"So nice to finally meet you," he says.

"Oh, um, thanks," I stammer, thrown off at how friendly he is to me, a complete stranger.

When he blinks, it's like I've been dazzled by the shiniest peridot gem. His eyes boast the most perfect shade of hazel green I've ever seen. But it's more than just the color leaving me tongue-tied. There's a genuine kindness behind them I don't often see when I make eye contact with someone I don't know. The way he stares catches me completely off guard, like I'm the only thing worth looking at in the surrounding area. It's impressive, considering the landscape is the very definition of breathtaking with the nearby lush green hills, cloudless blue skies, and multitude of palm trees. Not even the expansive lava field across the road, which appears practically endless as it stretches all the way to the horizon, seems to capture this guy's attention. Even I stop to gawk at it at least once a day.

I let my gaze linger on his eyes a second longer than what is considered polite. My stomach flips. I could fall damn hard for eyes like that.

For a fleeting moment, the Neanderthal part of my brain takes over. An image of me under him appears. Those hazel eyes pinning me, those thick lips stretched in a smile. A slight shake of my head erases the decidedly dirty thought like the drawing on an Etch A

Sketch. What in the world is wrong with me? A friendly greeting from a handsome man shouldn't send me into an X-rated daytime fantasy. I silently scold myself. This is apparently what eighteen months of self-imposed celibacy will do to a woman.

He sticks his hand out and I shake it, appreciating the firm yet gentle gripping method he employs. I'm so used to men offering weak handshakes that feel like a dead fish in my hand. But I dig this guy's style. He doesn't automatically assume I'm too weak to make his male acquaintance.

When he lets go of my hand, he looks back at his truck. "Apologies, I didn't think you were coming for another hour."

"What do you mean?"

He points his thumb at his truck. "It's all ready for you. Just be careful when you walk in because I tripped and knocked over a few metal bowls on the way out here." He runs a hand through his hair. "Afraid I'm still getting used to navigating my tall self within the confines of a van. Sorry, I mean 'truck.'" He holds a hand up. "I can assure you, everything is up to code."

I squint up at him, thoroughly confused. "That's great, but why are you telling me all this?"

"Well, I thought you'd like to know. You're the health inspector after all."

"Oh . . . no, I'm . . . I run a food truck."

I point to my truck, which is parked behind his. He pivots his frown to it, narrowing his stare, like he's just now noticing the giant food truck parked nearby.

"You're not the health inspector?"

I shake my head, hoping the movement comes off as good-natured and not dismissive. "Sorry, I'm not."

A long moment of silence passes where he takes another long look between me and Tiva's truck. I count to ten before the silence starts to turn awkward. New guy is clearly confused. Best to use a gentle, cheery approach when I inform him of the unofficial rules he's breaking.

I clear my throat. "I know this is probably awkward timing, but, um, you're not actually supposed to park here."

He whips his head around to me. A glare replaces his confused frown from before, and it is downright lethal. My mouth goes dry. It's a struggle just to swallow.

Silently, I remind myself that he's the newbie. He's just confused, and some people get annoyed when they're confused. I just need to explain myself, and then he'll understand. I power through the awkwardness permeating the air between us.

"See, I've had this spot for the past several months, and it's kind of an unspoken rule on Maui that food trucks don't park this close to each other if they're not in a parking lot or at an event. And seeing as I was technically here first—"

He turns around and walks back into his truck before I can finish speaking. My jaw hangs open in the salty ocean breeze. Did he seriously just do that?

I stand for several seconds, arms dangling at my sides, processing the moment. Maybe he's embarrassed and needs a bit of time before he moves his truck. I can certainly understand. I've made plenty of mortifying mistakes while learning the food truck ropes. This morning's menu mishap is small beans compared to the time I lost the credit card reader and could only take cash for a handful of days, or the time I mistakenly filled the sweet chili sauce bottles with sriracha.

I fold my arms across my chest, waiting for the engine to fire up. But nothing happens. Just more clanking sounds from the inside of his truck. I check my watch and see that a full minute has passed since he walked away from me. The longer I stand out there alone, the clearer it becomes. That midsentence exit wasn't embarrassment; it was a dismissal—of me. He's not going anywhere.

Heat makes its way from my cheeks all the way down to my chest. The whole time I was standing here, trying to be nice, he was disregarding me. I march up to the truck and pound on the cloudy glass window.

"Can you please move your truck?" I ask.

I catch his silhouette walking back and forth inside the truck, blatantly ignoring me. Steam levels my insides. What the ever-loving hell is this guy's problem?

I pound on the window with both hands. Politeness isn't working. It seems this newbie is in need of a harsher welcome. "Hey! Listen, you're in my spot."

This time when he walks out of the truck to meet me, he plants himself a foot away, resuming that killer glare from minutes ago.

"Maybe you couldn't tell by the way I've been ignoring you, but I don't care what you have to say," he says.

His irritated tone combined with the melodic English accent throw me off-kilter. I didn't expect to be arguing with a hot James Bond soundalike today, and it's messing with my head.

"Um, what?" I stammer.

"Oh, bloody hell. Do you really need me to explain? I'm not moving."

"Excuse me?" My voice hits that shrill register whenever I'm shocked and pissed at once.

"For fuck's sake," he mutters, glancing up at the sky. "I don't have time for this."

"Well, make time." My hard tone verges on a bark. "You're new here, right? I'll explain. I'm Nikki DiMarco. I run this food truck, Tiva's Filipina Kusina, with my mom, Tiva."

I almost mention that it's her day off, but I catch myself. Impossibly hot dickhead probably doesn't care about the details. Pursing my lips, I let the momentary embarrassment wash over me.

He deepens his scowl, and I'm jolted back to our confrontation. I point behind me to the rusty white food truck bearing Mom's name in bold red letters. Underneath the text is an artist's rendering of a plate of noodles and *lumpia*. He glances briefly at my truck, then back at me.

"Like I was trying to say before, you're not supposed to park right next to a competing food truck," I say. "It's kind of an unspoken rule here."

It's a struggle to keep my voice steady, but I want to be the calm, rational counter to this guy's angry petulance.

Crossing his arms, he shrugs. "Let *me* explain something. I'm Callum James, and I don't care. I'm staying right here."

Those arresting hazel-green eyes peer down at me. Funny, I used to think of green as a cheerful, enlivening color before this stranger turned hostile. Now green will forever be associated with "obnoxious" and "jerkoff."

"I don't know who the hell you think you are, but what you're doing isn't cool. At all," I say.

He smirks. The nerve of this jackass.

"Is something funny?" I say through gritted teeth.

He shrugs, letting his hands fall to his hips. Even through the loose-fitting T-shirt he's wearing, I can tell this prick is cut. It's obvious from his thickly muscled arms that are covered with ropelike veins, from the broad spread of his shoulders.

It's a quick second before that smirk widens to a smug smile. " 'Isn't cool at all?' Did you honestly say that?"

The rough, guttural register of his voice sends a sheet of goose bumps across my skin. Soft yet lethal. Like a bad guy in an action movie whispering threats to the main character who's tied to a chair.

He chuckles before letting his gaze fall along the length of my body. Is he seriously checking me out right now? A deep, seconds-long inhale and exhale is the only way I can cope.

*I will not punch this douchebag in the face.*

*I will not punch this douchebag in the face.*

I chant the silent mantra in my head while gritting my teeth.

"Hey," I bark. "Are you kidding me? Eyes up here."

His shoulders jolt slightly at my demand. At least he has the decency to look embarrassed. But a beat later it melts from his face, leaving behind a steely frown. He takes a single step forward, leaning his head down toward me. "Listen, petal. I don't care one bit if you think this is 'uncool.' "

When he makes air quotes with both hands as he says "uncool," I swallow back fire. The bastard called me "*petal.*" Where the hell is this guy from, *Downton Abbey*? Who the hell calls anyone petal anymore?

I open my mouth to unleash a tirade of expletives and "how dare you," but he cuts me off.

"I have just as much right to park here as you do. I'm not doing anything illegal, and I'm not moving. Get over it."

He spins around and saunters behind his food truck, leaving me standing there with my jaw on the ground, my fists clenched, and nothing to say.

How the hell did this happen? How was this guy able to shift from charming stranger one minute to insufferable bastard the next? How did he just destroy years of island food truck etiquette in minutes? How did a complete stranger leave me a mess of frustration and outrage?

The window of his truck slides open, and a man with a younger, friendlier version of the hostile stranger's face sticks his head out.

"Are you all right?" he asks in that same melodic English accent, his own hazel-green eyes glistening with concern.

At least this one's polite. I slap my hands on the metal countertop lining the window. His shoulders jerk up. "I'd like to speak with that ball of sunshine you work with."

His eyebrows jump up his forehead. "Um . . ." He twists his head back. "Oi, Callum!"

Callum walks up to the window, still sporting that sour, unfriendly expression on his face. Does this guy suck on lemon wedges before engaging other human beings?

When I wag my finger up at him, he doesn't even blink. The polite one does though before flashing him a panicked look.

"You want to defy local food truck etiquette by being a complete asshole? Fine."

The words punch out in a firm, steady tone. My fuck-off tone. Callum's disrespectful attitude is the last straw in my already shit-tastic morning—in my already shit-tastic life. I can't take one more thing working against me right now. So I won't.

"From this moment on, I'm going to make your life a living hell." I tilt my head to the side. "Deal with it."

In the split second after I speak, all I see are his eyes. Strangely, they still read kind, and it's enough to make me question for the briefest moment if I've been too harsh. But his brow furrows, his nostrils flare, and his mouth twists into the tightest purse I've ever seen. Never mind. If he were truly kind, he wouldn't have met my politeness with outright dickishness. I spin around and march back to my truck.

"Bloody hell, what did you say to her?" the polite one asks as I walk the six feet back to the other side of the clearing.

The only tidbit I hear before I'm back in my truck is Callum barking the name Finn. Judging by their resemblance, I'm guessing they're brothers. And Callum would do well to listen to his little brother Finn next time, as it might keep him out of trouble. Too late now though.

I tie on my apron and start prepping for lunch. Sunlight shines through the open window, illuminating the blade of my knife as I chop heads of cabbage. The adrenaline from our fiery exchange is a surprise source of energy. I shred the whole tray in half the time it usually takes.

All he had to do was show one ounce of courtesy. But no. He wanted to start a war. With a total stranger who was perfectly polite to him until he played dirty. A total stranger who's been through hell this past year and a half, who is tired of ducking from the constant stream of curveballs life chucks at her.

As of today, I'm done ducking. I'm fighting back.

He wants a war? It is motherfucking on.

# Chapter 2

War isn't always blood and guts, explosions and air strikes. Sometimes it's unspoken strategy, a sneak attack your enemy doesn't even notice. Sometimes it's quiet as a mouse, and by the time the other side even realizes they've been infiltrated, it's too late. The damage is done.

The makeshift cardboard sign I've propped against the far end of Hungry Chaps' food truck is exactly that: quiet, unsuspecting carnage. Day two of Tiva's Filipina Kusina versus Hungry Chaps, and my side's victorious already.

Mom and I enjoyed a steady lunch rush from 10 a.m. to almost 1 p.m., while Callum and his food truck only had a couple dozen in that same chunk of time—and it's all my doing.

I stick my head out of the window to call out another order. When I hand the customer their food, I sneak a seconds-long peek at my enemy food truck just feet away. The sign I threw together this morning is holding up well.

*"Mediocre Imperialist Cuisine!"*

The giant black letters practically shout from the ragged chunk of cardboard. They're probably visible from across the nearby lava field.

Mrs. Tokushige, Mom's best friend and our most loyal customer, mutters a thank-you when she comes to pick up her order of chicken *adobo* wings, all the while squinting at the sign.

"So strange they would think that sign would be good for business." She tucks a loose chunk of her thick jet-black hair behind her ear.

I bite my lip to keep from chuckling. I shrug and tell her, "*Bon appétit*," when I hand her the food. "Thank you again for letting us use your commercial kitchen, Mrs. Tokushige. You've helped us so much."

She flashes a kind smile before dipping her finger in the soy sauce–vinegar mixture of the *adobo* and tasting it. She lets out a satisfied hum. "Of course, hon. Anything for you and your mom."

She pats my hand, and I'm grateful again. Mrs. Tokushige is a widowed property owner who Mom got chummy with after first moving to Maui. They even belong to the same book club and mahjong club. I'm grateful to know her. Not only has she been a generous and supportive friend after we lost Dad, but she's been invaluable to our food truck, letting us use her commercial kitchen, which is right next to our condo, at a deep discount. I don't know if we would have made it had we been forced to pay regular prices to rent space.

"It's always open for you and your mom, whenever you want it," she says. "You're practically family."

She tiptoes up and smiles at Mom through the window. "Hi, Tiva! Smells yummy in there! And this *adobo* sauce, my goodness. Perfectly tangy and salty. I'll never get tired of it."

Mom beams. "Oh, Joan. You're sweet. Thank you."

Their conversation carries on while I inwardly gloat about my sneaky actions from this morning. It was petty as hell for me to arrive early to scrawl that sign. It was also petty to strategically place it at the perfect angle: leaning on the back tire of the Hungry Chaps food truck, facing away from the window and door. Callum and Finn can't see it from inside their truck, but customers get a full, unobscured view.

I catch a glimpse of Callum. He's sporting that same scowl he blinded me with yesterday. Not once does he let up, even when taking customers' food orders. I wonder if anyone has ever told him that acting pleasant and smiling at the patrons is necessary in the food service industry.

I duck back inside. "How many *lumpia* are left, Mom?"

She drops another order into the fryer. "We'll be out in an hour probably, if orders keep up."

I pat her shoulder, and she smiles. She and I have the exact same facial features: dark eyes, arched eyebrows, narrow button noses, high cheekbones. Even our smiles are the same. Our full mouths stretch across our faces in a straight line instead of curving up like most other people's. It's like gazing into a mirror of what I'll look like in thirtyish years if I opt for a bob hairstyle and maintain an excellent skin care regimen. Considering all the emotional and financial stress she's been through this past year, she's wearing it like a champ. She's a stunning mature woman.

She pats my lower back. "Don't slouch, *anak*. It's bad for you."

I'm a good eight inches taller than her thanks to my dad's genes. Emotion lodges in my throat, and I have to swallow. It's the one physical trait of his I have. I'd give anything for one of his burly bear hugs right now, the kind where I'm engulfed entirely in his broad back and arms, the kind that made me feel like a dainty little kid even in my twenties. I wonder what he would think if he could see us, his wife and his only child, trying to carve a place for themselves in the Maui food truck scene.

I wipe away the thought and turn to help the next customer in line, who orders a basket of *lumpia*.

"They love Tiva's *lumpia*." I flash Mom a thumbs-up. "Best on the island."

It's true. This egg roll–like Filipino dish isn't a unique dish for Maui, not with the island's strong Southeast Asian population. But Mom's mixture of finely ground pork with cabbage, carrots, rice noodle, and secret spice blend is a hit with everyone who orders them.

She glances down at a handful of empty paper trays on the counter, waiting to be filled. "I don't know about that. Just trying my best." She shrugs before brushing away a chunk of her hair that's come loose from her pinned-back style. Her deep brown eyes turn sad. "Now that we have this new competition close by, I have to try harder."

I un-grit my teeth and flash her what I hope is a reassuring smile. When I broke the news about the obnoxious new food truck business encroaching on our territory, her anxiety was immediate. I could see it in her frown, in the way her gaze immediately fell to the floor when I told her.

"People have been driving from all the way across the island to try our food," I tell her. "We'll be just fine."

Judging by the speedy way she turns back to the fryer without making eye contact, she's not convinced. And the truth is, as much as I'm willing to wage war on our new competition, I'm not certain we'll survive either.

An angry, English-accented bark causes us both to twist our heads in the direction of the Hungry Chaps food truck.

"What the hell are you talking about?" Callum booms.

When I stick my head out of the window, I see him stomping out of his truck in the direction of the cardboard sign.

"Mom, take over orders for a bit, okay? I'll be right back."

I zoom out of the truck and head straight for Callum, whispering apologies as I bump into people waiting in line to order. By the time I make it to Callum, he's red-faced, clutching the sign in one hand. The other one he points at me.

"You," he growls. "This is why we've had shit for business this entire day."

I march up to him until we're maybe a foot apart. He drops his hand; I rest mine on my hips and lean toward him.

"That's part of the initiation at this spot," I snarl back. "Deal with it."

His chest heaves, his mouth splits open, and a gust of hot breath shoots out. I swear, this guy is part dragon with his prickly personality and the rough way he introduces oxygen into his body.

"Stop saying that."

"Make me."

The unblinking stare he maintains would have been all kinds of intimidating yesterday when I barely knew him. Not today though. Today it emboldens me, because I know exactly what I'm dealing with.

"Imperialist cuisine?" His grunt is dialed back in volume, but not in intensity. His tone is a dare, a call to my bluff. Combined with his stance and body language, it's obvious what he wants me to do. Back off. Apologize.

Hell if I'm doing any of that. If a pissing match is what he wants, that's exactly what I'll give him.

"Pretty appropriate, don't you think?" My tone is a sarcastic kind of cheery. "Here you are, this big, bad, intimidating English jerk encroaching on territory where you're not welcome. That's the very definition of imperialist, wouldn't you agree?"

Once more his chest heaves. He tosses the sign aside. "That's some nerve you've got posting a sign like that."

"And that's some nerve *you've* got setting up shop when it's clearly against established etiquette."

It's a struggle to keep my voice below a yell when all I'm aching to do is scream at this jerk for his blatant disregard for rules.

"Like I said yesterday, there are no laws governing where we park."

Hot air pushes against my lungs. "And there are no rules governing the kind of signs you can post either."

"That's bollocks and you know it. You encroached on our space the minute you set that sign on our truck."

"Oh, don't give me some holier-than-thou lecture on encroachment. What you're doing—parking your food truck right next to ours—is the perfect example of encroachment."

He shakes his head, opens his mouth, then bites down immediately. Muscles press against the sharpest jawline I've ever seen. It matches his thorny personality perfectly.

"Oi, Callum!" Finn yells.

When I look up, I almost gasp. Two dozen customers crowd around us, most of them holding their phones up, recording our spat.

I mutter, "Fuck," under my breath at the same moment that Callum mutters, "Bloody hell."

Finn is perched with his head hanging out the food truck window, panic in his eyes. He motions for Callum to come back to the truck. Callum gives me one last glare before spinning around and stomping over to Finn.

I scurry back to my food truck as the crowd disperses, still aiming their phones at me. The anger from my argument has morphed into full-fledged embarrassment. I'm about to go viral and become the laughingstock of Maui's food truck scene. Freaking fantastic.

Mom greets me with her hands on her hips, her brow crinkled into a frown. "What in the world was all that about?"

I sigh and toss another batch of *lumpia* in the fryer. "I'll tell you later."

My public spat-gone-viral with Callum is a distant memory two weeks later. That's because almost every day since then, we've been bickering and pranking each other nonstop. The day after I posted my sign on the Hungry Chaps truck, Callum posted his own that said, "*Tiva's staff has been stricken with leprosy! Eat at your own risk!*" A taste of my own medicine, I suppose. That scared off customers for a good two hours until I found the sign, tore it apart, then gave onlookers a panicked explanation that it wasn't true. And then I promptly stomped to the Hungry Chaps truck and bitched out Callum. A few days later I got him back by letting the air out of one of the back tires. We of course had it out in front of every customer and onlooker in the vicinity. And of course it ended up trending on Instagram, Twitter, and Facebook.

You'd think customers would be driven away by our immature antics. Not so. In fact, business is booming. Every day both Hungry Chaps and Tiva's have lines snaking all the way out to the road. I can tell by the look in people's eyes, how they stare between our trucks as they order and eat, that they live to watch Callum and me lose it on each other. Drama has become our top-selling menu item, it seems.

I even worked up the nerve to watch one of our public spats posted online. I made it exactly ten seconds before pausing it. Hearing my shrill tone of voice, spotting that bulging vein in my neck when I wagged my finger at Callum, the unhinged look in my eyes . . . it was all a whole new level of cringeworthy.

As mortified as I am, I'm grateful for the uptick in business. This week we earned more than we have any other week prior. And recently, we've had a small crowd of customers milling around our trucks, waiting for us to open. So I guess there is an upside to all this ugliness.

My cell phone rings, and Mrs. Tokushige's name flashes across the screen. I put her on speaker.

"Good morning, Mrs. Tokushige."

"Good morning, hon!" she says in her patented cheery tone. "Sorry to ask on such short notice, but could you whip up some food for mahjong tonight? It's my turn to host, and I don't feel like cooking."

I chuckle softly to myself. Whenever Mrs. Tokushige hosts her friend group's mahjong game night, she places a carryout order from my food truck the morning of, even though she always promises to cook for them.

"I'll pay extra to make sure we get *lumpia*. I know how quickly it sells out," Mrs. Tokushige says.

"No need to pay extra. I'll make sure you have some." It's the least I can do for how generous she's been to us.

"Oh, and can you tell your mom we're doing it at seven tonight instead of six? Sally Nida has to watch her grandson late today."

The road turns bumpy and I slow down. "No problem at all."

"Such a good daughter you are, giving her the day off so she can rest."

If only Mrs. Tokushige knew that I practically have to order Mom to stay home. She'd work twelve-hour days every day if she had her way. But she needs at least one or two days of rest a week to do low-stress activities, like going for walks, playing cards, and reading. Since Dad passed away, she's thrown herself into working at the food truck with me, which is good. It's helpful for her to stay occupied, to have a focus other than missing him and worrying about money. But pacing herself is vital. I refuse to lose her to exhaustion after the horror of losing Dad.

I swallow back the lump in my throat. "I can handle it alone just fine. You know how she is. She'll push herself to exhaustion if I don't watch her. Can't have that."

"I'm sure she could use some time away after all that's happening with that new food truck," Mrs. Tokushige says. "The nerve of those boys to park next to you like that. And to argue with you all the time."

I pull into the clearing on Makena Road and park right next to the Hungry Chaps truck. Already, a couple dozen people mill around the area. I bite back a grin, the excitement coursing within me. I've never had a crowd of customers waiting to eat my food before I even opened for the day.

"You should report them to the local authorities," Mrs. Tokushige says, her voice booming with conviction through the speakerphone. "They shouldn't get away with the trouble they're causing you."

The thought's tempting, but I can't. As much as it pains me to admit, Callum is right. It's not illegal for him to park his truck next to mine, no matter how much I hate it. He's violated zero laws or policies. Even if I gave in and complained about him, it would be more trouble than it's worth. Food trucks on Maui are required by law to move every thirty minutes, but most don't to keep a steady business stream during the day. If I tattle on Callum, it could cause authorities to crack down on other foods trucks, costing them business. Getting back at him isn't worth hurting everyone else.

I politely thank her for the suggestion.

"I've heard the food from those British boys isn't even that great," she says. "I wouldn't know though. I'd never dream of eating there out of respect for you and Tiva."

I smile. "That's very sweet of you, Mrs. Tokushige."

We say good-bye and I put the truck in park. When I step out, I spot a sign posted next to the Hungry Chaps food truck, right next to where we normally park. I park, get out, then scan the text.

*". . . surpasses the daily nutritional guidelines for saturated fat and sodium. Though lumpia, turon, and other fried foods are delicious, they should be consumed in moderation. It is not recommended that you include them as a regular part of your diet."*

Lava pummels through my veins. The bastard posted a phony health warning against the food I serve. I should have seen this coming. Shame on me for underestimating the enemy.

I kick over the sign, then crouch down so I can rip it to pieces. It's a good several seconds before I hear Callum's angry shout.

"What do you think you're doing?"

He darts from the door of his truck to me. We're toe-to-toe once more, staring each other down.

I crumple a chunk in my hand and chuck it at him. It bounces off his impressive pec. "You are so out of line."

He crosses his arms across his broad chest. Smugness dances across the straight line of his mouth. "Nikki, I'm merely giving customers nutritional information about the food they're consuming." The cheerful uptick in his tone sounds almost innocent, as if he isn't trying to ruin my business. "Fried food isn't the best option for a lot of people's diets."

"You serve fried fish-and-chips, you dick!"

A deadpan stare is all he gives me. "We have a grilled fish option."

Throwing my head back, I growl. "You have no right to mess with my business. You have no idea how hard my mom and I have worked to establish ourselves here."

He tilts his head down to me. "And you have no idea how hard my brother and I have worked either. It's ridiculous for you to assume you're the only one around here who's trying to get their business off the ground. You think you have the right to monopolize this area?"

A gravelly throat-clear causes us to twist our heads to the side. Again, we're surrounded by spectators, and again, they film us with their phones. I choke down the urge to scream.

"If I may interject."

The throat-clearer raises his hand. Matteo Roderick from *Matteo Eats Maui* stands at the front of the crowd. He runs the most popular food vlog on the island and gets thousands of views every day. He dines at our food truck weekly, always giving us positive reviews online and on his social media accounts. Tourists visit our food truck often because of him, and for that I have to be grateful. It's why I resist the smart-ass remarks dancing on my tongue when he uses phrases like "flavor profiles" within earshot and when he offers unsolicited advice on how we should adjust our seasonings, why I ignore him even though he loudly chats while filming himself eating. It's why I haven't ripped his sandy-blond man bun from his giant head and tossed it into the ocean.

Matteo lifts an eyebrow. "As much as I love passionate discourse about culinary arts, I don't think this style of conversing is conducive to a pleasant dining experience."

I cross my arms over my chest, hoping it gives me an extra ounce of patience to deal with Matteo's long-winded and patronizing monologue. I notice Callum does the same. Matteo is maybe in his late twenties but talks like a snobby food critic who's approaching retirement age.

"I can only assume you two have heard of the Maui Food Festival coming up in May?" Matteo asks.

Callum and I nod. Everyone—every food truck, every restaurant, every tourist, every local—knows about the Maui Food Festival. It's the unofficial kickoff to summer, with every popular local place participating in it. Any eatery with any hope of making it on the island registers for the festival. Maui restaurants set up booths and food trucks congregate in downtown Lahaina to sell their dishes. People vote online for their favorite. Those that do well are guaranteed a boost in their business for the season, but the winner gets the sweetest prize: ten thousand dollars and a spot in a commercial for the Flavor Network.

"It's only the beginning of March, but you both plan to partake, I assume?"

Again, we nod.

Matteo clasps his hands together, as if he's about to pray. "Then I suggest a bit of friendly competition to settle this obvious dispute you two are having." He gestures to the clear blue ocean in the background. "This is a coveted spot, certainly. Why don't you let your customers decide? Whichever one of you scores the highest at the festival is the winner of this spot. How does that sound?"

Neither of us speaks. All we exchange is an uncertain glance between us before turning back to Matteo.

It's actually a solid idea. A hell of a stressful prospect though. I thought I hit the jackpot when I stumbled upon this open area months ago. I swallow back the urge to state my case, balling my fists at my side instead. I came across it first fair and square, and now I have to fight for it. I don't have a choice though. One steady, even breath and the muscles in my neck loosen from their tension knot. I'm not willing to leave this spot. I'll earn it all over again if I have to. It's absolutely not what I want to do, but our livelihood rides on this.

The crevice between Callum's eyebrow deepens. He almost looks amused. "So this is what it's come to?"

Something soft rests at the edges of his tone. It sounds a lot like hesitation.

"You clearly have no intention of backing off," I say.

"Not a chance in hell." All trace of doubt has left his voice, leaving behind that hard tone I've come to know so well.

"Okay, then," I say.

Matteo closes his eyes and smiles. "Splendid. And the prize is even bigger this year, since last year's winner was disqualified after it was discovered that they were secretly working with a chain restaurant to get free ingredients. Can you believe that? Such blatant cheating." Matteo tsks. "Festival officials are being even stricter about contest rules this year. The winner has to win on their own merits, which means no help from anyone. I hear that if there's even the slightest hint of eateries fraternizing with each other, you could be disqualified. That certainly won't be the case with you two."

Matteo chuckles, clearly pleased at his joke. I turn away to roll my eyes.

"They're taking the money forfeited by the disgraced winner last year and adding it to this year's prize," Matteo says. "That means twenty thousand dollars for the winner. That's really quite something, isn't it?"

Callum and I shoot identical WTF expressions at Matteo. On the inside, I'm pumped. Twenty thousand dollars is a game-changing amount of money. We could fix up our food truck, invest in some new supplies, and put whatever's left over into Mom's savings.

Callum pivots to me and sticks out his hand. "Shall we make it official?"

He wants to shake on it? I nearly scoff, but we have an audience. Best to be sportsmanlike for the cameras for a change.

When I slip my hand in his, there's a jolt. Electricity? Shock? The surprise comfort of skin-to-skin contact with the British hottie who can't stand me? Probably. The feel of Callum's hard, rough, warm hand against mine is a treat. I'm surprised. It's exactly the same firm, respectable grip he employed when he first shook my hand the morning he mistook me for the health inspector. I thought he'd for sure opt for a limp fish or douchey iron grip since our every interaction from that point has been hostile.

In these few seconds though, I'm not shaking the hand of the most disagreeable human being I've ever met. No, this is simply a hand on another hand, a small part of his body on mine. A devastatingly beautiful and cut body that I wish would show me a smidgen of kindness, like I showed him the day we met. Maybe if he had, we could have sorted this out and shared a laugh. My mind wanders some more. There would have been no arguments, no glares, no hurtful words exchanged. In my perfect world scenario, Callum would have agreed to move his truck elsewhere, but not before asking for my number. I would have given him a cute compliment about his accent and told him that my aunt and uncle live in London, which would have further broken the ice. Flirty texting would have most definitely ensued.

And then I catch him giving me *that* look again. That same split-second once-over he gave me the day we met, when we were arguing and I was incensed that he would dare to check me out in such a heated moment. Only this time, it doesn't enrage me. It sets me simmering, on fire in the best way. Like when you finally catch eyes with someone you've been gazing at from afar, and in that one look they give you, you know they want you just as much as you want them.

But then he furrows his brow and it's gone. When he releases me from his grip, my hopeful thoughts drift away with the gusts of salty ocean air. A million dollars says I was mistaken. He wasn't checking me out; he was sizing me up. I bite the inside of my cheek. Shame on me for fantasizing. It's pathetic, especially when the object of my fantasy so blatantly wants to destroy me, and the only thing Callum's dreaming about is taking this prime parking spot from me.

I breathe in, square my shoulders, and look Callum straight in the eye. "Okay, then. Bring it."

# Chapter 3

A pyramid of *lumpia* rests on the counter of our condo's kitchen, right next to the stove. Carefully, I maneuver one from the bottom of the pile and take a bite. It's a burst of all of my favorite flavors: the rich, well-seasoned ground pork, the tender rice noodles, the crispy shredded cabbage and carrots, the even crispier fried flour wrapper holding everything together, and the tangy sweet chili dipping sauce.

"Mom, I think you've done enough experimenting. All of these batches have been delicious."

I dip the other, unbitten end into a small dish of sweet chili sauce.

"You never know what people will want," she says. "Some like it with pork, some like it with chicken, some like it with shrimp."

Our post-work evening has been spent testing out different batches of *lumpia* for the upcoming Maui Food Festival. Ever since I told her we'd be competing to keep our spot on Makena Road, she's been in a food-prepping frenzy. Every night after work for the past week she's spent hours testing out new dishes, tweaking ingredients to get the flavors just right. Yesterday it was adjusting the level of fish sauce in the *pansit*, then attempting to perfect the ratio of rice noodle to meat and vegetables. Today it's coming up with different fillings for *lumpia*.

"Don't forget that batch you made with ground beef and raisins," I say after another bite. "That one was my favorite."

She frowns. "I'm not sure everyone will like the raisins."

"But that's the recipe you and Auntie Nora came up with. She cooked it for Uncle Nigel on their third date, and that was when he said he knew she was the one for him—because he could eat her cooking forever, remember? Customers will love it too."

"Maybe. But Uncle Nigel will eat anything," Mom says with a wave of her hand.

Every time she whips up a batch of this *lumpia*, it always makes me miss them. If only we had the time—and money—to visit them in London.

I finish eating and begin packing the rest of the *lumpia* in a Tupperware container. When I start to put the unused *lumpia* wrappers back in the fridge, she stops me.

"Don't. I'm going to make more."

"Mom," I groan and shove them in anyway.

Suddenly, I'm thirteen years old again and whining because she told me to go clean my room. But now I'm trying to convince her not to exhaust herself in the kitchen to no avail. We already spent two hours at the commercial kitchen this morning prepping food for today's service, then put in eight hours at the food truck. It's pushing almost ten at night, and she's been on her feet all day.

I shouldn't be surprised. She's always been someone who needs to be doing something. She's up at dawn most days, prepping for the day's work. On her days off she power walks and does calisthenics in the living room before most people finish their coffee. Sitting on the couch relaxing is never an option for her. It was one of the things about her that drove my couch-lounging dad crazy. Still, though, she needs to rest.

Gently, I grab her arm and turn her to face me. "When has anyone ever complained about your *lumpia*? Every kind we've ever served sells out. The same thing will happen at the festival, I promise."

She shrugs out of my grip. "You never know. Customers can get finicky."

She pulls the package of wrappers back out of the fridge and sits at the kitchen table with a bowl of egg wash. When she starts dolloping meat mixture on the wrapper, I know I've lost this battle.

I take the seat across from her. She blinks slowly, a telltale sign that she's tired. "Mom, look at me."

She refuses, still studying her assembly line of ingredients.

"You can't keep pushing yourself like this. It's not good for you."

The wrinkles in her forehead deepen. She still refuses to make eye contact with me. "Says who?" she mutters to the bowl of egg wash.

My stomach twists in a knot. That frustrated look, that annoyed tone. A fight is on the horizon, I just know it.

I rein in a frustrated sigh. "Says me. And your doctor. Remember what he said? How important it is for you to relax and de-stress, especially when you've been on your feet for hours and hours? You can't be keeping up this work pace."

"Did you hear that?" she hollers.

Her eyes are still on her hands, but I know exactly who she's talking to.

"Our daughter thinks she knows better than me, Harold." She shakes her head. The small gesture is as dismissive as it is disappointing. "How crazy, right?"

Most people would think it's weird that she regularly chats to the urn containing Dad's ashes, which sits on a shelf nearby in the living room, but I don't. She's been doing it since we lost him. It makes total sense to me. She does it because she misses him more than anything and it's her way of maintaining their connection.

Her hands move quickly, her dark, crepe-like skin stretching every time she rolls *lumpia.* She's knocking them out at a dizzying pace, faster than any machine could. She shakes her head and her eyebrows knit deeper.

"Mom." I take a centering breath before I continue. "If Dad were here, he would tell you the same thing. He was just as excited about the food truck as you were, but he was a stickler on not working yourself to the bone. You know that."

Memories of Dad hugging her from behind during one of her hours-long cooking or cleaning sessions in the kitchen filter through my mind. He would give her a gentle squeeze, a kiss on the cheek, then whisper how she needed to take a break. She would always twist around to smile up at him and take a break for at least a few minutes. Always.

My words don't carry the same charm as my dad's.

"I know what's good for me," she snaps, as if she didn't even hear what I just said. "To stay busy."

My hand falls on the table. "Mom, you *are* staying busy just by working at the food truck with me every day."

Finally, her dark eyes cut to me. "Not every day. You make me stay home one day a week, sometimes two. Like I'm a child."

I stand up and walk to the sink for a glass of water. It's the only way I can think to keep from unloading on her, to keep from saying what I truly feel.

Slowly, I sip until the glass is empty, then refill it. It does nothing to calm me. Turning around, I focus back on her, still rolling *lumpia.*

"That's not fair, Mom. You know how important your health is to me. You can't put in eight- to ten-hour days doing food prep in the morning and working at the truck, then continue cooking for hours when you're home. That's too much."

"It's not. I like the work," she says, her voice hard, her tone clipped. "Besides, we have to work extra hard to make sure we do well at the festival. You don't want to lose, do you?"

Her question, spoken in her signature impatient tone, leaves my head spinning. I know it all too well. She uses it whenever she's asking a question she doesn't want an answer to.

I bite the inside of my cheek to keep myself in check.

"Of course I don't want to lose. And we won't. I've got everything covered. Your help at the food truck is more than enough."

I take another sip of water and stare out the kitchen window of our Kihei condo. My gaze fixes on the indigo sky, the bright specks of starlight scattered throughout. Beneath the darkness above, I can just barely make out the hedge dotted in tropical flowers that marks this end of the condo property and the line of palm trees behind it. During the day in full-on sunlight, endless lush rolling hills complete the view.

Every time I look out our little kitchen window to the scenic view in the daytime, it's an instant mood lifter. I wish it were daytime now so I could use the view to calm me.

"I know you like to work, but you have to be careful," I say.

She waves a hand in the air, like she's swatting away a fly. "You don't know what I need, Nicole," she bites.

The knot in my stomach slingshots to my chest. When she calls me by my full name, I know I'm in deep. I slam the glass down on the counter. It's all I can do to keep from letting out the scream of frustration lying in wait at the base of my throat.

"Yes, I do." My voice booms against the walls. "Would you just for one second stop and realize that I might be asking you to slow down because I love you? Because I care about you and want you around for as long as possible? Because being on your feet like this for fifteen hours a day isn't what a woman your age should be doing?"

A wide-eyed stare is the only response I get from her. I should stop. I should take a breath, and get my voice back under control. But I can't.

I already lost my dad because he kept going, kept pushing himself, because he refused to go to the doctor for what he thought was a minor pain in his back, even though it had persisted for a year. By the time he went, it was too late. Only months were left.

I refuse to let her fall down that same path, to push herself into exhaustion, into some serious health condition that could have been avoided had she just slowed down. I refuse to stand by and watch my only living parent disregard her own well-being.

Tears burn at my eyelids, but I spin away, back toward the kitchen window, so she can't see my trembling lips. I've already lost my temper in front of her. I don't want to lose the rest of my emotions too.

Slow, quiet breaths ease the knot in my chest, my racing heartbeat. A gust of air flows in through the open window, immediately cooling my skin, which was hot with frustration moments ago. A crack of thunder sounds in the distance.

"We lost Dad because he didn't slow down until it was too late," I finally say. "I don't want to lose you for the same reason."

My throat strains to keep my voice steady. It's a challenge when all I want to do is sob, to make her understand that I'm not doing all this to hurt her.

More silence passes. Another long, quiet inhale ensures I won't lose myself. When I turn around, she stands up from the kitchen table, her back to me this time.

I would laugh if I weren't so distraught. We're so damn alike. We don't want anyone to see us vulnerable, to see us falling apart, not even each other.

"Fine, then," she says quietly. I can tell by the way she says nothing more, by the way she walks down the hall and to the bathroom without another word, that's she's more hurt than angry at what I've said.

Gripping the sink with both hands, I heave out a breath.

She may be upset with me, but she's still here, living and breathing. That's all that matters.

Downing another glass of cold water does little to quell this anger and sadness warring within me. I pivot to face the gray ceramic urn sitting on the bookshelf in the living room.

"Sorry, Dad," I whisper. "You know how stubborn she is. But I'm trying."

I clean up the kitchen, head to my bedroom, and do the one thing I know I shouldn't.

I crawl into my bed and close my eyes, my phone gripped in my hand. I swipe to the last voice mail my dad ever left me. The last memento of his voice I have other than the dozens of videos I saved on my phone and backed up on my computer.

*Sweetie pie, it's Dad. Listen . . .*

The seconds-long pause after he says "listen" always sends a lump to my throat. I could be in the middle of laughing, and if I heard his low, soft voice in that pained tone, I'd be left speechless, fighting the urge to collapse into a ball on the floor and sob.

*. . . I'm sorry to call you like this, but it's serious. I went to the doctor and I need you to call me, okay? As soon as you can. I love you, sweetie pie. Talk to you soon.*

Even with his diagnosis looming over him, he somehow kept that gentle tone. If it had been me who had just been given the worst news of my life—that I had stage four pancreatic cancer and months to live because nothing could be done—I don't know how I would have reacted. But I sure as hell wouldn't have that same composure he did during that phone call.

Somehow he was thinking clearly enough to know that going into the details of his diagnosis over voice mail wasn't a good idea. So he waited patiently those four hours until I fished my phone out of my purse after a night of barhopping. The entire staff at the Portland restaurant I was managing at the time was out celebrating after hosting a stressful corporate party. I was about to indulge in my third shot of tequila when I happened to glance at my phone, the voice mail alert flashing on the screen.

And then when I listened to his message—his voice a mix of love and worry—the floor fell out from under me.

Tears tumble down my face, soaking the pillow underneath my head, but I don't sob. I don't want to make any noise that would disturb Mom. Instead I swallow back every almost-sob that grips the base of my throat and stare at the ceiling.

Despite my tipsy state that night, the serious tone of his voice mail sobered me up real quick. I never knew my fingers could fly across a phone screen that fast. And then I was crouched down in the hallway of some random bar because the corner by the bathrooms was the quietest spot I could find.

And then he answered. Hearing his voice was comfort and terror all at once.

"Nikki-Nack!" He practically sang his nickname for me on the other line. I could tell he was smiling.

"Dad, what's wrong?" My voice broke before he said anything because, despite the joy in his voice, I just knew. It was so, so bad.

Shoving my face into my pillow, I let out a soft cry. After that call, I couldn't think. I couldn't breathe. I couldn't focus.

The only thing I was certain of in that moment was that I needed to be with him for however long he had left. That night, I packed my bags and told my boss at the restaurant, who was an old culinary school pal that brought me on to manage, what had happened. He and my other workmates were nothing but sympathetic and understanding. Told me to take my time and that when I was ready to come back, to contact them. I threw together a post on Craigslist to rent out my room in the house I shared with two of my friends so I wouldn't leave them high and dry. The morning after, I was gone.

I thought I'd be back. Portland was where I went to culinary school and earned a business degree. It's where I learned the ropes of the restaurant industry. I loved my work and my life there.

But that was before I saw how rapidly Dad declined and how gutted Mom was at losing her life partner. I couldn't fly back to Oregon and just pick up where I left off. I couldn't leave Mom to fend for herself, grief-stricken and with next to no savings after spending most of it on medical treatment for Dad.

My mind flutters to that last week he was in the hospital, when I sat next to his bedside, holding his hand. I bite my tongue, staving off the next sob that surely won't be as quiet. Behind the dark of my closed eyes, I remember how he smiled up at me from his hospital bed, despite the unimaginable physical pain he was in.

"Take care of your mom, Nikki-Nack. Okay?"

I nodded, promising him I would.

And then his smile turned wistful and sad. "Do a better job than I did at the end."

I scolded him, told him he had no right to say that, that he always did an excellent job taking care of her and me. Every word was true. He always had a steady job, worked long hours so she could stay home with me until I went to grade school. And he was even able to save enough to make her dream come true: retire in Maui.

It's almost funny how one trip to the doctor, one phone call, one evil cluster of cells changed all of that.

But I promised him. Taking care of Mom and carrying out his food truck dream is the least I could do after every single wonderful thing he did for us.

I play the message once more, wishing I could call him right now.

I take it back. I don't want the conversation; I want my dad. I want him here right now. If he were here, Mom and I wouldn't be bickering so much. If he were here right now, we wouldn't be stuck in a food truck together for eight hours most days, working our tails off to earn back all the money we spent to keep him alive just a little bit longer. He passed away three months after he was diagnosed.

Deep breaths ease me to a point where I can think clearly once more.

One thing's certain: I could never survive a pain like that again. It's why I impose days off for Mom like a drill sergeant. It's why I have no friends, no dates, no social life whatsoever. I can't handle another death, another loss, another person leaving me.

Minutes later I sit up in bed, forcing myself out of that familiar hole of agony and despair that gets harder and harder to crawl out of every time I let myself dip in. I wash my face, brush my teeth, and hope I've exhausted myself enough to sleep.

It's a tedious climb over the hill separating Big Beach from Little Beach, especially in the darkness of predawn. The steep incline of lava rock and sand are the perfect elements for a trip or tumble. But I've made this walk countless times in the year and a half that I've lived in Maui. I could do it blindfolded by now.

It's the only way to avoid the worst of the crowds, to come on a weekday right as the sun rises. Predawn visits to Little Beach have become my go-to getaway when I need to clear my head. Having spent my whole life in Portland, I never thought I'd ever be the kind of person who found nature soothing. But the peaceful vibes of Maui's beaches are what keep me sane. I need that today more than ever.

Last night's argument with Mom and the crying session in my bedroom has my entire body in knots. When I woke up an hour before my alarm clock this morning, I knew I needed to ease the tension within me if I had any hope of having a decent day at work.

Before leaving, I left a note apologizing for my outburst last night on the kitchen counter and wished her a pleasant day off. I know we'll move past this argument—we had worse arguments when I was a mouthy teenager. But having this day apart from each other will be good for the both of us. I can distract myself with work, and she can busy herself with her day-off hobbies. And then we'll start over again tomorrow.

As soon as my toes hit the sugary sand of Little Beach, every tense muscle in my feet and calves releases. I gaze up at the sun peeking above the horizon. One glimpse at the bright orange hue kissing the deep blue shoreline, and I'm as calm as the salty air around me. Eyes closed, I hum softly.

Thank heavens for last night's surprise rainstorm that caused the local news to send out panicked warnings to tourists. Sharks are more likely to be out in the murky waters caused by lots of rain. The truth is that even with the rain and murky waters, attacks are still rare. But nothing clears a beach of tourists faster than warnings of possible shark sightings. I'm thankful for how deserted Little Beach is this morning. Including myself, there are only three people here. This is definitely a day where I'm not in the mood to deal with a horde of phone-toting tourists elbowing one another for selfies on my way to the water. Even though we're technically past the busy season of winter, when more than a million tourists come from all over to get away from the cold and snow, Maui is still a popular year-round vacation destination. Crowds are common almost everywhere.

I drop my towel on the sand and dive straight into the waves. A rush of lukewarm seawater engulfs me. I hold the air in my lungs until my chest aches. When I break the surface, I gasp, then dive back in. Again and again I repeat, floating underwater until I can't hold my breath any longer, then bursting through the surface, screaming for more air. It's agony and heaven all at once.

On this beach and under this water, no worldly worries exist. Just a fiery sun kissing the crystal-blue ocean and powdery soft sand tickling my toes. A row of gnarled trees surrounds this small strip of beach, marking the boundary of my heaven. In this moment, despite all the trouble it's been to carve out an existence here, I'm thankful my parents picked Maui. Right now on this beach, in this water, against this sky, it is perfection.

A forty-something man with a killer tan and the body of a long-distance runner wades out of the water to his towel, giving me and the other swimmer at the opposite end of the shore a clear view of his naked rear end. Public nudity isn't legal on Maui, but everyone looks the other way on Little Beach, one of the few beaches on the island where people routinely shed their clothes. People can swim, tan, and walk around naked. As long as they don't make a fuss, no one bats an eye.

I tighten the strap of my navy deep-"V" one-piece. I've never been much of an exhibitionist, and I don't ever plan on being one, but I love the "Who cares? Do what you want" mentality of this beach.

Another ten minutes of diving underwater and I've had my fill.

I settle on my towel and gaze around me. The sun's Day-Glo orange hue bathes every surface around me. Propping myself up on my elbows, I scan the beach behind my sunglasses. Still just me and the lone guy in the surf, still knocking out laps up and down the beach at a dizzying pace.

When he finally crawls out of the water and makes his way to the shoreline, my mouth falls open. This man is the phrase "holy hot damn" in human form. And he's totally, completely nude.

Even standing twenty feet away from me, his hotness is as clear as the blue sky above. His tall form showcases loads of lean muscle everywhere. Biceps, shoulders, forearms, calves, quads. And abs. Oh dear Lord, those abs. In a soft whisper, I count them to myself. When I get to eight, I have to suppress a shiver, though inside I'm simmering with heat. I admit, I'm spoiled living on Maui. Six-pack sightings are an almost-everyday occurrence. Much of the population is fit and active, resulting in a higher than average number of hard bodies.

But this knockout has them all beat with his glorious eight-pack. If I were a pious woman, I'd run to the nearest church and offer a silent prayer of thanks for the visual.

My greedy eyes finally allow for a blink. I'm grateful the lenses on my sunglasses are reflective. If I weren't shielded by these giant black orbs, my wide-eyed stare would be visible from outer space.

Halfway up the beach, he pauses to take a deep breath, bracing his hands on his thighs—and I'm treated to a crystal clear view of the goods. Air lodges in my throat before I let out a boom of a cough. I clamp my hand over my mouth, hoping he can't hear me over the crashing waves.

I take it back. *This* sight is something to thank the heavens for. This man, this marble statue brought to life, is also blessed with one hell of a package. Holy hot damn indeed.

With each step forward he takes, my heart races. *Be cool*, I silently order to myself. *Slowly turn your head away and stare straight ahead at the golden sand, at the perfect blue sea, at the radiant horizon ahead of you. Quit gawking like a perv!*

From the direction he's walking, he's headed to Big Beach . . . which means he'll have to walk right in front of me.

I divert my gaze to my toes, which are buried in the sand in front of me. I will not be that gross creeper who violates the unspoken code of conduct on Little Beach by staring too long. I breathe, close my eyes, and count to ten.

And when I look up, Mr. Hot Damn is standing right in front of me, his towel draped over his naughty bits.

When I focus on his face, I choke for real this time.

It's Callum.

# Chapter 4

Endless water droplets dot his gently tanned skin, making him glisten under the early-morning sunlight.

"You." He sounds almost angry.

I wait for him to say more, but all that follows is silence.

"Um, yes," I stammer. I sound like a confused child.

I scour my brain for anything else to say, but nothing else comes to me. All I can do is open and close my mouth a handful of times. All the while Callum's laser-focused eyes drill invisible holes through me.

My body is on fire when I realize how creepy I must look in this moment. There Callum was, enjoying a predawn swim at a secluded beach, only to stumble upon his food truck nemesis eye-sexing him from just a few feet away. Judging by the angry wrinkle of his eyebrows, the way he refuses to break his scowl even to blink, the way he won't even speak to me, he is not amused. He is not impressed. He is simply exasperated by the sight of me.

Jumping up, I grab my towel and jog away, tripping all the way up and down the rocky hill to Big Beach. I run the distance back to my car and speed to the commercial kitchen to prep for the day's lunch service. By the time I finish loading the truck, I'm still huffing every breath. My heart is still racing. My body still feels like it's engulfed in flames.

Callum employed a genius new battle tactic this morning, and I bet he didn't even realize it. Everything in me screams retreat, to drive my food truck into the ocean, just so I'll never have to face him ever again. Somehow, I properly insert the key into the ignition and navigate myself all the way back to my spot on Makena Road without crashing.

I'm not so lucky the rest of the day though. Mom texts me a heartfelt thank-you after reading my apology note on the kitchen table, but I'm too flustered to form words, so all I send back is a thumbs-up emoji and a heart. When I open for lunch, I proceed to screw up the first several orders. And then I burn a half dozen dishes. Focus is impossible after an epic distraction like that.

It all counts as a victory for Callum. A few minutes in the presence of his flawless naked body, and I'm unnerved and scatterbrained for the foreseeable future. I can't bear the thought of ever looking at him again, let alone speaking to him.

When I close up for the day, I slowly, carefully drive back to Kihei. For a split second, I wish I lived in nearby Wailea so I wouldn't have to risk a motor vehicle mishap when my focus is this shot. But then I remember that I will never be able to afford any of the ritzy condos or vacation homes that make up the area. So I take a breath, focus extra hard, and make my way back to more affordable Kihei and the modest yet cozy condominium complex I call home. After I park, I lean my head over the steering wheel and groan. I am so, so screwed.

. . .

The warfare has turned psychological. Ever since I got that front-row view of Callum's impressive physique and even more impressive length the other day, I haven't been able to rid my mind of him. That's why I'm swimming at Baldwin Beach near sleepy Paia this morning instead of Little Beach. I'm scared that if I run into his naked form again, my head will explode. Best to keep my distance.

I walk out of the water, wrap myself in a towel, and stroll toward the far end of the beach, away from the small crowd of beachgoers. When I'm far enough away that I'm sure no one can hear me, I stop, then stare at the endless expanse of crystal-blue waves. On this clear day, the cloudless sky is so vibrant, it almost matches the color of the water. The wind picks up, and with it, the waves go choppy. I picked this beach to swim at because it was Dad's favorite on the whole island. He loved this nearly mile-long stretch of sand because it was never as crowded as some of the other beaches on the island. It was where we spread most of his ashes after he passed, save for the small amount we keep in a ceramic urn at home. My eyes burn as I look out at the horizon.

"I miss you so much, Dad. You have no idea." My voice is barely audible against the endless crash of waves. "It's so hard without you here."

I pull the towel tighter against me. Normally, a swim is enough to help me feel at peace. But lately, with the new food truck competition and the food festival on the horizon, I have to speak. I have to talk to him, even though I know he can't say anything back.

"I'm trying so hard," I sniffle. "I just . . . I hope I don't let you down."

My voice breaks just as the last word leaves my lips. I stutter a breath and take a peek around. Just a handful of sunbathers about twenty feet away and a jogger hitting the shoreline. Luckily, no one has seemed to notice the woman wrapped in a towel standing alone talking to herself.

Just then, something soft brushes against my leg and I glance down. A plump white cat with gray spots looks up at me.

"What the . . ."

It mews before working itself all along my ankles. Wiping away the tears, I chuckle, then crouch down to pet it. Unlike the random feral cats I'm used to seeing on the island, this kitty is crazy friendly. It stops and sits on the sand, letting me scratch its chin. Even through the ocean noise I can hear it purr. I'm smiling until the cat stands up and reveals a bloody stump that used to be its tail.

I scoop the plump cat up in my arms. The way it purrs even louder in my hold confirms that this little fur ball is probably a pet that's been abandoned or lost. The one animal hospital in Paia is less than a mile up the street from this beach. In my car, I make it in less than two minutes. When I burst through the doors of the clinic cuddling the injured cat against my chest, the receptionist behind the front desk peers at me over the top of her glasses with a suspicious stare. Clearly, she wasn't expecting a bikini-clad woman wrapped in a beach towel to walk into the office today.

"So sorry to bother you, but I found this cat on the beach with its tail mutilated. I think he belongs to someone. He's so friendly."

The cat's purr echoes in the tiny space. The receptionist must hear it, because she glances at the cat, her expression softening. "Let me see what I can do."

After twenty seconds of typing on her computer, she looks back up at me. "Looks like Dr. Choi has a bit of time between appointments. We can squeeze you in right now. Follow me."

We make our way down the hall to an exam room at the end. A

good two dozen framed photos of cats adorn the walls of the room. I'm staring at a photo of kittens fast asleep in a basket of yarn when the receptionist tells me Dr. Choi will be by as soon as he's done with an appointment. She shuts the door, and I set the cat on the exam table. Its green eyes dart around the room nervously. Chin scratches seem to soothe it though. It relaxes on the table, blinking slowly in appreciation of my pets. The door opens behind me and I turn around. When I see Callum decked out in blue scrubs, my eyes go wide.

"What the . . . You're Dr. Choi?"

"What? No."

"Then what . . . what in the world are you doing here?"

The shock of seeing him at a veterinary clinic rivals the shock of seeing him naked days ago. But it's a different kind of shock. This sterile room is like a reset, taking us out of our usual environment of the beach and food trucks. It's like we're characters in a play, and instead of being nasty to each other like normal, we have to pretend to be civil.

He tugs at the hem of his scrub top. "I volunteer here a few mornings a week."

"As a veterinarian?" I can't hide my disbelief. If that's the case, I hope he's managed a better bedside manner than the lack of people skills he displays at his food truck.

His jaw tense, he sighs, as if he's willing himself the patience to talk to me. "No. I assist the doctor with pets during exams. That sort of thing."

"Oh."

After that stilted exchange, he takes the two steps to stand on the other side of the exam table. When he reaches out to pet the cat, his hard expression softens. I loosen a bit on the inside too. It seems that Callum is definitely a cat person.

"Poor little bloke," he says, his eyes narrowing at the sight of the cat's bloody stump of a tail.

"I found him on Baldwin Beach. He just ran up to me."

Callum turns to the computer and starts typing info into a spreadsheet. "Must not be stray, then, if it's that friendly. A bit fleshy too. That's a good sign."

I chuckle and scratch the cat under its chin, which sends a loud purr echoing through the room.

Callum takes the cat's weight before typing some more, then fishes a few treats from a nearby jar to give to the cat. I lean down to offer it a few reassuring pets. When I raise my gaze back up, Callum's eyes dart from my bikini top back to the computer screen. Heat flashes across my chest. I suppose that's fair. I did spend a solid three minutes staring at his naked body on the beach, after all.

He dispenses another treat. "That's a good little love," he croons, stroking the top of the cat's head.

I'm almost dizzy at the gentle way he speaks. If he had used this tone on me the first day we met, I would have listened to anything he had to say.

The door opens, and in walks a fifty-something man with a thick head of black and gray hair.

"Thank you so much for agreeing to do this on such short notice," I say.

Dr. Choi nods. "No problem at all. I have a soft spot for cats, as you can probably tell." He gestures to the framed photos on the walls. "Looks like this little one's tail got a bit mangled."

I explain how the cat wandered up to me on the beach. Dr. Choi nods along while examining the injury.

"Well, this little one is lucky. The tail isn't severed at all, actually. That must have been an earlier injury that's been healed for a long while, fortunately. The bleeding is due to this nasty little cut at the end of it." He points to an inch-long gash under the cat's fur. "My guess is he probably got into it with another cat, maybe even a feral pig. They run wild in some spots here."

Callum holds the cat while Dr. Choi runs a scanner along its body to check if he's chipped.

"I'm not getting anything," Dr. Choi says. "Definitely looks like he's a runaway or abandoned by his family."

He flips the cat over to check to see if it's fixed.

"Oops!" Dr. Choi says. "Looks like this little guy is a gal." He frowns as he presses against her gushy tummy. "And if I'm not mistaken, she's pregnant."

My jaw falls open at the same moment that Callum's eyes go wide.

"Congrats!" Dr. Choi grins. "You've got a litter of fur babies on the way."

Dr. Choi explains that the cat is likely a couple weeks along, then says that the injured tail will be an easy fix with some stitches. He instructs Callum to hold the cat while he administers a vaccination.

My eyes glaze over as I observe the doctor and Callum work in tandem. There's no way I have enough money to pay for this appointment, let alone a slew of new pets. Anything more than zero dollars will send my tight budget into a tailspin.

I fall onto the nearby bench, speechless, as Dr. Choi takes the cat to a room in the back to stitch her. For a minute, I say nothing, processing the news that was just sprung on me.

"You all right?"

I glance up at Callum, the concern in his hazel eyes like a static shock to my system. I almost forgot about the kindness I spotted in them the day we met.

"This is . . . um . . ." I stammer another nonsensical sound.

He sighs, shoving his hands in his pockets. "I'll take care of it."

"What?"

"I'll take care of the bill."

I squint up at him. "But . . . why?"

He shrugs, turning back to the computer screen to type. "It's nothing, really."

My head spins. Why is he offering to cover this expense? It's not like we're friends.

"Last time I checked, vet visits cost money. That's not nothing."

He practically glares at the computer screen. "And?"

"And I just don't get why—"

The door swings open, and Dr. Choi walks back in holding the cat, a plastic cone around her head. "Good as new!"

Setting the cat on the counter, he explains the post-suture care and cleaning routine. The cone is to prevent her from licking her stitches. Callum swipes a cardboard cat carrier from under the counter and places the cat inside. I'm still speechless, unable to say a word after soaking in his offer to pay for the bill I just racked up.

"You're good to go!" Dr. Choi says. "Just check out with Brenda at reception, and she'll help you get the bill sorted."

"I'll show her out." Callum swipes the carrier from the counter and opens the door.

He marches in the direction of the reception desk with such long strides that I have to almost jog to keep up. I grip the towel at my hip to keep it in place.

"Hey!" I say in a shrill whisper to keep from making a scene. "Hey! What do you think you're doing?"

But he continues without a word, fishing his wallet out of his pocket when the receptionist smiles up at him.

"I've got this," I say quickly.

"No."

He doesn't even look at me when he speaks. When Brenda the

receptionist swipes his card from his hand and runs it through the card reader, I know I've lost. It's the most confusing, deflated feeling I've ever experienced. Yes, what he did was generous. But I don't understand why. Why in the world would he want to help me, the person he's supposed to destroy?

Brenda hands Callum a receipt, which he pockets.

She smiles as the cat presses her face against the carrier. "Did you decide on a name for this cutie-pie?"

I blurt the first word that comes to mind. "Lemon."

"Lemon?" Callum says, clearly confused.

Brenda chuckles sweetly. "Oh, that's just precious."

I thank her, grab the carrier, and move to the sitting area by the entrance. Callum follows me.

"I'll write you a check later. To pay you back," I mutter while fiddling with the handle of the carrier.

"Not necessary." He sighs, like he's annoyed at my presence, even though he's the one who decided to stand next to me. This guy is impossible to decode.

"Oh, it's necessary." I remind myself to rein in my irritated tone.

We're technically in a public place, and we need to maintain some degree of civility. Every time I fail to get a hold of myself around Callum, I end up in a viral video, and I don't want that to happen at the vet's office, of all places.

He crosses his arms, his frown a strange mix of amusement and impatience. Again, his gaze skims my chest, but only for a second before he refocuses. "Why, exactly?"

"Because I don't need a favor from you."

"It wasn't for you. It was for the cat." His curt words land like a slap to the face. Like I was a fool to assume he would waste such kindness on me.

It's so obvious now that I think about it. He volunteers at a pet clinic, which means he loves animals—which means he's the kind of person who would go above and beyond to make sure one of those animals is taken care of.

"I see." Somehow, I'm able to speak even though my jaw is tense as I attempt to stave off the embarrassment coursing through me. I swallow, taking care that my tone is as curt as his. "Thanks."

I turn away and head out the door without a second look back.

# Chapter 5

I toss then turn over in my bed. It's been a handful of days since the incident at the vet clinic, and I'm struggling to focus—and I know exactly why. Seeing Callum naked at Little Beach appealed to my carnal side. Seeing him go all cuddly over Lemon the cat appealed to my sentimental side. Experiencing those two sides of him was a lethal combo. I still don't like him, especially after he made it clear at the vet's office that he didn't see me as anything other than a feline guardian in need of his charity. But like has very little to do with intrigue sometimes. And it's safe to say that the part of my brain that appreciates Callum's body and his soft spot for pets is very, very intrigued. He's completely overrun my thoughts and emotions.

I hang my head over the side of the bed to peek at Lemon, who's snoozing underneath. That's been her resting spot of choice ever since I brought her home. I smile at the soft wheezing noise she makes.

I settle back on the bed. A tiny mass of heat simmers at the base of my chest, causing me to flush every single time I think about him.

It also makes an appearance whenever I catch a glimpse of him at work. It doesn't matter that each time I've seen him since the Little Beach incident he's been fully clothed, or that we haven't exchanged anything more than an accidental few seconds of eye contact. Even the recent uptick in customers and social media coverage due to our turf war have done little to curb the near-constant impure thoughts I'm having about him.

You'd think that having nonstop lunch and dinner rushes would keep my mind occupied—it doesn't—or that seeing our food truck blow up on social media due to our new rivalry with Hungry Chaps would be a distraction—it isn't.

It doesn't matter that whenever I check Facebook, Twitter, or Instagram, I'm bombarded with hashtags like #mauifoodtruckwars, #tivasvschaps, #EnglandvsPhilippines, and everything else related to our rivalry. Because all of that ends up being a reminder of Callum and the fact that I can't get him out of my head.

Flipping to my side, I pull a pillow over my face. At least Mom and I are getting along again. She accepted my apology after my outburst and is back to working a healthy number of hours. She went gaga over Lemon when I brought her home, too, which helped ease the tension between us. We've also developed a couple new recipes for the food festival and are testing them out at the food truck as featured lunch specials. Both regulars and new customers have been raving, giving us the confidence boost we'll need to bring our A game to the festival. Now if only I could get a proper night's sleep.

Every time I close my eyes, Callum's flawless form shows up like an ill-timed highlight reel. It takes at least an hour of tossing and turning to fall asleep, which then means groggy mornings. I can't handle another night of less than six hours of sleep.

Pushing the pillow off my face, I sigh.

If I were a guy, I know exactly how I would handle this. I'd jerk off, enjoy the temporary bliss, then fall asleep. Such a simple solution, but there's no chance. Callum is my competition, the person standing in the way of my business and my livelihood.

I close my eyes and breathe in the salty sea air wafting through my open bedroom window. I could never, ever do such a thing.

Could I?

Instead of scolding myself internally like I normally would when a bad idea crosses my mind, I let it unfold. Maybe indulging in one lustful, purely carnal moment wouldn't be the worst thing in the world. No one is holding me to these ridiculous standards other than myself. It's not like anyone would ever know that I pleasured myself with impure thoughts of my enemy. I wouldn't tell anyone.

Men do this sort of thing all the time. Why the hell can't I?

I adjust the pillow behind my back and eye the drawer of my nightstand. May as well give it a shot.

I pull out my vibrator and press it against the crotch of my panties. I don't even bother to lower the fabric. At this point, I'm so hot that not even a chastity belt could quell the flames inside me. Days of Callum's naked image bombarding me combined with the sweet memory of him cuddling Lemon have had quite an effect.

I close my eyes and lean back. Already I'm trembling.

I switch it to the highest setting. This will be quick and dirty. Nothing lingering or sweet about it.

The vibrations hit, and immediately my toes curl, my jaw drops, and I'm moaning up a storm. Thank Christ Mom is sleeping with the fan on high in her room due to tonight's heat wave. Fingers crossed it will muffle any and all background sounds.

Callum's face flashes across the darkness of my eyelids. Those hazel-green eyes, the ski-slope slant of his nose, that jawline sharp enough to cut diamonds. That mouth with those lips, thick lips I'd give anything to bite right about now.

Pressure builds from within my core, and I gasp. Holy shit, I'm nearly there. And it's barely been a minute.

I pull my hand away and gulp for air. This time I press gently and think of his body. All those hard lines and dense muscle, that warm-hued skin. That surprise between his legs . . . I mean, I should have known. Judging by his height and build, it's only logical that he's packing something impressive. But to see it in person, literally feet from my face, is a whole other . . .

I gasp. More pressure, more warmth in my midsection. This is a brand-new level of intensity. With each vibration that rattles through me, I'm pulled closer to the finish line. I'm panting now, aching for the end.

Good God, how is this possible? How is just the visual of Callum's naked body doing this to me? I can't stand this guy. Like, would-trade-one-of-my-body-organs-for-the-opportunity-to-punch-his-face type of dislike. But what he does to me physically is unlike anything I've experienced before.

I'm not one to fantasize about men I know in real life when I pleasure myself. The thought has always creeped me out. But Callum is the one exception. Because right now, just the thought of him has gotten me hotter faster than the thought of any other man on this planet.

Finally, it hits.

My stomach muscles clench, my calves cramp, and my head falls back. I'm shrieking and moaning at once, in between ragged gulps of air. All I see are white bursts. Stars, I think. Callum has sent me to outer space.

When I collapse back onto the blanket, I let out a pitiful squeal. I'm blinking nonstop because I can't see clearly. A full minute of panting follows.

That was . . . I have no idea what that was. No self-pleasure session has ever, ever gone that well, that intensely, that quickly in my life.

When my breathing falls back to a seminormal pace, I'm finally able to get my bearings. Every pillow is now on the floor. My sheets lie in a tangled heap underneath me. The hem of my tank top is bunched all the way above my belly button, and my panties are halfway off my hips. Even though there's no one here to see any of this, I still blush. I've managed to make the aftermath of my solo session look like two sex-starved individuals went at it. Go me.

I chuck my vibrator back into the nightstand drawer like it's on fire. When I crouch down to check on Lemon under the bed, she slow-blinks at me. Clearly, I woke her up.

I bite back a chuckle. "Sorry."

I pick up all the pillows, toss them back on the bed, straighten out my clothes, and climb under the sheet.

The heat inside me has officially cooled. My eyelids grow heavy. When I blink, I don't see Callum anymore. Every muscle in my body is relaxed, free of tension at the thought. Soon I'm asleep. It's deep and hard and everything good.

Until I start to dream.

Dream Callum is a million times nicer than real-life Callum.

Dream Callum spoons me from behind, my absolute favorite. How did he know?

He presses his clothes-free body against mine, a perfect shell for my hot and bothered self.

None of this is real. That doesn't make it any less divine.

He wraps his arms around me. They're so thick that when pressed against me, they cover most of my naked chest. Leaning back, I groan.

"You like that?" he asks.

I nod a yes, then moan again.

Those thick lips press against the back of my neck. "What do you want, Nikki?"

When his voice is this low, this gentle, it makes my eyes roll to the back of my head. The hottest sound in the world is Callum's English accent rolling off his tongue in a soft, guttural tone.

I twist my head around so I can get a better look. I make out those expressive eyes, his defined jawline, that perfect pouty mouth.

"You know what I want," I rasp.

"Naughty girl." A smirk completes his admonishment.

He starts a trail of kisses down the side of my neck, to my collarbone, across my breasts. I'm gasping, running my fingers in his honey-blond hair, which looks almost light brown in the dim glow of my bedside lamp.

Those thick lips make easy work of crossing my stomach, gliding down and across, skimming all the way to my hips. Goose bumps fly across every inch of me. When he makes it between my legs, I'm panting.

"I . . . Fuck."

I can't talk, I can't breathe, I can't see straight. Not when his mouth is this good. I'd give anything to explode right now, to let the pleasure waves wrack my body until I'm a panting, shrieking mound of flesh and bone.

But not yet. I have to get this out. He has to know. And I need to hear him say it.

All I can do to steady myself is tug my fingers through his hair. His smirk widens. He likes it when I'm a little rough, it seems.

His lips land on the inside of my right thigh, then the inside of my left. My head falls back at the feel of his soft lips against the most sensitive patch of skin on my body.

"Wait," I gasp.

I'm talking to the ceiling with my eyes closed. This won't do. When I finally connect with his hazel stare, he's no longer smiling. It's a frown, but also something more. Something hungry and desperate.

"I just . . . I want you to say you're sorry . . . for how mean you were . . . when we met."

It's a struggle among struggles to get the words out when all I want to do is press his face between my legs and relieve the fire inside me.

His brow lifts a touch, and his expression softens all the way to tender. And then he lowers his face right where I want him. "This is how I say sorry, petal."

Shrill beeping hits my ears. I open my eyes and turn my head to the alarm clock on my phone.

Alarm. That explains the unwelcome noise. I shut it off, press a pillow over my face, and groan. Cockblocked by my own phone.

"Damn it," I half yell, half groan.

My bedroom door whips open to reveal Mom peering at me with worried wide eyes. Her hair is pulled back, and she's donned one of my dad's old T-shirts, tied into a loose knot at the waist, and a pair of gray leggings. I've interrupted her morning calisthenics routines with my sex-dream-induced shouting, it seems.

"*Anak*, are you okay? Why were you screaming?"

Sitting up, I clutch a pillow to my chest. Why was I screaming? Well, I almost got what was most certainly mind-blowing dream oral sex from my nemesis, but my alarm so rudely interrupted.

I opt for a white lie instead. "I'm fine. I just had a leg cramp. Sorry to wake you."

Her hand falls against her chest and she nods, then pads out the door. Lemon scurries after her. Mom wishes Lemon good morning in a cheery voice, then there's a sound of cat food hitting Lemon's metal dish.

Great. I'm lying to my mom on top of having sex dreams about a guy I don't even like. And now I'm left with a phantom ache between my legs that I can't do anything about because I share a home with my mother.

I toss the pillow back on the bed and waddle to the bathroom, wondering how the hell I'm going to get through today's shift with the star of my hottest sex dream ever working ten feet away from me.

I weave through the maze of stalls at the Aloha Maui Farmer's Market near Kula. The pathways between the vendor stalls are bustling with shoppers checking out the mix of fresh local produce, prepared meals and snacks, and other random goods.

"Do they have any apple bananas?" Mom asks on the other end of the phone.

"They always have apple bananas." I hold my phone between my chin and shoulder, gripping the handle of the cloth grocery bag in my other hand.

"Good. Joan wants to make those smoothies at our next mahjong night," she says.

I tell her I'll pick up a few bunches of apple bananas and that I scored an entire crate of dragon fruit, which I'll pick up with the car later.

"Oh, that's good!" she squeals into the phone. "We can make that frozen dragon fruit puree and serve it this weekend for the customers. Everyone loved it the first day we tried it out. I want to do it with tapioca balls this time though."

Today we're pulling double duty. She's at the condo in Kihei trying out a new vegetarian *pansit* recipe while I'm scouring the farmer's market for new ingredients. She's convinced a new recipe will set us apart among competition at the Maui Food Festival. I'm just glad to be out of the house and away from the food truck. When I'm home, I worry about having more vivid sex dreams about Callum, which has happened a couple of times ever since that first night.

I slip my phone back into the pocket of my dress. Even though it's a Monday, the market is full to the max with locals and tourists. I can't even make a normal stride with the people around practically pressing up against me. I manage with baby steps, dragging my flip-flops against the ground.

But being in this up-country part of the island is a welcome break from my day-to-day of sweating it out while racing back and forth from Kihei and Big Beach. Kula stretches across the western-facing slopes of Haleakala, Maui's dormant volcano, which means it's cooler here most days. I take a slow, silent breath in. I could swear the air feels crisper up here, even though there's only a couple thousand feet of difference in elevation between here and the shore where I spend most of my time.

Gazing around, I spot Matteo the food blogger. He waves from his nearby booth, where he sells his special brand of essential oils. I offer a head nod, then bump into a blond woman in front of me, her hair in a messy braid.

"Shoot! I'm so sorry. I wasn't paying attention—"

She twists around to me, squints, then beams. "I know you!"

I focus on her vaguely familiar face, trying to remember where I've seen her before.

She squeals before grabbing my elbow and pulling me to the side and away from the crowd. "Nikki DiMarco, right? You and your mom Tiva run that food truck! Oh my God, I love your food! Your whole menu is to die for!"

I let out an embarrassed chuckle. Getting stopped by excited customers has been a common occurrence lately since every food blogger in Maui has posted about the feud between Callum and me. People ask for selfies with Mom or me—sometimes both of us—a handful of times every week. It's flattering but also unnerving. When we started this food truck, I thought my biggest stress would be cooking good food to earn enough income. I never dreamed I'd have to schmooze and take fan photos.

The bubbly blonde goes on about how the fruit salad is her favorite dessert.

"The vanilla whipped cream makes it so refreshing!" She digs her phone out of her purse and leans back a little, almost like she's afraid to ask.

"Would you like to take a selfie?" I ask.

Her grin stretches from ear to ear. "Um, duh!"

She wraps one skinny arm around my shoulder, yanking me into a side hug. I grunt at how hard she grips me. She's much stronger than her tiny frame lets on.

After taking a half dozen selfies on her phone, she squeals again.

"I follow your food truck on social media. I'm your biggest fan!" Holding up her phone to me, she swipes across the screen. "That's me, @hungrypenelope. I wish I could make it out to your food truck every day for every meal, but then I'd go broke."

When she laughs, I can't help but laugh along with her. As awkward as it is to be stopped while going about my daily errands, it's also flattering. The fact that complete strangers enjoy our food enough to tell us means everything. It makes all this craziness worth it.

I try to match her enthusiasm with a smile. "I love your handle, so funny. And you have such a pretty name."

She yanks me into another hug that's so tight I have to hold my breath. After she releases me, I catch her impressive one-hundred-thousand-plus follower count.

"Whoa," I mutter.

She waves her hand in the air, like it's no big deal. "Oh yeah. I do social media for a living."

I almost ask her what tips she could offer me so I can maximize our online exposure, but she speaks first. "I seriously cannot wait for the Maui Food Festival. Like, seriously. I'm already so excited! You and your mom have my vote, and my friends' votes too. You're our favorite place to eat on the island, hands down."

The smile drops, her face darkening. She peers over her shoulder before leaning toward me, like she's about to reveal a secret. "By the way, I think what Hungry Chaps did to steal your spot was so uncool. Like, majorly uncool. My ex-boyfriend was like that. Always pulling shady power moves. Completely not okay. Can you believe I moved all the way from Ohio to Maui for a jerk like that?"

She chuckles, clearly unfazed that she's spilling her relationship history to a practical stranger. Rather than feeling put off, I feel comfort. Penelope seems like a genuinely friendly person. I'm flattered she wants to share something personal with me even though we've only known each other minutes.

"But it was worth it because now I live in paradise and I found your amazing food truck. And now I've actually met you!" She lets out another squeal before her phone rings. "Shoot, I have to take this. FYI, I saw the Hungry Chaps guys milling around the market a bit ago, so steer clear."

Penelope walks into the crowd with her phone to her ear before I can thank her for the warning. Best to leave now before I encounter Callum. We tried to play nice at the vet clinic, but that only lasted minutes. The last thing I want is another public confrontation that goes viral. Even if it would drive up business, it's not worth the stress.

I head toward the other end of the market, then feel a tap on my shoulder. When I turn, there's Finn James in board shorts, a striped T-shirt, and slip-on shoes, looking like a preppy college student on spring break.

His face reads hesitant. Probably since the only other times he's seen me were when I was lashing out at his brother. Finn and I haven't even had a proper conversation in the weeks that we've been working next to each other.

I make an effort to lose the frown I know I'm sporting. Finn hasn't technically done anything to deserve my vitriol. It's not his fault his brother is a prick.

"Fancy seeing you here." He hunches his shoulders and tugs on the end of his shirt. He's leaner than his brother and a bit shorter, but easily clears more than six feet.

"It's an island. We were bound to run into each other at some point."

He lets out a chuckle that sounds more nervous than happy. "About all this madness at work." He stretches his arm out. He's holding a clear plastic cup of coconut boba tea in his hand. "Peace offering?"

I don't move to take the drink, opting to keep my arms at my sides. He stood on the sidelines for weeks while his brother and I waged a full-on food truck war with each other, and this is how he breaks the ice?

"You're joking, right?"

His hand springs back to his body. He clutches the drink to his side, like he's scared I'm going to smack it out of his hand. "I just thought that maybe—"

"Boba tea doesn't really make up for the fact that your brother has been a jerk to me since the day we met."

I spin around and slow-walk through the haphazard maze of booths. My well of patience is tapped dry for nonsense like this.

"Hey, wait! Nikki!"

When I turn around, Finn's brow is wrinkled to hell. He wears the worry on his face like a blemish. It just looks unnatural on his boyish face. "I'm sorry. Truly. I didn't mean to make light of things."

He shakes his head, glancing off into the distance before looking back at me, concern radiating in his eyes. Now that we're standing up close, I notice that his eyes are a touch greener than his brother's. I wonder if he's worried about someone filming our little scene and uploading it online. That's exactly what I'm thinking.

Thankfully, no one seems to have noticed us. Everyone is milling around the booths, chatting and perusing.

A heavy sigh moves through his chest. "You're right. Callum is an absolute knob sometimes, but he really does mean well."

I scoff. "So being rude and disrespectful is perfectly fine if he 'means well'?"

The frenzied way he shakes his head catches the attention of a nearby arts and crafts booth operator, who squints at him in confusion before looking away.

"No, that's not . . . Here, I'll try to explain. I was having a hell of a time getting my business off the ground here. I love food, I love cooking, I love feeding people. I've done it my whole life, and my dream has been to have my own restaurant in Hawaii. But I was clueless when it came to the business side of things."

He holds the boba tea up to me, but I shake my head. He takes a sip. "Long story short, I tried to do everything on my own at first—I wrote a business plan, applied for a loan, bought equipment. I drained my savings. I had no idea what I was doing, and before I knew it I was in debt to my eyeballs. When Callum got word, he dropped everything—his finance job, his flat in Chicago—to move out here and help me. I probably would have lost everything if he hadn't done that."

A crack forms in my steely hate for Callum. The knotted muscles in my shoulders loosen. What an incredibly kind thing to do for his little brother.

"He's completely turned things around for me. Did loads of research on the food truck industry, Maui's economy, the most popular tourist spots. Pretty much everything I should have done in the first place, but never even thought about. He was the one person who reached out to me when no one else cared."

"Not even your parents?" I say before I can catch myself.

He shakes his head. "No. It's just . . . our parents are good people. They loved us, took us on fun vacations, paid for our schooling. They had the money to do all the things that most parents want to do for their kids. But they had expectations too."

Finn pauses, possibly hesitating. "They're both in finance and thought working in food service was beneath me. They were thrilled when Callum followed in their footsteps—and the exact opposite when I told them that my career goal was to open my own food truck in Maui. But I didn't care. It was what I loved to do. So when my business here crashed and burned, they expected me to finally give up, to get a 'sensible' job, as they call it. But I wouldn't do it. And when I told them that, they made it very clear how disappointed they were by refusing to acknowledge that part of my life."

I keep from speaking even though I'm curious. My parents were always so supportive of whatever I wanted to do. When I said I wanted to go to culinary school after high school, they cheered me on. When I said I wanted to go to school online at night and earn my business degree while working in restaurants all day, they were just as supportive. I can't imagine what it would be like to have parents who disapproved of what you did for a living.

"Shit. That sucks, Finn."

The small smile he flashes holds a tinge of sadness. "It did. I honestly didn't expect money or for them to swoop in and save me or anything like that. All I wanted was their support. But they didn't have that to give." He clears his throat. "Callum did though. He always did."

He glances up and sighs. "I know he doesn't seem like it now, but he's a bloody good person. The best I know. I'm biased of course, since he's my brother." He chuckles before reining in his expression. "He didn't care how angry our parents were when they found out he quit his job. All he cared about was helping me."

Based on what Finn's told me about Callum, even I have to admit that's true.

"The way he went about things with you in the beginning was completely wrong," Finn says. "I even told him that. I told him I didn't want to stay at the spot on Makena Road because you were already there. But he wouldn't budge."

"Must be that douchebag finance persona he does so well."

To my surprise, Finn laughs. He wipes his brow with his forearm. Tiny beads of sweat on his skin shine in the sunlight.

"When it comes to business, he's a bloody shark. It's good because it's an effective strategy, but it's awful, too, because he turns into a complete bellend."

"You're right about that." I bite the inside of my cheek when I hear how borderline bitter I sound.

"Look, I know things are unpleasant right now. We're technically enemies. And in a couple months one of us is going to have to leave the spot. But you've noticed a big increase in your revenue, too, haven't you? It's like people can't get enough of this rivalry between you and Callum, and because of it, business is booming. I mean, it's odd and a bit terrible, but it's also brilliant."

For a second I think about saying nothing. He and his brother are my competition. They don't deserve to know the goings-on of my business. But they're not blind. Every day they see the long lines at my food truck. They know just how well we're doing, just like I know how well they're doing.

"You could say that," I say, shifting my weight from one foot to the other.

Finn shrugs. All the worry from his face disappears, and a gentle smile tugs at his mouth. "Then it's kind of a good thing overall, isn't it?"

I admit that it is.

His smile fades, and his eyes fall to the ground. "I'm truly sorry for how Callum's been. He's always been protective, especially after—"

A trio of elementary school–aged kids dart between us, screaming, "You're it! No, you're it!" We both stumble back a step. Finn chuckles, which makes me chuckle. I feel myself loosening from the inside out. He's got a lovely, joyous laugh. I wonder if his brother laughs the same way.

Finn runs a hand through his hair. It's shaggier than his brother's, but they both share the same honey-blond hue. "I just wanted to apologize to you and your mum for how all this started. There's no excuse for that, no matter how good it's been for our businesses."

My gaze falls to my feet. As much as I dislike Callum, his brother seems like a kind and decent person. He cared enough to apologize. And I can't fault him for his brother's personality. That's not in his control.

"I appreciate that. Thank you," I finally say. "I'm not a fan of how this all started, either, but you're right. It's working out so far for the both of us."

He shoves his free hand into the pocket of his shorts.

I glance down. "I'm also not a fan of his blinding hatred of me, but I suppose there's not much I can do about that currently."

A smile plays across Finn's lips. "You think he hates you?"

I nearly laugh at his shocked tone of voice. "Positive. Remember how he came at me that day we met? Remember every argument we've had in front of you? One hundred percent unadulterated hatred right there."

Finn bites back a grin. He opens his mouth to speak, then immediately shuts it. "I'll admit, Callum hates plenty of people. But you're not one of them."

Finn tips his boba tea at me before turning around and walking away. I'm tempted to holler at him so he can come back and explain what he meant, but he's swallowed by the sea of tourists and locals navigating the market before I can utter a word.

I'm left standing in an invisible cloud of confusion. Every single time I've interacted with Callum, his animosity for me has radiated like steam from a volcanic fissure. Why in the world would Finn say otherwise?

I wander through the crowd, half-heartedly scanning items for sale. Does Finn know something I don't? Did something change since Callum brushed me off at the vet's office?

My throat squeezes with longing, with a hope I don't often let myself entertain. Even so, I allow my mind to drift to distant thoughts, and something in my chest aches.

What I wouldn't give to have a polite conversation with Callum. A *friendly* conversation.

*You'd need friends to have one of those, Nikki.*

I swallow against the squeeze in my throat. Deep down I know it's true, but it doesn't make it hurt any less. I'm a friendless twenty-nine-year-old who was so panicked when I moved out to Maui that I didn't think to prioritize friendships. Relationships are a luxury you can't afford when you're fighting to support yourself and your mom after your dad's terminal illness threw everything into limbo.

But still.

The thought tumbles through my head. *It would be pretty damn nice to have a friend right about now.*

If Finn is right, if his brother somehow doesn't hate me, if he for some reason wanted to be friends, I'd say yes in a second.

I rejoin the slow-walking crowd, stopping at a baked goods booth. A young woman in cutoffs and a holey T-shirt offers me a sample of banana bread, and I accept with a soft "thank you."

When I look up, I freeze. Callum and Finn stand just ahead of me, but turned away. At their angle, they can't see my face, but I can see their faces.

"You're doing a bang-up job, Finn," Callum says, gently elbowing his arm.

Finn looks down at his banana bread sample, his face bright. "You think so?"

"Yeah. You turned things around, and now look how well your business is doing."

"You helped me a lot, Cal."

"You're the one who's thinking up the recipes. You're the one the customers love chatting with. Food and customer service are what's winning it, and that's all you. I'm proud of you."

When Finn looks up at him, the brightness in his eyes melts. "If only Mum and Dad could be, too, right?"

"Don't say that." Callum's tone takes a hard, serious turn. "They're proud; they just don't know how to show it. They don't know how to do anything that's not in the confines of a soul-sucking corporate office."

Finn chuckles, his face light again. "Right. Thanks, mate."

"Always." The look in Callum's eye says it all. Proud older brother.

Witnessing this moment of brotherly love makes me think that there really is something to what Finn told me minutes ago. Callum is capable of being soft—I've seen it with my own eyes. And if that's the case, maybe Finn's right. Maybe Callum is soft enough not to hate me.

Callum says something about leaving to change the oil in their car. Finn nods and says he's meeting a friend soon. He shoves the banana bread in his mouth, pats Callum on the back, and rejoins the bustling crowd.

Callum turns, and that familiar hazel-eyed stare captures me from just a few feet away.

He is shocked to see me. I can tell by the lift of his brow, how his hand drops to his side instead of grabbing the banana bread sample like he initially meant to.

He doesn't move. He simply stands facing me, an unfamiliar brand of surprise written all over his face.

I can work with surprise.

I lift my hand up in a small wave. He does nothing. I let one corner of my mouth lift in a shy, uncertain smile. Still nothing.

My stomach drops to my feet, but I wait. Our history may only consist of heated arguments, one nude beach incident, and an awkward run-in at an animal clinic, but he does not hate me. Finn said so. If that's the case, all I have to do is give this a few extra seconds.

Just then his brow makes the familiar journey downward. His

eyebrows pinch together, he presses his lips tight, and it results in the harshest scowl I've seen him make to date. There's no room for friendliness here, not when I'm miles deep in hostile territory.

I bite my lip in an attempt to erase my grin and force my arm back down to my side. It's too late though. I've already shown my hand. I'm someone aching for any semblance of kindness, friendliness. He knows that now. And he doesn't give a shit.

With his giant paw, he swipes a sample of banana bread from the table and heads right toward me. A whoosh of air hits my skin as he passes by, angry scowl still plastered on his face. No eye contact, no "excuse me." Just him walking right past me—right through me—as if I don't even exist.

The gesture lands like a punch to the gut. He's strong, unflappable, no-nonsense. I'm weak and pathetic, desperate for an empty gesture of kindness.

I ignore the ache in my chest and trudge ahead, weaving through the crowd on my way back to my car in the parking lot. Finn was probably just trying to be nice, to help me feel better after spending the past few weeks watching his older brother behave like an unconscionable dick.

*Callum hates plenty of people. But you're not one of them.*

A well-meaning lie, but a lie nonetheless.

# Chapter 6

I plop down in the driver's seat of my car, shove the key in the ignition, and hear nothing but a faint clinking noise. My heart drops, and my palms sweat. I know what this means, but this cannot happen. Not now. Not when I've just begun to make decent money. I've got a razor-thin budget and no room for emergency expenses.

I turn the key in the ignition over and over in direct opposition to all logic. Still nothing.

I punch the steering wheel. A group of people walking toward the farmer's market turn their confused glances at me. I lift my hand, my face hot, and mouth, "Sorry." They just frown. I don't blame them. I'd be confused, too, if I were them and saw someone pummeling their steering wheel. But right now I'm me, and the only thing I'm feeling is frustration because the battery in the ten-year-old used car I share with Mom has decided to die on my one day off this week—the day I was planning to run a list of errands so that the rest of my week could pass by smoothly.

Gripping both hands on the steering wheel, I lower my face to the center, forcing myself to breathe deeply. The slow, even rhythm is in stark contrast to the frenzy of worried thoughts making a mess of my brain.

Dead car battery means I have to call roadside service or Uber home if no one is available. I'll probably have to replace the battery, maybe even the alternator, too, if that's the root of the problem. So instead of running to the grocery store and testing out recipes at home like I planned to do today, I'll be stuck at a body shop, scrambling to find places in my budget I can pull from to pay for this surprise car repair.

I grind my teeth so hard I give myself the beginnings of a tension headache: dull pain starting at the base of my skull, slowly creeping down my neck. A beat later I yell out a groan. Of-fucking-course this would happen. Just when things were starting to pick up for me.

Just then there's a knock on the window. I jolt up with a yelp.

Callum's face greets me. "Car trouble?" His voice is muffled through the glass window, but I can still understand him.

"Um, yeah. Hang on."

I reach for the door handle, and he steps back to make room for me to climb out. I shut the door and cross my arms, facing him. "I think my battery's dead."

He stares, eyebrows in an impressive deep wrinkle. "I can give you a jump."

"No, thanks." The words spill from my mouth, like a reflex. As much as I desperately need a favor right now, I don't want it if it's from *him*.

He glances to the side, then crosses his arms. "Are you really in a position to refuse my help?"

My mind flashes back to how he swooped in at the vet's office and took care of my bill despite my protests and the condescending way he explained that it was for the cat's sake, not mine.

"I will always be in a position to refuse you." I practically spit the words through gritted teeth. He didn't even have the decency to acknowledge me when I waved at him minutes ago. He has no right to demand I accept anything from him.

He doesn't seem fazed by my curt tone though. In fact, for a split second it looks like his mouth quirks up. It falls away before I can be sure.

"Fine, Nikki."

He walks away down to the other end of the parking lot, and my breath escapes in a hot huff. One half of me is satisfied at seeing his broad form walk away. But the other half is scolding myself, frustrated that I couldn't just swallow my pride for one damn minute and accept his offer of help. Yes, he's a jerk, but now I've resigned myself to an afternoon of dealing with car troubles I can't afford.

Sweat beads on my forehead as the sun blares from above. I fish my phone out of my pocket just as a gray hatchback pulls up right in front of my car, the silver bumper just a foot from the scuffed fender of my Honda Civic.

When Callum climbs out of the driver's seat, my jaw drops. He pops the hood open, then nods at me. "Open the bonnet of your car for me, please. Now."

"Bonnet?"

"Hood. The hood of your car."

"Why?"

"Because I'm going to help you."

The muscles in my neck ease from their tension knot at the same time as my heart races. His voice takes a soft yet authoritative tone. I would never, ever admit this out loud, but that tone is killer—sexy, even. It's the perfect balance of commanding yet polite. I bet he could compel a fish to walk if he spoke in that tone. If he had used it when we first met, I would have been a lot more receptive to whatever he had to say.

I'm tempted to ask why again, but that would be risking my luck. This is a second chance to solve my problem with minimal fuss. I had better take it.

I stay silent and stand to the side, watching while he darts in his back seat to grab jumper cables. He doesn't ask me to help him as he sets everything up between our two cars or when he sits back in his vehicle and starts the engine. I don't offer either. I simply stand back, lean on my driver's side door, and watch him work. No matter how artificial this gesture is, I need it. And Callum knows it.

I cross my arms over my chest, momentarily self-conscious, wondering if he can smell my desperation. It's obvious judging by how quickly he picked up on my financial situation at the vet's office that he's been paying attention while we've been working in such close proximity. For one or two days a week it's just me at the food truck, because even though I'm a stickler on Mom's days off, we can't afford to hire anyone else, not even part-time. Our truck squeaks to a halt every time we pull up to our spot on Makena, a signal that we're in desperate need of new brake pads. The exterior is dingy on a good day. The white paint is peeling off, the painted-on images are fading, and there are dings and scratches galore.

I glance down at my outfit. A blue T-shirt dress that I've had for years. Not at all dumpy—more like well loved. And I wear it once a week, which means Callum has seen me in it many times before.

I'm flushed with embarrassment yet again. I'm like a humpback whale, but instead of a sonar distress call, my cry for help is my worn clothing and the rickety state of my belongings.

Fixing my eyes on him, I take stock. He's a casual clothes guy for sure. I've never seen him wear anything other than jeans, khaki shorts, T-shirts, and the occasional short-sleeve button-up. But they always look new, and I don't think I've seen him repeat an outfit yet. And that silver food truck he shares with his brother looks practically brand-new the way it shines like a seashell in the sunlight. Whatever finance job Callum had must have paid a pretty penny for him to drop everything and move to the state of Hawaii, one of the most expensive places you could choose to live in the US, so he could re-hab his brother's struggling small business.

Maybe Finn had money troubles before, but his big brother has seemed to make them all disappear.

He sticks his head out the window. "Now try it," he says in that same gentle yet firm tone, pulling me back to the present.

Hopping into my car, I shove the key in the ignition and turn it. The second it starts, I'm positively giddy with relief. The fact that it started so quickly means that my battery is still good, at least for a little while longer, and I won't have to replace the alternator. Instinctively, I almost grin up at him, but I catch myself. He already made it clear today he's not interested in seeing my smile.

I take a second and will my face back to neutral before stepping out of the car. He removes the cables and tosses them in his back seat. I stand by the hood of my car, alternating between crossing my arms over my chest and clasping my hands behind my back. Nerves swarm my stomach, like butterflies that are angry about being cooped up. I open and close my mouth a handful of times, waiting for the right time to tell him thank you. He saved my skin today, and for that, the very least I owe him are words of gratitude.

He climbs out of the car and turns to me. I open my mouth once more, this time certain I'll say the right thing, but he speaks first.

"You could say thank you, you know."

"What?"

He rolls his eyes, then slams the back door to his car shut. "That's typically what a person says to another person when they've done something nice for them."

His words fall out in a dismissive mutter. It sends me straight from simmering nerves to boiling over.

"You seem pretty fixated on manners and etiquette for someone who doesn't like to follow those rules himself." I spin on my heels and walk back to the front door of my car before turning to look at him once more. "I was actually going to say thank you. I was waiting for you to get out of the car so you could hear me clearly."

I duck into my car, dig through my purse for a twenty, then march up to him. "Here."

"What is that?" He scowls down at my hand, like I've just offered him a hit of crystal meth.

"Money." I say it in an obnoxious, overly clear tone, like he's a child and I'm explaining the concept of currency. Yeah, it's a dick move, but I don't have the patience or the capacity to try to be nice if he's going to operate in maximum prick mode during every encounter we have.

He shifts his scowl to my face. "I don't want that."

I try to shove it in his hand, but he yanks away. I try again, and again he darts out of my reach. Any bystanders watching us must think we're demonstrating some seriously awkward dance moves.

"Look, you wouldn't accept anything when you helped me with Lemon. Let me at least cover this."

He doesn't bother to speak, instead letting the disapproval on his face do the talking.

"Just take it," I blurt.

We stand facing each other while taking twin deep breaths, our chests heaving. Forcing money into someone's hands when they don't want it is tiring work. So is darting away from someone trying to give you money that you don't want, apparently.

"It's less than I would have had to pay a mechanic to do it anyway," I say.

"I don't want your bloody money, Nikki. Don't you think you'd be better off keeping that than giving it to me?"

I'm frozen at the disdain in his voice. It's clear in all of his features, actually. From the pitying way he looks at me, his brows creased, his mouth in a purse. Disappointment radiates from him.

It all comes tumbling back to me, the reminder crashing over me like a rogue wave knocking me underwater. He doesn't want a damn thing from me because I'm his lowly, pathetic competitor whose food truck is in shambles, whose used car is barely functioning, who can't afford hired help. He wouldn't dare take anything from me because he doesn't need it—unlike me, who needs so much because for so long I've been barely scraping by.

This must be his warped idea of charity. When he's tired of despising me, he can simply pity me. It reads like a whole new form of condescending.

"Fine." I shove the money in my pocket, hoping my cheeks don't flush so red that he notices.

I hop in my car and speed out of the parking lot, refusing to turn my head or glance in the rearview mirror. I don't want to give Callum any indication that he's on my mind.

After picking up the dragon fruit, I drive home, running through my mental Rolodex of new recipes I've been planning to try out for the festival. I've got a festival to prepare for—to win—and zero time to let Callum James faze me.

. . .

"So!" I point the pen in my hand at Mom, who sits on a stool at the other side of the kitchen counter. "The veggie *pansit* seemed to be a hit at the food truck last week, don't you think? When we tried it with tofu, not so much, so I say let's eighty-six the tofu *pansit* and officially add the veggie one to the roster for the Maui Food Festival."

She sips from her glass of water. "That sounds fine."

I scribble a note on the pad lying on the counter. "We'll keep a few old favorites, of course, like the *lumpia* and the chicken *adobo* wings. Any sort of finger food will be easier for people to eat when they're walking around."

She swats away a fly zeroing in on a nearby basket of ice cream bananas, nods, then rests her chin in her hand.

"What do you think of adding the veggie *lumpia* to the roster too?" I ask.

Roles have somehow reversed between us. Now I'm the one in full-on work mode all day, every day, our menu for the Maui Food Festival at the front of my mind always. Mom has taken a page out of my book and has been telling me to relax on a daily basis.

She frowns at me. "Sit down." She pats the stool next to her. I walk over and plop down.

This is the first time since driving the food truck to and from Makena that I've sat all day. Energy is coursing through me like electricity. I want to spend every free minute I have perfecting our recipes for the festival. Callum's blatant pity at the farmer's market was the boost I didn't know I needed. I refuse to lose our spot to him. And until we secure victory, I can't relax, unwind, or think about anything other than our food and how that ties into our future. It weighs like an anvil on my mind.

She puts her hand on top of mine, which rests on the white tile counter. "You've been working so hard lately."

"I want to make sure everything is perfect," I say. "We've got a lot riding on this."

"When's the last time you went out and did something fun? Something that wasn't about work or cooking or the festival?"

I open my mouth, but can't think of a single thing to say. Other than a handful of leisurely swims at the beach to clear my head, I haven't taken a break. Not once.

She responds with that knowing expression all moms seem to have. "All those times you tell me that I need to relax and do something fun to unwind, and yet you don't do it yourself."

I cross my arms. "That's different. I'm almost thirty. This is the time to push myself and work hard. You've spent a lifetime doing that, Mom. You need the rest more than I do."

"Everyone needs rest. Everyone needs to have fun."

"Working is fun for me."

It's only a half lie. I love seeing how our food truck business has grown. I love coming up with new recipes and seeing our customers go gaga over them. I love what she and I accomplish every day we work together.

But there's another part of me. The carefree part that used to spend days off hiking, bar crawling with friends, and napping. I've been ignoring that part for the past year and a half. Slowing down wasn't an option when we had medical bills, a funeral to pay off, and Mom's savings to replenish.

I bite the inside of my cheek to keep from admitting all this out loud. Of course it would be nice to indulge in a free day. I could hike one of the trails at Haleakala. Or finally make it to the Pipiwai bamboo forest and see if it's as stunning in person as it is in every single photo I've seen.

She frowns at me, the tan patch of skin between her dark eyebrows barely wrinkling. "Oh, don't give me that. You make me take days off from work so I can play mahjong with my friends and go to book club."

Reaching across the counter for her phone, she swipes across the screen, then slides it to me. "Now I'm making you."

I focus on the image, which is an airline logo. The letters "LHR" don't sink in at first, but then a second later, it registers. Heathrow Airport. A flight to London.

I squint up at her. "Mom, what in the world is this?"

She pats my shoulder before hopping off the stool. "You're going to London for a week to visit Auntie Nora and Uncle Nigel."

"Um, what?"

She runs a hand through my loose waves. "You deserve to go on a vacation. You've been working nonstop ever since you moved here to help me after your dad died."

She rounds the corner of the counter and heads for the sink to load the dishwasher. I trail behind her, stuttering. "But, Mom. England? The money . . . Taking time off from work . . . We can't afford this."

I'm still shaking my head, struggling to process the words she's speaking. How in the world can she just send me out of the country when we have a make-or-break career moment hanging over our heads?

"It's not costing us anything. Your auntie and uncle offered to pay. They miss you like crazy and are so excited to see you. You haven't seen them since you were what, twelve? Thirteen?"

I mumble a "yes." That's the downside of having family all over the globe. Unless you're made of money, regular visits are virtually impossible. It hasn't dampened our relationship though. Mom and I Skype or FaceTime with them a couple times a month, and Mom's been to London to visit them a few times in the last several years. It would be a dream to visit them. Just not now, not when we're preparing for the festival and money is so tight.

She files the last dish into the rack and shuts the door of the dishwasher. When she looks at me, I try to focus on her face, try to decipher if this is an elaborate joke. But nothing. Her expression is oddly relaxed.

"You're staying with them at their house, so you won't even have to pay for a hotel," she says.

Brushing past me, she heads down the hall to the bathroom. I tug her arm. "Mom, wait. Okay, fine, yes, a vacation would be nice, but I can't just leave you alone to take care of the food truck. That's too much stress. And we can't afford to close for a week, either, while I'm gone. What about prepping for the festival?"

She does her signature brush-off motion with her hand, like none of these are valid concerns. "Mrs. Tokushige's nephew just moved in with her, and he needs a temporary job. I talked to him the other night while we played mahjong, and he said he could help out at the food truck if we ever needed it. He used to work at a food truck in San Francisco, so he knows what he's doing. The festival is more than a month away, and all the dishes we've been trying out with the customers have been a hit. So don't worry."

I open my mouth, but she shakes her head, her favorite way to cut me off.

"And don't give me some lecture about how your dad would want me to take it easy. I'll still take my normal day off. I promise."

Just then Lemon rubs against my leg. "What about Lemon? She's pregnant."

Mom raises her eyebrow at me, a telltale sign that she's unimpressed with my excuse. "All she's been doing is eating and napping, and I don't think that's going to change for the week that you're gone. She'll be just fine."

I stutter once more. She must have been planning this for weeks behind my back. I'm impressed, shocked, and a little unnerved at her ability to orchestrate such elaborate plans in secret.

"Um . . ."

"No ums, no buts, no nothing. I worked in restaurants my whole life until I had you, remember? I'll be just fine." She pats my arm. "You deserve a break. Have some fun while you're gone, okay? Your flight leaves on Wednesday. I'll drive you to the airport before I go to work."

I try and fail to say something in response. So instead, I stumble the few steps back to the counter and stare at the flight information on her phone screen.

She stands up and points to Dad's urn in the living room. "I thought of everything, Harold. Aren't you proud? I'm the one telling people to slow down and take a break now."

She shuffles down the hall. "Better start packing, *anak*," she hollers from her bedroom. "Only two days until you leave!"

I've got no choice. It looks like I'm going to London.

# Chapter 7

I shove my carry-on in the overhead compartment and fall into the window seat. Leg one of my journey is down. Five hours in the air from Hawaii to Seattle, a three-hour layover at the airport, and now I'm finally on the plane to Heathrow.

I'm crossing my fingers for a smooth rest of the journey. It's been good so far. No crying babies, no delays, no bad turbulence.

I take a sip from my water bottle and pull a book from my purse. A fun, light read that should take up a chunk of this nine-hour flight. I crack it open to the first page, barely paying attention to the passengers shuffling through the aisle next to me. Everyone seems to be operating under some unspoken guise of decency I don't often see before a long-haul flight. People say, "Excuse me" and "Oops! Sorry!" when they accidentally bump into someone. Everyone is taking care to move out of the way to let others through, so as to avoid jamming up the aisles. A guy at the front of the plane even stops to help an older woman lift her suitcase into the overhead bin.

I let out a happy sigh. Maybe Mom was right. Maybe this trip will be the reset I need, the break from real life that will help me feel refreshed and return home reenergized.

Everyone takes their seats on the plane, and I turn back to my book. A heavy plop noise pulls my focus away. I turn to my left and see a backpack sitting on the seat next to me. When I look up, I almost drop my book. There's Callum James standing above me, chest heaving as he catches his breath.

"What the . . ." My voice is a rasp. It's the best I can do while my body struggles to process this influx of information.

Callum will be sitting next to me for the next nine hours.

His eyebrows crinkle together as he shoves the backpack above him. Lowering himself into the seat, he tugs on the seat belt. "Were you expecting someone else?"

His tone reads unamused. I can't possibly be the only one out of the two of us surprised that we're seated next to each other. Of all the people on this airplane—of all the people who booked a flight from Seattle to London on this day—how the hell did Callum and I end up seated together?

The universe is a sick bastard with an even sicker sense of humor.

"What . . . what in the world are you doing here?" I finally ask.

"Rushing to make my flight to London. What does it look like I'm doing?" There's bite to his low tone.

Rushing. That's probably why I didn't see him in the boarding area. I purse my lips, once again cursing the universe for allowing Callum to make this flight by the skin of his teeth.

Gripping both armrests, I prop myself up straighter and pivot my gaze around the cabin. Every other passenger is seated. The only ones moving about are the flight attendants.

I fall back into my seat, my head spinning. When I turn my focus back on Callum, the wrinkle in his brow is even deeper.

He tilts his head to the side. "Do you think I somehow orchestrated this?"

I shrug, flipping through random pages of my book. "Out of all the flights to London today, we managed to be on the same one sitting next to each other. Anything's possible at this point."

He scoffs. "If you say so."

I jerk my head toward him, ignoring the flight attendant standing just a few feet in front of us, pointing out the emergency exits while the voice over the intercom explains the safety procedures.

"Oh, don't give me that," I say. "We're stuck next to each other for the next nine hours."

"We'll manage, I'm sure," he mutters. He doesn't even turn to me when he speaks, opting instead to keep his gaze pointed at the headrest in front of him.

"Well, I won't."

I wave down the flight attendant nearest me. She walks up to our row, polite smile plastered across her face. I try to mirror the same friendly expression, but I'm wound so tight that my smile probably looks more like a wince.

"What can I help you with, miss?" she says cheerily.

"Would I be able to switch to a different seat? Whatever empty one you have? If it's not too much trouble."

Relaxing, unwinding, zoning out, all of that will be impossible if I have to share an armrest with the guy who's been a thorn in my side for the past several weeks.

Callum's chest heaves up as he takes a slow, deep breath in.

"Oh gosh, I'm not sure if I can do that," she says brightly. "See, this is a full flight. Unless another passenger is willing to trade seats, I'm afraid that can't happen. We're about to take off, but if you want, I can ask around once we're in the air."

Deflated, I nod and tell her that would be great. After I thank her, she walks away, leaving Callum and me in our bubble of tension.

He finally twists his head to me. A hint of amusement rests behind his stare. "Is a screaming toddler or an obnoxiously chatty seatmate really preferable to me?" he says.

"Seeing as neither one is threatening to put me out of business like you are, I'd welcome them with open arms."

I lean my head back and close my eyes, steeling myself for whatever comeback Callum has. But there's no reply. Only the hum of the engines gearing up as we speed down the runway.

We glide into the air, and I wait. For a snide remark, a scoff, anything to signal Callum's distaste for me. Still nothing. When I twist my head to look at him, he's staring at the seat ahead of him again. But his face isn't hard or smug anymore. Rather, something sorrowful taints his otherwise neutral expression. As we cut through the sky, I wonder what he's thinking.

A minute later, he turns to me. "Can we try something?"

"What do you mean?"

He sighs and runs a hand through his hair. "Look, I know . . . Can we just call a truce for this flight? No talk about work or the festival or anything else that's transpired between us."

Red ignites his cheeks when he looks at me. For a moment, I'm puzzled at his sudden blushing, but then the crystal clear image of him on Little Beach in his birthday suit flashes to the front of my mind. Oh right. I've seen him naked. Deliciously, deliciously naked. I tuck away the image. He probably doesn't want to talk about that either.

"Like a time-out?" I ask.

"Yes. Exactly."

I rub my face as the heat makes its way up my neck, my gaze falling to my lap. "I can agree to that."

"Shake on it?" He holds his hand out to me. "We'll be pleasant to each other for the rest of this flight?"

I clasp his hand in mine and nod. A phantom spark identical to the one that hit me the first time we shook hands glides through me. And then I remember just how quickly Callum let go of me the day we made our Maui Food Festival wager, like I was on fire. Like he couldn't bear to spend an extra second touching my skin.

This time, I'm the one who lets go first. "Deal."

An hour into our truce, my eyes are blurry from trying to make out the words on the page in front of me. Somehow just being this physically close to Callum has affected my ability to read. The text in this book may as well be Wingdings for as much sense as it makes in my distracted state.

I give up and shove the book back in my purse. I contemplate shelling out the money to pay for Wi-Fi on this flight so I can mindlessly surf the web just to distract myself, but I decide the expense isn't worth it. I scan through the free movies on the screen in front of me, but nothing catches my interest. And I don't think I could even begin to focus with Callum next to me.

Turning slightly against the headrest, I sneak a peek at him. He's staring at the screen of his phone, earbuds in his ears. What kind of music does this hot young curmudgeon like to listen to?

A different flight attendant walks by, eyeing him like a porterhouse steak. I roll my eyes, even though I sympathize with her appraisal. Jet-setting Callum is quite the eye candy in straight-cut trousers and a snug long-sleeve T-shirt the exact same shade as his hazel eyes. When she offers us drinks from her cart, I decline. Callum asks for ginger ale, but the smitten flight attendant says in an overly sweet tone that they're out.

"Can I get you anything else? Sprite? Coffee? Pepsi?"

"No, thank you." He focuses back on his phone.

She tucks her light brown hair behind her ears and leans closer toward him. "You sure?" She lifts an eyebrow. "Not even water? I'd hate for you to go thirsty."

Good Lord. Only one of us is thirsty, and it's definitely not either of the people currently seated.

"Um, Sprite is fine. Thanks."

She leans her hand on the seat in front of him. "I absolutely adore your accent," she says through a giggle.

His cheeks catch fire. "Oh. Thank you."

"I could listen to you talk all day." She grins, pours him a drink, then points to the call light. "Don't hesitate to flag me down if you need anything else."

She stares at him two seconds too long before finally walking on and helping the passengers behind us.

I can't contain the scoff that escapes my lips when I gaze out the window.

"Something funny?" Callum asks.

I turn to him. "Just amused at how obvious she was being with you."

"Glad my discomfort is funny to you."

His scowl lingers on me for one long second. Then it falls back to his phone.

That lethal look. That same dismissive glare he flashed me during the farmer's market when I dared to smile and wave at him. When I mistakenly thought we could be decent to each other for just one moment.

I bite down so hard, my jaw aches. "You're one to talk."

He squints at me.

"Don't talk to me about discomfort." I steady my voice so I don't cause a scene. "Your entire existence has made me uncomfortable. Ever since I met you, life has been a million times more unpleasant for me and my mom. Do you have any idea the kind of uncertainty you've sown into our jobs by taking over our spot? That thought is more than just uncomfortable."

When I pause to take a breath, I feel like I've finished the hill sprint workout at spin class.

"There you are every single day, parking right next to us, reminding us that in a few weeks we could lose it all. You wouldn't even listen when I tried to explain everything to you the day we met. I was just trying to be nice . . . Some trucks were awful to us when we started out, snapping at us because we didn't know the rules. Finally, someone clued us in, and things were so much better. All I wanted to do was help you, like someone helped me."

My heart is racing and I'm practically panting as I unload these words, these words I've been aching to say to him for weeks, but I've never had the nerve—until now. Now that we're trapped together in a metal tube with no clear escape, I may as well lay it all out.

"Remember the farmer's market? I was just trying to be nice again, and you glared at me like I was the vilest thing you had ever laid eyes on. You walked by me like I was nothing. Any idea how uncomfortable that made me feel? And how you refused to take that money I offered you at the vet's office and when you jumped my car? God, you were so condescending about it. I guess hard-ass Callum has no time to be even the tiniest bit decent to his competitors."

I stop before my voice has the chance to break. Why did I ever think he could be anything other than brash and cruel? That's all he's ever shown me.

Only one hour into this flight, and already our attempt at pleasantry is an epic fail. I death-glare at a cloud outside my window while quietly deep breathing my way to something resembling calm.

"I'm sorry, Nikki."

His quietly spoken words are a shock to the body. Good thing I'm already sitting, because if I had been standing, I would have fainted.

Pushing up his sleeves, he shrugs. "I didn't know you were trying to be nice. At the farmer's market, I mean."

"I was smiling and waving at you. Jesus, what's your version of nice?"

He sighs and fixates on the headrest in front of him. Then he whips his phone out and spends several seconds swiping before leaning over to show me. In an instant, warmth coats my arm closest to him. That's some powerful body heat he possesses if I can feel it despite the inches of space between us. I swallow to collect myself and look at the screen.

It's the selfie I took at the farmer's market with Penelope, the adorably enthusiastic fan of our food truck. Underneath our smiling faces is a caption: *Just met the amazing Nikki from @Tivas and OMG what an absolute doll! Can't wait to see her and her mom smash the competition at the #MauiFoodFestival! You're going down, @HungryChaps! Muahaha!!*

A devil smiley face ends the caption.

Callum rubs his forehead with his free hand. "I saw that right before I spotted you at the market." He runs a thumb across his cheek and chin, which are covered in thick golden stubble. "I thought you had something to do with her posting that. And then when you smiled and waved at me, it felt like you were mocking me. That's why I didn't acknowledge you."

"Oh." The realization takes a second to soak in. "I thought she just wanted a selfie. I didn't know she was going to post that."

"So all that was a misunderstanding," he says. He lets out a half groan, half exhale before pressing back into his seat.

"Looks like it."

We say nothing for a solid minute.

He coughs, then clears his throat. "I'm sorry for the way I made you feel at the vet's office. And with your car. I don't . . . I was truly just trying to help you. I didn't mean anything disrespectful when I told you to keep your money. When I help someone, I never, ever accept money when they offer it. I always tell them to keep it, that it's better off with them than with me because all I want to do is help."

With his clarification, the residual anger burns away like clouds dissipating after a storm.

"Huh." It comes out like a bewildered huff of breath. "I thought you were taking a swipe at me because of my financial situation."

He squints at me. "Your financial situation?"

I roll my eyes. "You don't have to pretend, Callum. From the state of my car and my food truck, it's obvious money has been a bit of a struggle." When I look back up at him, his hazel eyes are bright with concern. My resolve starts to soften. "I mean, it's not as bad now. We're not rolling in the dough, but ever since this unofficial competition started, business is picking up. I guess everybody wants to eat at our trucks just to see if we'll go off on each other. Crazy, huh?"

I let a small laugh slip; he does too.

He glances back down at his phone and clicks on the Instagram story for Hungry Chaps. A silent video plays of Finn plating up a basket of fish-and-chips against a glittery star filter.

"Glitter and stars? I didn't know that was your guys' style." The words are out of my mouth before I can catch myself. But I can't help my curiosity. Callum was obviously the one who filmed the video, since Finn was in it, but I would have never pegged him for a guy who would choose such a flashy filter.

When he looks up at me, I fully expect to be scolded for peering at his phone. But then he just shrugs. "Finn thought it would be funny. He runs all our social media accounts and seems to know well what customers like to see. I'm not really into Instagram. I have my own account, but I lost interest the day I made it."

There's a muffled announcement from the pilot about a bit of rough turbulence ahead.

"Would you be up for playing a game?" he says, out of the blue.

I squint at him.

Stretching up out of his seat, he tucks his phone into his pocket. "There's a game Finn and I used to play when we were youngsters. The Question Game. We'd take turns asking each other questions, and we'd have to answer them, no matter what."

"Okay . . ." I have no idea where this is going.

"It might be nice to talk about something other than work and us fighting about work."

Can't argue with him there.

"We can try to be quiet," I say.

He raises an eyebrow at me. "You really think we can make it for the next eight hours saying nothing to each other?"

No. "Yes."

His gaze glides to my collarbone, then back up to my face. I wonder what that long glance was about.

"Don't you want to at least try to see if we can get on temporarily?"

It's a weird idea, using a childhood game to keep the peace between us. But it's better than my strategy of stewing silently next to each other for the rest of the flight.

"Fine. I'll play."

He points at me. "Ladies first."

"Okay. How does an English guy like you like living in Hawaii?"

He clears his throat. "It isn't how I thought it would be."

"How did you think it would be?" I try to sound as sincere as possible. I honestly want to give this attempt at civil conversation a fair shot. And I honestly want to know.

"A lot less yelling at people in public during work hours, for one," he says.

I snort a laugh. "What else?"

"Three questions in a row? That's impressive for someone who didn't want to talk at all a minute ago."

"Easy, tiger. If you keep hassling me, it's back to loaded silence."

His grin morphs into a smirk. "I was hoping for more days spent on the beach."

I nod and try not to picture him walking out of the ocean like a naked ripped sea-god.

"Join the club," I say. "I never in a million years thought I'd be living in Maui and running a food truck with my mom."

He relaxes into his seat, his head lolling against the headrest as he turns to me. The gesture makes this feel like some strange brand of pillow talk.

"You're not from Maui?"

I shake my head. "Born and raised in Portland, Oregon. My parents lived there until they retired. They wanted to live someplace warm year-round and chose Maui."

"So you moved to be closer to them?"

"Sort of. Not at first." I heave a sigh, wondering if it's the smartest thing in the world to be so vulnerable in front of my competition. I opt for a shortened, sanitized version. "My dad was diagnosed with pancreatic cancer not long after they moved. He didn't have much time left when they figured out what was wrong with him. So I dropped everything to be with him until he . . ."

I don't say the rest. I don't have to. By the pained look on Callum's face, he knows exactly what happened.

"At the time I was managing my friend's restaurant in Portland, and I loved it. But I couldn't stay. I couldn't leave my mom alone in Maui, struggling in her grief under a mountain of medical bills. My dad's treatment wrecked a lot of their savings."

"So you gave everything up to take care of your mum?"

I nod, easing through a slow breath. As long as I stay measured and even in my tone of voice, I won't break down.

"I promised my dad before he died that I would. And even if I hadn't, I couldn't have lived with myself if I had just abandoned her to fend for herself. I'm an only child, and the rest of her family is scattered all over the place. Her sister, my aunt, is the person I'm visiting in London actually." I look down at my lap when I speak. I clear my throat, taking the extra moment to collect myself. "Plus, running a food truck was my parents' dream. They always talked about doing it when they retired. But now it's a way for my mom and me to spend time together while we support ourselves."

I pause to take a breath, wondering if sharing this next part will make me feel even more vulnerable than I already do. "And it's a way for me to live out my dad's last wish."

When I look up, his obnoxiously gorgeous face is twisted in an unfamiliar expression. Not pity, exactly, but not sadness. Something kinder. Empathy, I think. That wrinkle in his brow, the tenderness in his eyes, it's like he understands exactly what it feels like to have your heart ripped out, your insides set on fire, when you lose a piece of your family forever.

"That's incredible, Nikki. I bet that would make your dad so happy."

I nod a thank-you. In the past it's been so wrenching to talk about any of this. But speaking to Callum sets me at ease. How weird.

"Do you miss Portland?" he asks.

"A lot. Everything is so different there, from the quirky style of houses to the hipster food to the insane traffic and the nine months of rain. I never realized just how pleasant daily sunshine was until I moved to Maui."

"Coming from England, it was a shock for me too."

"I'm still getting used to it—and the number of hotels and resorts and vacation condos that seem to be everywhere," I say. "Hopefully, I can go back to Oregon for a visit someday. I burned a lot of people I was close to when I moved though."

"How do you mean?"

"When I got the news about my dad, I went into autopilot mode. The only thing that mattered was getting to Maui so I could be with him during treatment. I gave my notice at my job, packed my stuff, and left. I didn't even say good-bye to most of my friends and co-workers. I just sent them texts telling them about what happened with my dad and that I had to leave right away. Most of them called to check up on me a few times the first few months I was gone, to ask if I was okay and if there was anything they could do for me. I never followed up with them. I've never even called them back to catch up or say hello. It was pretty cruel, looking back on it."

This is the first time I've admitted all of this out loud, and it still makes me want to crawl out of my skin. I was the world's worst friend.

"It's been over a year since I've talked to any of my friends on the mainland," I say quietly.

Callum shakes his head. "Nikki."

The sound of my name spoken in his soft, low tone is made melodic by his accent and sends a tingle through me.

"You didn't do anything wrong. You had a family emergency and had to act quickly. I'm sure they understood."

"I'll never know."

"You can reconnect with them. People get back in touch all the time nowadays."

"Maybe." Maybe someday when things are secure, I'll have time for friends again.

"You should consider it," he says softly.

It's a thought that's crossed my mind a million times. I have every single one of their numbers still saved in my phone. But what kind of jerk would I sound like if I called up my old workmates after almost a year and a half of zero contact?

Callum's gaze falls to his lap. When he looks back up at me, his face is twisted into a pained expression. "Nikki, if I had known you lost your dad when we first met, I wouldn't have acted like such a . . ."

"Wanker?"

He breaks into the widest grin I've ever seen him make, and it's pure, unfettered joy. It must be contagious, because now I'm grinning too.

"You're using my lingo. Love it," he says. "Is that what you thought of me when you first met me?"

"No. You were nice to me when you thought I was the health inspector. But when you started being mean, yeah. It was straight to wanker."

He chuckles, not the least bit offended at my honesty.

I let out a small laugh. "I'd say sorry, but I know you thought the same of me."

"Not really," he says, his gaze fixed to mine.

"Yeah right."

"It's the truth. I liked you straightaway."

"Not possible. You were pissed at me, just like I was pissed at you."

For a second he looks away, like he's trying to rein in the smile that's so close to splitting his face. When he turns back to me, the lightest shade of pink splashes across his cheeks.

"You made me angry. But I liked it."

My mouth goes dry. "You did?"

"I have a bit of a thing for gorgeous women who take the piss out of me."

"Really?"

The break that follows is like silent flirting. He's gazing at me and I'm gazing at him. The expression on his face is an intriguing mix of shy and smug, like he's unsure if admitting that to me was a good idea, but he wanted to do it anyway.

His admission flatters me as much as it intrigues me. Yes, it's a bit nutty that I'm well on my way to liking a guy I loathed two hours ago. But this little bit of honest flirting has gone a long way toward repairing the rift between us.

"Should I keep calling you wanker, then?"

Callum lets out a throaty chuckle. "I suppose my personality isn't fit for the hospitality industry."

"It's pretty damn well suited to finance."

Confusion mars his face.

"I ran into Finn at the farmer's market right before I saw you that day. He gave me a quick rundown of your professional past. Everything made a lot more sense when he told me you were an ex-finance guy."

Callum lets out a groan, then a soft laugh. "Of course Finn would do that."

"It was sort of sweet the way he defended you. He said you were the only one who offered to help him when he ran into trouble with his business."

Flush creeps from behind the thick stubble on his face once

again. Inside I'm cheering. It's weird to pay a compliment to the guy I've been warring with the past few weeks. But it's also intriguing. The gentle curve of his smile, the easy posture he assumes when we share about our backgrounds make me wish we could talk like this always.

"So in all your finance experience, did you also train how to cook and operate a restaurant? Because you do a pretty bang-up job."

"A bit. I learned to cook by helping my gran at her bed-and-breakfast growing up. Finn and I would do the cooking and cleaning as teenagers."

"Seriously?"

His eyes cut to me. "You sound surprised."

"That sounds so . . . quaint. And heartwarming. Very unlike you."

He chuckles. "We enjoyed it. Got to plan the menus together. The guests loved whatever we'd come up with. We'd trade off being head chef every other night. Finn loved that. Though he loved it a lot less the nights I was in charge. According to him, I'm bossy."

"No way." I try for fake surprise. He rewards me with a wink.

"Finn was a bit reckless in the kitchen growing up," Callum says. "He avoided countless grease fires thanks to me."

"You've got the protective-big-brother act down," I say.

There's a long pause. He looks away from me, then clears his throat. "There's a reason for that."

"Which is?"

Another extended pause. He takes a breath. "Finn was hit by a car when he was five years old. He was riding his bike, and a drunk driver crashed into him. He nearly died."

"Oh God." I cup my hand over my mouth.

"He's fine now, of course, but he was in a coma at first. I sat by his side every day in the hospital, holding his hand, hoping that he'd just wake up and get better. I thought I was going to lose him, my only brother. My only sibling."

The hard clench of his jaw, the glistening of his eyes give away just how hard he's struggling to keep it together while telling me all this.

Like a reflex, my hand falls to his forearm. Inside, I'm cringing. The urge to comfort happened so fast, before I could think twice and hesitate. I expect a frown or for him to ask just what the hell I think I'm doing. But none of that happens. All he does is close his eyes and nod.

"Thank you," he whispers.

We've broken the touch barrier previously with handshakes, but this time, there's substance to our contact. We're sharing emotions, memories, pain. Silence floats between us once more, but this time there's comfort. And it's mutual.

A minute passes, and I still say nothing. I just keep my palm on his forearm and wait for him to feel ready to speak.

"He woke up two days later to his obnoxious, overprotective eight-year-old brother holding his hand," Callum says.

"I bet he was over the moon to see you by his side."

Callum's eyes take on a friendly sheen when they focus on me. "It took a few moments for him to process what was going on. Then when he did, when he saw me, he smiled."

There's a tingling heat between my hand and his arm. I give him a final pat, then slip my hand back to my lap.

"Of course he did," I say. "His big brother was right there watching over him the whole time."

He drains the rest of his drink and hands the empty cup to a passing flight attendant with a small smile and a polite thank-you.

"I suppose ever since then, I've been in protective-brother mode. Whenever people tried to pick on him at school, I'd jump in to defend him. When I was abroad for work, I'd call him every week to check up on him. Even now, he's twenty-seven and I'm thirty, yet I'm still doing it. When I first moved to Maui, I was only meant to stay to help him for a few months, to help him get his footing. Then I'd move back to Chicago. But I've pushed back my moving date so many times. It's just nice to be close to him for a change and work with him. And see him doing so well. It's ridiculous, but . . ."

"It's not. I totally get it."

He shakes his head. He knows I know what it's like. Me uprooting my life to be closer to my mom is proof.

"I'm sure he'll be glad to be rid of his overbearing older brother in a couple of months."

"So you're for sure moving back to Chicago then?"

He nods while glancing away. "After the Maui Food Festival."

I almost ask why he'd go back if he's enjoying his current setup so much, but I bite my tongue. Given how his eyes darted away when he mentioned it, he probably doesn't want to say more.

I touch my hand to my face. "Wow. The Question Game goes deep. You should have warned me."

Another soft smile from him. Inside I'm glowing, like a giant Christmas tree with all the lights on full blast.

"Growing up, Finn and I would mostly ask ridiculous questions, like if our favorite superheroes could beat a lion or a bear in a fight."

I let out a boom of a laugh, then notice the sky outside turning deep blue. It's almost nighttime already.

Callum's expression turns sheepish. "I'm sorry things got so personal."

I fix my gaze on him. "I'm not."

Getting personal helped us connect. Something new has been

forged between us. I felt it through every moment of prolonged eye contact with Callum in this conversation, every time he leaned in close enough that I could feel his delicious body heat on mine. I felt it when I touched his arm. We're not enemies anymore, not by a long shot. At this point, after all the light flirting and sharing of emotional memories, we're well into liking-each-other territory. Friends doesn't seem like the right word though. It feels a lot like we're bordering on something else entirely.

As I hold his gaze once more, I wonder if he feels this shift between us too.

But I don't have to wonder. We're still playing. I can ask.

I breathe. "One more question."

# Chapter 8

I exhale. "So um . . . this thing . . ."

Callum looks at me with renewed intensity.

"Do you feel . . ."

I attempt a steadying breath, then promptly lose my nerve. "So when are you going to come visit Lemon?"

His lips part, but he says nothing for the first few seconds. He swallows. "I didn't know I was welcome to see her."

"You're the reason I have her. Of course you're welcome."

His smile is small but warm. "How is she doing, by the way?"

"Good. She mostly sleeps, eats, and wakes up for me to pet her, then she goes back to sleep."

"Sounds like a typical cat." He taps his fingers against his knee. "I'd love to see her when we're back in Maui, if that's okay?"

"I'd like that too." My voice is too raspy for my own good, but I can't help it. That stare, the soft way he speaks. I'd say yes to anything he'd ask right now.

Swallowing, I force myself back on track. "So why are you headed to London?"

"Our cousin Henry is getting married."

"Finn didn't feel like coming?"

"He doesn't get on with Henry. I don't, either, to be honest. He's very much a blokey type whose life revolves around beer, football, and football chants."

"That's the most British sentence I've ever heard."

His laugh fills our end of the cabin. It makes my heart beat faster.

"I don't know how he ever managed to convince his fiancée to marry him. But family is family. Besides, it's been an age since I've been home last. I owe everyone a visit."

"But Finn gets out of it?"

"That's just his personality and everyone understands. I can't really blame Finn. Henry's a bit of a bellend."

I honk out a laugh so loud, it spooks the flight attendant pushing a food cart by us. "Wow. That's some salty language coming from a distinguished former finance professional."

He rolls his eyes. "Finance is hardly a distinguished profession."

"But it pays pretty damn well, from what I've noticed."

"You've got some balls bringing up money." He chuckles.

"You dropped everything to move to Maui, a place that's notoriously expensive. It doesn't take a genius to figure out that you made bank before your food truck days."

He rubs his neck, clearly uncomfortable with all this money talk. So I switch gears.

"But in all seriousness, you're pretty amazing, Callum. Finn also filled me in on how your parents were upset when you quit to help him, but you didn't care. That's really sweet. Like, unbelievably sweet."

Once again, his eyes fall to his lap. He's dashing when he's bashful. "Well, if it comes to choosing between pleasing my career-obsessed parents or working with my brother, I choose my brother. Always."

My heart thuds. "Do you miss anything about your old job?"

"The paychecks were nice, but that's not enough to make me give up an opportunity to work with Finn. It feels a bit like old times, when we were teenagers working for our gran. I think she'd be proud."

"I know she would." I look away and out the window when I realize the weird conviction in my voice. What an awkward thing for me to say, someone who has never met his grandmother.

I count to five and turn back to Callum, ready for a change of subject. "You probably don't miss having to wear a suit all the time. Finance guys wear suits, right?"

"I definitely don't miss that," he says.

The expression on his face turns soft, and for a moment, I pause. Maybe I don't have the guts to ask him about this shift in our dynamic, but I'm feeling bold enough to repay the flirty compliment he paid me before about giving him a hard time.

I fix my stare on his eyes. The perfect balance of hazel and green. "That's too bad," I say before turning back to the window. If I have any hope of pulling this off, I can't keep eye contact with him. "I bet you look really freaking good in a suit, Callum."

Again I count to five before turning back to check his reaction. I turn back and see the corners of his mouth turned up into a flustered grin. He is totally into it.

His gaze sharpens. "How about you? Do you miss dressing the part of restaurant general manager?"

"Tons. I loved it. I wore little black dresses every night."

Callum's cheeks are fiery red when he swallows. His eyebrows lift a touch. "Every night?"

I nod, glancing away when I feel my own cheeks warm. "As much as I love wearing comfy clothes at the food truck, I do miss dressing up and feeling pretty."

"You're always pretty, no matter what you wear."

It's no longer just my cheeks that are warm. His low growl sets every inch of my skin on fire.

The cheery flight attendant from earlier walks up to our row, still beaming. "Miss, I managed to find someone to trade seats with you, if you're still interested."

Callum directs a pointed look at me. Because he already knows, even though I haven't uttered a word. I don't want to sit next to anyone other than him.

"I changed my mind," I say to her. "I think I'll stay."

When I open my eyes, it's still dark in the cabin. I don't remember when I fell asleep, but it wasn't long after I declined the flight attendant's offer to trade seats. Callum and I chatted some more, flirted some more, laughed some more, and then my eyelids started to feel heavy. The last thing I recall is pressing against the headrest of my seat and closing my eyes.

But right now my head is propped on something firmer than the headrest. A few more seconds, and my eyes adjust to the dimness of the cabin. I register something underneath my cheek.

Callum's shoulder.

A sharp intake of air is my only response. I immediately clamp my mouth shut to keep from making too much noise. With each second that passes, I'm more alert. I notice the rhythmic, up-and-down movement of his chest, a telltale sign that he's deep in sleep.

Slowly, I lift my head up and away from him. He responds with a soft moan, then it's back to that gentle hum of air going in and out. It rings like a soft purr in my ear.

I shake my head and scoot closer to the window, wondering how the hell I felt comfortable enough to fall asleep on him. It's a struggle to process through the sleep-fog, but I get there.

Our breakthrough conversation. It's the fact that through the Question Game, we revealed intimate personal truths about ourselves. The fact that flirting with him was surprisingly fun. The fact that we went from rivals to friendly flight companions to something else in a matter of hours. It's the fact that his shoulder feels better than any pillow I've ever fallen asleep on. Despite how glorious it all feels, it seems entirely inappropriate to use Callum as a human pillow in this moment. Dozing off with your head on someone's shoulder is a decidedly couple-y thing to do. And Callum and I sure as hell are not a couple.

I steal another glance at Callum. Peaceful, slumbering, delicious Callum. He hasn't budged an inch since I jolted away from him. Maybe he's one of those people who sleeps so deeply that not even an earthquake can rouse him. If that's the case, maybe it wouldn't be the worst thing in the world if I were to lay my cheek back against his shoulder and see if I can fall asleep again.

Gently, I rest my head against him. He still doesn't move. The rhythm of his breathing stays the same, which is an immediate relaxer for me. All of my limbs loosen, and my eyelids grow heavy once more. An internal switch has flipped—I'm sleepy again. His body is like my own personal tension reliever. If I were a ballsy woman, I'd snake my arm around his and nuzzle my nose into his neck. I'd take deep breaths of his sandalwood cologne and let that soothing aroma lull me to sleep.

But that would cross every line imaginable, and already I'm pushing it. Right now, his shoulder will have to do. Before I know it, I'm out.

A loud, muffled voice speaking a string of unintelligible words is my wake-up call. Eyes still shut, I groan. Do they train all airline crews to speak as quickly as possible so no one can understand them? Then a cheery flight attendant hops on to announce that we're thirty minutes from landing at Heathrow. My eyes spring open. It's then that I realize I'm still propped against Callum's shoulder.

"Sorry," I mumble and pull away from him while wiping the side of my face. Please, please don't let there be any of my drool on him.

Sunlight bathes the interior of the cabin, and I do a quick scan of Callum. No drool marks on his shirt or pants. I let loose a relieved sigh.

He twists to me, sleepy grin on his face. "Sleep well?"

He tugs at his hair, which is matted in the back where he was leaning against the headrest. The front is only slightly mussed. It's decided. Callum James has the most adorably sexy bed head in the universe.

Nodding, I turn away and run my tongue along my teeth. My breath must reek.

I swipe two sticks of gum from my pocket and shove them in my mouth. "Sorry, I um . . . I didn't mean to fall asleep on you."

A slight wrinkle appears on his forehead, but it quickly fades. "It was rather nice actually."

"Really?"

The plane makes a sudden drop, and we clutch our armrests in unison. A minute later, all is calm once more.

He looks at me, and his smile reads tender, sincere. "I quite liked you sleeping on me, Nikki."

Saying nothing, I let his words float in the air. Now that comment from Callum is something else entirely. Is that a last-hurrah type of comment since our truce is set to expire the moment we touch land? Or is it an invitation to see if our current something else can turn into something more?

A full minute of turbulence has us bouncing up and down. As we begin our descent, I contemplate staying silent, holding back.

Only ten more minutes of our time-out. When the seat belt sign dings, everyone will file off the plane and we'll be back to our hostile status quo.

He peers over at me, pointed look on his face. "How was it for you?"

"I liked a lot of things about this flight actually," I say. It doesn't come off as desperate as I thought it would while mulling over the words in my head. In my growly early-morning rasp, I almost sound smooth.

"So maybe we could—"

The wheels hitting the ground cut Callum off. The two of us bump around in our seats until the plane comes to an abrupt stop.

I wonder if he'll finish his sentence while we taxi. I bite my lip to keep from saying anything. But minutes pass and he says nothing.

My heart falls to my stomach. He's lost his nerve. Or maybe I misheard what he said in the first place, and he wasn't going to say anything at all.

The seat belt sign dings. Almost everyone around us stands up and cracks open the overhead bins.

I stand up to that awkward hunched-over position I assume at the end of long-haul flights so I can stretch my arms and legs without hitting my head on the ceiling.

*Be cool*, my inner monologue commands. *Aloof. Carefree. It was just a time-out, a way to avoid killing each other during this flight. Don't push your luck. It means less than nothing.*

I flash what I hope is an easy, relaxed smile while typing the passcode into my phone and fumbling with a random app. "I think this marks the end of our time-out. It was fun."

Fun? Birthday parties are fun. Pub trivia is fun. Falling asleep on Callum's muscled shoulder during a transatlantic flight? That's a new form of bliss I didn't know existed until last night.

Callum's frown returns. "Is that all you want, Nikki? One time-out and nothing else?"

His forward question ties my tongue in a knot. What I really want is to fall asleep spooned against him, this time on a king-size bed, without our pesky clothes in the way. But I can't say that out loud. He'll think I'm a sex-crazed deviant, and that would be bad.

Or maybe . . .

I notice a flash behind those killer eyes, like he can read the X-rated thoughts playing in my head. Interesting. I may not be alone in my naughty wishes.

He leans down to me until our faces are nearly touching. "Don't tell me that after our conversation, after falling asleep on each other, a time-out is all you want." The muscles in his sharp jaw twitch. "Because I certainly want more."

"Oh." The hot air in my lungs escapes as a slow hiss.

"Here."

He grabs my hand, which still has my phone clutched in it. The firm yet gentle way his palm cradles the back of my hand makes it impossible to breathe. He somehow knows how to touch, how to hold, how to bring my heart to a complete standstill with five seconds of contact.

He types his name and number into my phone, then dials himself. Then he releases me, saves my number to his phone, and meets my gaze once more. There's renewed intensity in his eyes. It's eagerness, confidence, and some mystery emotion I haven't quite worked out yet. I've never seen it in all the times that we've looked at each other.

"I'm here until Tuesday, and I'd very much like to see you outside of this plane," he says. "Call me if you're interested."

He grabs his bag from the overhead compartment, then smooths the front of his shirt with his free hand.

I shove my hands in my pockets to keep from tearing at the fabric and exposing that perfect chest, that flawless highway of light skin, hard lines, and even harder muscle.

I lick my bottom lip, then shake my head. I'm surrounded by strangers, families, children. My feral behavior is beyond ridiculous. I'm in public and need to keep the eye-fucking down to an absolute minimum.

Must regain control. I inhale slowly, steadily. "You think that's a good idea? Us meeting up?"

As much as my body wants it, it can't be a good thing. Our respective livelihoods depend on us ruining each other. Getting involved with each other outside of work, no matter how hot, would blur the lines for sure.

Quarters are so close in this cramped row of seats that when he leans toward me, it's practically a hug. I can feel the heat from his body skimming across my skin. We're barely two inches apart and this is how he feels? How hot would he feel if we were naked, skin-to-skin, under bedsheets, his body on top of mine?

A moan tickles the back of my throat. I suppress it. Airplane. Families. Children. Public decency laws.

That foreign look in Callum's eyes takes on a familiar sheen: dilated pupils that are also cloudy. I've seen it many times in many men. But this is the first time I've ever witnessed it in Callum's. And it has a name: lust.

His chest heaves. He lowers his mouth to my ear. "No. It's a bloody bad idea. But I'm keen on bad ideas if it involves you, Nikki."

Callum steps out of our row and strolls down the aisle toward the exit, without a second glance at me. Turning the corner, he disappears.

I'm relieved. Because those words he whispered in that low rasp cause me to fall back into my seat, and I don't want him to see the effect he has on me after just one transatlantic flight.

I'm going to need a minute to recover. Or ten.

I take a steadying breath, noticing the flirty flight attendant staring daggers at me from the front of the plane. She must have observed the exchange between Callum and me just now. There's no mistaking our eye contact, the closeness of our bodies, the way he held my hand in his when he typed his number into my phone.

Callum just threw down the gauntlet. The only question: am I bold enough to be bad?

I trudge up Primrose Hill, Callum's words from two days ago still fresh in my head.

*I'm keen on bad ideas if it involves you, Nikki.*

Even two days of sightseeing in central London and exploring the Camden Town neighborhood where my aunt and uncle live did little to distract me. His words have been at the back of my mind the entire time.

I still haven't reached out to him. He hasn't reached out to me, either, but that's not a surprise. He left the ball in my court. It's one hundred percent up to me where we go from here. And still I have no idea what to do.

Despite Callum's very sexy distraction, visiting my aunt and uncle has been the recharge I didn't know I needed. My first night here they treated me to an epic dinner at their favorite Indian food spot, and they've been hugging me nonstop since I arrived. Just sitting and catching up with them has helped take my mind off the stresses from back home. Spending time together is like a cuddle for my soul. I make a mental note not to let so much time pass until our next visit.

Maybe next time, we'll have enough money so that Mom can come visit too.

I reach the top of the hill and take in the view of lush green hills around me. In the distance, countless skyscrapers and the iconic London Eye mark the horizon. The half dozen people standing around me take photos and videos. I'm not the only one taking advantage of this mild and sunny spring day. Joggers and walkers scatter across the park. There are parents pushing strollers and dogs playing fetch with their owners.

I snap a few photos of the skyline, then take a selfie. I start to shove the phone back in my pocket, but an idea hits and I pause. What if I send it to Callum? A friendly text and a selfie is a harmless way to break the contact barrier without setting any expectations.

I type out a quick message and send the photo before I change my mind.

Primrose Hill is gorgeous. All of London is actually. Why on earth did you leave? 😉

Instead of staring at my phone in eager anticipation of his response, I shove it in the back pocket of my jeans and walk back down the hill. Halfway down, it buzzes. My heart thunders when I check and see it's a text from Callum.

CALLUM: Because the weather here is miserable. You've caught us on an off day when it's sunny. You look gorgeous BTW

I bite my lip, grinning to myself as I stroll around the park.

ME: It's hard to beat Maui's perfect weather 😉 Also, thank you. How are you?

CALLUM: I'm stuck in a pub watching my cousin and his knobhead friends do shots before the wedding. I was hoping I could text you for the next few minutes to avoid talking to them

I laugh softly to myself, then quickly text back.

ME: Of course. And yikes, sorry to hear that

CALLUM: Having a nice time with your family?

ME: Yes. They've been taking me all over Camden Town. My aunt and uncle had errands to run today, so I'm checking out the Primrose Hill area on my own. Such a cool neighborhood they live in.

CALLUM: You're not far from me. My cousin's family rented out the Grazing Goat pub for the reception tonight. It's in Marylebone, only a few miles away.

My hand holding the phone tingles. Now that's a sign from heaven if I've ever seen one. Callum is within reach. If I want him, all I have to do is say so.

Three gray dots appear at the bottom of his most recent message, then fade away. Again they reappear. Again they fade.

The disappearing dots are an odd comfort. It's a sign that he's just as nervous as I am. It's the unlikely confidence boost I need.

ME: What you said . . . Before you walked off the plane . . . Did you mean it?

It's the best I can manage when my nerves are whirling like an out-of-control carousel. The wording of my message makes me sound like an uncertain teenager. But I don't care; I just want an answer. Before I try anything with him, I need to know for sure what he said wasn't a one-off or his idea of a joke.

My phone buzzes with his immediate reply.

CALLUM: Every word, Nikki

My fingers fumble to form a coherent response, but I come up with nothing. So I simply send "OK."

If I weren't walking the perimeter of a public park, I'd be cradling my face in my hands and groaning at how pathetic my texting game is. I fight through the embarrassment, staring with interest at a red phone booth.

When my phone buzzes this time, I'm too nervous to look at it. What in the world do I expect Callum to say when all I send him is a pathetic "OK" as my reply?

I force myself to read his response anyway.

CALLUM: You're awfully chatty today 😋

ME: Sorry. I'm out of practice at this whole flirt-texting thing LOL

CALLUM: Ah, I see. Try this: Yes, please, Callum. I'd like nothing more than to do some very, very bad things with you 😉

I chuckle out loud this time. With each text he sends, I'm more at ease, more comfortable at the thought of amping things up between us.

ME: LOL you are ridiculous

CALLUM: I am . . . but am I also right?

I step to the edge of the sidewalk to keep out of everyone else's way. Staring at his words on the screen, I take a breath. This is it. Take a chance or blow him off. My fingers hover over the keypad for a second before I swallow and take the plunge. I type those three letters that I know will kick things off officially between us and hit "send" before my nerves can convince me to do otherwise.

CALLUM: Lovely. Free tonight? I'd like to see you.

With steady hands, I type my response.

ME: When and where?

# Chapter 9

The moment I walk inside the Grazing Goat, I scan the room for Callum. It doesn't take long to find him. Even in a restaurant packed to the brim with sharply dressed wedding guests, he stands out. His broad, tall, leanly muscled body cuts a dashing figure in the black fabric of his tailored suit. There's just a peek of white from his dress shirt and the sheen of his silver tie. I was right. The Great Gatsby in all his West Egg glory would look downright slovenly standing next to Callum James in this suit.

He stands at the edge of the bar and turns around, spotting me. A soft smile tugs at his lips. His gaze fixes on me like a spotlight. Those bright hazel eyes light me up from the inside out.

He strides the few steps to where I'm standing. There's no hug, no cheek kiss, no bodily contact of any kind. And that's one hundred percent fine. We're standing in a room full of his family and friends after all. It would be awkward if he had to explain that he invited his work rival to this family engagement. Standing this close to Callum, so close that I can feel that delicious heat from his body hitting mine, is a worthy alternative.

"You made it," he says.

A roar of cheers from across the room captures our attention. A handful of tux-clad men hold pints of beer above their heads, yelling something nonsensical in unison. The guy at the end leans down to kiss a woman, who is rolling her eyes but smiling. The bride, I assume, since she's wearing a white ball gown.

Callum frowns, then touches the small of my back. "Here."

He leads me to an empty side room. The expression on his face turns sheepish. "I love my family, but Christ am I done with the drinking and shouting and toasting."

"It's all right. You look really good, by the way. Like, really, really good." There I go again sounding like a bumbling middle schooler with no game whatsoever. I power through the urge to face-palm.

Under the dim mood lighting of this side room, his skin flushes light pink. "Thank you. I hardly ever wear getups like this anymore. Feels weird."

"It looks the exact opposite of weird." My eyes move in a slow scan down the length of his body. "You'd give James Bond a run for his money."

He lets out a chuckle before doing his own visual scan of me. "And you look . . ."

Automatically, I cross my arms over my chest. I didn't plan to attend a wedding while on vacation in London, so I made do with dark skinny jeans, a black blouse, patent leather heels, and a cream trench coat. I'm not the best-dressed person in this room by a long shot, but I'm proud of how put-together I look on such short notice.

"I didn't pack anything that was even close to suitable for this type of thing," I say. "I told my aunt and uncle I was meeting a culinary school friend for drinks at a nice pub, so I had to try and look the part."

I bite the inside of my cheek when I remember how I lied to them. But no way in hell was I going to tell them the truth: that I was meeting up with my rival who I'm wildly attracted to.

He rests his hand under my chin, tilting me up to look at him. I shiver at how I still have to look up at him, even though I'm in heels. I love, love, love how tall he is.

"You're the most gorgeous woman within a thousand-mile radius."

I mumble a thank-you, and his hand falls away. "So um . . . did you . . ." Words are damn near impossible after a compliment like that. "Did you want to get a drink or something?"

His eyes fall to my collarbone, which is exposed thanks to the open cut of my blouse. "No."

Our stares connect, and everything around me, within me is ablaze. It's that same look of lust he left me with before stepping off the plane the other day.

"What do you want, Callum?"

He uses his mouth to answer, but not with words. With a hand at my waist, he pulls me against him, then presses his lips against my collarbone. The soft contact turns my legs to jelly. It makes my chest ache and my breath catch. It's been so long I almost forgot what arousal felt like. Almost.

My hands tangle through his hair as I struggle to steady myself.

The heat of his lips on my skin causes me to choke on my next intake of air. So, so soft. And then there's the gentle scrape of his teeth. Thank heavens he's holding on to me, because my legs are completely, utterly useless.

"I want you, Nikki. Now." He leans back up, eyes still on fire.

Through a ragged breath, I manage to speak. "Let's get out of here, then."

. . .

Callum unlocks the door to a renovated multistory Victorian in Marylebone, a few streets down from the Grazing Goat.

I take in the massive foyer and the white marble floor that leads to a hallway straight ahead. A spiral staircase sits at the other side. There's a small yet opulent chandelier made of prism-like crystals dangling from the ceiling. It's a dazzling contrast to the off-white wall and the black-and-white photos of various London landmarks hanging along the hallway. Understated yet upscale decor.

"Wow," I mutter. "Your parents have a nice place."

"I don't want to talk about my parents."

Callum shrugs out of his suit jacket. Then he places his hands on my shoulders, slowly slipping my trench coat off. His lips land on the side of my neck, and my eyes roll back. There's a phantom pulse between my thighs. It's settled. Side-of-the-neck kisses are the hottest thing ever.

"You're sure they're not coming home tonight?" I say between a gasp and a moan.

Callum doesn't bother to lift his mouth from my neck when he answers. "Positive. They're staying with our other relatives at a hotel near the restaurant."

"Thank fuck."

His chuckle rumbles from his mouth to my skin, all the way down my throat. That ache that started at the restaurant intensifies, radiating from my toes to my fingers. When he softly runs his teeth against the sensitive part of my neck that meets my shoulder, every joint in my body turns to goo. Something inside me catches fire. It starts as a slow burn, a simmer, engulfing me from the inside out. If this is what his mouth can do to me when we're standing fully clothed at his front door, just what am I in for once we get to his bedroom?

"So you don't want to talk about your parents. What do you

want to do instead?" I tease. There's a foreign rasp when I speak. I sound like I'm doing a Jessica Rabbit impression.

"I want to find out what you look like when you let loose, Nikki," he says in a whisper-soft growl against my skin. I try my hardest not to howl.

He swoops my hair to the side, kissing the back of my neck. I reach behind me, running my fingers against his scalp, through that delicious mass of thick hair.

"I want to hear how you moan, how you pant and groan when you're turned on." He trails his perfect mouth down the back of my neck. "I want to watch how your body trembles when you're overloaded on pleasure, your mind free of all those everyday worries."

Everyday worries. Like work, family, future.

"Um . . ." My hands fall away from him, and I turn so we're facing each other.

A simple, seemingly benign combination of words, but it brings up every stressor from back home that I seem to have forgotten ever since our truce on the plane.

He takes a step back, giving me space. Concern flashes through his gaze when he looks at me now. "If you changed your mind about this, it's okay. I understand. Really."

I'm instantly cold at the loss of contact. And that's when I know: I want him right here, right now. Any and all consequences can go straight to hell.

I shake my head, panicked at the thought that I've given him the wrong idea. All those worries from home don't matter right now. Callum and I have managed to look past all that since leaving Maui. Now, we see who we really are, what we really want. And that's each other.

"That's not it at all. I don't want to leave. It's just . . ."

It's just that I don't know if one night with him will be enough.

After all this buildup, all our flirting, this newfound connection between us, I suspect I'm going to want more.

But that's impossible. In a few days, we'll both be in Maui and life will be back to normal. I have no right to hope for anything other than tonight.

This temporary time-out is all we get. And it needs to be enough.

Callum steps toward me, closing the space between us. "Tell me what you want."

I tug at the bottom of his shirt. "I need to hear you say the words."

My chest heaves with every breath I take. The simmer inside of me is now a million invisible flames. It's more than an ache; it's need. I'm practically panting at how much I want him.

"Tell me this is bad, but you don't care. Tell me you know what a terrible idea it is for us to do this because of our history, because when we go back to Maui, we'll have to forget this ever happened," I say. "Tell me that you're willing to do it anyway. Because . . ."

Gently, he takes my chin between his thumb and index finger. "Right now I don't care about any of that. I just want you."

He finally presses his mouth to mine. Somehow it's better than I imagined it would be. He teases at first, the tip of his tongue lapping at mine like I'm some delicious ice cream cone he can't stop licking. He's taking it slow, savoring me.

Given the expert way he worked my neck with his lips earlier, it's no surprise he's a dynamite kisser. I wasn't expecting this level of mind-blowing though.

My insides are bursting at the intensity of this simple yet addicting kiss. Holy Christ, why don't all men kiss like this? Slow, steady, tantalizing rhythm. Efficiency is overrated. Taking your time is where it's at.

Pressing my palms against his chest is the only way to steady myself against the dizzying effect of Callum's nuclear kiss.

Seconds pass, maybe even a minute or two. Then there's a pickup, a leveling up of intensity. Callum's tongue is getting very, very filthy, and I love it.

His hands, which started at my waist, are now in my hair. I'm gripping his wrists for dear life, like holding on to them is the only way I can keep myself alive and upright.

We're both panting, both letting out soft moans every time the tiniest bit of air slips between our mouths.

I'm the first one to pull away. I need a minute. For oxygen, for my brain to process all the arousing sensations his mouth sends to my body.

With his hands holding my cheeks, he smiles down at me. "How's that?"

"That's . . . that's . . ." I'm seeing stars as I wobble on unsteady feet. Words are simply not enough, but they're all I have. "Why did you wait this long to kiss me?"

"Anticipation. It does a body good."

"Whatever you're doing with your body is damn good."

He laughs, his face bright with amusement. "Is that so?"

"We'll talk more about it later. I want to go upstairs. Now."

Callum leads me upstairs down another stunning white marble hallway to a closed door at the end. He takes me to some random bedroom, shuts the door, tugs off his tie, and I forget where in the world I am. Because that gesture—that simple act of his forearm pulling fabric from his body—has me hypnotized. He's got the right idea. Less clothes, more skin.

"Wait." I walk up to him. "I want to do the rest."

A slow smile crawls across his lips, and his hands fall to the side. Button by button, I release him from the crisp cotton. The white falls away, leaving behind the light honey glow of his skin. I run a hand across his chest. It's as deliciously firm as I dreamed it would be.

He raises a brow at me. "Don't look so shocked. You've seen all this before."

"I never got to touch you though."

My gaze fixes on his stomach, which is taut with endless hard lines. My mind flashes back to how breathtaking he looked standing before me on the beach, seawater dripping down every naked inch of him.

He leans down for another kiss, our tongues tangling as I claw at his belt, then the zipper of his pants. They're on the floor in a hot second, leaving him in burgundy boxer briefs that are snug enough to show off that impressive bulge I remember so well.

He squints down at me, chuckling. "You act like you've never seen me before."

"Have *you* seen you?"

He walks me backward until the backs of my legs hit the bed. I plop down on the edge; he kneels before me. The movement causes a flashback to the very first sex dream I ever had about him. Him on his knees, his face between my thighs, driving me every kind of wild.

The corner of his mouth quirks up as he unbuttons my blouse. "You look like you want to say something."

Am I that obvious? I shake my head, shivering when he slides the flowy fabric off of me, leaving me in a black lace bra. He leans in, scraping his teeth against the front of each cup. I hiss out a breath. The ache inside me pulses so strong, I have to clutch the mattress to cope. His mouth isn't even on my skin yet, and already I'm going bonkers.

Slipping a hand behind my back, he flicks off my bra, tossing it to the side. Then his hands are on my jeans, and they're on the floor in seconds.

He fixes his gaze to my breasts, and his eyes glaze over. "Fucking hell."

I never thought my chest was worth swearing over. My boobs are on the small side of average, no more than a handful. But the way Callum gawks at them, like he's a starving man staring at a turkey leg, makes me feel like a goddess.

I tug a hand through his hair. "You're making me blush."

His hazel eyes pin me. Even in the dim lighting of the bedside lamp, they shine, their intensity undeniable. "You're stunning, Nikki. Every inch of you."

Leaning forward, he runs his tongue over my breasts. With each lick, I'm panting, tugging at his hair, clawing at his shoulders. My chest swells for the millionth time at just how damn good Callum's mouth feels on me.

As fun as it was to dream about Callum, being with him in real life is a billion times more satisfying.

When I've exhaled every molecule of air, he trails his kisses down my stomach. He presses a massive hand on my torso, pushing me flat on the bed. Already my senses are lost in a pleasure fog. Every time Callum's lips land on me, my brain short-circuits.

"I had a dream like this," I finally say. I'm too turned on to be embarrassed anymore.

"So that explains that look on your face a bit ago."

I nod.

"Tell me about it."

I shake my head, regaining a smidgen of dignity. "You'll think I'm a creep."

"Well, now I have to know." He lowers his face to my thigh. His breath on my skin drags a groan out of me.

"I had a sex dream about you after I saw you naked at the beach," I finally say.

"Really?" he growls against my skin, amusement coloring his tone.

He kisses up the inside of my left thigh, then plants his mouth at the top of my right thigh. That sensitive spot in between pulses so hard, I can feel it all the way in my ears.

He turns his head, breath warming that spot between my legs. The muscles in my thighs twitch at the anticipation. He's so close. So freaking close and still he won't give it to me. What a damn tease.

"I want to hear about your dream." There's a smile in his tone. He sounds pretty smug at the thought of being the star of my fantasy.

"You were . . ." My chest heaves when I pant. The way he teases, the way he builds up is both torture and heaven. He knows exactly what I'm aching for, but he won't budge. Not until I give him what he wants.

I lean up, locking eyes with him. "You were apologizing to me in my dream by going down on me. For being a jerk when we met."

My heart thunders in my chest as I wait to hear what he thinks about what I've just admitted. But he doesn't reply with words. Just a satisfied smile. Then he drops his head back down, pulls my panties all the way to my ankles, and finally makes contact.

I fall back against the bed, gasping at the soft, hot, wet feel of Callum's mouth on the most sensitive spot of my body. This is way, way better than any dream.

The slow circles he makes with his tongue send heat through every inch of me. Callum is the master of slow burn, setting me on fire from the inside out with just his tongue. It doesn't seem to matter where he chooses to taste me. Every single time his mouth makes contact, I'm engulfed in flames.

I'm gasping, whimpering, moaning his name. He hums his approval. He speeds up, then slows down. Then repeats it again and again. Everything he does, it's all divine. With my body on fire, my brain in a pleasure-mush state, I can't form words; only sounds.

Pressure builds behind the heat, like I'm boiling over. I twist both hands into the pillow supporting my head. It's either that or rip the hair from his scalp, because I absolutely cannot handle this level of ecstasy.

Callum increases the pressure and then throws in a wild card: suction. Holy hot damn. My whimpers turn into screams. The pressure between my legs builds and builds until every limb is shaking.

Just then he eases up, and I finally catch my breath. But then he's back at it, humming against me. I could swear I hear him chuckling.

Before I can be sure, he's amping up the pressure, speeding up until I'm thrashing. I don't know how much longer I'll be able to hold on. Seconds, maybe. But minutes? No way on God's green Earth.

More pressure, more suction, then bam. Explosion.

The simmering slow burn is nowhere to be found. This is a volcanic eruption of ecstasy. It's every muscle ablaze, tensing as climax claims me. It's me shouting, gasping, panting, tugging at the bedsheets, tugging at Callum. It's babbling, going cross-eyed, ending in a sweat-soaked pile in the middle of the bed and never, ever feeling more satisfied than in this moment.

My heart races as I struggle to breathe like a human again.

Callum crawls up the bed, covering my body with his. The wet warmth of his bare skin on my bare skin is heaven.

He rests his arms on either side of my head. Our faces are inches apart, but that's still too far for me.

"Now that I know about your dream, I don't feel as bad about the things I was thinking about you."

"Such as?"

"The first time I saw you, my jaw nearly dropped. I thought you were beautiful. And then we fought, and I couldn't get you out of my head. I screwed up every order that day. Finn nearly sent me home. I was useless."

"Is that so?" I lean up on my elbows, pressing a light kiss to his mouth.

"You aren't the only one who's been dreaming about this," he says.

The crinkled sound of foil tearing has me grinning. He positions himself against me, just barely making contact. The anticipation is almost too much.

"You're going to make me wait? After all this?" I say, hoping the breathy way I speak comes off as teasing as I intended.

He lifts his eyebrow just before clenching his jaw. Then he closes his eyes and presses his forehead against mine. "It's more for me than you."

His strained, low tone makes it clear. He's pacing himself so he doesn't lose it too soon. Clutching my arms around his biceps, I breathe slowly, deeply. After a beat, he slides in. My mouth contorts as I gasp a "whoa."

He doesn't thrust at first. He remains still, kissing me deeply. We're sloppy tongues and nibbles and swollen lips until we can no longer breathe. Callum pulls away, drawing in a slow breath. Then he starts.

His movements are smooth and measured at first. Each slide has my eyes rolling to the back of my head. Softly, he grips my jaw with his hand.

"Hey. Look at me."

I bite my bottom lip, trying my hardest to keep his gaze. But it's a battle. There is so much bliss with each thrust of his body into mine that I can barely hold on.

"You thought about this," I gasp. "About us."

He nods. I notice he clenches his jaw, then slows down. This is intense for him, too, it seems. It's a comfort to see him hanging on by a thread, just like me.

"And I thought you hated me," I say before gasping.

"I never hated you." Somehow he manages to keep the slow, even pace while talking. "But I *can* dislike someone and also think she's hot. I'm a bloke, remember?"

I giggle through a moan. He's hitting somewhere deep and fucking hell, it's amazing.

Digging my nails into his back earns me a hiss, then a groan. "I don't hate you anymore, Callum."

"Good." He leans up, deepening the angle between us. "Because I don't hate you, either, Nikki."

I hold my breath while he hooks his hands under my thighs. When he resumes, it's faster, harder, and a whole new level of euphoria.

I press my eyes shut just as they start to roll back. That spot. That elusive spot every man had such a hard time locating is front and center now. I silently dub him the G-spot whisperer. Another deep thrust hits it again. Good thing I'm not trying to speak anymore, because I've lost all my words. All I have to offer are huffs of hot air and whimpering. Lots and lots of whimpering.

The edge of Callum's mouth turns up, and I have to swallow to keep from choking at the divine sight. He looks like a god in this moment. His skin is a golden glow, painted in specks of sweat, highlighting every single cut muscle he possesses. And his expression—a cross between concentration and satisfaction. It's hard physical work what he's doing, but he relishes it. I can tell by the glimmer in his eyes, the way his hands cradle my legs so I'm comfortably supported. I can tell by the pinch of his jaw, those soft grunts he lets loose, that this is blowing his mind too.

For the second time in one night, pressure builds inside me. The feeling is almost too much, but all I want is more. These long, deliberate thrusts are the greatest physical sensations my body has ever experienced. I could explode at any moment, but I want this to last. Forever, if possible.

Arching my back, I press my head against the pillow. I cry out, sounding like a rabid banshee.

A muttered curse falls from his lips. "That's it. Don't hold back."

Pressure and heat collide, and I couldn't hold back if I tried. The deep thrusts keep coming like an endless loop of crashing waves. Callum and my G-spot are new best friends, it seems. Over and over, he hits it. Over and over, the sensations build to an overwhelming peak. His pace shifts from impressive to phenomenal. If Callum were a sex doll, I'd buy a dozen. His stamina, his technique, his adoration of me and my body, it's all perfection.

When I burst, I'm even louder than before. And just like before, I'm ablaze from the inside out. Ecstasy pulses through every inch of skin and bone. My blood pumps hot, like lava flowing through my veins. Every muscle tightens, then loosens. Panting, I clutch Callum's forearms and watch his face as he hits his own peak.

He's a million times quieter than I am, and it's endearing as all get-out. His teeth clench, his face reddens, his brow wrinkles, and every vein in his neck bulges. There's a grunt, then a low groan. It's so very masculine, and I wholeheartedly adore it.

Collapsing on top of me, he buries his face into the side of my neck. I wrap my arms and legs around his torso, my rapid panting finally easing.

"Good God, Nikki," he wheezes into the pillow.

"Speak for yourself."

He chuckles, rolls off of me, then grins as he settles to my side. I burrow my face into his chest, and he wraps his arms around my torso.

Afterglow sets in, and I'm instantly drowsy. After a while, through the fatigue, Callum's words from earlier seep in.

*I just want you.*

I drift off, wondering what exactly the cost of bedding my enemy will be, how badly I'll burn.

# Chapter 10

I wake cradled against Callum's bare chest, sunlight warm on my face. Eyes closed, I hum, satisfied. Then I check my phone on the nightstand and breathe a sigh of relief. No panicky texts from my aunt and uncle checking up on me. Thankfully, I had the foresight to text them last night just before falling asleep and tell them that I lost track of time during drinks and would stay with my "friend." Again, that familiar tinge of guilt for lying to them hits, but I remind myself that their heads would explode if I told them the truth.

Underneath me, Callum stirs. When I peek up at him, he's smiling. In an instant, every part of me relaxes.

"Morning," he half yawns, half groans.

His open mouth is now just an inch from my face. I take the opportunity to nibble on his lip.

"Mmm," he moans, letting me carry on for a few seconds before capturing my mouth in a slow, filthy kiss. "Now that's a way to wake up."

I gaze up at him, contentment coursing through me. Every muscle is relaxed, and I'm comfortably tucked in that happy-drunk mood that comes after epic sex and a hard sleep.

My stomach growls, a reminder that I haven't eaten in the past eighteen hours. I was so nervous to meet Callum last night that I skipped dinner.

"Are you hungry?"

He looks at me, his eyes puffy from sleep. Still devastatingly gorgeous. He squints. "I am."

I open my mouth to ask what he'd like to do for breakfast, but he grabs my wrists, pinning me to the mattress. There's a slow trail of kisses down my chest.

"I thought you wanted breakfast," I say between gasps. The feel of Callum's lips trailing down my stomach is hands-down the hottest way to wake up.

"I do," he says, his open mouth at my hip.

He resumes that filthy morning kiss, only this time between my legs. Callum is a quick study, remembering all the techniques from last night that sent me over the edge. Slow, long swipes of his tongue, that delicious suction technique that I'm going to tell him to patent once I regain my ability to speak. I'm squirming and panting, which soon gives way to shouts. It takes less than a minute and I'm gone.

He finishes with a soft kiss on the inside of each thigh. When he looks up at me, that smug smile remains.

"You were saying something about breakfast?"

Breakfast was a mistake.

Breakfast, which was a relaxed full English at his favorite pub in Marylebone, hooked me. Callum in his hometown is downright charming. Conversation flowed easily, and I didn't want it to end.

So it didn't.

We took a walk at Hyde Park, then stopped at a bakery for almond croissants, then he offered to show me around Marylebone the rest of the day. And I couldn't say no. Because who the hell could say no to a hot English guy who's dynamite in bed, an excellent meal companion, and who looks at me like I'm the only woman on his radar?

And that's exactly why I'm sitting across from Callum in the supposedly delicious Max's Sandwich Shop, which looks more like a hipster dive bar.

An animated, mad scientist–looking guy in glasses nods at us from behind the counter, then takes our order. We grab a table for two in the corner.

"You're going to love the ham, egg, and chips sandwich," Callum says. "It's Finn's favorite."

"Is that what inspired the ham, egg, and chip toasty on your menu?"

He whips his head around to peer at the counter, which is empty.

"The guy who took our order headed back to the kitchen," I say. "Is everything okay?"

"I just didn't want him to overhear and think I'm stealing his recipes. He might ban us from eating here, and then I'd never be able to eat the greatest sandwich ever made again."

I roll my eyes. "Come on. It can't be that good."

"Just wait."

"Honestly, the sandwich you serve is amazing. Your idea to put a layer of fries between the ham and the egg is mind blowing."

"That was Finn's idea actually. And you've eaten our food?"

Heat crawls up my cheeks. "It was a moment of weakness."

He narrows his eyes at me.

"Okay, fine. I wanted to know what I was up against, so I asked one of our customers to order food from your truck and bring it to me. Want to know why I despised you for so long? Because one bite of that sandwich and I knew we were in trouble. You and your brother serve incredible food."

The grin he lets loose is so sweet, it borders on boyish. "I'll be sure to tell Finn," he says.

I cross my arms, fighting to keep my pout from being too obvious. But then Callum leans across the table and grabs my hand. He laces his fingers through mine, and I forget to breathe.

"Your food is mind-blowing, Nikki."

I pick at a loose thread in my jacket. "What dishes have you tried?"

"Your *lumpia*, *pansit*, the *adobo* wings. Finn and I also asked a customer to order from your truck one day to size you up. We waited till we closed one night and inhaled it all in minutes. I drove home with steam coming out of my ears because I was angry at how amazing you and your mum's cooking is."

I grin down at our joined hands. It's one of the best compliments I could ever want, when my biggest competition admits how good I am.

*Competition.*

The joy is gone when I remember what's at stake, how we've upped the ante by sleeping together last night and spending all day together.

And then I remember that promise I made to myself a little over a year ago, when I lost one of the most important people in my life.

"Listen, we should—"

The mad scientist sandwich maker returns, a wax paper–wrapped sandwich in each hand. I thank him, then stare at the table. Callum starts to tear open his sandwich, some delicious-smelling creation with kimchi, bulgogi beef, and fried sweet potato noodles. But when he notices me fumbling with my paper, he stops.

"What's the matter?"

"I don't mean to spoil this day. Spending it with you has been the best, but aren't you concerned about what's going to happen when we go back home and this time-out officially ends?"

When he frowns, I clarify. "We're competitors, Callum. When we get back to Maui, we'll be going head-to-head with each other every day, just like before. The Maui Food Festival is in less than a month. One of us is going to lose at the end of it. We can't exist like this when so much is at stake."

He frowns. "What exactly is at stake?"

I peel the wrapper off my sandwich. "My mom's retirement savings. My career. Our livelihood."

My feelings, my emotional well-being, the fact that I can't have anything close to a relationship because I know beyond a shadow of a doubt that I won't have the strength to make it through the inevitable end.

"How exactly?" he asks.

"Don't you remember what Matteo said about last year's winner? They lost the prize money when everyone found out they buddied up with another restaurant. You think they'd just let it slide if they found out about us?"

He squints at me, like he's waiting for me to explain further, but I can't fathom how he doesn't understand what I'm talking about.

"Look, twenty thousand dollars could change my and my mom's life. I don't want . . . I can't afford to lose out on that if somehow we win, and people find out that Tiva's and Hungry Chaps were screwing around with each other."

It's not just that though. My doubts run deeper, but I'm not brave enough to say this next part out loud.

If Callum and I were crazy enough to make it official, it would most certainly end. Once a winner is declared, one of us will have to vacate that spot in Makena. That would sow resentment, jealousy, maybe even hatred. It would be the end for us, and I would be destroyed, just like I was when I lost my dad.

I won't—I can't survive another loss.

I take another breath to steady myself. No sense spilling all my emotional baggage to Callum. He doesn't deserve to get bogged down in my past, in my pain. I opt for a PG-rated version of the truth.

"I like you, Callum. But my work and my mom are my priority. I can't compromise on those; they mean too much to me. I just don't have the energy to add anything more to my life right now when I'm juggling so much."

Callum takes a sip from his beer bottle. His face turns stony, but after he swallows, he's soft again. "So what exactly does that mean?"

"It means I can't do a relationship."

His eyes shine as he gazes at me. "We don't have to make this into some big thing, Nikki. I'm willing to keep things physical and casual, nothing more. I'm going back to Chicago after the festival anyway. Until then, we can keep work at work and quietly see each other in our free time. If that's what you want."

I sip from my beer bottle, hoping the icy liquid cools the flush running through me. Just the mention of us in bed brings back all the hot memories from last night and this morning. It's been forever since I've been with anyone, and I almost forgot just how divine it feels to enjoy regular orgasms, to wake up cuddled next to someone you're insanely attracted to.

I've done hookups before, but not in an official no-strings-attached agreement like this. Can I manage this with Callum? Can I have him in my bed at night after competing against him all day, every day?

I have no idea.

I pause for another sip of beer. Maybe since we're stipulating that this is casual and there's an expiration date, we can swing it. I sure as hell would like to try.

"I'd like that," I say. "But only if you're okay with it too."

"I'm fine with it." This time when he smiles, it looks more like he's pursing his lips.

"We'd have to be discreet about the whole thing."

"I'm not going to run and tell any food bloggers or vloggers, if that's what you're worried about."

"Of course not. Sorry, that's not what I meant at all."

A beat of tense silence follows with us just looking at each other. Callum takes a gigantic bite of his sandwich. I finally dig into mine and moan at the burst of flavor. It's the perfect bite of ham, malt vinegar mayo, fried egg, shoestring fries, and focaccia bread. I offer him a bite, but he declines with a wave of his hand.

I swallow. "I just don't want to be gossip for the foodies. And I don't want to jeopardize this career opportunity. I know getting first place at the festival is a long shot, but I want to try—I want to commit myself to it one hundred percent."

"It's not a long shot. You have just as good a chance as anyone," he says without looking at me.

His lack of eye contact reads like I've offended him. I refuse to do this unless he's genuinely into it. I reach out and touch his hand. When he looks at me, the softness returns to his face; that kindness in his eyes still radiates.

"You sure you're okay with this?" I ask.

"Yes." He pauses to take another bite, then raises his beer in a toast. "Cheers on it?"

I let out a slow breath to ease the tiny knot that's suddenly settled in my chest. There's no reason to be anxious. There's nothing wrong with a casual arrangement. I said it's okay, and he said it's okay. We're two adults who are just being direct about what we want. We're competitors-turned-friends-with-benefits.

I clink my bottle against his. "Cheers."

Callum leads me with a hand on the small of my back through the doors of the Washington, a pub in Camden Town. It's the day after we agreed to be friends with benefits, and we seem to be settling into things nicely. His parents are out to dinner with friends this evening, so he invited me over to take advantage of the empty house. And that's exactly what we did for a solid two hours. We took advantage of his bedroom, the living room, and the shower. It seemed like the fitting thing to do the day before his flight back to Maui.

With our physical needs sated and our appetites raging, we take a booth in the corner of the pub. Callum goes to the bar to fetch us beers while I reply to a text from Mom.

Having a good time? Doing anything fun?

I swallow back the sudden bitter taste in my mouth. Just the thought of her finding out about my newly formed no-strings-attached arrangement with Callum sends me into hives. I stick to the truth but leave out any incriminating bits.

ME: Yes, it's been so awesome! I went sightseeing with Auntie Nora today while Uncle Nigel was at work. They're out to dinner with friends tonight, so I'm exploring the neighborhood right now. I'm taking them to brunch tomorrow to thank them for having me, then we're going to Leadenhall Market.

MOM: Sounds fun. Be careful, Auntie will try to grab the bill at brunch. Or if you pay, she'll try to slip you money later on.

I sigh. Ever since I was a kid, Mom and Auntie Nora have fought over bills at restaurants and other expenses. It's only natural she'd try to do the same with me now that I'm an adult and can pay for things.

But even though I appreciate her generosity, she and Uncle Nigel have done enough by flying me to England and letting me stay with them. The least I can do is treat them to a meal.

ME: I'll be ready. Want any souvenirs?

Callum returns with two pints just as she texts back that she wants a refrigerator magnet with the Union Jack flag on it. I chuckle and show him the text.

He lets out a soft laugh. "Really? A magnet? Your mum doesn't realize you don't have to travel to London to get one of those? She can order one online."

"Even if I told her, she wouldn't care. She would still want me to get her one from here."

We take long sips of our beers, and I peer around the pub. It's bustling for a weeknight, with the after-work crowd filing in for a drink before heading home.

"I totally dig the pub culture here, by the way." I tilt my head to the line forming at the bar. "We have happy hour in the States, but nothing like this."

"It's ingrained in us from an early age. Any excuse to day drink." Callum takes another sip.

A trio of middle-aged men make their way to the table across from us, pints in hand. I focus on the one seated nearest us, who has an old-school flip phone tucked inside the leather cell phone holder on his belt.

The memory of my dad sporting the exact same look pops in my head. I cup my hand over my mouth to stifle my laugh so the table doesn't hear.

Callum's face is pure confusion when he looks at me. "What's so funny?"

"It's nothing. Just . . ." I nod to the table, and he twists to take a look. "My dad used to wear his cell phone on his belt just like that guy. It drove me and my mom crazy. He was the most stubborn person ever when it came to technology. Like, our family phone plan would let us upgrade every year, and every year either my mom or me would get a new phone. Not my dad."

I laugh again, remembering the Father's Day surprise she and I planned for him a few years ago.

"For Father's Day we got him this basic smartphone. When he opened it, he was so confused. He looked at it like it was some alien gadget he had never seen before. We tried to explain that it was a simple smartphone. I started to show him how easy it was to use, but he shook his head, politely said 'no, thank you,' and then held up his flip phone. He said that was as high tech as he ever wanted to be."

Callum looks at me, his eyes bright, his smile wide, and bursts into a laugh. "So he was pretty set in his ways, then?"

"He was." I let the memory of that Father's Day soak in. "Good thing I thought to get him a backup present in case he didn't like the phone."

"Which was?"

"A new leather case for his flip phone."

We fall into uncontrollable cackles that draw a handful of annoyed glances from nearby tables. But I don't care. Sharing this memory with Callum is worthy of loud laughter. Catching my breath, I sip my beer.

I place my glass back on the table and catch Callum staring at me. "What?"

"Your entire face lights up when you talk about your dad."

"Really?" Sheepishness tinges my chuckle. "I thought it would seem sort of sad talking about him this way."

"Why?"

I take a moment before speaking. "I don't talk about him with anyone other than my mom. I don't really know how often you're supposed to speak about someone after you lose them or if you're supposed to speak about them at all. Or if it's weird and just too sad."

From across the table, Callum grabs my hand. "There's no such thing as normal when it comes to something like this, Nikki. Normal is however you feel."

His touch is a security blanket for my nerves. I may not be sure of my emotions or what to do, but I'm certain that I feel comfortable in Callum's presence, even when talking about a tough subject. And that counts for so much.

"Honestly? It felt really good to talk about him with you."

That admission earns me an affectionate squeeze from his hand. "Then tell me more."

"He loved that show *M*A*S*H*. Even though it ended in the eighties, he would watch reruns almost every week. Drove my mom up the wall."

Callum beams wide. "That's hilarious."

"But he made up for it. He brought her flowers every Friday after he came home from work. He was always up for a card game—any card game. He loved jogging in the mornings and camping and fishing. He used to smoke, but he quit when my mom got pregnant with me. He said he didn't want to continue any bad habits like that when he had a child counting on him."

I pause and sip again, my chest tight with the memory surfacing just now—one of my favorite memories of my dad.

"At my culinary school graduation, he made this sign and held it as I walked across the stage. It said, 'Congrats, Chef Nikki-Nack! You did it!' "

I look up to see that Callum's smile has softened. More wistful than amused. "Nikki-Nack."

"His nickname for me."

"That's adorable."

The tightness in my throat, the burn in my eyes, it all dissipates at how intently he listens to me.

"It really was," I say softly.

I open my mouth to speak again, but the only thing that comes out is a soft squeak. I press my mouth shut, shaking my head. It's the best I can do since I can't say sorry. Everything is a reminder that he's not here and he never will be.

Callum squeezes my hand once more. "Hey. It's all right. You don't have to say anything. Just take your time."

I look up to see his face twisted in concern. I nod, grateful that he seems to understand exactly how I feel, exactly what I need in this moment.

It's another quiet minute with just the pub chatter filling the silence between us before I say anything. "I talk to him sometimes still."

Biting my lip, I fixate on the wood grain of the tabletop, wondering if I've crossed the line to full-on weirdo now that I've admitted that out loud.

But he answers without missing a beat. "I used to do that with my gran after she passed."

"Really?"

He nods, the expression on his face warm. It makes any semblance of doubt about myself fly right out the window.

"I was living in Chicago when she died, so I didn't get to say good-bye to her. Whenever I was home and visited her grave in the beginning, I would have a chat with her. Tell her about my day, what was on my mind, how much I missed her."

Hearing him share his own memories with his grandmother makes me want to pull him into the tightest hug. It shows he's not judging me; it shows he can relate to what I've been through.

"There's an urn with his ashes at the condo I share with my mom," I say. "Whenever I'm stressed or sad, I say a few words to him."

His mouth curves up in a gentle, understanding smile.

"Mom and I spread most of his ashes at Baldwin Beach—his favorite beach. Every time I'm there, I stand at the far end of the beach, away from all the crowds, and say hi. That's actually what I was doing the morning I found Lemon."

"That's wonderful, Nikki."

We share another quiet moment, and it's not the slightest bit awkward. The silence between us marks a whole new level of intimacy. I haven't been able to talk about my dad with anyone other than my mom.

I meet his eyes once more.

"You can talk about him with me whenever you want, you know," he says.

"You sure?"

He nods. "We're friends. We should be able to talk about these sorts of things."

"Friends with benefits."

He raises an eyebrow. "The friend part is still key, Nikki. It's what helps make this whole arrangement work."

I let his words soak in. It would be a nice change of pace to have a friend in all of this too.

"I'd like that."

He smiles softly. "Grief is complicated. Take all the time you need. I'm here for you. Always."

"Thank you."

I sip from the untouched water glass on the table, lacing my fingers in his. Maybe this entire setup between us—rivals turned bedmates turned emotional confidants—is naive and foolish and totally unconventional. But it feels right. I'm at ease in a way I never have been ever since losing my dad. And that has to count for something.

Callum glances at the bar. "Shall we play a bit more of the Question Game, then?"

I let out a small laugh. "Sure."

He turns back to me. "Who would win in a fight: you or Matteo?"

"I'm insulted you even have to ask. Me. I'd tug on his man bun, exposing his throat for my attack. It would be game over."

"I like your style."

"My turn: how often do you swim naked at Little Beach?"

Thankfully, he doesn't balk at the question. Now that we're sleeping together, I figure it's okay for me to broach the subject.

He rolls his eyes good-naturedly. "About once a week. Why? Are you interested in joining me?"

"Maybe."

I sip more of the water while he drains the last of his beer.

"Who would win in a fight: you or Finn?" I ask.

Callum scoffs. "Ridiculous. Me."

I give my best mock frown. "You sure? Finn looks like he keeps in good shape."

Callum's jaw tenses, and I have to swallow back a laugh.

"You're joking, right? I'm three inches taller than him and weigh a stone and a half more."

I shrug, looking around the bar, pretending like I'm unimpressed with that fact. "If you say so."

He lets out a frustrated laugh. "You're taking the piss. Nicely done."

I point to his empty glass. "Another?"

He nods and says thank you as I stand up to take our empties to the bar. I ask the bartender for two more pints and check my phone, smiling to myself. It's a wonder how seamlessly I shifted from sad to happy in Callum's presence. I rack my brain, but I can't remember any guy I've dated who I could be so emotionally open with, who made me feel equally at ease whether I was sad or happy.

Someone's hot breath hits my neck, interrupting my thought. I shudder, then look to my left. A thirty-something man with glazed-over eyes sports the creepiest smirk I've ever seen. He's so close that we're brushing shoulders. The stench of alcohol hits my nostrils. Every muscle inside me tenses at his proximity.

"Can I buy you a drink, love?"

I turn back to the bartender, who is just now getting to filling my drinks. "No, thank you." I stare straight ahead, hoping that my refusal to look at him signals my obvious disinterest.

His hand lands on my back. "Come on, then," he practically sings. "You look a bit worked up. A drink might loosen you up."

He leans into me even more, and I bump a nearby stool to try to get away from him. "I said no. And don't touch me."

The drunken offender's hand falls away and so does his smile. He takes a step back, and the breath I've been holding flows out in a huff. The bartender sets the drinks down in front of me, but I don't just want to scurry away from this guy. I want him to know just how much of a prick he is for invading my space. I have a right to be at this pub without being harassed.

I turn to him. "Is that disgusting approach usually a hit with the ladies? God."

Drinks in hand, I spin around to walk back to my booth, but then I feel his hand on my shoulder. Again I'm cringing. I'm also cursing myself. I should have just walked away without saying a word. Now I've provoked this angry drunk.

But just as quickly as it came, his hand is gone. Behind me there's a grunt, then a thud. I spin around, stunned at the sight of Callum pinning the drunken prick by the throat to the bar.

"You don't touch her."

Callum's growl captures the attention of every patron in the pub. His face is red, his jaw is tense, and his body is on edge, ready to unleash hell if the drunken guy so much as blinks wrong.

He probably wouldn't have to work very hard to leave an impression on him. Callum's got several inches and many pounds of lean mass on this jerk. The way he's able to handle him so effortlessly tells me Callum could probably break him in half with one hand tied behind his back.

My throat goes dry taking in the scene in front of me. Thank fuck Callum happened to be watching. Just thinking about what the guy would have done if he hadn't intervened has me in a cold sweat. He was comfortable enough to put his hands on me, a complete stranger, when I rejected him. Who knows what else he was capable of doing?

The drunken guy tries to speak, but nothing other than a gurgle comes out. Probably because of Callum's death grip on his throat.

"Oi! What's going on here?" the bartender shouts as he darts to our end of the bar.

With his eyes still on the drunken offender, Callum speaks. "Your customer grabbed my friend. And since you weren't keeping an eye on things, I thought I'd handle it."

Callum's death glare cuts to the bartender, who is all wide eyes and no blinks.

"Sorry, mate," the bartender says. He directs two other bartenders to haul the offender out of the bar.

Before he hands over the drunken offender, Callum leans his face even closer to his. "Do not put your hands on a woman like that. Ever."

It's a whispered threat, but it's more lethal than a shout. Callum practically tosses him to the two bartenders, who deposit him on the sidewalk. A few tables break into applause and whistles. Callum doesn't even crack a smile though. He simply walks back over to me and touches his hand to my elbow.

"Are you okay?"

I nod, every nerve within me short-circuiting. "Fine. Thank you."

"Bloody creep," he mutters, looking in the direction of the door.

The bartender hands me back my cash, saying our drinks are on the house. Callum nods at him, then turns back to me. His hazel eyes study me with concern.

"We don't have to stay," Callum says. "We can leave if that makes you feel more comfortable."

*Comfortable.*

The word settles deep into my chest. It's clear as day to me now: comfort is Callum next to me. I can be anywhere in any situation, and as long as he is next to me, I'll be okay.

"I'm not above accepting a free drink." I look up at him. "I want to stay."

He chuckles, then carries our beers back to our booth. We pick up right where we left off, our conversation flowing easily. But inside me something's different. Is a casual arrangement supposed to feel this intimate, this quickly? Because right now casual feels a lot more personal. And I think I like it.

# Chapter 11

Almost two weeks back home in Maui and our no-strings-attached arrangement is still intact. To my surprise, we haven't crashed and burned. Days are spent like they were before the trip to London that changed everything. We cook and serve food parked next to each other, never exchanging a word during work hours. It's a huge disappointment to the food bloggers and social media fans who visit our trucks daily to enjoy a meal, phone in hand, ready to catch our next squabble and upload it. But there's nothing salacious to capture.

Our evenings, however? Our evenings are very, very salacious. We take turns sneaking to each other's places. Things are tricky since we both live with other people, but we've worked out a system. When Mom's at mahjong or book club, Callum comes to mine. When Finn is out, I go to his. The minute we shut the door, clothes are off, and we're a tangle of limbs and skin and hot breath until we realize what time it is.

The anticipation of seeing Callum outside of our food truck battlefield is what powers me through most days. It's why I'm standing at the front door of his condo in Wailea this evening, shuffling my feet, stomach in a million happy knots as I wait for him to answer. I knock for the second time, cardboard cat carrier clutched in my other hand.

He answers, his smile wide when he sees me. Then his gaze drops to the carrier, and he full-on beams.

"Lemon!" he practically squeals.

We walk inside, he shuts the door, and I let her out of the carrier. At first her eyes dart around the space, conveying the typical hesitation all cats have when you bring them to a new place. But then Callum scoops her up and scratches under her chin. She's purring instantly.

"Thought it was time she visit her co-owner's home," I say.

Callum mock frowns at me. "It's impossible to own a cat. They own us."

He sets her down on the floor, then points to the nearby dining table where four bottles of pink champagne rest.

"Wow. Do you woo all the ladies like this?" I joke.

He rolls his eyes. "Finn helped a chef friend cook at a private party in Kaanapali the other night and they went home with all of the leftover alcohol. He's gone on an overnight hike, so he asked me to get rid of a couple bottles."

"The perks of private dining. Damn, I miss those days."

"Well, I'm chuffed to bring you a taste of the past."

One corner of his mouth quirks up, showcasing the hottest slanted smile I've ever seen. I lean against the nearby kitchen island to keep myself steady as I quietly swoon.

"Wondered if you were in the mood for a champagne-drinking contest?"

I chuckle. "Why, exactly?"

He raises a brow at me; my grip on the counter tightens. "Why not?"

He swipes a bottle from the table and pops off the top. The cork shoots across the room, the boom sound spooking Lemon. Even with her pregnant bulging tummy, she scurries down the hallway at lightning-fast speed.

"Sorry, love," Callum hollers after her before taking a long sip. He wipes his wet lips with the back of his hand, eyes on me the entire time.

I'm giggling as I reach for the bottle and take a swig for myself. I swallow. "What would a champagne-drinking contest entail?"

He grabs another bottle and leads me to the nearby living room of his open-concept condo. With the minimal furnishings of a four-person dining table, microfiber sectional, coffee table, and wall-mounted flat-screen, his condo is considerably roomier than mine. The condo I share with Mom boasts less square footage, yet we've got twice the amount of furniture in our living and dining rooms.

He plops on the couch and pats the seat next to him. I cuddle into him, and he hands me the freshly opened bottle.

"We watch one episode of *The Office* US, then one of *The Office* UK." He flips on the TV. "Whoever finishes their bottle first during those two episodes wins."

I nudge him with my elbow. "Not fair. We both just took a drink from your bottle."

He rolls his eyes, still smirking. Then he swipes my bottle and takes a five-second-long chug before handing it back to me. "There." He huffs a breath, chest heaving. "We're even. You ready?"

I squint at him. "What does the winner get?"

"Sexual favors from the loser."

I tap my bottle against his. "Bring it."

. . .

Ten minutes into the pilot episode of *The Office* UK, I'm all giggles and my bottle is three-fourths empty. The alcohol and the bubbles have gone straight to my head. Callum's got just a few gulps left, though, which means I'm for sure losing this contest. I don't care though. Tucked under his shoulder, his arm wrapped firmly around me as I'm comfortably tipsy, I'm winning by a long shot. I get to cuddle with Callum, then ravage him in bed. Something stirs inside me. Not warmth, not even comfort, but something deeper.

"You know something? I think I like the American series better," I say.

"No surprise there."

"Let me guess. You prefer the UK version."

He takes a long swig of champagne. "Of course. The original is always superior."

I shake my head before leaning so close to his face that we're almost touching noses. "No way. Have you ever had Extra Crispy KFC chicken? Way, way better than Original Recipe."

"If you say so."

I cross my arms. He kisses the tip of my nose, and I burst into a smile.

"You're adorable when you're petulant," he says.

I fall back against the couch and take another gulp of champagne. I gaze up at him.

"And you're adorable with this whole romantic champagne setup."

He peers down at me. "Romantic?"

"Anytime there's pink champagne involved, it's romantic."

"Not sure if I agree with that."

I roll my eyes. "Do you drink pink champagne with your brother? Or your friends?"

He shakes his head.

"Point proven." I take a gulp and feel the slightest bit dizzy. I focus back on the TV. "So tell me, Mr. Pink Champagne. Did you prefer Jim's grand gesture of surprising Pam with a house in the US version? Or did you like Tim's quiet gesture of gifting Dawn new art supplies during the UK version's Christmas special with a note encouraging her to pursue her dreams?"

My tipsy and random question doesn't seem to faze Callum at all, because he replies immediately. "Jim, hands down. I've got a soft spot for grand gestures."

"Really? I would have never guessed." I hiccup. "I liked Tim's style better. Sweet and thoughtful but also low-key." I beam up at him. "Look at us, switching allegiances so quickly. Just a minute ago you were ready to toss me off the couch because I admitted I liked the American version better."

He runs his hand up my bare leg.

Eyes closed, I let out a satisfied hum. "This was a great idea."

He peers down at me then glances at my bottle, a smirk on his lips and in his eyes. "You think so? Even when you're about to lose?"

I shrug and take another gulp. "I still get to fool around with you at the end of this, you sexy, sexy man. I'm the real winner in that sense."

Just then Lemon jumps on the couch, cuddling between the two of us. He pats her plump pregnant stomach, which triggers an idea.

"Hey, I was thinking. We should work out some sort of custody agreement for Lemon."

"How so?"

"You took care of all of her medical bills. You should get to keep her part of the time. We could do the week-on, week-off thing. Like divorced parents."

"Not the most positive spin you could've put on it."

"Screw spin. Are you interested or am I keeping Lemon and her future baby kitties all to myself?"

He kisses my cheek before giving Lemon a head scratch. She nuzzles his knee appreciatively.

"I would love that," he says.

"Great. I'll leave her here tonight and get her next week."

Callum scratches under her chin while peering down at her. "You hear that, Lemon? We're officially one big happy family."

I swig more champagne. "One big drunk happy family." I giggle so hard, I nearly drop my bottle on the floor.

He straightens to a sitting up position, takes the bottle from me, and leans forward to deposit it and his own bottle on the coffee table.

"But the contest . . ." I say before hiccupping.

"Let's take a break." His tone is low, soft.

Hugging me tighter against him, he gives Lemon another pat. Then he presses his lips against my forehead. I close my eyes, a happy hum emanating from my throat. His lips on me, our bodies pressed together, our cat between us, and two cheap bottles of champagne. Such an easy recipe for a perfect night. I let the moment sink in, then promptly melt into the couch.

"This is perfect," I say. "Like, literally perfect."

He gazes down at me with cloudy eyes. I'm guessing he's tipsy, too, but less so than me since he's got the body of a muscled warrior. "Is it?"

"I like doing this with you. I wish we could do it every night."

It's a nervous moment while I wait for him to say something. But only silence from him. Great. I made things weird with an unintentionally touchy-feely comment.

To recover, I stand up and grab my bottle from the coffee table, then quickly down the remaining champagne. I spin around, narrowing my gaze at him. An amused expression dances across his face.

"I believe I just won the contest. You know what that means?"

He smirks before gently scooting Lemon next to him on the couch. "Not sure if that counts, petal. We were in the middle of a break."

I bite my lip, giddy at the very English nickname he's chosen for me. This is feeling more and more like an actual relationship by the minute, and it's nowhere near as terrifying as I thought it would be.

I quickly tuck the errant thought aside. Everything seems ideal when you live in a fantasy world like this, when you don't actually have to do the dirty work of a relationship, like arguments, sharing chores, splitting bills, enduring annoying relatives, all that. When a relationship is simply hanging out and mind-blowing sex, it's easy to idealize—because you're only experiencing the best parts.

I'm thankful for the reminder my tipsy self manages to give. I focus back on the task at hand: bantering with Callum in the lead-up to sexy fun times.

I shrug. "Too bad. Those are the rules; you said so yourself. Whoever finishes their bottle first, wins. I finished mine first, which means I won. Which also means . . ."

I twist my head in the direction of the hallway to his bedroom. Just then Callum stands up and grabs me by the waist.

"Which means I owe you a favor," he says.

"You do."

I press against the front of his shorts and lick my lips at the hard feel. Mischief dances across his face. Any awkwardness from the moment prior is gone. We're back to playful and horny.

"What would you like?" he growls.

I scrunch up my face in mock indecisiveness. "What are my options?"

He leans down, softly pressing his lips to my neck. "Anything and everything," he whispers.

My answer is wordless. It's just me tugging him by the shirt to get his mouth to mine. After a minute of rabid kissing, I finally voice my request. "Your bed. Now."

In a split second, Callum bends down and tosses me over his shoulder. He heads in the direction of his bedroom. On the way, he slides his hands up my shorts, squeezing a palmful of my ass. I squeal and giggle.

"Whatever you say, petal."

I dunk another basket of *lumpia* into the fryer, unable to wipe the smile from my face. It's only been two days since Callum and I last hooked up, but our meetups have become my own personal sexy rewards program. Bust my ass during the day, act professional around all these customers, then when evening falls, I treat myself to a naked Callum making me howl into the wee hours of the morning.

One downside to my secret hookups? Lying to my mom about what I did in London and what I do with my free nights now. And where I've taken Lemon. Thankfully, she's bought the lie that I've made some new friends who are curious to see what owning a cat would be like and want to try it out before making a final decision.

Leaning out the window, I hand the baskets to the waiting customers and see the napkin dispenser that's usually on the ledge is now missing. Looking up, I spot Callum leaning out of his food truck to hand off an order. Then he catches my eye and winks. I turn away quickly before anyone can see me smile.

The missing napkin dispenser is payback for when I swiped all the malt vinegar bottles from the ledge of his food truck yesterday. Despite our secret hookup arrangement, we still have appearances to keep up. After a couple weeks of acting civil to each other, we realized customers would eventually notice our sudden change in behavior—and probably post about it online. And if the Maui Food Festival organizer caught wind of my and Callum's new arrangement, we'd both be disqualified from the contest. So every few days we resume some small-scale form of fake fighting. I adore it. It's a whole new form of flirting between us.

Mom turns to hand me two orders of *lumpia*, pulling me back into the moment. She smooths her hand over the blue bandana she's wearing as a makeshift hairnet. "So energized, *anak*." She turns back to the counter to scoop an order of papaya salad. "I knew a vacation was a good idea. It really recharged your batteries. You've been in a good mood every day since you got back."

If I don't make direct eye contact, keep my hands busy, and speak in vague statements, I can get away with withholding the truth. But skirting the issue is all I can do. If she grabbed me by the shoulders, pinned me with her stare, and asked me what was really going on, I'd cave. I can't look her in the eye and lie. So I don't look at her at all.

Just then, Mrs. Tokushige comes to the window. "Nikki! How was your trip to London? You two have been so busy lately, I haven't had the chance to ask."

I smile while pretending to check on the silverware containers. "London was a lot of fun," I say.

She pats my arm. "I'm so glad. You deserve some time away. Like your mom said, you work so hard."

Mom perks up. "It's good, too, that you're going out more now that you're back. Having hobbies, meeting people, it's all so important."

If only she knew what I'm actually doing when I tell her I'm headed out for the night. I nod, making a split second of eye contact with her before I spin away to wipe down the counter. Anything longer and I'll break.

Mrs. Tokushige pulls Mom into a chat about the new thriller she's reading for their book club. I leave to take out the garbage to the trash can, which sits equidistant behind both food trucks. I dump the bag and turn back to my truck, catching Callum's eye as he leans out of his window to hand a customer their food.

The corner of his mouth darts up when he spots me. That familiar fire ignites within. It's like I'm running around with some glorious sex-induced fever that leaves me giddy twenty-four seven.

I walk back to my truck and lean on the counter, sipping from my water bottle. My phone buzzes in my pocket. A text from Callum.

How about something different tonight?

He sends a link and I click on it. It's an advertisement for a masquerade-themed block party in Paia. I swipe through the photos and read the captions. A night of music, dancing in the street, and drinks.

My thumb hovers over my phone screen as I hesitate. Every time we've met up since returning to Maui, it's been in private with no one else around, at either his place or mine. To show up in public together could pose a risk. If some food blogger or customer saw us together and it got back to the Maui Food Festival organizers, they could think we're together and we'd lose our shot at the prize money. No way is it worth the risk.

I text him my concern, and he answers right away.

I have our masks ready to go. We'll be hidden in plain sight, promise. All you have to do is show up at my condo at 7. What do you say?

While I mull it all over, he texts again.

Come on, petal. It'll be fun 😉

The use of that nickname pushes me over the edge. I lean out the window to sneak a peek at him. He's standing at the window of his food truck, his head buried in his phone. He looks up but is careful not to show any discernible happiness in his expression. The wink from before was risky enough in front of everyone.

Something extra dances behind his gaze the longer he looks at me. It's a sneaky slyness that his hazel-green eyes hide well. I suspect I'm the only one to notice it, because not a single nearby customer pays us any attention. We're indulging in our secret out in the open, yet no one even notices. Just his eyes on my eyes—it's all I need.

Tearing my gaze from his, I turn back to my phone.

What color dress would go well with my mask?

# Chapter 12

"Whoa," I mutter as Callum pulls his car into Paia.

It's just after sundown when we arrive to the block party, and this normally sleepy beach town has morphed into a mini Rio de Janeiro during Carnival.

The entire main drag through town is closed to cars. During the day it's a low-key tourist destination. People mostly pass by it on their way to drive the insanely popular road to Hana. Some stop to check out the restaurants and shops, and to take photos of the Old West–style buildings lining the main street, which are painted in an array of pastel colors. But tonight it's overrun with a crowd of masked people jumping and gyrating to frenetic dance music.

We get lucky and take a street parking spot right as a car pulls out. Callum stares ahead at the rave-like celebration commencing in front of us.

"Fucking hell," he mutters, his eyes wide. His expression is what I imagine he would look like if he saw a fireball flash across the sky.

I nudge his shoulder. "This was your idea."

Twisting his head to face me, he grins. "Are you ready?" He

hands me a mask from the back seat of his car. It's a basic black eye mask with pink feathers shooting from either side and looks perfect with my black minidress.

"Hell yes, I'm ready."

I secure it on, then watch as he sets his own in place. It's a gray one that covers half his face, like in *Phantom of the Opera.*

I gaze down his chest and legs. He's opted for a crisp, short-sleeve button-up and gray chino shorts. It's the perfect smart yet not-too-dressy outfit for an outdoor dance party. I lick my lips. Even with his face shrouded, he's still positively delicious.

We climb out of the car and walk toward the block party. Callum grabs me by the hand and leads me through the mass of swaying bodies. The sea breeze picks up, whipping my hair around my face. Callum turns to me and tucks my hair behind my ear.

Even though I can't see most of his face, I can tell just how much he's enjoying being out and about. His mouth is curved up into that telltale half smile he sports every time he's happy yet wants to play it cool.

"Thank you." I squeeze his hand.

We stop at a nearby booth selling some rum, pineapple, and coconut concoction in a coconut shell. I hand the seller cash and hold the straw up to Callum's mouth. He takes a sip, making a satisfied exhale when he swallows. "Very, very good."

"Hey, cool accent, man."

Callum gives the guy a thumbs-up as he flashes the hang loose sign. We continue down the block. The song booming through the salty sea air is some EDM tune I don't recognize. I bop along anyway, swaying my hips as we walk.

"I didn't know you were such a good dancer," Callum says as we walk along the outskirts of the dancing crowd.

I pull him by the hand, moving us away from the crowd, and

take a few more pulls of the fruity drink. It's more dangerous than it tastes, because already I'm feeling tipsy. I haven't had a strong cocktail in about a year.

"I used to go out dancing all the time with my friends when I lived in Portland. Not so much anymore."

"That's a shame," he says. "I love seeing you let loose."

His words from that night in London—the night we first hooked up—echo in my head.

*I want to find out what you look like when you let loose.*

I take a step forward so that our bodies are nearly pressed together. "That's funny coming from someone so straitlaced."

"It's bloody sexy seeing you move like that," he growls.

I bite my lip a bit to keep myself under control. "Let's keep going, then."

Callum pulls me by the hand to the very edge of the dancing mass. He takes a sip of the drink before letting me finish it off. I set the coconut at our feet, letting the alcohol and the electronic beat pulse through me.

He presses his front against me, swaying his body slowly at first. The beat speeds up, and I move my hips faster. One of my hands clutches Callum's shoulder; the other holds my long hair back and out of my face. With the elastic band on my wrist, I tie it up into a ponytail.

Callum leans his lips to my ear. "Always prepared," he muses.

"Always."

Under the influence of alcohol and electronic dance music, I feel a whole new kind of ease, moving my body however and wherever I feel. I haven't felt this good—this free—in ages.

Maybe it's the juice-laden alcohol pumping through my system. Maybe it's because I haven't been out like this in almost two years. Maybe it's the fact that I've got this hot man pressed against me in public and I can touch him, grab him, and grind against him, without a single worry as to what anyone around us will do or say. Because of these masks, we're hidden in plain sight. And it drives me the best kind of crazy.

Spinning around, I press my backside against his front. I lean my back into his chest and grip the back of his neck with my arm. He peers down at me gazing up at him; our stares lock. Despite the barrier our masks provide, I can tell exactly how he's feeling. It's all in his eyes. Those normally hazel-green stunners are dilated to hell. Jet-black spheres overtake the green. The way I'm moving my body, the show I'm putting on for him, it's having quite an effect on him.

Something hard presses against my ass, sending a grin to my face. He's really, really enjoying the effects of me grinding on him, it seems.

"Fuck," he grunts.

Immediately, I stop grinding against him, moving myself just a few inches away. "Getting all worked up?" I shout over the thundering beat.

"A bit," he mouths, then chuckles. He is adorably flustered.

I turn around to face him, my head still mildly dizzy from quickly downing that gigantic cocktail and the music thundering around us. With my arms wrapped around his neck, we shuffle our feet back and forth in a slow dance. It doesn't matter that our soundtrack is upbeat or that everyone else around us is jumping and raving. Nothing outside of me and Callum exists right now.

A few minutes pass, and then Callum takes a breath. "All good now. Thanks," he yells over the music.

I nod and pull him by the hand back to the coconut stand for a refill. We share a few sips, then Callum looks at his phone. "Christ. We danced for nearly an hour."

It only felt like minutes.

"Is that how you always used to dance?" His eyes bore into me.

I chuckle. "Hell no. When I went out dancing with my friends, there was a lot more jumping and a lot less grinding."

"Ready to go again?"

I take another sip, which sends me into solidly buzzed territory. "I'm a little tipsy, actually. Any more dancing, and I'll be on the floor."

Callum swipes the drink out of my hand before taking a long gulp. He looks in the direction of the beach. I can't see it from where we're standing, but every time there's a break in the music, I can hear the soft crash of the waves. I close my eyes, humming at the soothing sound.

"How about we take a walk? Maybe stop by the beach for a bit?"

"Okay."

The sound of the ocean churning intensifies as we make our way down the street to Baby Beach. A gust of ocean wind hits my skin, and I smile. When we reach the sand, we take off our masks.

"You know, there's a spot not far from here in Paia called Secret Beach," I say. "It's clothing optional. You could come here and do your naked swimming if you ever get tired of Little Beach."

"I'll keep that in mind."

I gasp and clutch at him with both hands. "We should go skinny-dipping together now! Wouldn't that be fun?"

I tug down the straps of my dress, but Callum grabs both of my hands, stopping me. "Not now. You're drunk. It wouldn't be safe."

I make a pouty face up at him, even though I'm not even sure he can see my expression in the darkness. I can barely see his.

"Some other time. Promise," he says, then pauses. "Baldwin Beach is just down the road. That's where your dad is, right?"

Just the mention of my dad catches me off guard. But not in a bad way like it would have before. There's such softness, such reverence in Callum's tone when he speaks about him. It makes everything inside of me run warm.

"Yes."

"There's a million gorgeous beaches here. What made Baldwin his favorite?"

"The color of the water. He said he loved how it looked almost turquoise."

"Next time you talk to him, tell him it's my favorite too."

"I will."

I wonder if he can hear the smile in my voice. I can hear the smile in his. For a long moment, we say nothing. The ocean and the breeze are the only sounds around us. It's soothing.

"You seem happy right now, Nikki," Callum says, his voice a hair louder than the crash of the waves in front of us.

A bout of alcohol-induced dizziness hits, and I lean into him, resting my head on his shoulder. We fit perfectly in bed, when dancing, when cuddled on the couch, when we're standing side by side.

"That's because I am. This moment is just . . ." I trail off, unable to find the right word.

This moment, this night, it is everything. I didn't know how much I missed going out, socializing, dancing, feeling like a normal twenty-nine-year-old woman.

I close my eyes, enjoying the light buzz running through me. I grip his arm tighter. "Sorry for how tipsy I am. It's been a while since I've drunk this much of the hard stuff."

"Don't be sorry," he says. "I'm having a nice time."

I shift, pressing my ear against his chest. The shallow breath he takes hits softly against my cheek.

"Spending time with you is my favorite thing to do, Callum. *You* are my favorite."

The words just slip out. It sounds almost like relationship talk, and that's a no-no for us.

"Is that so?" he asks.

I tilt my head up to get a better look at him. My eyes are finally starting to adjust to the dark. Judging by the upward curve of his mouth, he isn't offended at all by my slipup.

The dizziness eases, making way for that drunken giddiness that eventually accompanies my buzz. "This is so, so nice. Standing here with you. I haven't done this in forever. You know it's been almost two years since I've gone out dancing?"

"You did mention that."

"Oh, right."

He chuckles.

I can't seem to stop babbling. "I'm glad I did. I'm glad you made us come out tonight. It feels so . . . so . . ."

"Freeing? Good?"

"More than good. Incredible." Loosening my hold, I run a hand up and down his arm. He lets out the softest moan. "You feel incredible, too, you know that?"

I glance up at him, my eyes finally adjusted to the darkness. He peers down at me.

"I just . . . everything about you," I say. "Being with you is like being home. You feel like home to me. No one has ever made me feel that way. No guy, at least. Well, except for my dad."

Did I really just say Callum felt like home? Did I really just compare him to my dad? I've lost all control over my mouth and my words. What am I even saying anymore?

The dizziness is back, and I clutch tighter to him. I close my eyes, hoping the spinning doesn't start. If that happens, that means I've left pleasantly drunk territory and will definitely start vomiting.

Thankfully, the world doesn't tilt and spin, but I can't seem to stop talking. My mouth is a spigot of words, and I've torn the knob clean off. "I wish we could do this all the time, Callum. You're amazing. You're hot and protective and sweet and hardworking and thoughtful and you like cats and . . ."

Planting my feet into the sand, I look up at him once more. I can't see his full expression—only his furrowed brow is visible in the darkness. But judging by his silence, I can tell he's confused and weirded out by everything I'm saying. And even in my drunken state, I know why.

I've crossed a boundary. Me gushing over him isn't casual hookup territory at all. I'm talking like he's my one and only. I'm blurring the lines, and he doesn't like it. I don't like it either. I should know better—I'm the one who set the boundaries.

But this night? This moment? It is a perfect storm of feelings and alcohol and romance and ambiance. I broke the rules and let myself get pseudo love drunk.

Callum clears his throat. "And?" he repeats with an edge to his tone.

I shake my head, letting out a laugh that's all nerves and pitchy. "Nothing. Sorry. That was the alcohol talking."

A long silence follows. When he finally speaks, all he says is, "Okay." Nothing more.

I let out all the air I've been holding in a slow, silent hiss. I'm relieved. I don't want to talk about how I just made a fool of myself in front of Callum because I caught feelings for a split second in a drunken haze.

Staring straight ahead, he bites his lip before speaking again. "Ready to head back to the car?"

"You're okay to drive?" I ask.

"I only had a few sips. I'm fine."

We put our masks back on. He takes my hand in his and leads me up the beach to the street. We don't talk the entire walk to the car or when he starts to drive back to his place.

We both yank off our masks and toss them in the back seat in silent unison. With each mile we cross, I sober up. I need to think fast. I need to fix this rift I just caused between us.

"I'm . . . I'm sorry for what I said. I didn't mean it. It was just the alcohol and the mood and the fact that I haven't been out in forever. I'm sorry if I made you uncomfortable."

We hit a stoplight, and he eases on the brakes. He twists his head to me, the look on his face blank. Does he think I'm a stalker now? Is he annoyed that I didn't just drop it back at the beach? Am I making something out of nothing? I'd give anything to know what's running through his brain.

"You mean that?" he asks.

"I do. I'm sorry that I gave off the impression that I wanted more. I don't. I'm happy with the way things are right now."

That last sentence falls out of my mouth so stilted that I cringe. Drunk me momentarily wanted something more, but sober me knows better. Sober me knows what's on the line if we ever veer off-track.

Callum nods. "Right." The word rolls curtly off his tongue.

When the light turns green, he speeds ahead. In the silence of the drive, I wonder why it's so hard for me to believe my own words.

# Chapter 13

A few days past my drunken slipup, we're back to normal. The morning after the block party, Callum didn't mention a word of what I said the night before. I didn't either. When I found my sriracha and sweet chili sauce bottles missing the next day, I breathed a sigh of relief. Then I stole the container of lemon wedges from the counter of Hungry Chaps food truck during a carefully timed garbage haul, and that was that. Things were back to normal. We dove right back into flirty texts and no-nonsense hookups, and I couldn't have been more relieved.

I look through the window of my food truck, spotting Callum standing in his own truck's window. All he gives me is a lift of one eyebrow, but that low-key flirt is more than enough to get me through the rest of the day.

Tonight I'm heading to Callum's place after my shift. Finn is helping a chef friend with a late-night pop-up in Napili tonight, then camping at Haleakala, so I'm due at Callum's at 9 p.m. sharp. And it's doubly good because tomorrow is Easter, which means we're closed, which also means I don't have to rush home after fooling around like usual.

Mrs. Tokushige saunters up to the window for her usual lunch order. "Ay, Tiva." She narrows her eyes at Mom, who's finishing a *malasada*. "Do you know how much sugar is in those things? You should know better!"

I let out a laugh. "I think one doughnut is fine, Mrs. Tokushige. You see how well she eats the rest of the day."

The concerned expression on Mrs. Tokushige's face eases. "I suppose you're right. You never can be too healthy at our age, though, Tiva."

The two exchange a knowing expression. I decide it's the perfect time to take out the trash to avoid whatever squabble they're about to get into.

I haul the bag out to the garbage can just as a petite dark-haired beauty saunters up to the Hungry Chaps food truck, right in my line of sight. She slaps both hands on the metal ledge. Callum's brow jumps, as do his shoulders.

My eyes go wide. She's all smiles and curves with a deep olive tan and thick black hair that falls all the way to her waist. She's a whisper above five feet tall, but she's got the spirit of a giant. It's obvious in the way she waltzed to the truck and the unflappable eye contact she's making with Callum. She's practically bursting at the seams with that effortless, raw confidence stunning women like her seem to have in spades.

In her presence, I suddenly feel like a gawky baby giraffe struggling to stand.

"Hungry Chaps, huh?" She raises her brow at Callum, who's now frowning. "How clever."

She strains her neck to read the menu tacked on the side of the truck. But I can tell by the exaggerated arch of her back that it's a move to display her ample chest, which is barely contained in her black crop top. It complements her microscopic jean cutoffs perfectly, which showcase two perfect slivers of tanned butt cheek.

"I might need your help choosing something. I'm having trouble deciding." This stunner has the most insincere, whiny drawl I've ever heard. I don't know anything about this woman, but she strikes me as the kind of person who would fake indecisiveness just to get a hot guy like Callum to talk to her.

I swallow, my mouth sour.

Callum studies his notepad. "Fish-and-chips are good. So is the steak pie."

The moment she leans her head up closer to him, he leans back inside the window of the truck, staring like she's some mystery science project.

She grins wide. "One pie for me, then."

He scribbles her order and starts to turn away, but then she reaches up to grab his forearm.

The heat inside me turns bitter. I order it away, but to no avail. I have no right to feel jealous in this moment. Callum isn't mine. We're just friends with benefits. And this no-strings-attached arrangement means he can see her—or any other woman he wants. I knew that from the get-go. But to see it play out in front of me throws me completely.

Now the entire inside of my mouth is sour. Every time I swallow, I taste poison.

"Yes?" Callum remains still in her hold. I'm beyond shocked he doesn't shrug her away. He's not one to let a stranger grab him out of the blue. But she's not a typical stranger. She's sexy and flirty and easy on the eyes.

"I don't get to hear accents like yours very often," she says. "Can you say a little more before you go and take care of my pie?"

If I weren't clenching my jaw so hard, it would be on the ground. That's some ballsy innuendo. I'm sure this living doll is dying for Callum to do naughty things to her pie.

I'm also guessing that, looking the way she does, she doesn't normally have to work this hard to get a man's attention. She's not letting it faze her though. Callum is indisputably hot. I watch women ogle him all day, every day. But rarely do they saunter up with even a fraction of the gumption she possesses.

The edge of his mouth twitches up. It almost looks like the start of a smile.

"How about, 'Your food will be ready in ten minutes,'" he says.

Her free hand falls to her bare clavicle, and she audibly swoons. Her other hand remains clamped on his skin. My stomach lurches. I want to vomit.

She narrows her deep brown eyes at Callum, like a puma eyeing an injured deer. She bites her lip, practically moaning.

"Lovely. I'm dying to hear you talk more. After your shift maybe?"

My heart thuds so hard against my chest, I'm certain it's going to burst out and land on the dirt several feet away from me. Steam is hissing from my ears and my skin is lava. I want to march the ten feet to where this sex kitten stands and pull her gorgeous hair out of her scalp. Because how dare she. Callum is mine and—

I nearly crumple to the ground. He is not mine. He never was and he never will be. This all-consuming possession I feel for him is completely irrational and not one bit okay. He has every right to say yes to her proposition. And I have zero right to feel this way.

That moment of romantic feelings that swooped through me at the Paia block party and the night we spent drinking champagne at his condo should have clued me in. They're both signs that we need to cool off ASAP.

I spin on my sneakered heel and march back to my truck where Mrs. Tokushige and Mom chat happily about the Easter dinner Mrs. Tokushige is planning. I'm thankful they don't notice the change in my demeanor. They would definitely ask questions, but I don't want them to think anything is amiss.

I pull out my phone from my pocket, then text Callum.

Hey. Something came up. Can't meet tonight. Sorry.

I turn it on silent, then resume taking orders and slinging baskets of food. Hopefully, Callum read my text before saying no to that oversexed Tinkerbell. Because now he's free to take her up on her offer to listen to him talk while she preps her pie for him.

I grit my teeth even harder, wondering if he'll say yes, all the while praying he says no.

"I'm tired, *anak*. Going to bed." Mom squeezes me in a hug.

I glance at the clock on the oven. "It's not even eight thirty."

She yawns. "I need as much beauty sleep as I can get at my age."

I wonder if Mrs. Tokushige's warning about health at their age scared her into an earlier bedtime.

"Be careful if you go out tonight, okay?" she says.

She pats my hand, then heads down the hall to her room. Lemon follows her, scurrying into her bedroom before she shuts the door. I stare at the screen of my laptop propped on the kitchen counter, my eyes burning. Watching funny cat videos on YouTube isn't what I planned to be doing tonight, but I didn't feel like doing much else after watching Callum get hit on by Maui Barbie.

I press my lips together, then wince at their dry feel. I'm in need of a ChapStick intervention.

When I pull my purse on my lap to dig some lip balm out, I notice my phone flashing. This is the first time I've looked at it since turning it to silent this afternoon. I spot three missed texts and two missed calls, all from Callum. My stomach drops.

CALLUM: I was really looking forward to seeing you. Everything all right? Let me know you're okay at least?

CALLUM: Can you tell me what's going on? I haven't heard from you all day.

CALLUM: Petal. Are you angry at me or something?

The tiniest ping of guilt hits the center of my chest. He's clearly not out with anyone if he's texting and calling me this much.

I text him back.

ME: Sorry for making you worry . . . Nothing's wrong, I just felt a little weird today.

His reply is less than a minute later, further proof that he is definitely at home in his condo, not out with some hottie. My emotions are a cocktail of relief and embarrassment. I jumped on the irrational jealousy bandwagon way the hell too soon.

CALLUM: Weird how?

For three solid minutes, I try and fail to draft a suitable explanation. Anything I send over text would sound positively insane right now. Because how exactly would I explain my ridiculous behavior?

I got irrationally jealous at seeing another woman flirt with you, even though you're not mine, and you have every right to do whatever you want with whomever you want. Oops!

So instead I write:

ME: It's hard to explain over text.

Seven seconds later, he replies.

CALLUM: Then tell me in person. Come over.

When Callum answers the door, he's stone-faced. Just like the day I met him, just like all those times we argued and bickered.

I never thought I'd see him make that face with me ever again. But how can I expect him to act any other way when I've been so foolish?

He shuts the door behind me. I gaze around the living room, taking in the sparse furniture. I've seen this space a million times before, but tonight I examine it with renewed interest. Anything to put off the inevitable. We're about to have a very, very uncomfortable conversation about my adolescent behavior, and I don't know if I'll be able to stomach it.

I scan the other end of the condo, where the wooden dining table sits.

"You have a very spacious place," I say, glancing everywhere but his face. "Have I ever mentioned that?"

Callum steps from behind me, raising an eyebrow. I have no choice but to look at him now.

"Is that why you came over? To talk about my flat?"

I shake my head and drop my purse on the tile floor. My eyes drop to the light peach hue of the tile resting under my bare feet. My nerve still evades me. "I'm sorry I blew you off today."

"Don't talk to the floor. Talk to me." There's an edge when he speaks, a hardness that hasn't been there since we started getting along. But I've brought it back with a single moment of jealousy. Well done, me.

Slowly, my eyes make their way up to his. I take my time, though, indulging in a scan of his thighs, that broad chest clad in a bright blue T-shirt. The color makes his honey-kissed skin glow even at night.

I wish we could stop this uncomfortable conversation and go to his bed instead. I wish I could rip that shirt off his body and make him forget all about what a baby I was today.

"I'm sorry. I guess I just . . ." I have to take a second and swallow.

It feels like I'm free-falling into those grass-green pools masquerading as his eyes.

I can't bear to say the word. Because if I say jealousy, the jig is up. He'll know everything. He'll know that I'm getting attached to him; he'll know that I'm reneging on the agreement that I came up with to keep things casual.

And admitting that out loud would be a betrayal for me too. I promised myself I wouldn't get close to anyone. It's not worth the feeling of loss, the soul-crushing sadness that consumes every fiber of my being knowing that I'll never, ever have that person again.

My dad's death was a caution. People come and go. The worst thing you can do is let yourself get close because of the pain you'll inevitably feel when they leave. And I refuse to go through that kind of agony again.

I clear my throat, renewing my focus. "It was just that . . . earlier today, I had a weird moment of . . ."

"Of?" he says, that razor-sharp edge still present in his tone.

Biting the inside of my cheek, I gaze in the direction of the kitchen, staring at nothing in particular.

I go for the long version of the truth, just to avoid that pesky eight-letter word. "It was weird to see that hot girl flirt with you today. That's all."

I wring my hand even though there's nothing wrong with it, just to have something else to do other than stand here and bask in my self-inflicted humiliation.

For several seconds, he says nothing. He simply stares down at me, his face still hard as stone, giving nothing away.

"You were jealous?" The way he says it, it's not teasing. It's like he's reading off a grocery list to double-check that he hasn't missed anything.

I mutter what I think sounds like a "yes."

"Did you honestly think I was interested in her?"

I shrug. The lines between his eyebrows may as well sign a lease to stay. I have a feeling I'm going to be on the receiving end of countless Callum frowns during this conversation.

"She grabbed your arm and you didn't pull away. It seemed like you liked her touching you."

He sighs, like he's disappointed in me. "Finn told me I needed to be nicer to the customers. I was trying to listen to his advice."

His explanation makes sense. It doesn't make this hurt any less though.

"I made plans with you tonight," Callum says. "Do you think I'd break them to pursue someone else?"

My head falls back in a groan. "I have no idea, Callum."

His fingers grip my chin, and he directs me to look at him. The firm contact sends heat pulsing through me.

"Why were you jealous, petal?"

I pull my face out of his hand. "I don't want to talk about it."

He steps forward, pressing against me, his hands at my hips. His chest heaves against mine. He breathes, then I breathe, then we do it all over again until we're panting. It's both heaven and agony.

"Tell me," he growls. "I want to know why."

"No, you don't."

"Why?"

"Because . . ."

My voice shakes with the need to tell him how I really feel. I want to tell him that I'm jealous because I care about him more than just some casual arrangement. I want to tell him that I don't want to share him with anyone else. I want to tell him that I think of him as mine, even though he's not and never will be.

"Why do you even put up with me?" My attempt at a diversion fails, because he answers promptly.

"Because you're one of my favorite people on this island. You call me on my shit and it's sexy as hell. You're passionate and caring. You work hard, you fight hard, and you love hard. Not to mention you're gorgeous." His hands press into me harder, and it's heaven. "Do you want me to keep going?"

I shake my head. Any other time I could listen to him talk about what he adores about me all night long. But that's not what I want right now.

"What do you want, Nikki?"

It's the millionth time he's asked me this. I remember the first time he posed that same question while standing in the foyer of his parents' empty house back in London. He asks me what I want almost every time we hook up, and I usually show him with my hands or mouth. But now the words sound like a completely different language in this conversation where we're both fire-breathing dragons ready to demolish the other.

"I want you, Callum. Right now."

His left hand slides to my forearm. "You're burning up," he growl-whispers.

Hot with jealousy, simmering with arousal. The flames are the same; it's just the feelings that change. And he's the root of them all.

"I can't help it," I pant. "You do this to me. Every single time. I'm burning whenever I'm around you. I act like the biggest fool because of you."

That's the watered-down truth of my behavior today. That's as much as I want to tell him.

He leans down and his mouth lands softly on the side of my neck. My eyes flutter as I let the tingles make their merry way down the rest of my body.

"I suppose I should cool you off, then," he says against my shoulder.

He takes me by the hand to the bathroom in the hallway. He

turns the knob in the tub, and a rush of water shoots from the showerhead. We both shed our clothes in silent unison. There's no need for words right now.

Callum steps in the shower before I can get a proper look at him. It doesn't matter how many times I see him naked. I'm forever in awe. Under the brightness of the overhead light and the sheen of the water, he is stunning. Like always.

I claw at the wet muscle in front of me, and he captures my mouth in his. We're kissing so hard, so rabidly that I can hardly breathe. The only air I get is through tiny gaps between our mouths when our movements are too rough.

I breathe, he breathes, and we do it over and over.

He's grabbing at my waist, the fleshy curve of my hips, my generously rounded backside. I give his chiseled chest one last eager grope with both hands. And then I stroke along his always impressive length, speeding up with every groan and grunt he gives me. It's two minutes until he's done for.

I rinse my hand in the stream surrounding us, but then he grips my hips and directs me to sit on the ledge at the far end of the shower. I watch him kneel down in front of me, biting my lip to suppress a groan. The water is lukewarm right now and that's a good thing. I'll need to cool off soon.

He pushes his face between my legs and works his magic. Endless swirls and licks and sucks. I'm howling. It echoes against the walls of the bathroom, the only appropriate soundtrack to the filthy actions taking place in this steamy haven. Legs shaking and muscles twitching, I explode. He doesn't dare let up, digging his fingers in my thighs.

Still no words. It's exactly how I want it, how I need it.

He helps me up, we rinse, towel off, then reconvene in his bed. He cuddles me into his chest. Every muscle inside me that was formerly tense is now relaxed into goo. This is the effect Callum James has on me. I'm a wildfire one minute and Play-Doh the next.

"I'm sorry for how I acted today," I whisper against his chest.

"It's all right, Nikki. I just wish . . ."

When he doesn't finish right away, I open my mouth to ask him what he wishes, but I stop myself. I don't want to know. Because if he told me what I want to hear, I'd be stuck. How could I date the man who could put me out of business?

And that's not even the worst part. The worst part is that I'm so into Callum, that in the right weak moment, I might actually choose him.

A weak moment a lot like this one, where I'm tucked against him in the dark, surrounded by his mass, protected, his entire body feeling like home.

But then I'd be the worst daughter who ever lived, and I have a promise to keep. I refuse to break it.

Before he can finish, I kiss him. I pull the bedsheet over the two of us and close my eyes, hoping his silence lasts until I fall asleep.

When I open my eyes, Callum's lead pipe of an arm is on top of me, and I'm tucked securely underneath. I close my eyes and let out a long, silent breath so I don't wake him. It's so damn comfortable under here, under Callum, under his super soft bedsheets.

There's a soft wheeze above my head. One pleasant surprise after all this time together is that he doesn't snore like a freight train. His breaths are soft and slow, almost rhythmic. I turn my head to see the few inches of space between us. Everything about waking up next to Callum in his bed is soothing bliss. The feel, the sounds, that delicious musky spice his body somehow naturally produces.

But then my bladder reminds me that it's early morning and I'll burst if I don't do something about it soon. Holding my breath, I slowly roll out from under him, slip on his T-shirt, and quietly pad to the attached bathroom.

I relieve myself and wash up, catching a glimpse of myself in the mirror. My cheeks sport a healthy amount of pink still. Leftovers from last night when I embarrassed myself in front of Callum by admitting my jealousy to his face. I take a breath, thankful that he's not yet awake so we don't have to face the awkward aftermath. Because what do you say the morning after you almost spilled all your feelings to your fuck buddy?

I stand in the open doorway, gazing at his sleeping form like a creep. My heart thuds. What the hell will I say now? I can't drag him into the shower for more sex. I mean, I want to, but he'll see right through that. And then he'll ask me about last night, why I got all angsty and emotional. And I may not have the strength to lie.

I take two slow deep breaths before taking a step toward the bed. And then I hear keys jangling at the front door.

"Oi, Cal!"

Finn's voice booms from all the way at the other end of the condo. Callum slingshots into a sitting position, rubbing his eyes.

I grip the edge of the doorway. "Hide me!" I shriek-whisper.

Callum slow-blinks. "Wait just a—"

I karate chop the air in front of me to silence him. "No! No time. Finn can't know that I'm here. Hide me. Now!"

"Callum, you still sleeping, you lump?" The sound of Finn's voice grows louder.

Callum jolts up from bed and ushers me into his closet. "Sorry, he said he was going to be gone today and tomorrow. I didn't know he'd be coming back."

I tuck myself in the farthest corner and point my wide-eyed stare at him.

Callum grabs a pair of boxers from the floor of his closet and pulls them on. He wobbles, nearly falling over, he does it so fast. Leaning against the closet doorframe, he steadies himself.

"Just . . . just hold on, I'll get rid of him."

Callum shuts the closet door just as I hear the whoosh of his bedroom door flinging open.

Finn's chuckle hits my ears and I hold my breath. Please God, don't let him see me. Given how close he and Callum are, I don't believe he'd rat him out even if he did find us together. But the fewer people who know about our secret, the better.

"It's nine thirty, mate. I didn't know you slept in this late anymore."

With the amusement in Finn's voice clear, I let out the air in a slow hiss.

Callum clears his throat. "Did you barge into my bedroom just to make fun of me for oversleeping?"

There's a soft patting noise. Probably Finn smacking Callum on the back. "Of course not. Look, I have a dilemma and I need your help. Do you remember Ted from uni and rugby club back home?"

"How could I forget," Callum mumbles. I imagine him running a hand over his tired face.

"You know how he manages Travaasa Hana? Well, he needs someone to take over the Easter dinner service at the resort this evening. He rang me in a panic about how the chef he hired fell through at the last minute and he doesn't have anyone to cover. Can you do it?"

"Can't you?" Even as I sit hidden away in the closet, the curt way Callum grumbles makes me flinch.

"We're fussy when we oversleep, aren't we?"

In my head I can picture Finn holding his arms palms up at a scowling Callum.

"Sorry," Callum grumbles. "I just . . . you caught me a little off guard, Finn."

A heavy sigh fills the silence. "I can't take it, Cal. I already committed to that camping trip with Grace and her friends. I don't want to back out now, even though I'd kill to cook at Travaasa."

"Meeting her friends already?"

The lightness of Callum's tone makes me think he's half smiling. It makes me smile too. There's another soft smack sound, probably Callum playfully hitting Finn this time. I wonder if Finn is blushing.

"You know how it goes," Finn says, the grin obvious in the flustered way he speaks.

"I don't actually."

There's a few seconds of silence.

"Well, that's no one's fault but your own," Finn finally says.

"Don't start, Finn." Callum's tone turns curt once more.

"It's so bloody obvious how you feel about her," Finn says. "You've got history together. Why don't you just tell her already. No use in putting it off like you've been—"

"I don't need my little brother to lecture me on my love life."

My ears perk in the silence that follows Callum's comment, delivered in his trademark hard tone. Who the hell is Finn talking about? Is Callum seeing someone else besides me? Maybe he's rekindling something with an ex? Finn did mention the word "history," and that's a for-sure code word for exes. Maybe that's why he rejected sexy Tinkerbell yesterday, because he's still carrying a torch for someone in his past. But last night Callum made it sound like there wasn't anyone else, though maybe he was just trying to spare my feelings because he could see how upset I was . . .

I force myself back to the present. No. None of that is my business. Callum and I are just hooking up, that's all. He's moving back to Chicago soon anyway. And since we're not even close to being a couple, he has every right to see exes, other women, whoever he wants—which it sounds like he's doing from what Finn says.

I silently thank Finn for his abrupt entrance. That wave of emotions I've been battling the past twelve hours ends right now. I need to just enjoy our no-strings-attached arrangement for the uncomplicated and enjoyable setup that it is and stop longing for more.

There's a throat clear, then Finn speaks. "Do you want to do the dinner service tonight? Or am I calling Ted back to break his heart?"

"I'll do it," Callum says.

Finn says something about forgetting a bag he packed for the camping trip. Soft footsteps lead out of the room. A minute later there's an exchange of muffled voices, then the front door closes.

Callum opens the closet door. "You all right?" he asks.

I nod my head. "So you're cooking at Travaasa Hana tonight? Congrats."

I gather my rumpled clothing from the floor.

"Look." He catches my wrist, turning me to face him. "About what Finn said earlier—"

I hold up a hand and plaster what I hope is a convincing smile on my face. "It's okay. We don't have to talk about it."

And for my sanity, I really, really don't want to. The fact that I almost spilled the beans last night in my jealous state when he very likely has someone else on his mind is proof that I need to keep myself in check. No more emotional slipups. From now on, no matter how mushy-gushy I feel, Callum and I are to remain in the friends-with-benefits zone.

He releases my hand, and I go back to dressing myself. When I turn around, I'm greeted with the sight of Callum sitting on the edge of the bed, legs hooked over the side. His honey-blond hair is ruffled, his five-o'clock shadow is extra scruffy, his eyes are puffy, and he looks more delicious than any breakfast-in-bed option I could ever ask for.

There's something expectant in his eyes. The corner of his mouth hooks upward. "Are you busy tonight? I'm going to need your help."

# Chapter 14

When Callum and I walk into the lobby of the Travaasa Hana resort, I gawk. There's an open courtyard with a perfectly square fountain in the middle. Plush benches and chairs are positioned throughout, along with lush greenery that sets a decidedly tropical vibe. The color palette is warm all the way, with shades of orange, yellow, and brown filling the open-concept space.

A muttered "whoa" slips from my lips.

Callum grins down at me. "I can't believe you've never made it to Hana in all the time you've lived here."

I twist my head around the opulent space for the millionth time. My eyes catch on the four identical spouts at each corner of the fountain. Each one spits perfectly arched streams of water into the air.

"If I had known just how spectacular this place is, I would have come here sooner."

We walk up to the front desk, and Callum asks for Ted.

"You sure you want me here?" I ask.

"Positive." Callum winks at me.

"I'll have to thank Finn later for being so smitten with Grace that I got to steal his cooking gig."

Despite the awkward moment we shared after Finn inadvertently gave away that Callum is most assuredly enjoying other women's company in addition to mine, I jumped at the chance to help him cook dinner. I haven't done a high-end dinner service since my Portland days, and I'm aching to dive back in. Plus, I have the day to myself since Mom is spending Easter with Mrs. Tokushige's family. Now that Callum and I are focused on a mutual goal of salvaging a fancy holiday dinner, we're distracted from our awkwardness. Even the car ride here was tension-free since we spent it planning tonight's menu.

A tall, flustered pale guy who looks about thirty shuffles from the back, rounding the reception counter to meet us.

A relieved smile stretches across his face before he pulls Callum into a bear hug. "Thank fuck you're here, mate. The guest chef I booked for tonight couldn't make it because his flight was canceled. I don't know what I would have done if you hadn't said yes."

Callum ruffles Ted's short-cropped brown hair. Ted softly punches his arm, and they exchange a laugh.

"Happy to help." Callum gestures to me standing at his side. "This is Nikki, one of the most talented chefs on the island."

Now I'm the focus of Ted's relieved smile. He shakes my hand. "You know that's quite a compliment coming from him, right? He never compliments anyone, not even his friends."

I catch Callum's eye roll. My heart thuds with giddiness. "Really?"

Ted narrows an eye at Callum, then turns back to me. "I'm officially jealous, but seeing as you're saving my skin tonight, I'll let it go."

Ted huffs out a breath, pulling the lapels of his suit jacket.

I look at Ted. "Don't worry. We planned the whole menu on our drive here."

"Thank fuck."

"Is that your new catchphrase?" Callum asks.

I swallow back a chuckle and follow Ted as he leads us across the lobby to the dining area. When we reach the kitchen, my jaw unhinges. It's a stainless steel haven with shiny appliances everywhere I look. A trio of kitchen workers decked out in white jackets glide across the kitchen cleaning and prepping. Ted clears his throat, and they all look up.

"Sorry for all the chaos of this morning, everyone, but these two are here to save the day." Ted gestures to us. "Callum and Nikki are two food truck rock stars from the west side of the island who have graciously offered to take over dinner service tonight. I have no doubt that they'll serve up a brilliant meal for our guests."

Callum and I shake hands with the staff and look in the fridges and walk-in to figure out what we have to work with for tonight.

"I know food bloggers are a notoriously critical bunch," Ted says. "But I have faith in you."

I whip my head back to Ted. "Did you say food bloggers?"

He nods. "Apparently, some big-shot Maui vlogger arranged tonight's dinner as part of a social media retreat for a bunch of local food bloggers. Matteo something or other."

I nearly fall into a nearby shelf, but Callum catches me by the arm before I topple the endless stacks of metal bowls.

"Wait, so . . . so every major food blogger in Maui is going to be dining here tonight?" I stammer.

Ted nods, an easy smile on his face.

That means every major food blogger is going to see Callum and me together, which will unleash a wave of gossip about us. If they see us cooking side by side after only ever seeing us fight before, they're going to jump to some pretty dramatic conclusions—and will certainly post about it online. It might lead to an uptick in business like before, but if the organizers of the Maui Food Festival catch wind of this—which they probably will if someone here publicizes it—they will likely assume we're working together and disqualify us from the contest prize. No way in hell will I let that happen.

I hold up a hand to Ted. "One sec."

I yank Callum's arm, pulling him back into the hallway outside of the kitchen. The door swings shut, giving Callum and me a semblance of privacy.

I smack his arm, but it barely registers as a pat against his solid mass. "Why the hell didn't you tell me we'd be cooking dinner for every foodie with an Instagram account in Maui?"

Callum holds his hands up. "I didn't know. Finn didn't mention it this morning when he told me about it. You were there, remember?"

We pause and take twin deep breaths. It's only marginally soothing.

I wring my hands. "Remember how they recorded our arguments and posted them online? They'll be chomping at the bit to upload a photo of us together tonight just so they can cook up some drama and get more hits to their blogs."

"So?"

"Callum, seriously?"

My voice echoes through the hall, capturing the attention of a resort employee walking on the opposite side. Both Callum and I mutter sorry at the same time.

"If the organizers of the Maui Food Festival find out about us serving together, they could see that as fraternizing and disqualify us from the festival. I need a fair shot at that money, Callum. So does my mom. Don't tell me you and Finn wouldn't want a proper shot at it too."

He blinks for a second before refocusing on me. "I understand. I want that too."

"Then we can't let this get out. We can't let anyone see us together."

He shakes his head, the muscles of his jaw pressing against the lightly stubbled skin. "Fine."

Hot air fills the space between us. We're both fire-breathing dragons again.

"Now how do we fix this? How do we make sure this doesn't get out and that no one sees us?"

Leaning his head back, he closes his eyes and pinches the bridge of his nose. When he opens his eyes, there's renewed focus in his stare.

"I'll explain the situation to Ted."

I shoot wide eyes at him.

Callum frowns. "I'm not going to tell him our personal stuff. God, Nikki. What kind of person do you think I am?"

I look away, fixating on a nearby plant before Callum says my name in that low growl I die for. I turn back to him.

He clears his throat. "I'll tell Ted that things need to remain quiet because of the upcoming festival. I'll tell him that we're going to stay in that kitchen the entire night and that no one is allowed in other than staff."

The invisible fist squeezing my chest loosens. "Perfect. Thank you."

He grabs my hand, and that fist disappears completely. The warmth I felt when I woke up next to Callum in his bed resurfaces.

"It's going to be fine, Nikki. Promise."

I turn around and head back for the kitchen. "I hope so."

. . .

I finish plating the final deconstructed *lumpia* on a small plate, then smile up at the server. "They're ready."

I eye the plates I've assembled. Each plate boasts a crispy fried wrapper at the bottom, then a generous tablespoon of flavorful ground pork sautéed with minced carrots, cabbage, and water chestnuts. It repeats for three layers, a sprig of cilantro topping each one.

I say thank you to the servers when they swipe the plates from the kitchen and file out to the dining room.

Callum flashes a thumbs-up from the stove. "Excellent job."

A breath lodges in my throat. This is the first time I've had the chance to look at him longer than a few seconds since prepping and cooking began. The awkwardness of last night and this morning feels a million miles away. We make a surprisingly good cooking duo.

We prepped smoothly side by side, as if we'd been working in the same kitchen together for years. There was no bumping into each other, no crowding each other's work spaces. Just an effortless, unspoken harmony.

The other best part: being back in a full-size restaurant kitchen. Nerves grabbed hold of me the second I started mise en place, but it all came flowing back to me the minute I grabbed that first clove of garlic and began mincing.

All I had to do was focus on the moment. Focus on the moment with the food in front of me. Focus on the moment with the man standing next to me.

Now that the appetizers are out, I can breathe. I stare at the line of empty white dishes lining the metal table in the middle of the kitchen, then glance up at Callum. We're good again. We're hookup buddies—friends—and temporary cooking partners. Nothing more, nothing less. And as long as I keep that at the forefront of my mind, I can indulge in a seconds-long glance at him. We've got five minutes until we start cooking the main course, and I want to take every moment to soak in the exquisite visual he's giving me.

"You really know how to work a kitchen," I say.

He crosses his arms against his chest. Perfectly tanned forearms jut from the rolled sleeves of his crisp white chef's jacket. Saliva coats my mouth as I take him in. He looks like some sort of male model–chef hybrid. The relaxed way he leans against the metal edge of the stove, easy smile on his face, it's more like a still from a glamorous photo shoot than a real-time moment in a busy kitchen.

"You say that like you're surprised," he says.

"I'm not. It's just cool seeing you in action. All those years of working in your gran's bed-and-breakfast have paid off."

"That helped me with my cooking skills more." He turns to check on the temperature of the oven as it preheats. "I learned how to work a kitchen after spending my early twenties in restaurants."

He gently wrings out his hands at his sides. Automatically, my eyes fixate on his thick fingers and how deftly they move.

"So that's how come you're so good with your hands," I say.

His lips twitch upward ever so slightly. "It is. I can chop, sauté, dice, whisk, knead. Massage. And rub. Among other things."

I bite my lip. This feels like some sort of indecent kitchen pillow talk. My eyes skim the shiny metal surface of the nearby prep table. If only there weren't a handful of servers due back in the kitchen at any minute, I'd demand he bend me over the shiny cold surface and show me for the millionth time just how good he is with his hands. That's a decidedly friends-with-benefits thought.

I shake my head and glance at the clock. Only four minutes of ogling time left.

"You look like you've got something on your mind." It's as if he can read the naughty thoughts crowding my head.

My eyes fall to the floor. It's time to rein in the pornographic kitchen euphemisms and focus back on the task at hand.

"I just hope they like the deconstructed *lumpia*. It's a little pretentious. I don't know why I didn't just cook my regular recipe."

Callum swipes a stainless steel saucepan from the shelf above him and sets it on a spider burner. "We tasted it before it went out, remember? How many times do I have to tell you that it's bloody delicious?"

He flips on the burner and tosses a stick of butter in the pan.

I fetch a vat of diced scallions from the walk-in and set them next to the stove. I look up at him. "Thank you. That means a lot."

He gazes down at the butter, which is slowly melting into a rich foam. "That idea you had to stack the fried wrapper sheets between the minced pork was genius. Foodies go wild for that stuff."

Heat finds my cheeks, and not just because Callum's hot body is an inch from mine. But because of how genuine his compliment is. I've been so fixed on perfecting the comfort food menu for the food truck and festival that I haven't had much time to experiment with more daring recipes, like I did in my old job. My stomach was in happy knots the entire time I prepared my appetizer. I've missed playing around with creative recipes.

"Is that what the foodies at the restaurants you worked at told you?" I ask.

Callum shakes his head, chuckling. "I worked in pubs. Those aren't the kind of places foodies care to go to."

"Not true. Even foodies know that pub grub is some of the tastiest food there is. Anyone who turns their nose up at fish-and-chips and meat pies doesn't have a clue what good food is."

Callum winks at me before pulling a tray of single-serving-sized chunks of mahi-mahi from the walk-in. "Will any of your recipes from tonight be showing up at the festival?"

I ladle the scallions into the melted butter, then wag my spoon at him. "Nice try. I'm not revealing anything."

Callum shrugs while staring at the pot of butter, a gleam in his eye. "Just curious."

"I'm not going to ask you if the tempura-crusted mahi-mahi you're making for tonight's entrée is something you're planning for the festival. That stuff is sacred and I don't play dirty."

He sets the tray of fish on the prep table, places a hand on my hip, and pivots me to face him. His other hand rests under my chin. The sound of metal clashing on metal hits my ears. All of a sudden my hands are empty. I must have dropped the spoon on the stove when Callum pulled this deliciously suave move on me just now. But I don't care. It's an excuse to have his hands on me. I'll take it.

"Oh, you play dirty, Nikki." His eyes bore into me. "Just not in the kitchen."

The kitchen door swings open, causing both of us to take identical steps away from each other. Callum turns to the prep table while I stare at the scallion butter like it's the most intriguing substance in the universe.

A server darts to the wine rack in the corner for a fresh bottle, then the door swings open once more.

"Everyone's loving the canapés," Ted announces, beaming. "Well done, Nikki!"

He skips over to Callum and slaps him on the back. "I hope your part of the main is as good as her starter, mate."

I sneak a peek at Callum, who's biting back a grin. He turns back to the stove top and begins to sear the fish. "I hope so too."

Ted leans against the prep table, still grinning. "Those deconstructed *lumpia* were like magic. At first everyone was annoyed that the original chef couldn't come, but once those came out, the muttering died down. I heard nothing but chewing and humming. Music to my ears."

Another server walks in and deposits an empty tray in the sink just as the server carrying wine walks out. No chance of finding out just how down and dirty Callum wants me to go with the kitchen now functioning like Grand Central Station. Instead I put my head down and focus on preparing the best possible main with Callum: tempura-crusted mahi-mahi on a bed of pineapple fried rice.

For a solid hour, we cook and plate, the bodies passing in and out of the kitchen our white noise.

Callum wipes a rogue droplet of his ginger soy reduction from the rim of the plate with a tea towel. He stares with laser focus, even as people move around him. I wonder if all those years working in finance gave him the nerves of steel he seems to possess. I can't remember seeing anyone this unflappable in the kitchen.

We hand off plates to waiting servers one by one, and it's like a perfectly choreographed dance. Plate after plate changes hands over and over, until Callum and I are left alone in the kitchen, standing side by side, our hands on our hips, staring at the door.

"We did it." He speaks through a rough sigh.

"It was stressful, but . . . exhilarating."

"So." He unbuttons the top button of his chef jacket. I suppress a moan. I'm back to burning up.

"Decided that your bestselling food truck fried rice was too good for my lowly seared fish?" His playful tone makes me chuckle.

I lightly smack his shoulder. "Most of the people in that room have eaten every item on our menu week after week. The last thing I wanted was for one of them to figure out we cooked this meal together."

As soon as I say it, I wish I could take it back. It sounds so harsh.

His mouth is a straight line. He offers a single nod. "Right."

I touch his wrist. "I didn't mean it like that. What I meant was I don't want to be the focus of their gossip. I really enjoyed cooking with you, Callum."

He pulls away from me like I'm made of fire. "You're right. It's best that no one finds out about us. Like you said."

On the inside, I'm cringing so hard. *Really enjoyed cooking with you.* I sound like a home economics teacher.

The longer I look at Callum, the more obvious his hurt is. He refuses my eyes, occupying himself with washing dishes at the sink.

"Callum, I didn't mean—"

"It's fine." His tone is a soft bark, but I get the message loud and clear.

His hunched shoulders, the way his back is turned to me, the way he refuses to look at me say it all. I've hurt him, and he doesn't care to even look at me right now.

The longer I stand there engaging in this staring contest with his back, the more unbearable my faux pas becomes. I scurry through the door and out of the kitchen, unconcerned that I'm breaking my own "do not leave the kitchen" rule.

I stumble a few steps before noticing the dull roar of comments coming from the dining area.

"Crazy delicious," someone sings.

"The flavors are on point."

Curiosity takes hold of me, and I dart behind a nearby plant so I can eavesdrop more without blowing my cover. From behind the overgrown ficus, I strain my neck for a look at the diners. The soft murmur of conversation fills the room. Every single person at the tables is chewing or raving about how good the food tastes. Inside I'm bursting. Every foodie big shot in Maui is head over heels for my and Callum's food.

I scan across the room and zero in on the familiar blond man bun I've been looking for. Matteo shakes his head back and forth, eyes closed, lips puckered while chewing. An older man in a sport coat sitting next to him starts to speak, but Matteo cuts him off by holding up his hand.

Everyone else at the table stares at Matteo, brows raised, eyes unblinking, waiting for him to say anything. I do an internal eye roll. The way his foodie groupies hang on his every word in person and on his blog is a bit over-the-top.

After several seconds of making "mmm" sounds and exaggerated faces, Matteo swallows and smiles. He opens his eyes, patting the arm of his sport coat–clad companion.

"My sincerest apologies, Jonas, but sometimes when you're enjoying an otherworldly bite of food, all of your senses must be focused on it to fully appreciate the flavor overtaking your body."

His companion nods, as does everyone else at the table.

Matteo holds up a forkful of fish. "Just take this exquisite bite of fish. The way it plays on your tongue—the salt, the richness, the luscious texture."

A wave of "oohs" and "aahs" travels across the table.

"And the crunch on the outside." He practically sings the words. "Goodness me."

Matteo chomps on his forkful. The rest of his dining companions do the same, then rave about the perfect flavor.

Matteo takes his butter knife in his left hand and brushes a mound of pineapple fried rice on his fork. He holds it up in front of him, catching the light of the nearby overhead chandelier. It's like he's an appraiser scrutinizing a gemstone in the light.

"And this rice. My oh my, this rice. The perfect complement to the delicately fried fish with its sweet chunks of succulent pineapple and salty bacon." He slaps his free hand on his knee and lets out a throaty chuckle that booms against the dining room walls. "Who would have thought to add bacon as a twist in fried rice? Not me, ladies and gentlemen. Not me."

After his monologue, he rewards himself with the bite of fried rice. Everyone else at his table follows suit, taking bites, then raving.

Despite Matteo's rambling, I'm beaming. He may be ridiculous, but he loves Callum's and my food. And that matters. It means the most discriminating palate on the island thinks my last-minute attempt at an upscale dish is damn good. That means he'll rave about it on his vlog and his website. And even though he has no idea it was me who helped prepare the meal, it's still validation. It's proof that even after flipping my life upside down, I can still go back to my roots—my passion—and cook a solid high-end meal.

I wait a beat and walk quietly backward until I'm out of the line of sight from the dining room. I spin around to head back to the kitchen, then bump chest-first into someone.

"Shoot, I'm sorry—"

The woman I collided with flips her blond hair out of her face, straightening out her dress. "It's okay, I . . . Holy crap, Nikki?"

Penelope, the Instagrammer I took a selfie with at the farmer's market all those weeks ago, beams at me.

# Chapter 15

"Oh, um, hi." I tug at the hem of my chef's jacket.

Why the hell didn't I just stay in the kitchen? Ted was raving about how good everyone thought our cooking was. That should have been enough. Did I really need to blow my cover just to satisfy my need to see it for myself?

"What are you doing here?" Her berry-hued lips stretch into a smile so wide, just looking at it makes my cheeks ache. Understanding crosses her face. "Oh, wait, did you cook the meal tonight? Oh my gosh!"

"Well, I um, technically, yeah."

She grabs my hands in hers, squealing softly. "Oh my gosh, Nikki! Amazing meal! Seriously amazing! So different from your food truck meals, but just as good. You know what I mean?"

I nod and let out a choke of a laugh. I fail to match her enthusiasm once again, but I need to play it cool. If I seem weirdly tense, she might think something's up.

"I know exactly what you mean. And thank you," I say in a hurried tone.

"So who's the other chef? Your mom? You are seriously a dynamite team. Your food is the absolute best!"

The silver bracelets on her wrists jingle with each excited shake of her arms.

"Well, um, that's the thing. It's supposed to be a secret." I hope my smile doesn't come off as too pained. "I filled in as a favor at the last minute, and we don't want any special recognition in the run-up to the Maui Food Festival. You know what I mean."

She nods, her face turning serious. "Oh, of course. You can count on me. I won't peep a word, promise!"

She pulls me into a hug, and I nearly tumble to the floor. My God, tiny Penelope is stronger than she looks.

When she leans out of the hug, she still holds me by the upper arms. "How crazy that we—"

The kitchen door swings open and out steps Callum.

When Penelope gazes at Callum, I know the jig is up. In the few seconds he stands in front of us, she stares at him, standing there in his white chef jacket that's identical to mine. Then she looks back at me, her widening eyes and mouth making it obvious that she's putting two and two together.

"Wait . . . you two are working together?"

The wonderstruck expression on Penelope's face is reminiscent of when a little kid is told that Santa isn't real.

"But I thought . . . You don't even like each other . . ."

Callum's brow raises. "This is all your fault, Penelope."

I mouth, "What are you doing?" at him.

Penelope seems to be going through the same thought process, because she's staring at Callum with her eyebrows all the way at her hairline.

He crosses his arms over his chest.

"Wh-what?" she stammers.

"Remember that selfie you posted of you two with a caption calling out Hungry Chaps?" Callum says. "Well, this is the outcome. Nikki and I had it out over that, but now we've come to an understanding."

Penelope furrows her brow. "And now you're cooking together?"

"Something like that." Callum lifts his eyebrow for just a half second, but the message it sends is indisputable.

His cheeky little nod is more than enough to clue her in. She's beaming again and turns to me. "Oh my gosh, it's like those enemies-to-lovers romances! Those are my absolute favorite!"

I tug her arm, finally understanding what Callum is doing. Sometimes the best way to hide is out in the open. Penelope is already a fangirl. If I can convince her to keep this a secret as a friend and fan, she'll feel special. And our secret will be safe.

I turn Penelope to face me. "We have you to thank, Penelope. You brought us together. Sometimes we even call you Cupid."

The lie doesn't flow as smoothly as I hope, but she's too excited to notice, thankfully.

"You do?" she squeals.

I nod. "But we have to keep this quiet, okay? The Maui Food Festival's coming up, and we don't want this to ruin our chances. People will think we're just a cute love story and make unfair assumptions about us working together. But we are still two separate food truck businesses. We don't mix that part of our lives at all."

I bite my tongue as soon as I say it. *Love.* Way wrong word to use, but maybe it will sell us better to Penelope.

"You don't mix—except for tonight." She winks. "Say no more. It's our little secret. I won't breathe a word until you two are ready to make things public."

I wink at her. "You'll be the first we tell, promise. We just want to get through the festival before, though, okay?"

"Okay!"

She pulls me in for one last squeeze of a hug, then softly punches Callum in the shoulder before yanking him into one of her death-grip hugs. Even though he's twice her size, he winces at her strength.

"You nabbed a good one, buddy," she says.

Callum can't seem to contain the grin tugging at his mouth. "Don't I know it."

Penelope makes a zipper gesture with her lips, waves good-bye to us, then scurries back down the hall to the dining room.

I pat Callum on the chest. "Bold move deciding to let her in on us."

"It's obvious how highly she thinks of you," he says. "She doesn't want to let you down."

"Way to think on your feet. I was sure we were busted as soon as she saw us together."

He raises his eyebrow at me. "So according to Penelope, I'm the lucky one in this arrangement."

"She speaks the truth."

He chuckles and turns toward the kitchen.

"Wait." I catch his wrist. "About earlier. I didn't mean to sound so harsh. Cooking here with you was a dream. I'm so sorry if I made it sound like anything else."

His mouth curves up in a soft smile. "Thank you. I feel the same way about working with you."

We say nothing, the tension between us from earlier melting like an ice cube on a hot sidewalk. With his hand on my waist, he pulls me against him and leans down so we're nearly mouth-to-mouth.

"Come on," he rasps. "We've got dessert to plate."

. . .

Ted walks into the kitchen, arms outstretched. He pulls me and Callum in for a double hug.

"You two blew everyone away tonight!"

I slip out of Ted's grip and step away, leaving him to strangle-hug Callum. Ted boasts a tall and thin frame, but he has the hug-strength of a grizzly bear.

Callum pats his back and Ted lets go.

"So it went well, then?" Callum says, straightening his shirt.

A wide grin rips across Ted's face. "More than well, mate. Bloody brilliant. Everything from the starters to the mains to the dessert was a hit." He turns to me. "Nikki, remind me to get that *turon* recipe from you. You gave multiple mouth-orgasms tonight with that one."

I cup my cheeks in my palms to keep the blushing at bay.

"Is it really just bananas, brown sugar, and *lumpia* wrapper?" Ted asks.

"Yes, but it's fried, and that's what makes it."

Ted raves about the tempura crust on the fish, then whips out a room key card from his inside jacket pocket. "And this is my way of saying thank you. The most luxurious bungalow on the resort property, free of charge for you two tonight." He pats the key into Callum's hand, then winks at us. "Have fun."

Ted whips out his phone before hollering "Happy Easter" at us and waltzing out the door.

My eyes cut to Callum, who immediately puts his hand up in surrender. "I didn't say a word to him about us, I swear."

I press my lips together to muffle the squeal aching to let loose. I've never, ever stayed in a resort this luxurious before, and tonight I get to enjoy it on the house, with Callum.

"I don't even care. We get to stay at a luxury resort tonight. For free. I'm pumped."

Callum leans his mouth to my ear. His lips barely graze my skin, but I still shiver. It's a whisper of a kiss but just as hot as everything else he's ever done to my body. This is a whole new level of arousal.

"How about we go play dirty, Nikki?"

My eyes flutter and a moan rips from my throat. "Yes, please."

We do the world's fastest cleanup of the kitchen, thank the staff and servers for their hard work, throw our chef jackets in the dirty laundry bin, then slip out to be as discreet as possible.

The roar of conversation and elevator music wafting from the dining room drifts all the way down to our end of the hallway.

Callum touches my arm mid-step. "Bollocks, I forgot my phone."

I grip his wrist, pulling him down to me. "Hurry back. We've got some dirty business to take care of, remember?"

I leave him with a chaste peck on the lips, but my stare combined with my firm grip on his body give away just how eager I am to get filthy.

A mischievous gleam shines behind those hazel eyes. He practically sprints back into the kitchen. I lean against the wall to check my phone and see a text from Mom.

Hi, anak! How was your friend's dinner?

I text back while fighting the guilt warming through my chest. What I told her earlier today was half-true—I *was* helping a friend with Easter dinner service at Travaasa Hana. I just hid the fact that the friend was Callum.

ME: It went well, everyone loved the food. How was Easter with Mrs. Tokushige's family?

MOM: Good! Very fun and too much food. Her family's so nice. They all wish they could have met you though.

ME: I'll meet them next time, promise.

I take a deep breath, thankful that I don't have to look her in the face when I tell her the next part.

ME: The manager here comped me a room tonight as a thank-you for serving dinner last-minute, so I'm going to stay here and drive home in the morning, okay?

MOM: Sounds fine. Have fun, love you

I text "love you" just as Callum walks back out. He takes me by the hand. Warmth coats every inch of my skin. It's like I'm standing outside, eyes closed, face turned up to the sky, soaking up endless rays of sunlight.

Hand in hand, he leads us through the back entrance to the ocean-facing bungalows. A gust of salty sea air washes over me. Closing my eyes, I breathe it all in. This time, I enjoy the slight burn of the salt in my nostrils, how it glides down my throat and to my lungs. The guilt disappears, and I'm smiling once again.

"What the . . . Whoa."

My eyes scan the room, like I'm the Terminator trying to slowly process all the images around me. This bungalow is the single most luxurious space I've ever set foot in. Honey-hued bamboo floors and furniture set give off an elegant yet tropical feel. I walk over to the sliding glass door, which takes up nearly the entire opposite wall of the room. When I pull it open, the crash of waves echoes softly through the room. The deep blue ocean rests against the indigo-hued evening sky, making this a tranquil nighttime scene. But it's the plush king-size bed calling my name. I fall into the center of the impossibly soft sheets, burying my face in the softness and moaning.

The soft buzz of Callum's phone hits my ears. "Speaking of 'whoa.'" I twist around to gaze up at him. He holds his phone up. "Ted just offered us a job."

I sit up in the bed. "He what?"

Callum stares at his phone screen, his eyes sparkling as he grins. "He asked if we'd be interested in cooking dinner one night a week at the resort together."

Callum glances up, his wide smile the most joyful I've ever seen it.

"Um, hell yes!"

I jump up and down on the bed while Callum looks on, chuckling. "Before you break what is most certainly a several-thousand-dollar bed, do you want to see the hot tub?"

I jump off the bed and onto the floor. "There's a hot tub?"

Callum points to the balcony, and I dart through the open sliding glass door.

"Holy hell, there's a hot tub!" I gaze up at him, smiling through my dropped-jaw shock. "This is . . . Oh my God! Okay, screw the bed, I'm taking a dip in there right now."

Shedding all my clothes, I step into the tub, which is thankfully secluded from all of the surrounding rooms by the line of palm trees crowding this end of the balcony. I hold Callum's gaze as I grip the sides and slowly lower myself in. I hum at the shock of hot water hitting my bare skin, how it instantly soothes my sore muscles.

For a tiny second my mind slips, and I wonder if Callum has ever shared a hotel room like this with anyone else before, but I push it away. That's not relevant to us or to this moment. I need to enjoy this for what it is: a sexy night with a sexy friend.

Callum turns back to his phone. "I've relayed our acceptance to Ted."

He glances up, his eyes snagging on my bare chest. A second later, his stare glazes over. I give myself an imaginary pat on the back for how well I've captured his attention.

When I'm all the way in, I tilt my head at him, giving my best taunting stare. "You're not just going to stand there and gawk, are you?"

Seconds later, his jeans, T-shirt, and boxer briefs are in a heap on the deck and he's slowly lowering himself into the hot tub. I relish the slow movement the water forces him to take, because it allows me to gaze at his naked body longer. He lets out a groan as he settles across from me.

Bracing my hands along the edge, I lean my head back and sigh. "Your friend Ted is my new favorite human being."

A splash hits my ears, then his hands land on my body. I glance up just as Callum settles me onto his lap. I bite my lip, positively giddy at the opportunity to straddle him naked. I moan at the feel of our hot bodies against each other, our slick skin making the movement impossibly smooth. Wrapping my arms around his neck, I press my forehead against his.

I close my eyes. "If someone told me the day we met that we'd eventually share a hot tub together, I would have laughed in their face." Opening my eyes, I lean back to get a proper look at Callum. "I thought you hated me."

He flinches. "Nikki, you know I—"

I rub the back of his neck with my hand. He closes his eyes and moans.

"It's okay. We're good now."

He presses his mouth where my neck and shoulder meet. The light kisses and suckles he blesses upon that spot turn me into a whimpering fool. Seconds pass before I lean away to look at him. He stares back with that intensity that seems to come and go so easily. But this time there's purpose in his eyes. It's obvious in the slight furrow of his brow, in the clench of his jaw.

"Are we good, Nikki?"

"Absolutely."

His hands fall to my waist. I shiver despite the temperature. His feathery-soft touches always do that to me. With both of us wet, my sense of touch is heightened. Every tap of his finger, every swipe of his hand on my body feels a million times more sensitive than usual.

He shakes his head. "This isn't my idea of good."

"Then tell me your idea of good." I swallow his breath when I speak, we're that close. "Please."

He leans his face to my face, and we're somehow even closer than we were a second ago. I'm certain he's going to kiss me. But instead of sliding his perfect tongue into my mouth, he speaks.

"Good would be doing this with you every day. Good would be getting you to admit when you're jealous and want only me. Good would be calling you mine."

Digging my fingers into his shoulders, I'm practically shaking. Just when I thought we were firmly back in friends-with-benefits territory, he throws me for a loop with a statement like that.

If we're both on the same page—if we're both game for more—could we really make it work? Could he really give up whoever else he's seeing casually for me? What about the festival? What about his plan to move back to Chicago?

Softly, he bumps the tip of his nose against the tip of mine, then presses a kiss to the corner of my mouth. Every thought, every question, everything that's not this kiss fades away.

I pull away. "Are you saying . . . What are you saying, Callum?"

He lunges for my mouth, and we're kissing so hard, I'm robbed of all oxygen. I lose track of time, location, what day it is, my senses.

Pressing a hand against his chest, I steady myself. "Say it again," I say between broken breaths.

*Say I'm yours. Say you want to be mine. Say nothing else matters.*

He leans his head back, his chest heaving as if he's run a marathon. "Nikki, I . . ."

*Say you want me all day, every day. Only me.*

In the background my phone rings, but I don't care. His clouded stare and the slow smile that crawls across his face read pleasure-high. With both hands on my cheeks, he pulls me in for yet another breathless kiss. Then he slides one hand between my legs, and I'm crying out in an instant. But then he stops.

"Is that your phone that keeps ringing?" he pants.

I say a quick apology, then swipe my jeans from the nearby pile of clothes. I dig the phone out of the pocket. "I'll turn it to silent. Sorry."

But then I see a slew of missed calls and texts from Mrs. Tokushige.

"Hang on," I mutter, swiping my finger across the screen. "This is so weird. It's my mom's friend."

I pull up the text messages and almost drop my phone in the hot tub when I read Mrs. Tokushige's text.

Your mom was rushed to the hospital. Please call me as soon as you can.

A shriek lodges in my throat. Callum clasps my hand. When I look at him, the inky, enlarged pupils of his eyes read sheer panic. "What's wrong? What is it?"

But I can't talk. I can only cry and scramble clumsily out of the tub, grabbing at my clothes. I drop the phone in his hand and watch all the color drain from him when he reads the text. And then I feel his steady touch on my arm. He speaks. But all I can do is cry and hope to God he's telling the truth, that it's not just empty words to make me feel better, like I suspect.

"It's going to be okay."

# Chapter 16

Callum leads me through a long white corridor with his massive hand pressed on my back. I've lost count already of how many of these sterile tunnels we've walked through since arriving at Maui Memorial Medical Center minutes ago. The same ball of despair and nerves that hit when I would visit my dad as a patient here takes hold. We pass the corner where he lost consciousness while being wheeled to a nearby exam room for an MRI. That was a month before he passed, when he was so weak that walking was almost too much for him most days.

My heart thuds, my head spins, my palms sweat. Just the thought of Mom being here makes me want to puke. This cannot be happening.

We make it to a random waiting room with green chairs, and I spot Mrs. Tokushige sitting in the corner. She stands as soon as she sees me.

"Oh, my dear," she croons while pulling me into a hug.

I fought the lump in my throat the entire drive here, and I don't have the strength anymore. When I speak, my voice finally breaks. "What happened?"

She wipes a tear from my face with the folded-up tissue in her hand. "I'm not sure, dear. We were all cleaning up in the kitchen, and all of a sudden your mom fainted. We couldn't wake her up, so we called 911. She thankfully came to before the paramedics arrived, but then she had trouble breathing."

"Is she all right? Can I see her?" My head spins with a million more questions, but I swallow the rest of them back.

Mrs. Tokushige nods, her topknot shaking with the movement of her head. "She's in room 547 at the end of the hall."

Her gaze floats to Callum, who stands behind my shoulder, but she says nothing.

Callum turns to me. "You go ahead," he says. "I'll wait here for you."

He moves to stand next to Mrs. Tokushige, who nods at me. "The doctor should be in there with her still," she says.

When I walk in the room, I have to cling onto the doorframe to keep from collapsing. She rests on the bed, eyes closed, her chest rising and falling with each labored breath. Under the harsh fluorescent lights her tawny skin appears sallow. I swallow back a sob and walk over to her bed. Other than a few minor ailments detected at her annual doctor checkups, she's never once had a health scare. The last time she checked into a hospital was nearly thirty years ago when she gave birth to me. By all accounts she's an active and healthy sixty-something woman.

Through blurry eyes, I try to focus, but tears rush my waterlines. What she was before today doesn't matter. Because right now she's barely conscious, lying in a hospital bed, looking like the most helpless creature I've ever seen. And I need to accept it.

A young woman in green scrubs and a white coat stands next to her, reading over a chart before looking at her IV. She glances up. "You must be Mrs. DiMarco's daughter."

I wipe my face with my hand, nod, then walk over to her bedside. I scoop her hand in mine.

"I'm Dr. Alma, the physician on call."

I shake her hand with my free hand and introduce myself.

"Your mom is a little woozy from her fall, so she's resting right now. Do you want to step outside and we can talk while she gets some rest?"

I follow behind the doctor, who is barely five feet tall and looks younger than me. She closes the door behind her. I glance down the hall and spot Callum standing next to Mrs. Tokushige, who's sitting down in one of the chairs. Despite the free fall my nerves are doing, one look at Callum is a moment of calm. That unrelenting pressure in my chest that's persisted ever since reading Mrs. Tokushige's text eases a smidgen.

"You all right?" he mouths.

I nod and turn back to the doctor.

"It looks like your mom has an ulcer in her stomach and is severely iron deficient. Has she mentioned anything about feeling tired lately? Any mention of bloody stools or vomiting blood?"

I shake my head. "What? No. I mean, I don't think so. She hasn't said anything about that. And she hasn't been acting differently either. She's been keeping herself busy and active like normal."

Dr. Alma offers a head nod that reads sympathetic. "She doesn't seem like the type who cares to slow down."

"Definitely not."

"Unfortunately, she's lost a lot of blood due to her ulcer, so we're going to give her a blood transfusion to replenish what she's lost."

The thoughts spinning through my brain halt like a needle on a record. "Blood transfusion? But . . ."

Dr. Alma purses her lips. "I know that sounds serious, but it's pretty routine in a situation like this. Her ulcer is causing considerable blood loss. But once the transfusion is complete, she'll feel a lot better. It's also likely that she's anemic, so we'll put her on an iron supplement as well. But don't worry, it won't interfere with her diabetes medication at all."

The needle flies off the record completely, shattering against the inside of my skull. "Diabetes . . . What? My mom doesn't have diabetes."

Dr. Alma frowns. "Ms. DiMarco, your mother is a type 2 diabetic. Didn't you know that?"

I shake my head and hold the nearby wall to steady myself.

She blinks before reining in her expression. "I think you two have a lot to catch up on."

She says she'll be back to check on her later in the evening. I walk back into the room, confusion hanging over me like a damp fog as I focus my eyes back on Mom.

The door squeaks shut behind me, jolting her awake. She squints at me, then pushes herself up onto the pillows. "*Anak*. Hi."

I stand at the head of her bed, balling my hands into loose fists. Sadness has flipped to frustration. How could my own mother keep her health problems a secret from me?

Her brow furrows when she focuses on my face. "What's wrong?"

I shove a fist through my hair and tug. The split second of pain does nothing to dispel the frustration mowing over my insides. I wring both hands at my sides before folding them across my chest. I can't get angry, though, not when my mom is lying in a hospital bed.

"Were you ever planning to tell me about your diabetes diagnosis?" It's a struggle to keep my tone calm, but I manage.

"Eventually." She shrugs, like it's no big deal she's been hiding a major medical issue from her own daughter.

I swallow, willing myself to remain measured and steady. "Don't you think it's important that I know?"

Glancing down, she smooths the bedsheet with her hand. "My health is none of your business."

The scoff I let out is almost as loud as my voice. "Seriously? You are so out of line with this." My hard tone ricochets against the hospital room walls. I deserve to know why the hell I was kept in the dark. "How long have you had diabetes? Why have I never seen you take your meds or check your blood sugar? And why the hell did you never tell me?"

I take a breath, but it does nothing to calm me. "And like hell it's none of my business. I'm your daughter. It's my job to take care of you. How am I supposed to do that if you keep your health a secret from me?"

She pushes the blanket off her chest and crosses her arms. The movement reminds me of a child who doesn't want to go to bed yet. It's fitting though. This moment is a role reversal for the record books. Here I am standing over my mom, scolding her for doing something unbelievably careless that could have cost her her life. She's handling it about as well as I did as a kid when she or Dad lectured me.

"Okay, maybe I should have told you, but I didn't want to worry you. I saw how upset you were after we lost your dad. I saw how you turned your life upside down for him, for me. I didn't want to put you through that again."

I toss my hands in front of me. "Mom. You can't hide your health problems from me because of Dad. He would have freaked if he found out you were hiding this."

She sighs, an ounce of defiance melting from her face. "You're right about that. But I just didn't want to worry you. You already do so much for me."

I pause for another deep breath. "From now on, you need to be truthful about everything."

"Fine." She scratches her elbow. "I was diagnosed just after your dad died. I didn't want to add to the bad news, so I kept it to myself. I take my meds in my bedroom so you don't see. I check my blood sugar in the bathroom and my bedroom so it's not in front of you. And I'm very careful with my diet. You see that I don't eat junk food very often?"

I nod my head, biting my tongue to avoid another outburst. But I'm struggling to grasp the fact that for more than a year and a half, she kept this a secret from me.

"My doctor even said that if I continue doing well with my diet and exercise for a few more months, I might be able to go off my meds."

"Fine, Mom, yes. You're a healthy eater and that's great your doctor thinks that. But God, what if you had collapsed in front of me and the medical staff asked me if you were taking any medications? Or what if they asked me what illnesses you had? I wouldn't have been able to give them the right answer to any of that. That's so unbelievably dangerous. Don't you get that?"

"I admit, it wasn't the best idea, but you try to control every part of our lives ever since your dad died. It gets tiring after a while."

I scoff, my jaw on the floor. "I'm not trying to control anything. I put limits on certain things you do because if I don't you'll drive yourself into the ground. And look: I was right. You keep me in the dark about your diabetes, you hide your health problems from me, and see what happens? You end up in the hospital."

"Nicole Elise DiMarco, I may have made a mistake, but I'm still your mother. You don't take that tone with me, young lady." She wags her finger up at me. "You don't know better than me about everything."

"Maybe I do. Maybe just because I'm your daughter doesn't automatically mean you always know best. Maybe you should listen to me. Maybe you should be open and honest with me about your health. Is that too much to ask?"

"Open and honest, Nikki? Really?" Turning her head toward the window, she says nothing for nearly a minute. I don't either. The silence is louder than when I was nearly shouting a minute ago.

She finally turns back, her dark eyes on mine, her voice steady. "I know you mean well. But it's just too much sometimes. It made me not want to tell you certain things. I was afraid I would stress you out even more if I told you about my health problems. I know it was wrong of me to hide it from you, but I didn't want you to worry about me even more. You moved here for me. You gave up your job, your friends, your life in Oregon, your dreams to help me. I feel like such a burden on you sometimes." Her eyes glisten under the overhead lights. "I've brought so much worry to your life. I didn't want to add more."

Bracing my hands on the railings of the bed, I lean down to her. For the past year and a half I thought I did such a good job making it seem like I was happy here, all the while hiding the constant strain of trying to make a life and a living.

I open my mouth and contemplate saying that she's mistaken, that every day is a joy, that I don't worry nearly as much as she thinks I do, that she's wrong to think otherwise. But when I focus on her stare, I can't lie. Not anymore. She knew all along that I never wanted to be here in the first place.

I opt for a sanitized version of the truth. "Mom. I'm here now. I don't want to be anywhere else, because you are my priority."

I let out a slow exhale, relieved that my voice sounds as calm as I hoped it would. I pat her hand. "I'm going to get a coffee. I'll be right back."

When she looks up at me, I spot a hint of understanding in her eyes. Maybe it was never my dream to run a food truck at nearly thirty with my mom. But this is my life. I chose it. I'm working hard to succeed in this new path. I'm making my own way now. I'm happy with the independence I've forged and the fact that I can spend more time with her. And I hope that when I tell her that, she'll believe me.

I slip out of the room and head for the cafeteria. Hurried footsteps trail behind me. I turn and see Callum.

"Mrs. Tokushige had to leave to go be with her family, but she wanted me to tell you that she'll visit tomorrow to check up on your mum." He grabs my hand in his. "Is she okay?"

I fill him in on her ulcers and her anemia diagnosis, as well as the fact that she's been lying to me about being diabetic.

"Fucking hell," he mutters.

"That's a more succinct and colorful reaction than mine, but that's how I felt on the inside."

We walk to the cafeteria, and Callum buys me the biggest coffee they have.

"Thanks," I say when he hands it to me. I stop a few doors down from Mom's hospital room. "I just can't believe she would lie to me about this. And for her to say she did it because I try to control her life, that's just insane."

Callum pulls his lips into his mouth. His eyes dart everywhere but me.

"What?"

He shakes his head. "I think she may have a point, Nikki."

I stop mid-sip. "Excuse me?"

"Please don't take this the wrong way, but all I'm saying is that I can sympathize a bit with what your mum is saying."

I take a long sip of the muddy water that somehow passes off as hospital coffee.

He clears his throat. "I'm not saying what she did was right. It wasn't. It was dangerous, and she absolutely shouldn't have hidden it from you. But you can be pretty fierce and intimidating sometimes. I can understand why she was scared to tell you."

Something in my chest tightens and drops to my feet. A familiar guardedness creeps back inside me. It's that same feeling that used to consume me when we spent our first few weeks of acquaintance arguing and sabotaging each other.

"What are you talking about?"

His eyebrows pinch together. "Nikki, please don't get defensive."

I shake my head and start to walk forward, but he lays a gentle hand on my forearm, stopping me.

"Do you think I wasn't paying attention all this time that we've been parked side by side? You made your mum take days off work. You were so diligent about her taking breaks every single day." He runs his other hand through his hair. "Even when I would come over to your house those nights when we . . ."

An elderly woman in a walker passes by us in the hallway. We fall silent and flash her dual polite smiles.

Callum waits until she's out of earshot before he starts speaking again. "Even on those nights your mum was gone from your place, you made sure she was doing some activity that you thought was good for her."

"And what's wrong with that?" I yank my arm from his grip. "I care about my mom, Callum. I want her to be safe and healthy. That makes me a bad person somehow?"

"No, that's not—of course you're not a bad person, Nikki. You're one of the best people I know."

Warmth surges up my chest, a direct counter to the anger mowing over my insides.

"All I'm saying is that you should try to understand what your mum was thinking when she made the decision to hide that from you. Maybe if you ease up a bit, she'll be more open with you."

" 'Ease up'? Callum, I really don't need to be lectured by you."

My hard tone echoes softly against the hallway walls. Just like that, any semblance of warmth inside me evaporates into thin air.

"I admit, I'm protective of my mom, but she's literally all I have. Remember?"

My voice breaks on the last syllable of "remember."

Callum's eyes are alight with worry. "Nikki, I didn't mean it like that." He lifts his arm and moves like he's going to reach for me, but then jerks it back to his side. "You have me too. You know that, don't you?"

I bite down so hard, my jaw aches. "Do I, Callum? Because anyone who's with me needs to support me, not criticize my relationship with my only living parent." I take another gulp of coffee. It burns down my throat, sour as vinegar.

"Of course you do." His low tone turns bitter.

"Well, right now it feels like all I have is someone who wants to fuck me, then judge me."

I don't mean the words I say or the angry tone I take. But my emotions are a dumpster fire after seeing Mom in the one place I never, ever wanted her to end up.

Something that looks a lot like shock jolts through Callum's expression.

"Is that what you honestly think of me, Nikki? I'm just some piece of meat you shag? Nothing more?"

The truth? Not even close. My burst of jealousy yesterday, the ache I felt waking up next to him this morning, the hope that consumed me in the hot tub while I waited for him to say just how much he wanted me and only me . . . it's all proof that Callum means so much more.

I bite the inside of my cheek, take a silent breath, then count to three.

"I can't do this. My mom needs me." I spin to the trash can and toss in my empty cup, just so I don't have to look at him.

I turn in the direction of her room, but Callum's hands find me once more, this time on both of my upper arms. He turns me to face him, eyes desperate. The frustration is bubbling within him. There's invisible steam practically pumping out of his ears.

"How can you say that? After what we said to each other tonight? After last night? After—"

I shrug out of Callum's hold. "Don't."

My attempt at a whisper comes off more like a bark. A trio of nurses down the hall shoot us confused stares. Callum drops his hands from my arms.

I gaze up at him, willing my voice to sound steady and calm. "Please. I have to go."

He replies with silence, a stony look on his face. But then he blinks and I see it. Sadness and disappointment, all caused by me.

He spins away and walks down the hallway, not once looking back at me.

# Chapter 17

"How was work, *anak*?"

I drop the food truck keys on the dining room table and kick off my sneakers. Every day I've arrived home, and every day I've been greeted with the same question from Mom.

"It was good. Busy. Mrs. Tokushige's nephew Kyle has been a big help though."

It's only been a handful of days since she's been released from the hospital, and already she's got cabin fever. It was a struggle to convince her to stay home and rest, but thankfully, her doctor said a few days' break from work was mandatory. She listened but has spent every day off busying herself with food prep. Each morning I wake up to chopped veggies, marinated wings, and *lumpia*, ready to load from the commercial kitchen into the truck. It's like she's working remotely in a weird way.

Instead of reminding her to ease up, I thank her each morning. If keeping busy is what makes her happy, then I need to let her do that.

I walk to the kitchen for water and fight off my instinct to pepper her with questions, like if she ate enough during the day and what her blood sugar readings were. Mom and Callum were right. If I want her to be open with me, I need to give her the space she deserves.

I manage a reasonable, "How are you feeling?"

She opens the freezer and peers inside. "Good. I just went down to the commercial kitchen and whipped up some extra orders of *lumpia* and wings in case you need them."

She pulls out her blood sugar testing kit. She plops onto the nearby barstool, then pats the seat of the one next to her. When I sit, she goes through her evening routine of pricking her finger, dabbing it on a paper strip, then inserting it into the meter to get a reading of her glucose level. Ever since we had it out in the hospital room about her keeping her diabetes a secret, she's made it a point to do her readings in the morning and evening in front of me.

The meter beeps and she turns it to me. "See? One hundred and seven. I had a snack a little while ago, so that's pretty good."

I pat her arm and smile at her. "That's good, Mom. But you don't always have to do it in front of me. I trust you."

She glances up at me. "I know you do, but I want to show you that I'm not hiding anything. I'm taking care of myself. I feel good, I feel healthy, but I promise I will tell you if I'm feeling bad again."

I slip my arm around her and pull her into a side hug. "Thank you. That means a lot."

Her openness brings a much-needed level of comfort to our relationship. It means she's working hard to repair the rift caused by her keeping her health status a secret. Each day I rein in my control freak tendencies when it comes to her health. There's no need for me to micromanage now that we're approaching each other with this new level of honesty.

But still, bits and pieces of our conversation from that night in the hospital float to the present, weighing on me like a cinder block.

*You moved here for me. You gave up your job, your friends, your life in Oregon, your dreams to help me. I feel like such a burden on you sometimes.*

She's being open with me about what she's going through. Now I need to be open with her.

I glance at her as she speedily puts away the kit. She starts to stand up from the stool, but my hand on her forearm stills her.

"Stay sitting for just one more sec, okay?"

"What's wrong?" she asks.

I sigh, then look her straight in the eyes. "Nothing. I just need you to know something. You didn't ruin my life. When Dad got sick, I moved here without thinking twice about it. I moved here because I wanted to be with him and you. I won't lie; it was hard leaving my job and friends behind. But it was worth it. I wanted to be where you and Dad were. And that's true even now. I don't want to be anywhere else. I want to stay here with you, okay? Never doubt that."

Her eyes glisten under the bright lighting of the overhead fixture.

I squeeze her hand. "I mean it, Mom. I may not have envisioned my life to turn out like this, but I wouldn't want it any other way, okay?"

She pulls me into a hug so tight, I can barely eke out a breath.

When she finally releases me, she wipes away the tears from her face, smiling.

"Stop feeling bad," I say. "I need you to be your chipper self when you come back to the food truck tomorrow and at the Maui Food Festival this weekend."

She beams, hopping up from the stool. "Oh, *anak*! I can't wait. I've missed seeing the customers and spending all day cooking by the beach, smelling that salt air, hearing the waves crash right next to us. And the festival! I've been putting some finishing touches on the new fruit salad recipe I came up with. Here, let me show you."

She mentions something about adding sprigs of mint just as my phone beeps with a text message. My heart jumps to my throat when I see it's Callum.

Hi. Are you all right? How's your mum? I haven't heard from you.

This is the first time either one of us has reached out ever since our argument at the hospital. But it's not like I haven't thought of him. Every single night I fall asleep to Callum's gorgeous face, his taste, the memory of his body pressed against mine. The pillow I shove between my legs is a sorry substitute, but it's all I can manage.

Because to text him or call him would mean we'd have to talk about our argument, and I can't handle the pain of that.

I stare at his text again. I'm lucky that we've been able to maintain our status quo of zero interaction while working side by side every day at the food truck. Whenever we make eye contact, Callum is always the first to look away. But it's never enough to erase the emotion radiating from him like a bonfire. Sharing the same swath of dirt every day, working in our separate food trucks, just a handful of feet separating us, won't hold up forever. We have to communicate at some point.

I look up at Mom, who's dicing a mango at lightning speed, completely oblivious to the warring emotions taking place inside me.

I take a breath and reply.

Hey . . . sorry I haven't messaged you, things have been busy. She's good, thanks for asking. She feels well enough to be at the food truck tomorrow.

She leans over the counter to hand me a spoonful of mango salad to try. Again my phone dings.

CALLUM: I'm relieved to hear that. But what about you?

I clear my throat, my face heating even though he can't see me. We're miles apart right now, and he can still tell I'm deflecting.

ME: I'm fine.

CALLUM: Liar.

I don't want to fight via text, so I set my phone down on the counter and help Mom with the fruit salad. Another few minutes pass before my phone buzzes with two new text alerts.

CALLUM: Sorry. I just miss you.

The next message is a photo of Lemon sitting on his couch, looking up at the camera.

CALLUM: Lemon misses you too. She wants to know if you'd like to come over and cuddle her, because she's sick of the big guys with the strange accents.

My heart melts on the spot.

ME: I would love that.

CALLUM: Then come over. Please. Promise I won't bring up anything upsetting . . . I just want to be close to you, hold you . . . anything to make you feel better.

With those words, I'm convinced. Callum somehow knows exactly what I need even when I refuse to say it.

ME: On my way

When Callum opens the door to his condo, all I can focus on is his face. It's marred with worried wrinkles.

"Hi," I say softly, unsure if I should apologize before stepping foot in his home. The last time we were face-to-face this close, we were arguing at the hospital. I owe him a sorry for how I lashed out, for sure.

"Come on in," he says.

I follow him inside to the kitchen counter, where two bottles of sparkling white wine sit. I'm about to ask what's the occasion, but he turns to me, gently grabbing my hand in his.

"I'm so sorry for what I said at the hospital. I was out of line. You were stressed out, and I should have just supported you instead of arguing with you."

My chest clenches. "It's okay. I'm sorry too. And also . . ."

His eyebrows knit as he gazes at me, his eyes full of kindness and worry.

"You were right," I finally blurt. "About me needing to ease up on my mom. I have been, and she's been more open with me. Things are so much better between us."

The warmest smile pulls at his beautiful peach lips. "That makes me so happy to hear, Nikki." A long moment passes, and his mouth turns down. "About the other things we said . . . at the hospital . . ."

The memory of me hurtfully reducing him to a fuck buddy and nothing more is front and center in my mind. I'm practically on fire with how embarrassed I am for calling him that. But I don't want to rehash that now, not when it's been nearly a week since that night at the hospital, and our biggest competition—against each other—is just days away. I want this time with him to be as untainted with the complications of reality as possible.

"Do you want to talk about it?" he asks.

"Not really."

He nods his understanding. "How are you feeling? Really feeling?"

Instead of answering, I let go of his hand and wrap my arms around his torso. I burrow my face into his chest as he slips his arms around me. The warmth is intoxicating, more powerful than any alcohol or drug. If only I could stay locked in Callum's embrace forever. Life would be so much easier.

"I just . . . I feel so much better when I'm with you," I whisper into his skin.

He presses his nose into my hair and takes a deep breath. "Same."

I lean back so I can look up at his face. "I know . . . I know we have so much to talk about . . ."

I stop short before I can speak and ruin everything. So much is hanging heavy in the air between us. Our relationship in its current state is an awkward limbo between bedfellows and something more. It's bound to change with the festival this weekend and when one of us has to move from our spot in Makena . . . and then whenever Callum moves back to Chicago. But I don't want to think about any of that. All I want to do is have this evening together and exist in this perfect bubble we've created. Reality can wait a little bit longer.

"I just . . . I can't . . ." My voice wobbles and my eyes water.

Callum presses his lips against mine, quieting me instantly. After a long beat, he pulls away. "It's okay. We don't have to talk about any of that. I told you I wanted to help you feel better."

He glances to the bottles on the counter. "How about a sparkling wine drinking contest and a few episodes of *The Office* to take your mind off things?"

My smile is one of joy and relief. He knows me so well. I blink away the tears and nod. "That sounds perfect."

We each grab a bottle, pop the corks off, then settle on the couch. Lemon crawls out from under the coffee table and hops on my lap.

"Hey, my girl." I pat her pregnant tummy as Callum powers on the TV. "How has she been this past week with you and Finn? She looks like she's ready to pop."

"She's made herself right at home. She's even started sleeping in Finn's bed with him."

"Good thing Finn doesn't hate cats."

"He's got a soft spot for them, just like me."

I down a sip of the wine. "How did you explain the arrangement with the cat? You know, since we're still keeping you and me under wraps."

Callum stares at the TV screen, jaw tight. "I told him I'm fostering cats from the vet's office periodically." He clears his throat. "He seems to buy it."

"I'm so glad," I say quietly.

Episodes queued up, we settle into our go-to position on the couch: Callum in the corner, me cuddled under his arm, Lemon tucked between us. We make it two episodes before both of our bottles are nearly empty. I sneak a glance at Callum, and my heart thuds.

*Perfection.*

It's the one word I've been searching for all day—these past few days actually. Every day I've been without Callum, it's felt like something is missing. But now that we're together, it's clear. He's my lost piece. When I'm with him, everything's right. Everything's perfect.

Picking up Lemon with my free hand, I deposit her on the other end of the couch. Then I swipe Callum's bottle from him and set both of the bottles on the coffee table.

"What are you . . ." He loses the rest of his words when I quietly straddle his lap.

A dizzy spell from the wine hits me, but I steady myself with both of my hands on his shoulders. His eyes lock with mine, and before he can say anything else, my mouth is on his.

It's another breathless, desperate kiss, just like all our other ones. But for me, at least, it feels different. For me it's a silent acknowledgment that after tonight things may change. After tonight, it's only two days until the festival. After that he's headed back to Chicago. For sure there will be disappointment and stress, maybe hurt feelings, maybe even anger.

But tonight there's no trace of any of those. Tonight, as Callum and I pull at each other with eager hands, yanking our clothes from our bodies, it is perfection.

Perfect is the way his hands grip my hips, steadying me as I grind myself on his lap, only the thin fabric of our underwear separating us. Perfect is his tongue teasing my tongue, refusing to stop, spurred on by how many times I moan and cry out. Perfect is my hands lost in his hair, his throaty groans every time I tug. Perfect is that stripped-down look in his flawless hazel eyes every time our gazes connect, letting me know that this means something to him too.

Soon we've shed all fabric. Inside I'm burning, aching, begging for release. So I reach between his legs to guide him inside of me.

"Wait," he blurts, then reaches to the other end of the couch where his rumpled trousers lie.

He glances at the empty spot on the couch where Lemon was sitting. "We must have scared her off."

We both share a chuckle as he fishes his wallet out of his pocket, then he pulls out a condom. I swipe it from him, rip the wrapper open with my teeth, then lean back as I slide it on.

Callum fists the arm of the couch and grits his teeth as I make my move. "Fucking hell, Nikki, that's . . ."

"Perfection," I let out in a breathy voice. I groan at how he stretches me out in the best possible way.

With both hands on my cheeks, he pulls me to his face once more. "Exactly."

I start out slowly, moving up and down with both of my hands on his shoulders for leverage. It's barely a minute before Callum flashes that hyperconcentrated look in his eyes. He leans up. With one hand on my hip and the other still cupping my face, the corner of his mouth quirks up.

"Nikki. I . . ."

The new angle hits a deep spot, and I fall forward, barely able to contain myself. My lips land on his, cutting him off. I start to kiss him until I've got no more air in my lungs.

I direct my hand down low to that spot that's been on fire ever since I straddled Callum. Right now it's begging, pleading for attention. I move my hand softly at first, swirling a slow rhythm until the heat morphs into pressure.

Callum's eyes fall to where my hand is. "Yes. Just like that," he growls.

Faster and faster I swirl until every blink gives way to blurry vision. Then it comes.

Through all the convulsing, all the whimpering, all the panting, one thing is clear: this climax is perfection, and the reason why is because it's with Callum.

He holds me up as I thrash against him, refusing to let himself break until I've gotten mine. When I come down, his body tenses, his jaw bulges, and his eyes go hazy. But somehow he's still got me. His muscled arms shroud me like a warm blanket. Under them, I'm safe. Under him, everything is perfect.

We hug each other as we fall over into a lying position on the couch. Our breathing shallow, we take a second to reposition ourselves. He's the big spoon like always, and I'm tucked tightly against him. It's my favorite position to fall asleep in. I stretch against him, my eyelids heavy with each blink. I let them close for real this time, the soft lull of Callum's breath above me soothing me like a lullaby.

From behind me, he leans his mouth to my ear. "I have to tell you something."

"Mmm?" is all I can manage from my drowsy haze.

"Nikki, I . . ."

Before he can finish, I'm sound asleep.

# Chapter 18

Every time I look up, it's the same sight. A sea of food trucks at the Maui Food Festival. Usually from this spot in downtown Lahaina, you get a clear view of the harbor dotted with dozens of boats, but not today.

I retie my apron while scanning the crowd. It's wall-to-wall people, and it's barely noon. After just two hours, it's packed to the max. Today there are a million food trucks and booths set up side by side, as far as the eye can see. People saunter at a snail's pace from eatery to eatery because walking at a normal speed when it's this crowded is out of the question.

I relish the nonstop workflow though. It's the only way to distract myself from my last mind-blowing night with Callum. Since then, we've been so busy with festival prep that we could barely find the time to text each other, let alone see each other in person.

I force the focus back to the chaos in front of me. I can't think about Callum or how much I'd rather be in bed with him than sweating my skin off and cooking for every stranger that passes by.

Our last night together was just that: one night. Today is what matters.

Today we find out if Tiva's Filipina Kusina keeps our coveted spot on Makena Road, or if we have to scramble to find someplace new. I'm sweating like a sinner in church. God bless this black tank top and its ability to hide all the dampness leaching from my pores.

Even breaths and swallows help me keep my composure. All I can manage are nods, polite smiles, and pleasantries whenever I take cash or hand out food, nothing more.

Behind me, Mom fries endless orders of *lumpia* and chicken *adobo* wings.

"Three orders of fruit salad, coming right up! Two orders of chicken *adobo* wings, coming right up!" She practically sings every order.

A group of regulars stops by to say hello and welcome her back after the health-related hiatus she took.

She pats my hand. "I was under strict orders from my daughter and my doctor to rest for a few days. But now I'm back and I'm ready to feed my folks. Now who's ready for some *lumpia*?"

Soft cheers boom from the small crowd.

Every time she hands a customer their order, she beams. Not an ounce of hesitation is traceable in her cheery attitude. She's a fitting balance to my nervous energy.

She taps my shoulder. "Isn't this great? So many people want to try our food." She looks up at a customer as he takes a bite of chicken wing. "How is it? Good?"

He nods, sauce smeared across his lips. "So, so good, Tiva. I already voted for you ladies online."

She gives him a thumbs-up while I offer a soft "thank you." The Maui Food Festival website has an active poll for attendees to vote on their favorite eateries. My hand itches to grab my phone out of the pocket of my jeans and check the results every five minutes. The Hungry Chaps truck is all the way on the opposite end of this row. I can't see them, which means I can't gauge how they're doing. Checking the results as they come in would be an easy way to satisfy my curiosity.

Instead, I clench my fingers into a fist and resist. Obsessively checking the poll two hours into the festival will do nothing other than send my blood pressure to the mesosphere. We have the whole rest of the day left to work, and I can't lose myself to distraction. My only goal for the next six hours is to cook the best dishes possible so every person that eats our food votes for us.

Penelope saunters up to the booth, her wide smile so bright it rivals the unrelenting sun beating above.

"Nikki! You're kicking some serious ass!" She holds up her phone to me. "So many people are raving about your food on social media. They're hashtagging Tiva's left and right!"

Mom turns as soon as she hears her name, beaming when Penelope shows her all the photos of our food that people have been posting to Instagram and Twitter.

"You're killing it, Tiva!" Penelope high-fives her before ordering a *halo-halo*. "It's so hot and I've been craving this."

I dispense a generous serving of crushed ice, *ube*, sweetened beans, coconut, and evaporated milk into a paper cup and hand it to her. She tastes a spoonful, closes her eyes, and moans. The "mmm" she lets slip sounds more like a growl than a hum. Leaning over the counter, she whispers in my ear, "Your boy toy is in the zone. I went over to wish him luck. The look on his face was intense."

A high-pitched chuckle falls from her lips. All I can do is say, "Oh wow."

She leans back, keeping her tone low. Tipping her spoon at me, she gives me a knowing smile. "I told him I was coming over to say hi to you, and he got all flustered. His cheeks got pink and everything. He's so into you. It's adorable."

When I glance up above Penelope, I freeze. Callum stands front and center, just a few feet from me. I wasn't expecting to see him at all today.

Penelope twists around to sneak a peek, then turns her megawatt smile back at me. "Looks like someone misses you." She winks before walking into the crowd.

Callum approaches the counter, his hazel eyes on me, making me feel like the only person on the planet.

"Can we talk?" His face is a mess of worried lines.

"Is something wrong?" I manage to sound mostly composed.

I notice he hasn't shaved since I've seen him. The scruff on his cheeks looks like the beginning of a beard. I don't even like beards, but on him it is scrumptious.

He runs his tongue along the glorious thickness that is his bottom lip. "I need to tell you something."

Leaning around him, I hand a waiting customer their order of wings.

"Can it wait?" I say, my eyes veering in every direction other than in front of me.

I'm not strong enough to tell him no when he's standing so close, his body heat skimming my skin, his gaze making my knees go weak.

"No. I need to talk to you now."

I glance around. No one else is at our truck right now, making this our first lull of the day. It also means no one is paying attention to our exchange, which I'm silently thankful for.

"Meet me behind my truck in a minute," I say.

When we reconvene, we're out of sight of the bustling crowds.

"What is it?"

He shoves his hand in his pocket and pulls out the stick of Chap-Stick I usually keep in my purse. "You dropped this at my flat the other night."

I swipe it from his palm and put it in my apron pocket and almost laugh, confused as to why he chose now of all times to give it back to me. "Thanks, but you didn't have to give this to me today. You could have waited."

Shuffling his feet, he glances at the ground. "I thought you might, um, need it. For your, uh, lips."

"Okay . . ."

I wait another second, but he says nothing. His eyes dart from me to the ground to the side and then back at me.

"Well, thanks."

I turn away to walk back, but then he speaks, stopping me.

"I'm not going back to Chicago. After the festival, I mean."

I take a step toward him. "What?"

"I'm staying here in Maui."

"You are?"

He nods.

"Don't you have a job and an apartment waiting for you?" I'm stunned at how hard my voice is in this moment. I should be happy. The guy I have feelings for, the guy I fantasize about on a regular basis, the guy I want more than anyone else in the world is staying here. But all I can process is shock.

Despite what I've said, the expression on his face reads tender. "I don't care about any of that."

My heart lodges in my throat. It also ceases beating. "What are you . . ."

His chest heaves with a single breath, and his hazel eyes lock on me. He steps forward and takes my face in his hands. Instantly I'm calm, I'm soft, I'm at ease.

"I want to be with you, Nikki. I want to stay here in Maui and give us a proper shot." His voice is a cross between a whisper and a growl. Soft and scratchy.

"But that's not what we agreed to."

His hands fall away from me. Confusion takes over his formerly affectionate expression. "I know that, but . . . Don't you feel this thing between us?"

I feel it every time I see him, every time he's in the vicinity, every time I see his name light up my phone screen. It's all proof of just how much this thing between us has grown. I care for Callum more than I've cared for anyone I've ever been with.

But I can't do more than what we're doing now. That would require a commitment, an emotional investment. It would require me steeling myself for the inevitable day that I lose him. And I don't have the strength to do that.

Callum continues to gaze at me, eyes hopeful, waiting for me to say that yes, I feel every single thing he feels right now.

But all I do is shake my head.

"I know you feel something for me, Nikki." His stare and his voice turn determined. "I can tell by the way you melt against me every time I touch you. I can tell by how happy you are every time we're together. I can tell by the way you looked at me in the hot tub that night, when I started to tell you how I felt about you—about us. I can tell that I mean something to you. You're just scared to commit because of what happened with your dad."

"Excuse me?"

"It's so bloody obvious you're scared of getting close to someone, of losing someone again." He tugs a hand through his hair, an outward display of the frustration that's clearly coursing within him.

"Don't!" My voice booms through the festival noise. Callum has no business bringing up my dad in a situation that's strictly me and him. I can't believe he would even try. "Don't say another word about my dad. And don't try to armchair diagnose me."

In two steps he's close to me again. "It's okay to be scared, Nikki. I'm scared too." His face, his tone, it's all soft now. "But fuck it, I want to give us a shot. Because that's what you do when you lo—"

For a split second, his eyes widen, but then he reins it in quickly when he furrows his brow and pulls his lips into his mouth.

I can't unhear what he said. The beginnings of the "L" word.

"What did you say?" My voice is a scratchy whisper.

His chest heaves when he takes a breath, and then he takes my hand in his. "I . . . I'm in love with you," he finally says.

I open my mouth, but nothing comes out. Just a shudder of a breath. My hand goes limp in his. It's lucky he's holding on to me, because his words are an invisible truck hitting me at full speed. I'd be facedown in the dirt if I were standing on my own.

*Callum is in love with me.*

*Callum is in love with me.*

No matter how many times I silently repeat it to myself, it still rattles me to the core.

"You . . . you're in love with me?"

My brain flashes back to our last night together, to the last words he spoke before I fell asleep.

I hold my hand up at him. "Wait. The other night . . . did you say . . ."

He nods. "I said I loved you. But you were asleep."

The words send shock waves through my body and brain that are so powerful, all other sensations are rendered null and void. He leans forward until our bodies press together, and then he runs his hand through my hair before settling back onto my cheek.

It's a long moment of us standing and staring. Opening and closing my mouth does no good, because zero words materialize. It's his touch. It has some sort of mythical hold on me, and I need to think clearly in this moment. I step back and out of his reach.

The wrinkles in his forehead deepen. "I can't take another second of pretending like I don't love you. Fuck this bloody contest, fuck all this food truck nonsense. I don't care about this ridiculous festival or who wins or loses or the money or where I'll be able to park from now on. I couldn't care less about some random place where Finn and I can sling food. All I care about is being with you. Can't we . . ." He pauses, his chest rising with a single breath, his throat moving with a single swallow. "Can't we just forget about all this and be together?"

His words take a moment to soak in, but once they do, I want to scream until my lungs implode.

All these months I've spent working to perfect my recipes, those weeks I drove around when I first moved here trying to find the perfect spot for our food truck, the hours I've spent worrying about money and my mom and how in the world I'll make a life in a place I never thought I'd be, every late night, every early morning, every dollar I spent to keep this business running . . . the promise I made to my dad before he died. I'm supposed to forget about all that? *No.*

I swallow, barely able to keep from yelling. "Maybe running a food truck was a fun little hiatus from your finance life, but it is everything to me, Callum. I came here to help my mom and keep a promise to my dad, not abandon my family the moment I catch feelings like some lovestruck teenager."

The harshness in my voice makes me cringe. This conversation needs to end. If I keep going like this, I'll say something even worse.

"Let's talk about this after the festival," I mutter.

The expression in his eyes runs hot. I can tell by the way the veins in his neck bulge that he's trying to keep himself in check. Still his tone remains hard, desperate.

"Are you honestly telling me that you can't fit me into your life, Nikki?"

My head spins. It's like a million invisible walls are closing in on me. "I can't do this right now, Callum."

I dart around him to walk back to the truck. He catches me with a hand on my bicep before I can make it more than a few steps, spinning me to face him. "You're willing to throw us away? Because you're scared?"

When I look at him, my chest throbs like it's going to collapse. I've already told him I can't take this; he can see how much it kills me. Why does he have to push?

When I say nothing, his face twists and his hands fall away from me.

"I see." His voice is strangled. "I suppose that means we're done, then."

The finality of his words makes my knees buckle. But I can't seem to move my mouth. To ask him to stay with me. To give me more time.

His pained gaze lingers on me for a long second. Then he walks away.

*We're over.*

When I'm certain that my legs won't fall out from under me, I stumble along the back way, turn the corner at the last food truck in the row, and stop dead in my tracks. A dozen people stand with their phones pointed at me. I have no idea how long they've been standing there recording my and Callum's blowout, but even if they just caught that last little bit, they've captured a gold mine.

I blink and register Callum scowling at our audience.

"Fuck off," he booms.

The crowd disperses like cockroaches scattering at a beam of light. The damage is done though. That will be uploaded to countless blogs in no time. We'll be island gossip for sure. Who knows the effect it will have on the rest of today.

I head back to the truck and grab the nearest pair of tongs. It's a minute before I even notice Mom standing perfectly still in front of me, not moving.

"*Anak*." Her voice is even, calm. It's not the uplifting tone it normally is, and it's so damn unnerving.

I ignore the ache in my chest, the burn in my eyes, and focus on the scene in front of me: people standing at our truck, waiting to order food. Like a robot, I take their orders.

"*Anak*," she repeats, her voice softer this time. "I heard shouting behind the truck. What was all that about?"

"Nothing." I don't bother to look up. My gaze is fixed on cash-filled hands outstretched at the counter. I have orders to take, food to prepare, a festival full of people to serve. There is no room for anything else.

"Nikki, I think you should—"

"Not now, Mom." My tone is so hard, the customer in front of me flinches.

The sound of her defeated sigh hits my ears. Out of the corner of my eye, I see her walk back to the fryer.

I gaze up at the customer, who's staring at me wide-eyed. I take the money from his outstretched hand and dispense more orders. Another second passes. Somehow, some way, tears don't fall, and I'm grateful. Falling apart for the rest of today is not an option. I've already lost my cool during the biggest event of my career. I can't cry too.

And I don't. Every time the burn hits my eyes, every time my chest squeezes tighter and tighter, I breathe in.

*Not now.*

It's a mantra I silently repeat to myself over and over until the last customer leaves and the festival comes to an end.

Not now. Not ever.

# Chapter 19

I toss the last of the supplies into the truck and shut the back door before spinning around and taking in the view. Every booth is empty, and every food truck has pulled away. I'm the only one left. I stretch my neck before checking my phone and see a text from Mom.

Made it home safe. Mrs. Tokushige said you did a wonderful job today! So proud of you, anak!

Thankfully, Mom didn't put up a fight when I asked Mrs. Tokushige to give her a ride home after the festival while I stayed to clean up. I think she could tell by my frosty demeanor and the way I made zero chitchat for the rest of the day that I was barely hanging on by a thread for some mysterious reason. I needed some time alone to collect myself. And that's exactly what I've been doing for the past three hours since the festival ended. I offered to stay and pack everything up myself because I wanted the alone time to process the tailspin of the last several hours.

Everything festival-wise was a dream. Customers raved about our food. I lost count of how many people stopped by and said they voted for us. It was a heartening distraction from what a disaster I was on the inside. Even though I managed to maintain my professionalism the whole rest of the day at the festival, the damage was done. The Maui food scene now knew what I'd been up to in my personal life these past couple of months. Every time I took an order and handed out a plate of food, I wondered what that person was thinking. Were they at my truck because they genuinely wanted to enjoy our food? Or was I a sideshow to them? Were they only there to gawk at me because they heard about Callum's and my soap opera breakup?

I shove open the driver's side door and push away the thought. It doesn't matter. All there is left to do now is drive home, down a cold beer, and pass out in bed to avoid thinking about how Callum and I are done forever.

"Nikki!" a voice shouts from behind me.

I spin around and spot Penelope jogging toward me. I hop back out of the truck and start to ask what's wrong, but she cuts me off, pulling me down into another one of her death hugs.

"You did it!" she yells, her voice giddy.

She breaks the hug, grips me by the shoulder, and holds me in front of her.

I stare at her painfully wide smile and try to muster a small one of my own. "Did what?"

She shoves her phone an inch from my face. "You and your mom! You got the highest score at the festival! Look!"

My stomach leaps up my chest when I focus on the screen. At the top of the Maui Food Festival webpage are the results of the poll. Tiva's Filipina Kusina sits at the top in bright red letters, the number ninety-seven next to our name. My breath comes out in a huff. I can't make words.

"Holy . . . wow . . ."

I don't let myself blink when I look at the results. I don't want that bright red number going anywhere.

Still grinning wide, Penelope nods her head while laughing giddily. "Hell yes, holy wow! You freaking did it!"

Slowly, I nod my head. Processing is still a struggle, but after another few seconds of Penelope's giddy squeals and congratulations, it finally sinks in. We won. Mom and I, we did it. We established ourselves as the top eatery on the island, beating every other restaurant and food truck in the festival. We just won twenty thousand dollars. Nothing else even close to matters.

I wait for the wave of emotion to hit, for the joy, the relief, the adrenaline rush of success to paint me from the inside out. But it never comes. Inside every muscle is tense. My blood pumps like slow-moving sludge. There is not one iota of joy, happiness, or excitement inside of me.

"This calls for champagne!" Penelope says.

She pulls away and chatters on about a new cocktail place near her apartment. Her words fade into the background, though, the longer I stand there.

*Champagne.*

The last time I had champagne was with Callum, cuddled next to him on his couch, just before we screwed each other's brains out. I'll never, ever have champagne with him again—I'll never have anything with him again.

Our win means he and Finn won't share a food truck spot with us anymore.

I won't see Callum's face every time I look up from the truck window. I'll never get another eyebrow wag that serves as a secret smile between us. We'll never share another champagne-drinking contest, another kiss, another cuddle, or another flirty conversation.

Hot tears burn my eyes. Penelope doesn't seem to notice as she's still chattering away, looking up an address on her phone. I pull out my phone from my pocket, call up the Maui Food Festival site, and check the results once more. And then I see it. I zero in on the text that rests below Tiva's ranking. Hungry Chaps is in second place, scoring two points lower than us.

"Um . . ."

Penelope glances up at me. "What?"

I turn my phone to her, remarking just how close Callum and Finn were to beating us.

She shrugs, a look of ease lighting up her face. "A win is a win. Besides"—she beams and pats my shoulder—"he's your boyfriend. He loves you and he'll be happy for you, promise."

She winks before looking back down at her phone.

The word "love" hits like a fiery ember to my skin. It's what unleashes the floodgates. My face twisted, I let out a sob.

Penelope's eyes go wide. "Oh my . . . What's wrong, Nikki?"

I shake my head while holding my hand up, as if to wave her away. It's the trademark move so many people pull when they're upset but don't want to be fussed over. But Penelope stays still, rubbing my arm with her hand.

"It's okay," she says. Her stare has flipped from joyful to concerned. "Just take a breath."

Covering my face with my hands offers only a tad more privacy as I sob out in the open. But I can't help it. I should be jumping up and down in triumph. I should be texting Mom and Mrs. Tokushige the good news. I should be driving to the nearest bar with Penelope to toast my victory.

But the way my stomach churns, the way my chest aches as if it's on fire, makes all that impossible. Because there's only one thought crowding my mind.

I've lost Callum forever.

This time when Penelope pulls me in for a hug, it's gentle. So are her words. "Nikki, what happened?"

When I catch my breath, I tell her everything.

No matter how many times I glance out the kitchen window of my condo, my gaze always goes back to the computer screen. My fingers always type in the same phrase:

*Tiva's Filipina Kusina*

The results that pop up on the pages are never the ones I want to see. Nothing about our win at the Maui Food Festival or how good our food is. Just endless comments on Twitter and Instagram about me and Callum. Our secret affair, our very public fight, our very public breakup. It's only been a day since the festival results were released, and everyone seems to have forgotten that we're the winners. Instead the topic trending on Maui social media is the disintegration of my and Callum's secret relationship.

I thought falling into a sobbing pile of tears in front of Penelope yesterday would be my all-time low. How I wish. I hit a whole new low every time I check Tiva's Twitter or Instagram accounts and read the incendiary comments people leave.

I polish off my glass of beer while eyeing the results page of my latest search. Audio clips of Callum and me lashing out at each other circulate like wildfire. Thankfully, no one was able to get a clear video of the two of us having it out, but the sound they recorded is plenty hurtful. I let myself listen to part of one clip that some newbie food vlogger named @IEatEverything posted, but I muted it halfway through. I couldn't take it. I couldn't relive hearing my and Callum's raised voices, our wrenched words, our private pain on display for strangers to listen to, like some demented heartbreak song played on repeat.

I grit my teeth while scrolling through the endless tweets.

Who knew these two were dating? #mauifoodfestival #foodtruckromance #torridaffair

Someone caught feelings. Hate when that happens #ouch #brokenhearted

I can't bear to think this British stud is heartbroken. What kind of monster breaks up with a hunk like that? #pickmeinstead

Nikki from @Tivas is an ice queen for leaving that hottie out to dry. Yo, Callum! I love @HungryChaps! Hit me up! I'll cheer you up! 😉 #DTF

My eyes go crossed reading all the declarations of love for Callum and admonishments aimed at me. But they have no clue about our history, our feelings, what we endured. They have no right to make judgments about me or Callum. They don't know a damn thing about us.

Halfway down the results page, the comments grow even snarkier. My jaw aches with how hard I'm biting down.

Bet they planned this for the publicity. Perfect timing with the #mauifoodfestival. The whole thing screams scripted drama #dontbelievethehype

Two rivals having a secret affair in the run-up to the biggest competition of their careers, then a public breakup?? #manufacturedromance #fake

Public argument + wrenching breakup = free publicity and more business for @HungryChaps and @Tivas, amirite?? #fakeAF

I grip the edge of the counter until my fingers ache, wondering if the Flavor Network, the cosponsor of the Maui Food Festival, has seen any of this. Holding my breath, I make a silent wish that somehow, some way, this major TV network doesn't have a social media department. Because if they catch wind of any of this, it's all over. They'll think Hungry Chaps and Tiva's conspired together to secure their top finishes, and disqualify us like they did with last year's champion. I hold in a breath then let it burst out, annoyed with myself. All the deep breaths in the world don't make one bit of difference in this disaster.

I close every social media tab, then check my email. A new message pops in my inbox. Someone named Charlotte with a Flavor Network email address. The dread that hits my stomach is instant. I know exactly what this message is going to say even before I read it. I do a half-hearted skim of the text anyway.

> . . . clearly a talented chef who is passionate about food . . . recent social media activity has alerted us to a possible violation of the Maui Food Festival rules . . . which is why we regret to tell you that we're rescinding the prize money and commercial offer . . .

I blink through the burn in my eyes, but a tear escapes down my cheek anyway. Sniffling, I lift the hem of my shirt and wipe it dry. That's it. All those months of thinking up new recipes, all the backbreaking days of cooking and prepping, all those hours on my feet, carving out a social media presence . . . it was all for nothing. Everything Mom and I earned eighteen hours ago is gone.

Down the hall her voice echoes. "*Anak*, are you hungry?"

She walks to the kitchen sink to fill a pot of water. "We should start planning how we're going to use the prize money. The truck definitely needs some work, but I also want to get a new fryer. And can you believe we're going to be in a commercial? I already called your aunties and uncles and told them. They're so excited!" She spins around to me, grinning. "What do you think?"

Her smile drops as soon as she registers my tear-soaked face. She darts over to me, but I stand up before she can pull me into a hug. I don't deserve any affection for what I'm about to tell her.

"I'm sorry, Mom. But we . . . The festival changed their mind. We didn't win. They took back the prize money."

Her perfectly arched eyebrows wrinkle together. "What are you talking about?"

We stand facing each other, the stool between us. "It's just . . . I did something . . . I messed up. Really bad. It's all my fault."

Her frown turns serious. "That's ridiculous. You didn't mess up anything. You and I did a great job yesterday at the festival. Everyone loved us."

I pause to wipe my face with my hands before dropping them at my sides in defeat. She reaches over, taking my hand in hers. In her eyes, there's a calm I didn't expect to see. A reassurance, understanding.

"It's okay. You can tell me."

Her sweet support in this moment is more than I can take—it's more than I deserve after what I've done to ruin our big break. "I know, Mom, but—"

The shrill ring of my phone cuts me off. I huff out a few steadying breaths as the ringing dies out, thankful for the pause to collect myself. A second later, it drones on once again.

I swipe my phone from the counter. "Let me get rid of this. Then I'll explain."

Penelope's name flashes across the screen before I answer. "Hey, Penelope." My throat strains to keep my voice at a pleasant tone. Penelope doesn't need to endure an in-person breakdown and an over-the-phone breakdown from me two days in a row.

"I just wanted to say, don't worry about a thing," she says. "I'm on it."

"On what?"

"I know your phone has probably been blowing up with notifications after that statement the Flavor Network just sent out concerning your win at the Maui Food Festival."

I let loose a heavy sigh. "I actually haven't seen their statement yet. I got an email from them, though, which I'm sure says much of the same, so I think I'll skip the post." Closing my eyes, I pinch the bridge of my nose.

"I've got it all under control," she says.

Penelope's voice still boasts its bubbly inflection, but there's something firm behind it now. Whatever she's talking about, it's clear she's a thousand percent sure she's got it handled.

"What do you mean?"

"You know how I said before that I did social media for a living?"

"Yeah." I glance at Mom, who now boasts a confused frown as she listens to my side of this conversation.

"A lot of my clients are TV networks. One of them is Chic TV." There's a smile in her voice when she speaks. "You've heard of it, right?"

"Um, of course." Chic TV is the most popular lifestyle channel on cable television.

"Chic has been interested in dipping their toe into something cooking related for a while now. They were going to team up with the Flavor Network to do a cooking show last year, but Flavor tried to screw them over during the contract phase of things, so Chic pulled out. They've held a grudge ever since. And this is the perfect opportunity to get them back."

My head spins trying to keep up with everything Penelope says. "Oh . . . what does that mean?"

Penelope chuckles. "Sorry, sometimes I get so excited about something that I don't explain it fully. Check your Instagram."

I pull up Instagram on my laptop and see that Tiva's has been tagged in a post from the Flavor Network's account. It's a photo of the crowd during the Maui Food Festival with a brief caption explaining why they rescinded our prize. Thankfully, there's no mention of my name or Callum's, just that Tiva's was caught breaking the festival rules and that we were disqualified.

Mom leans closer to the laptop screen and squints. "A violation of the rules? What are they talking about?"

I shift the mouthpiece of the phone away from me. "I'll explain in a minute," I whisper.

"Ignore the Flavor Network's post," Penelope says. "Chic just tagged you in something. Be sure to read the whole caption."

I go to Chic TV's Instagram account and see their latest post: a photo of our food truck.

"Oh wow! That's us!" Mom says before I read the caption:

We here at @ChicTV had a great time at the Maui Food Festival! Maui, you've got some seriously delicious eateries! Congrats to @Tivas for kicking major a$$ and winning the grand prize! Sadly @theFlavorNetwork has gone back on its promise to deliver prize money to the winner for a second year in a row (something's #fishy about that, #amirite?). But @ChicTV would love to deliver where @theFlavorNetwork has fallen short. @Tivas, we'll give you your rightful prize money if you promise to shoot a commercial for our network this fall. What do you say?

A sharp intake of breath is all I have as a response. My head spins at how Penelope has flipped our course completely for the better.

"I just got off the phone with the food division at Chic TV a half hour ago, and everything is official. Someone from the contracts department will email you soon with all the details. The ball is officially rolling on this, so you don't have to worry."

I can't speak. All I do is breathlessly stutter.

"Shoot, are you okay?" Penelope asks.

"It's just . . . Penelope, how did you do this? Why did you do this?"

"Because it's my job. And because you're my friend."

This time when my eyes water, it's not because I'm angry or heartbroken. It's because I'm overwhelmed with joy that someone as kind and successful as Penelope would even consider me their friend.

The word "friend" settles somewhere deep inside my chest.

"Look, I know I came off like a weird fangirl when we met at the farmer's market," Penelope says. "You're an amazing cook and run the best food truck on the island. Everyone in the Maui food scene was blown away by you, myself included." She pauses for a breath. "I know we haven't known each other long, but my friends are important to me. Whenever I can do something for them, I try. And that's what I'm doing now. Trying to be a good friend."

At her words, I crack my first smile of the day.

"I know it's hard making friends when you move to a new place," she says. "I'm so happy I found you here in Maui."

After nearly two years of struggling on my own, I have a friend. "That means a lot, Penelope. Do you maybe want to get a drink tomorrow after I finish up at the food truck? I owe you for how you helped us today. And for listening to me wail yesterday."

It's something so simple—two friends spending time together. But it's been so long since I've experienced that. And I miss it.

She drops to a more wistful tone. "I really am sorry about you and Callum. You can talk to me anytime about anything. And you don't owe me. I would love to get a drink with you tomorrow though."

"Seriously, Penelope. You are beyond amazing."

I promise to text her when I get off work, she promises to think of a good place to meet, and we hang up.

I turn back to face Mom, bewilderment clear as day on her face. But I can't be too surprised. I went from crying in front of her to smiling in the span of a few minutes.

I take a breath. "It's going to be okay now. Penelope fixed everything. We still won, and we're still getting the money. We're just going to do the commercial for a different network. Chic TV instead of the Flavor Network."

That joyful smile from before spreads across her face. "She did? Oh my gosh, we are? Oh, Chic TV is way better than the Flavor Network! They're so stylish! And that's your auntie Nora's favorite channel, remember? Oh, I can't wait to tell her! I'm going to call her now actually."

She scurries to the bedroom for her phone, leaving me alone again in the kitchen. When I turn to close my laptop, my eyes catch on a comment right under the Chic TV post about us, and my hand freezes midair.

@HungryChaps: What @theFlavorNetwork did was a travesty. @Tivas won fair and square, with zero help from anyone—not even us. Well done, ladies.

Inside I soften at the public congratulations from Finn. It's beyond gracious of him to make a statement like that on Hungry Chaps' Instagram account.

And then my eyes fall to the comment below his. A user by the name of @FoodAndFinanceLad. My chest swells when I process it. That must be Callum's account—the account he said he's never once used, until today—to leave this comment.

More than well deserved. Nicely done, petal.

A flower emoji ends the comment. I can barely breathe.

I click on the profile, and sure enough, there are no other posts or stories. Just that one comment. No question, this is Callum's account.

I grip the counter to steady myself. Even after our fight, even after our very ugly and very public demise, Callum somehow found it in him to congratulate me with the Instagram account he never uses—and it's thrown me for one hell of a loop.

# Chapter 20

"Everything okay, *anak*? You seem a little off." Mom sets a glass of water on the kitchen table for me.

"I'm fine." I take a long sip. It's a lie, but I've got no energy for the truth.

Because the truth is too painful to talk about. I'd have to admit, like I almost did the other day right before Penelope swooped in and saved us, that I had a secret relationship with our rival, broke up on the worst possible terms, and reeled about it in silence until he left a sweet comment for me out of the blue on social media that had me questioning everything. I'd come off like a traitor *and* a basket case.

She plops down in the chair to my left, her focused stare fixed on me. "You don't seem fine. In fact, you haven't seemed like yourself lately. Want to tell me why?"

I let out a long exhale, saying nothing. It does little to ease the concern painted so clearly on her face. She stares with a furrowed brow, her dark eyes boring into me like lasers.

"Just tired, that's all," I say. "It's just a lot dealing with all those bloggers constantly hanging out at our truck."

This time when I speak, it's the truth. This first week of having our food truck spot on Makena Road back to ourselves has been like navigating a paparazzi press line. Every day a dozen bloggers visit our truck to ask me two things. The first is how I feel about being dropped by the Flavor Network only to be picked up minutes later by Chic TV. Penelope was kind enough to give me a heads-up on that one. When we met for drinks, she warned that social media influencer wannabes may pester me in the hopes of getting their fifteen minutes of fame by latching onto the food truck that will soon be in a commercial for a popular network.

The second most common thing they ask about is Callum, our relationship, our fallout, how I feel now that he's vacated our spot. And every day I serve customers while pretending that I don't hear their invasive questions float within earshot as they crowd our truck. I never knew ignoring people could be so exhausting.

But it's even more than that. It's the fact that every day I park our truck in that spot, I hope against hope that the Hungry Chaps food truck will be parked there. Even though it will never, ever happen. When they didn't show up that first day back, it was expected. It didn't ease the knot in my chest at all though.

And every day since, the knot has grown bigger and tighter. Today I can barely breathe when I think of Callum and me sharing that spot, how for weeks we worked less than ten feet from each other during the day, then ravaged each other at night.

Yes, we're done. Yes, we fought. Yes, we both said terrible things to each other. But that doesn't erase our passion, our feelings, how he made me happier than anyone I've ever been with. How he was the only person other than my mom who I could talk to about my dad.

Another labored breath and my chest feels as though it will collapse under the weight of this invisible agony.

It's all crystal clear now: I love Callum.

I would happily endure a million nosy vloggers all day, every day, if I had Callum in my line of view. If I could look up and see him flashing a half smile at me from the window of his food truck.

Mom's voice pulls me back to the present. "Those bloggers or vloggers or whatever they're called are certainly irritating. But I don't think that's the only reason why you're so sad."

When she inquired on the first day why everyone kept asking me about Callum, I froze. I never wanted to tell her about us, even when I thought we had lost our festival prize and I was about to force myself to come clean. I brushed off her question, saying the vloggers were desperate for a story and making things up about us. She nodded and didn't mention it again. But for a split second there was that knowing look in her eyes, like she could tell I was hiding something. She gives me that same look right now.

"I'm not sad, Mom. I just miss Lemon."

An eyebrow raise is all my explanation gets. It was the same eyebrow raise she gave me when she asked about Lemon not being at the condo anymore and I mumbled some half-assed excused about Penelope wanting to take her for a while. In actuality, Lemon is still with Callum because she just happened to be staying with him when we ended everything between us. I haven't had the nerve to reach out to him and ask if I can see her or if we could somehow resume some sort of fair visitation schedule. The pain from our split is still too raw.

"I'm your mom. I know when you're sad. And I also know that it's because of a very tall, very handsome English boy."

My eyes go wide, but I rein them back in after a blink. "Mom, I told you, that's not . . ."

She flashes her best deadpan stare. It's been a while since I've seen it. Not since I was seventeen and she walked in on me curled up in a ball on the floor of my bedroom, thoroughly hungover after a night of sneaking alcohol at my best friend's house.

"Nicole Elise DiMarco, I may be from a different generation, but I'm no fool. I know when my daughter's in love, just like I know when she's not telling me the truth."

There's a pop in my jaw as it falls open. I snap my mouth shut.

Her hand falls over mine. Both her eyes and her tone turn tender. "Did you really think I didn't notice what you were doing all those nights you went out? Did you think I didn't notice all those times at work when I caught you smiling to yourself for no reason at all?"

"But . . . how?"

"I caught you two looking at each other a few times at the food truck. Whenever you saw each other in those moments, you just looked so happy. I knew something was going on." Her burnt umber eyes fall to her lap. "And then the other day Mrs. Tokushige sent me all these links to videos about what happened at the festival between you and Callum. She was so worried about you, how you were dealing with all this."

I let out the breath I've been holding. "Oh."

Patting my hand, she flashes a small smile. "The way he looked at you those times I noticed, it's the same way your dad would look at me. You can't fake that sort of feeling, that love. And you can't hide it for very long either."

She motions for me to drink the rest of the water in my glass. I do even though my head is spinning. My face heats at all the times she spotted my smug expression after a night with Callum. I had zero clue.

"Wow, Mom. I'm a little embarrassed at how I underestimated you."

She swipes the glass from the table and refills it at the sink. She turns to look at me. "You should be more embarrassed at how you two ended it with each other." Again she sighs. "It's no surprise you pushed him away. You've been pushing everyone away ever since your dad died. Except me."

I'm speechless once more, just a string of stutters and breaths.

When she looks up at me again, her eyes glisten. "Your dad would be so sad to know that he made you this afraid of love."

Her voice breaks at the end, and she glances down at her hands while I let the shock of this revelation fully soak in. And then I reach for her hand, squeezing it gently. My eyes dart to his urn in the living room. My heart sinks to the floor. Because I bet she's right. He would be devastated that I used him as an excuse to push someone so wonderful away from me.

I steady my voice. "Mom, don't cry. Please. It's more . . . complicated than that."

Even behind glistening eyes, her stare doesn't lose its punch. "Is it? You love him, and he loves you. It doesn't get simpler than that." For a moment she stops, lips pursed, shaking her head. "You think if you don't let people get close—no friends, no relationships—you don't have to face losing them someday," she says. "That's no way to live."

Another truth bomb that takes a silent minute for me to process.

"You should call him," she finally says.

"I can't. You watched the video of our argument. You heard the things he said to me and the things I said to him. They were awful. I don't know if we can come back from that."

"People in love hurt each other, unfortunately. But you learn to forgive. Your dad and I learned that long ago."

"Mom, you and Dad bickered over what takeout place to order from or where to vacation. Not this sort of thing."

"You think we never argued about anything serious?"

"Not in front of me. You were pretty much the perfect couple."

An amused chuckle falls from her lips. "We weren't even close to perfect."

"You sure made it seem that way. Everyone agreed. All my friends thought you were the cutest married couple they ever met because you always seemed so in love."

"Oh, we were in love." She takes a long sip of water from my glass. "But you're wrong to think we never had any real problems."

Tapping her fingers on the tabletop, she gazes into the kitchen. "Your dad broke up with me right before we got engaged."

My mouth falls open. "I never knew that."

"I laugh thinking about it now. It was so ridiculous. So typical. We were young, barely twenty-one. Looking back, it made complete sense, and I don't blame him at all. But at the time, I was so hurt." She wags her finger at me. "In fact, if you had come to me at twenty-one and told me you were getting married, I would have told you not to, to take a break, anything to get you to wait longer. Getting married too young is the kiss of death for so many couples." She folds her hands on the table and her gaze turns serious. "I wanted to get engaged, but your dad got cold feet. Said he wasn't ready, that he wanted to see other people. So we broke up. And he did exactly that."

I hold my breath, unsure if I want to picture my dad in his younger years sowing his wild oats.

I shake my head, refusing the visual. "Wow. What a jerk. That sounds so unlike him."

"Exactly what I thought at the time." She twists around in the direction of Dad's urn. "You had a bit of a jerk streak when you were younger, Harold. Thank goodness you were handsome enough to make me forgive you." She turns back to me. "I cried myself to sleep for weeks, I was so heartbroken. But then a month later he showed up at my doorstep unannounced. I was shocked. He looked terrible, like he hadn't been eating or sleeping. He said he made the biggest mistake of his life by letting me go. He wanted me back right then and there."

"Are you serious?" I grip the edge of the table with both hands, eager to hear more.

"Dead serious. But I wasn't going to let him off the hook that easy."

My fingers dig into the engineered wood. It's like I'm listening to a page-turner on audiobook. "What did you do?"

Chuckling, she shrugs. "I told him no way I wanted him back. And then I went on a bunch of dates with a few other young men."

"But . . . you said you were heartbroken over Dad. You said you wanted him back."

"I did, but I wanted him to know I had options too." She waves a hand in the air. "I wanted him to see that I wasn't that easy to win back—that he would have to work for it. He got the message loud and clear after that. And a few weeks later, he asked me to dinner at this lovely little bistro in downtown Portland. And then he proposed."

"Wow," I say, breathless. My seemingly perfect parents had a borderline dysfunctional lead-up to their marriage.

She reaches across the table, patting me softly on the cheek. "See? Your dad and I weren't perfect at all. The way we got engaged was a mess. But we both admitted our mistakes and worked hard to do better. And we did. If we messed up, we apologized. We forgave each other too many times to count. And we never gave up on each other."

She stands up from the chair and walks over to me.

"And you shouldn't give up on Callum. You two have been through a lot. It takes time, but you can fix it."

My head spins with this eye-opening revelation. Contrary to my lifelong belief, my parents weren't always a shining example of a lovey-dovey, zero-conflict relationship.

Placing her hand on my shoulder, she gives a gentle squeeze. "What I told you wasn't meant to shock you. It was meant to give you hope."

Her words are a flicker of light in a pitch-black room. The mess I've made is salvageable. Maybe. Hopefully.

She leans down to hug me. "Just think about reaching out to him, okay?"

"I will."

I stare at my phone screen, thumb hovering over Callum's name in my contacts. Seconds pass. Still I do nothing.

The seemingly tiny task of moving my finger feels as impossible as dog-paddling across the Pacific or scaling Everest. I stand up from my bed for the millionth time. I've repeated this song and dance all morning. I've tried to call Callum while standing at the kitchen counter, in the hallway, outside on the balcony of the condo, but it's always the same. I freeze, terrified at the thought of what he might say. Or won't say.

It's one day after the pep talk from Mom, and I thought I was ready to attempt to contact him. So, so wrong.

Every time I look at his name in my phone, my stomach punches itself. Even so, I take a deep breath, close my eyes, press his name, and hold the phone to my ear.

And then I hang up and toss the phone on my bed.

Wringing my hands and pacing the room doesn't seem to help my racing heart. Planting my feet on the ground, I face the shiny black rectangle in the middle of my bed. It's one phone call. One. I can do this.

"I can do this," I mutter softly to myself as I pick my phone back up and dial again.

This time I grip the wrist of my phone-holding hand with my other hand. Insurance. A backup plan. It's the only way I can make sure I don't hang up and toss the phone out my bedroom window this time.

When the ringing turns to voice mail, relief sets in. I breathe. I can leave a message.

There's a beep. I open my mouth, then promptly freeze. "Hi, um . . . this is . . . um, well." I clear my throat. "This is, um, Nikki. Hi . . . I . . . well, I . . ."

I'm covering my face with my free hand, leaning my neck back, and trying my hardest to stifle a groan through gritted teeth. This is hands down the most disastrous voice mail message ever recorded.

It's a few more "um"s and "uh"s until I give up and end the call.

My brain and mouth have failed me. But of course they would. Because how in the world could I sum up my feelings about our relationship in a single voice mail message?

It's not even close to possible.

Again I flop on the bed, my head spinning. The ringtone of my phone blares. It's Callum. I answer the phone, but I'm too scared to say anything.

"Um, Nikki?" Callum says after a second.

"Um, y-yeah?"

Callum is on the phone. With me. We're finally speaking. And I have no idea what to say.

We share a strained silence as I work up the nerve to say something, anything to get a conversation rolling between us.

"How's Lemon?" It's the only neutral topic I can think of.

He clears his throat. "That's actually why I'm calling. Can you come over? There's something you need to see."

. . .

I'm on autopilot the whole drive to Callum's, speeding past the slow-moving traffic. I didn't think to ask him what was wrong with Lemon, and he apparently didn't think to tell me. I park at his place in Wailea and run all the way to the door. I take a second to catch my breath before knocking. The door opens before I can even raise my arm. And just like that, with one look at his face, I'm breathless yet again.

His blank expression turns into a frown when he sees me. "Come on in."

Inside, I'm one giant stress knot. Now that I'm actually here with him, I'm on the spot. I don't know what the right thing to do or say is. So I just quietly follow him.

He, too, seems to be taking the silent route as he leads me to the bathroom down the hall. When he steps aside to let me look through the doorway, I'm speechless, but for an entirely different reason.

Next to the wall lies a cardboard box with a fluffy blanket stuffed in it. Lemon sits curled in a ball, three tiny fuzzballs pressed up against her stomach.

"She had her kittens?" I practically squeal.

I dart over to her, careful to kneel down slowly to avoid spooking her. She looks up at me with sleepy eyes, blinking every few seconds. When I scratch under her chin, she purrs instantly.

"Last night while we were asleep," Callum says behind me.

"Lemon, you're a mama," I whisper to her. "Congratulations, my girl."

I turn back to Callum, who sports a gentle smile. Seeing Lemon with her babies is like a reboot to our dynamic. It's easy to put all of our nonsense on hold when there's an adorable litter of newborn kittens to focus on.

"Finn woke up to use the loo this morning and saw her in the middle of the bathroom floor with these three little ones."

"No way." I let out a laugh of disbelief.

Callum nods to the box. "That was the best makeshift nursery cat bed we could come up with."

"You guys did a great job. She looks really happy."

I bend down again to pet Lemon and take in her litter. One is white with gray spots like her, one is all gray, and one is all white. With my index finger, I take a moment to give them all gentle pats.

"They are so cute it hurts," I say.

Callum lets out a soft chuckle, the sound like a hug to my heart. A dam inside of me breaks, and all of the old feelings come rushing back. Even though I'm facing away from him, I have to close my eyes while I let the ache inside of me pass.

When I turn back to him, he's standing in the open doorway with his hands in his pockets. "I thought you'd want to see them. I'm sorry I didn't let you know sooner. It was a bit chaotic dealing with everything at first, but I called you straightaway once I got everything sorted."

"Totally understand." I cross my arms, my gaze falling to the tile floor.

Now that the cuteness of the kittens has been discussed, we're back to this awkward shuffling of not knowing how to act around each other post-split.

I look up at him. "I'd like to help take care of the kittens, if that's okay."

"Absolutely. They are just as much yours as they are mine."

I nod, the pressure in my chest easing at the flow of our conversation.

We agree that they'll stay with Callum the next couple of weeks, then I'll take them to stay with me for a few weeks. We also agree to get Lemon spayed.

I reach into my pocket to grab some cash. "Here, let me pay for some of Lemon's food. She's nursing three little ones now."

But before I can even slip my hand out of my pocket, Callum takes a step forward and puts his hand over mine. I look up and we lock stares. He's just a few inches from me now, so close I can hear him breathe.

"You know I'm not going to take that." His voice is low, steady, kind, perfect. I miss hearing it; I miss being next to him so much.

I nod, tucking the money back into my pocket. He lets go of me and steps back to the open doorway. I take a seat on the edge of the tub and focus on the cats to steady myself. The cold porcelain against the backs of my legs is a welcome reset . . . until I remember that Callum and I shared countless naked sessions in this bathtub. When I glance up at him, he's flushed, his eyes scanning the empty tub behind me. I wonder if he's thinking about those same memories.

"What should we name them?" I ask, just to focus on something else.

"I'll leave that up to you."

"You sure? You didn't seem too crazy about the name Lemon when I first came up with it."

He gazes lovingly at the box before darting his eyes back to me. "It's grown on me."

"Let's wait awhile. It's been an eventful day already." I fixate back on the kittens.

He nods once. "Good plan."

I swallow, willing the heat inside of me to dissipate. It doesn't. In fact, the longer I stay in his presence, the hotter I feel. I need to say something before I combust. The messy aftermath of our argument is nowhere near resolved, but I need to tell him that I love him. He deserves to know.

I clear my throat. "We should talk. Don't you think?"

"About what?" Callum's frown throws me.

"About us," I say. "About what happened at the festival."

Disappointment flashes across his face. It makes my heart plummet to my feet.

When he purses his lips, I can tell he's choosing his words very, very carefully before he breaks me.

"Can we take a time-out on all of that?" he asks.

*Time-out*. Just like the one we took on the airplane. He suggested that one too. Only this time, it's not going to lead to flirty conversation and a newfound closeness between us. This time-out is going to hurt like hell.

"I think today should be about Lemon and her kittens," he says. "I don't want to taint the joy of it by bringing up ugly moments from the past."

His explanation is a total shock—and completely sweet. One part of me is aww-ing that he wants to keep today pure for Lemon and her kittens. But the other part of me is devastated that he rejected my attempt to hash things out between us.

I stand up. "I should go."

Callum moves from the doorway to let me out. I power walk to the front door, but just as my hand grips the knob, his voice stops me.

"Nikki, wait. I'm sorry, it's just—"

When I turn around, he's got that same pained expression on his face as the day we fell out at the Maui Food Festival. It's the same pain I feel now at his rejection. I steel myself anyway.

"It's fine."

I spin around, shutting the door behind me without another word.

# Chapter 21

It's okay, *anak*." Mom stirs a pot of soup on the stove top. "Give it some time."

It's barely seventy degrees—hardly soup weather. But the normal fall-like temperatures that compel people to cook hearty soups don't find their way to this part of the island. So anytime it dips below eighty, she thinks it's perfectly fine to whip up her specialty: a giant pot of chicken soup with bok choy, wild spinach, and whatever herbs and spices she has on hand.

She throws in a handful of pork rinds, and my mouth waters. The salty strips get all chewy in the broth, lending a yummy texture and flavor. Usually, she's right. Her soup has never failed to turn my mood around. But I'm not sure if it will work this time.

"Mom, I appreciate your pep talk and the soup, but you don't have to coddle me. I know how grim things look."

She pours a few ladles full of soup into a large bowl and sets it on the counter by the kitchen bar. I dip my spoon in, blow on the steaming liquid, and take a sip. The salty, satisfying liquid coats my throat. I close my eyes and hum in delight. She's right. My problems haven't magically disappeared, but having this soup to enjoy is the comfort I need right now.

Spinning around from the stove, she frowns. "No negative attitude allowed. You think you could magically make things better in one day?"

She shakes her head, turning back to the pot of soup. Carrying her own bowl of soup, she takes the stool next to me. "He told you he loved you, and you rejected him. That cuts deep. It takes time to earn back trust after that. Be patient."

We finish our soup in silence. I let her words soak in, wondering if she's right.

I do a mindless scroll through my phone. Chic TV has tagged our food truck in another Instagram post, and I smile reading all the congratulations from commenters. Tweets and messages inquiring about my and Callum's relationship are sprinkled throughout the mostly positive comments. I roll my eyes every time I come across an especially snarky one. But then I skim a few rebuttals from Penelope and smile to myself. It feels good to have a friend again.

A notification pops up that I have a message from a new follower. When I open the message, I almost drop my phone in my soup bowl. It's from Madeline, my old housemate in Portland and one of my best friends from my old job. She and I spent countless late nights and busy shifts together, always laughing and venting about our days when we arrived home.

> Hey, Nikki! I know it's been ages, but I follow Chic TV on Instagram and I saw that you and your mom won the Maui Food Festival! Congratulations!! So incredibly happy for you both! And I'm super excited to see that you're going to be in a commercial too! Just wanted to say that I've been rooting for you this whole time and I'm so, so proud of you ☺

With teary eyes, I find the last text she sent me, which was more than eight months ago. I never even bothered to answer her.

MADELINE: Hey. I just want you to know that I'm still thinking of you. Always. I don't mean to bother you when you're grieving, but please reach out when you're ready. Take all the time you need, okay? I'll always be here for you, Nikki.

My eyes burn. When I blink, a tear falls. But I'm not sad. I'm hopeful. If spending time with Penelope has shown me anything, it's that friendship is worth the effort.

I can still have my friend back. All I have to do is reach out. And that's exactly what I do. I open Instagram again and reply to her message.

> Hey, Madeline. Thank you so much. You have no idea what it means that you reached out to me ☺ I know it's been forever . . . I don't know what to say other than I'm sorry. Life's been kicking my ass, but I'm figuring it out. I totally understand if you're not up for reconnecting, but I wanted to say that I really miss you, I hope you're doing well, and I'd love to call you sometime if you're up for it.

I hit send and hope for a miracle.

"Not again," I mutter, looking down at my phone.

The number flashing across the screen makes me want to chuck it out the food truck window.

Still no contact from Callum. The only phone calls I seem to get lately are from bloggers wanting details about my and Callum's failed relationship or because they want us to name-drop them during our commercial slot with Chic TV, which we're filming at the end of the summer.

I dismiss the call and shove my phone back in my pocket. I don't have time for this madness when I have a gaggle of nosy vloggers and wannabe paparazzi crowding my food truck space. They've been hanging around, cutting in front of the customers in line, shoving people aside, and shouting questions at me sporadically throughout the day.

How any of them obtained my phone number is beyond me. Apparently, some of these food vloggers in Maui are aspiring to be paparazzi scum given how ruthlessly they've been behaving.

The warmth of Mom's hand on my arm is a tiny comfort. She looks up at me. "You ready to start the day, *anak*?"

I take a breath and nod.

When I open the window to the food truck, I'm promptly greeted with our usual line of customers. But at the very front are a handful of food vloggers I recognize from local blogs and YouTube channels elbowing one another. When they look up and see me, they shove their phones and cameras in my face.

"Nikki! Congrats on your win at the Maui Food Festival! Would you be willing to mention my blog in your commercial?" a high school–aged boy asks. I roll my eyes and say nothing.

A woman in sunglasses and a fedora shoves the high school kid to the side with her free arm, her other hand pointing her phone at my face. "Was your relationship with Callum real, Nikki? Or did you do it for the publicity?"

Mrs. Tokushige and Penelope stare daggers at the back of the fedora's head. Seeing them show up here day after day is much-needed comfort in this madness. There are a few more questions shouted from the crowd. And then someone asks if Callum is as skilled in the bedroom as he is in the kitchen. That's when my blood turns to magma.

I slam my hands on top of the metal countertop. "Listen the hell up!"

My shout silences every last one of the vloggers. The high schooler looks on with a shocked expression and mutters, "Yes, ma'am."

"My personal life isn't up for discussion. I'm also not interested in name-dropping any of you in a commercial when you've been harassing me and my customers every day since the festival. I'm here to cook and serve food, and you goddamn piranhas are crowding around my truck, making it impossible for my mother and me to serve our customers. Either get the hell out of the way so my customers can order, or else."

There's silence, followed by soft mutters. A scrawny white guy in the back of the crowd tucks his phone into his pocket and crosses his arms, stubborn written across his frown. "Or else what?"

Leaning my head back, I puff out all the hot air pent up in my body. He's the pissant who asked about Callum's bedroom performance. I swipe a bottle of lemon-lime soda from the counter and give it a dozen of the most violent shakes I can manage. I stomp out of the truck and up to the offending vlogger.

Even when I'm standing two inches from him, he has the audacity to smirk. But when I twist off the cap, a stream of soda smashes him square in the face. My frustration dissipates with each violent burst of carbonated liquid.

Stumbling back, he heaves a breath, then coughs. He wrings his hands, then rubs his eyes. "You have—you have no right!" he sputters.

I can't help but laugh, then turn around to the other vloggers. They all stand with dropped jaws and wide eyes. Slowly, they back away from the spectacle I've created, their gazes locked on me the entire time. It's like I'm some wild animal they've been warned about.

*Slowly walk away! No sudden movements! If you're not careful, she'll assault you with carbonated beverages!*

The offending vlogger wipes the moisture off his face with his arm. "That's assault! I'll call the police on you!"

I step forward so far into his space, he stumbles backward. Good. He's been in my space—on my food truck turf every day, acting like an entitled and rude asshole. It's time he gets a taste of his own medicine.

"And tell them what?" I bark back. "That you've been harassing me and my customers all morning—all week actually? Please do. You'll save me the trouble of picking up the phone. I was going to report you to them anyway."

Mrs. Tokushige walks up next to me, the look on her face something between determined and ferocious. "He elbowed me yesterday when I was standing in line. I think he's the reason I've got this bruise on my arm."

The stubborn vlogger is now irate. His wide eyes dart from me to Mrs. Tokushige, then back to me.

"So you've been physically assaulting people as well? I bet the police would love to hear that." I glare at him.

Penelope hops over to my other side. "The other day that guy tried to slip me a twenty to get me to tell him secrets about you. Scum."

"Bribery too?" I say. "Another interesting fact to relay to law enforcement."

I pat Penelope on the shoulder, thankful that she's more than just a customer now. We regularly meet up at each other's places for drinks and chats. I vent to her about the Callum situation and random life stresses. I learned her relationship with her ex-boyfriend ended the month after she moved to Maui for him when she caught him cheating. She almost booked a ticket back to her home in Cincinnati, but she decided to try making things work here on her own. So she put her Instagram hobby to professional use and started a social media consulting company, which explains her killer Instagram following and how she's free most days to take her lunch all the way out at my food truck in Makena. Right now, she's the greatest friend I could ask for.

I wink at her, then turn back to the offending vlogger, who opens his mouth to speak, but then starts coughing up leftover soda.

"I'd love to see you cited for your shitty behavior," I say. "Call the police. I dare you."

Instead of dialing the police or saying anything, he stomps past us and down the road, muttering curses along the way.

I hug Mrs. Tokushige and Penelope. "Thank you both. Seriously. He's been driving me insane. They all have actually."

Penelope pulls me into another hug. "I've got your back. And nothing will keep me from your delicious cooking, not even some douchebag paparazzi wannabe."

I turn to address the remaining vloggers. "Anyone else have anything to say?"

They all stand quietly while shaking their heads "no."

"Good. I have customers to feed. If you want to eat something, line up just like everyone else. If not, please get the hell out of here."

The remaining vloggers take their place in line.

Penelope walks back to the truck with me. "That's probably not going to be the last time they'll try to bother you."

"I know. But the prospect of being attacked with soda bombs should scare them off for a few days, though, right?"

Penelope chuckles and I hop back into the truck, where I'm greeted with Mom's disapproving frown. I can hear the words before she speaks them, about how unladylike it was for me to react that way, that she didn't raise her daughter to act like a barbarian just because someone was rude.

I sigh. "Okay. Let me have it."

A soft hand lands on my arm. She flashes a smile. "You gave that jerk exactly what he deserved."

She pulls me into a hug. My phone buzzing in my back pocket interrupts our embrace. Another unfamiliar number.

I muster my newfound boldness, endorsed by my mom, and pick up the phone. "I swear to God, if you call me one more time—"

"Um, is this Nikki DiMarco?" It's a shaky English accent on the other end of the phone. Not Callum's though. My chest throbs.

"Who is this?"

"Ted, from Travaasa Hana." He clears his throat. My face promptly bursts into flames. "Sorry, is this a bad time?"

With my free hand, I cover my eyes. Like that will do much good while I'm dying of embarrassment on my end of this phone conversation. I just snapped at the general manager of the Travaasa Hana resort. Well done me.

"I'm sorry, I thought you were someone else."

"It's quite all right." He lets out a good-natured laugh. "Things have been stressful lately, haven't they?"

His soft tone, the obvious empathy in his voice helps dial back the embarrassment a touch. I wonder if he's read all the crazy stuff online about Callum and me. I wonder if he's seen the shaky video of us having it out at the festival. Last I checked, which was a few days ago, the video that @IEatEverything posted was up to nearly fifty thousand views. So yeah, he's probably seen it.

I swallow back the urge to groan out loud.

Ted clears his throat again. "I was wondering if you were still interested in being our featured chef at the resort once a week."

"Oh."

Memories of the night Callum and I served a surprise three-course Easter dinner at a high-end resort on a total whim swoop through me. I blink and see Callum's full lips stretched into a satisfied smile when we finished serving, every single diner raving about our dishes. I blink again and see his naked form in the hot tub of our room. I remember his hands on my body, his breath on my skin, his heart beating so hard, I felt it inside me.

I hear the words he spoke to me in that delicious guttural whisper.

*Good would be doing this with you every day. Good would be getting you to admit when you're jealous and want only me. Good would be calling you mine.*

Given the way he shut me down at his condo the other day and how I haven't heard from him since, he wouldn't be interested in working with me ever again. A lump lodges in my throat. It's a second before I can collect myself and answer Ted.

"I'm sorry, Ted. I can't. As much as I want to, I just don't think I can handle prepping another dinner with Callum. We had a falling out, in case you hadn't heard."

The awkward pause and throat clear on the other end of the line tells me he did indeed hear about it, just as I suspected.

"I'm sorry, I should clarify," Ted says. "Callum won't be part of this. I want to contract you and only you to serve a weekly dinner at the resort restaurant. Would you be interested?"

When the words sink in, I nearly drop my phone. "I don't understand . . ."

Ted waits a beat before speaking. "Look, I'm sorry to hear about you and Callum not working out, but between you and me, he voluntarily stepped down when I called him about it a few days ago. He said he didn't want to do the weekly service because he didn't have it in him. He said you would do a better job of it anyway."

I'm rendered speechless once more.

"Honestly, Nikki, he doesn't give out compliments easily."

I remember Ted making that exact same comment the night Callum and I collaborated on Easter dinner.

"I've been friends with Callum for years, and I've never known him to gush about anyone like he does about you," Ted says. "It's certainly a significant gesture that he would do something like this."

Ted's words trigger an image of Callum and me cuddled on his couch guzzling pink champagne while watching *The Office*. Our playful discussion of romantic gestures replays in my mind, how I said I preferred low-key ones—kind of like what he's done for me just now.

My heart thuds. I swear it reverberates all the way to my throat. Maybe this is his way of showing he remembers what's important to me—that I'm still important to him. Maybe it's a signal that we can be something more. And maybe it's my turn to show him how much he still means to me.

Ted clears his throat, cluing me in on the fact that I've said nothing for several seconds. I refocus.

"So what do you say? Are you still interested in my offer to have you cook at Travaasa?" he asks again.

He explains how much it will pay, and I have to bite my tongue to keep from squealing. Adding that to our weekly food truck earnings and the festival prize money would give our savings the boost we need. Ted also mentions the prospect of heading special event dinners throughout the year. I have to remind myself that it's unprofessional to cheer loudly while on the phone with my prospective new boss.

This is it. This is the opportunity I've been waiting for, the chance to showcase just how much I can do when someone gives me an empty kitchen, a fridge full of ingredients, and creative freedom. It's the big break I've been aching for since I set foot on Maui.

I take a breath and finally speak. "I'm absolutely interested."

Ted says he'll email me the official offer and contract soon. I hang up, feeling an ounce lighter than I did when I answered the phone.

I turn to relay the news to Mom, who takes a break from taking orders to squeal, then pulls me into a jump hug.

"Oh, I'm so proud of you!"

She chats about how she's going to book a holiday dinner at Travaasa for her book club so she and her friends can try my gourmet menu.

I smile till my cheeks ache. Then I go to the truck window and wave over Penelope to see if she can help me pull off the idea that popped in my head while talking to Ted.

"So this is going to sound nuts, but hear me out."

"You ready to do this?" Penelope glances at me as we sit side by side at my dining room table.

"Definitely."

I smooth the low ponytail that's slung over my shoulder with one hand, then run my other hand over the fabric of the silky blouse I'm wearing. This is the most dressed up I've been in weeks. But today's the day I need to pull out all the stops.

"Okay," she says. "Then let's get started."

She adjusts her phone, which sits atop the table, so that there's a clear shot of her and me on the screen.

I'm about to make the grandest gesture I can think of. For Callum. My stomach is doing roundhouse kicks at the thought of how personal I'm about to get.

In the end, it will all be worth it. I hope.

I glance at Mom, who's watching from the living room. She flashes that same encouraging smile she used to give me when I was nervous about a test or presentation in school. "You're going to do great, *anak*."

"Thank you, Mom." I really, really hope so.

Penelope pulls up Instagram on her phone, then starts to stream a live video. My heart thuds against my chest harder than ever before. I've never done a live interview on social media before, let alone one where I'm about to get this personal. From the inside of my chest it feels like my heart and lungs are playing the bongos. The frenzied movement even shakes the fabric of my white blouse. But that's just the adrenaline talking. I *want* to do this.

Penelope tucks her blond hair behind her ear then smiles at the screen. "Hey, everyone. I know you're used to seeing live videos of me chowing down on yummy food or filming gorgeous sunsets, but we're trying something a bit different today."

She turns her attention to me. "Today I'm over the moon to have Nikki DiMarco with me. She runs the delicious Tiva's Filipina Kusina food truck with her mom, Tiva. It's the best eatery on Maui, as evidenced by their recent Maui Food Festival win. But sadly, that's been a bit overlooked due to the way a lot of food vloggers and island paparazzi have been prying into your personal life."

"That's true, unfortunately," I say.

"And you wanted to set the record straight."

I nod, reminding myself to breathe. Even though it's only me, Penelope, and Mom in the condo right now, I can practically feel the eyes of thousands of viewers on me at this moment.

But that's what I want. I want everyone to hear what I have to say once and for all.

Penelope flashes another gentle smile that helps ease the nerves whirring inside. "The floor is yours."

I inhale, then exhale, then dive right in. "First of all, thank you so much for letting me do this. I guess I could have done this on Tiva's Instagram, but we have a fraction of your followers. And whenever you post or do a live video, you get an insane number of views and likes and comments. And I want as many people as possible to see this, because this is the only time I'll ever openly discuss my relationship with Callum James from Hungry Chaps."

With a single inhale, my heartbeat slows. "I met Callum when he and his brother, Finn, parked next to my truck near Big Beach almost four months ago. We started out as rivals, nothing more. That competition between us was one hundred percent real. So was the Maui Food Festival wager we made. I'm guessing most of the people watching this now saw videos of Callum and me arguing. Those were one hundred percent real too."

When I think back to those ridiculous antics we pulled on each other, I don't cringe like I used to. Instead, my chest aches. I pause to take another breath and steady myself.

"Our relationship was also real."

I glance down at my hands folded in my lap. I wonder what Callum is doing right now.

"Close quarters can breed attraction just as effectively as it can breed contempt," I say.

Even though Penelope knows all this, she stares at me with wide eyes, like she's hearing it for the first time. I bet she's wondering if I'll elaborate for everyone who's watching. I won't. That unlikely chance of Callum and me being seated together on the plane ride to London is what changed everything. But I'm not sharing that with them. That's personal, something I'll lock away forever next to my heart, in that little space I keep Callum. It's special and secret and belongs to no one else.

Another breath and I continue. "Every single thing that happened between Callum and me was real. Our initial dislike for each other, the tension between us, our attraction, our arguments, our relationship."

Our kisses, the glances we stole during busy workdays, the desperate way we touched each other every single time we were together in private. The love between us, even though I waited too long to acknowledge it.

I rest my hands on my hips to steady myself. Looking at the ground seems to help. I take a much-needed breath. "We didn't fake a single thing."

This time when I breathe, I feel as light as the breeze flowing in through the window. Everything I've been holding in, everything I've been hiding, every secret that's been cooking me from the inside out these past few months is out. It's the most freeing feeling.

I finally let myself look at her phone screen. My eyes bulge when I see that several thousand people are currently viewing this livestream.

And then I decide to go with this newfound open attitude and look straight at the screen. "Any questions?"

It only takes a few seconds for the first question to pop up.

Penelope leans in to read it aloud. "Do you still keep in contact with Callum?"

For a second I contemplate answering with "not really," since I have technically spoken to Callum since our breakup . . . just not recently. But that answer is sure to garner a wave of speculative follow-up questions that could lead to even more rumors, so I squash it. Instead I just shake my head and say, "No."

"Do you know where he is? What he's doing now?" Penelope reads.

"Unfortunately not."

She hesitates before reading the next question. "Do you think there's any hope of reconciliation for you two?"

"I . . . I hope so."

"Do you love Callum?" Penelope practically winces when she reads it. She knows the answer. I told her. But she also knows how heartbreaking it is for me to bring up the word "love" when it comes to Callum because of how badly I messed things up the one time he told me he loved me.

I can feel my answer in every bone, every muscle, every beat of my heart, every inhale, every exhale, every blink. When it's this deep inside, it's obvious on the outside too. It's in my eyes, my body language, the tone in which I speak. I bet every single person watching me now can tell I'm still in love with Callum. Because I am. And I hope when he sees this, he'll believe me.

"Yes, I do love him."

"Is one more question okay?" Penelope asks in a gentle whisper.

I nod.

"If you could say anything to Callum right now, what would you say?"

"I would tell him that I'm sorry for how I hurt him, that I've never loved anyone the way I love him." I pause to steady my voice. "I would tell him that my biggest regret in life is not giving us a fair shot when he asked me to. And if I could go back and do things differently, I would in a heartbeat."

With the last of my words comes more silence. I blink, and then come the tears. Just a few, and I quickly wipe them away. But I'm not embarrassed. I didn't anticipate crying today, but I did. Because I was open and honest and free. That's nothing to be ashamed of. That's me being me.

I sniffle, wiping my nose on my arm. "I think that's all I can manage. Sorry."

Penelope's eyes glisten with tears when she looks at me. "Don't be sorry." Then she hugs me. "You're amazing, Nikki," she whispers in my ear. "I'm so, so proud of you."

When she lets me go, she wipes her eyes then addresses the phone screen. "Well, that's it, everyone. Thanks for joining us."

Penelope ends the video just as Mom hurries over to hug me too. "I'm so proud of you, *anak*. Callum will love it." She sniffles, then leans away so she can cup my face in her hands. Tears shine in her eyes. "I just know it."

Doubt lingers at the back of my mind. My grand romantic gesture of publicly declaring my love for Callum was a risky call for sure, but I had to try. Now all that's left is to wait and see what he does.

Penelope zips to the bathroom while Mom announces she's going to fry up some *lumpia* to ease our nerves after such a tense event. I stand next to her in the kitchen and help her with the prep.

"Our girl really put herself out there today, Harold. For love," she says as she dunks a half dozen *lumpia* in hot oil. "You'd be so proud of her."

# Chapter 22

I weave my way through the booths at the Aloha Maui Farmer's Market in a daze. Three days since my romantic grand gesture and no word from Callum. Penelope even saved my live video on her Instagram highlights in case he didn't catch it right away. But it doesn't look like he's going to see it at all. If that's not a crystal clear sign that I've misread absolutely everything about us, then I don't know what is.

I survey the array of fruits, vegetables, and other yummy goods surrounding me to distract myself from that sobering fact. Keeping busy in the aftermath of his silent rejection is a must. Even though we were never officially together, our time apart hurts worse than when I called it quits with any past boyfriend. Filling my time with work, menu planning for Travaasa Hana, farmer's market visits, and spending time with Penelope is the way I cope.

Swimming at Big Beach helps too. No more early morning swims at Little Beach though. Too much of a risk of running into Callum. Given his radio silence, he's made it abundantly clear he wants nothing to do with me.

I survey a *lilikoi* at a nearby stand, wondering if the passion fruit *semifreddo* I'm planning to serve for dessert at Travaasa Hana will wow like I hope. It's two weeks until my first solo dinner service, and I want to blow everyone away.

My phone buzzing in my pocket pulls my mind back to the present and away from imaginary meal planning. An alert from Instagram. When I see it's a message from Madeline, I let out a squeal so giddy that the people next to me gawk like I've grown another head.

Nikki! Oh my gosh, you have NO idea how happy I am to hear from you! Please, don't apologize. I'm beyond thrilled you got in touch with me! How are you? Have you filmed your commercial yet? What else have you been up to? Sorry I didn't message you back sooner; things have been so busy! But now I'm all good! OMG OMG OMG Tell me everything!

The smile on my face won't budge. Even after all this time, Madeline is happy to hear from me. And she still wants to be my friend.

I start to type a response answering all of her questions, but stop when I realize I want to call her. I want to actually speak to my friend. So I tell her.

ME: SO happy to hear from you, Madeline! I have so much to tell you!! Can I call you sometime?

MADELINE: Um, hell yes! Are you free tonight? I can call you after I get done with my shift at the restaurant

Just the mention of my old restaurant sends a jolt through my chest. I want to hear about Madeline, about the restaurant, about absolutely everything.

I tell her that I'm open for a chat this evening and can't wait to catch up. She responds with a half dozen smiley face emojis.

A squeal pulls my attention to the crowd behind me. I slide my phone back in my pocket and watch as a crowd of market goers slowly forms to watch a couple standing in the scenic grassy area several feet away. A handsome Thor look-alike with short curly hair is down on one knee, ring box in hand, smiling up at a pretty *hapa* woman. She's late twenties and beaming, tears in her eyes, blinking like she can't believe the sight in front of her.

It's all the telltale signs of a proposal: her cupping her mouth with both hands, tears of joy streaming down her cheeks, nonstop nodding before he can even get the question out. Everyone—even those in the nosebleed section in the back of the crowd—knows what he's about to say.

"Will you marry me?" he asks.

"Tate! Of course I will!" she sob-laughs.

The entire crowd bursts into applause at her answer. Her fiancé slides the dazzling ring on her finger before popping to his feet and pulling her into a hug. There's a kiss that I suspect is more passionate than those two would usually indulge in publicly due to the occasion. Because they're seconds into their engagement and basking in one of the happiest, most romantic moments of their lives.

The blissed-out couple finally turns to the cheering crowd around them, their faces displaying twin gigantic smiles. Even I join in on the clapping. I may be navigating a romantic low at the moment, but their joy is contagious. This couple is insanely in love, and any decent person should acknowledge that.

The man standing in front of me lets out an enthusiastic "whoop" while clapping, then spins around. My smile drops. It's Finn.

The stunned expression on his face when he sees me lasts only a second. He softens to a polite smile. "Exciting times at the farmer's market."

I don't say anything. It's not possible with my tongue at the back of my throat. Finn, the brother of the man I love—the man I lost—is standing in front of me. What on earth could I possibly say to him?

When I'm silent for a solid five seconds, he clears his throat. "We need to stop running into each other like this." He laughs, the stilted sound a giveaway for how uneasy he is. "Because, you know . . . remember the last time we, um, saw each other at the market?"

I let out the breath I'm holding, and all the muscles in my neck loosen. This is clearly just as awkward for him, but he's making an effort to be pleasant. I should too.

"How have you been, Finn?"

"Good. Busy."

"How are Lemon and the kittens?" I'm dying to visit them, but I'm not sure how I can bridge the gap of Callum's rejection to ask if I can take them for a while.

He beams when I mention them. "Adorable. It turns out the gray one's a girl and the two others are boys."

I'm about to ask if they're leaning toward any names yet when a stunning brunette woman saunters up to Finn. He turns to her, scoops her hand in his, and pecks her lips. I have to physically restrain myself from saying "aww" out loud. Finn and his lady are ridiculously cute together. There must be something in the water. Everyone around me has been bitten by the love bug, it seems.

She smiles at me and sticks out her hand. "I'm Grace."

Returning the pleasantry, I shake her hand. Then I pause while still gripping her. The memory of hiding in Callum's closet while he talked to Finn slingshots to the front of my mind. This is the woman Finn was gushing about.

"Oh, *you're* Grace!"

They're both speechless at my comment. I have a lot of explaining to do.

"I um . . ." I attempt a smile. "This is going to sound terribly creepy, but do you remember Easter weekend when you two went camping at Haleakala?"

Confusion mars their faces as they nod. I quickly explain how I overhead Callum's conversation with Finn while I was hiding in his closet, back when we were trying to keep our relationship under wraps.

Grace chuckles while Finn bursts into laughter.

"Wow. You were quite committed to keeping things with Callum a secret, weren't you?" he says.

"We figured it would be easier that way," I say.

Grace excuses herself to check out the jewelry stand next to us.

Finn shakes his head. "Maybe you thought it would be easier, Nikki. But all Callum wanted was to make things official with you."

"It took me a while to see that," I mutter. "I thought we both were fine with the casual thing. I know I wasn't his one and only."

This time the wrinkles in his forehead read confused.

"You don't have to cover for him, Finn. While I was hiding in the closet, I overheard you two talking about that other woman he was seeing."

"What other woman?"

"Don't you remember? That same conversation when you were talking about going camping with Grace, you asked when he was going to spill his guts to that woman he was into, that woman he had history with."

Finn tilts his head to the side, his face making a seamless transition from confusion to clarity. "Nikki. I was talking about you."

Finn's words from that morning echo in my head.

*It's so bloody obvious how you feel about her. You've got history together. Why don't you just tell her already. No use in putting it off . . .*

"Ever since Callum met you, you've been the only woman on his radar," Finn says. "And despite everything that happened between you two, you still are."

My throat tightens. I want to believe Finn more than anything, but he could be mistaken. We were able to hide a good chunk of our relationship from him for a while. Maybe he's in the dark about Callum's true feelings now too.

Finn pats my shoulder.

I sniffle. "I guess it doesn't matter now since my grand gesture for him was a total fail."

"What grand gesture?"

I give him a brief summary of the live video on Penelope's Instagram where I declared my love for Callum, hoping that he'd hear about it over social media and reach out to me.

A bewildered look flashes across Finn's face. "I doubt Callum has even seen it."

"How do you know that?"

"A couple of the volunteers at the animal clinic in Paia quit, so we've been helping out there when we're not at the food truck. Even I haven't had a chance to keep up with all the social media happenings, and that's part of my job for Hungry Chaps. And if I missed out on it, Callum certainly has. He's pretty much been working from sunup until bedtime this past week. This is our first day off in a while actually."

My head spins at this influx of new information. If what Finn says is true, if Callum really has been too busy to see my grand gesture, then I may still have a chance.

"He's home right now. You should go see him." There's a glimmer in Finn's eye, like he knows that despite his reassuring words, the only way I can be completely sure is to hear it from Callum.

He turns to Grace, and they wave good-bye.

The tiniest sliver of hope bursts inside of me. If Finn's so sure about this, maybe I should believe him.

I take off in a jog to my car and head for Callum's condo. With each mile I clock, my breath quickens. I speed along the road, taking each turn and sharp corner like I'm a deranged race car driver. It's not reckless driving; it's purposeful. I've got a man to declare my love for. I ease my foot off the gas pedal when I reach ten miles past the speed limit. I highly doubt that if I were pulled over for speeding, the officer would care for my excuse of breaking the law in the name of love. I can just imagine the eye roll before the officer sternly scrawls my ticket.

I dial it back to the speed limit and take a deep breath. My heart is racing, my hands are clammier than ever, and I'm gripping onto my steering wheel like I'm trying to strangle it.

When I pull up to his street, I force myself to take another deep breath. I spot his car in the driveway, and my heartbeat takes on a frenzied pace. Should I blurt "I love you" when I see him? Should I start off with a calm and casual, "Hello, how are you?" instead? Should I run up and kiss him first?

"It's okay," I coach myself with a whisper. The thundering in my chest and all my warring thoughts come to a halt. The words will come to me when I see him.

I zero in on the door to his condo. Slowly, I peel my hands off the steering wheel and reach for my car door handle.

Just then his condo door opens. Out walks a stunning redhead. My hand freezes on the handle of my door, and my heart seizes in my chest. He follows closely behind, the grin on his face just as wide as hers.

This time when I try to breathe, the air lodges in my throat, like I'm choking on a piece of cement. It's like I'm paralyzed, unable to cry or scream, even though my body aches to do both. But all I can do is gawk with unblinking, unbelieving eyes at the scene in front of me.

Halfway to his car, she stops to show him something on her phone. A warm breeze swoops up her fiery locks. She looks like a beauty queen with her porcelain skin, those delicate facial features, and killer curves. The kind of woman both men and women stop dead in their tracks to stare at because you wouldn't believe a human being could look so beautiful unless you saw it with your own eyes.

I stare not in envy, but in utter sadness. Because the sight of this gorgeous woman means one thing: I'm too late.

The two stand close to each other, close enough to let me know that this isn't a friend. No matter what Finn thinks about Callum's feelings for me, this is someone special.

Seconds later, the two throw their heads back in laughter. A funny video or text message, I presume. They stand and chat, still smiling, still laughing. And I watch it all, slinking low in my seat, like an obsessed stalker who can't believe her eyes.

But I have to believe it. Because it's true.

Callum is off the market. It wouldn't matter if I ran up and kissed him, then told him I loved him. He's no longer available. He's with her now because I was too much of a closed-off jerk to recognize what I could have had when he offered it to me.

And because of that, he will never, ever be mine.

He leads her with his hand on the small of her back to the car and opens the door for her. I wait until they're both in before I peel out on the road, speeding away in a cloud of burnt rubber. The toxic stench assaults my nostrils every time I take a breath, but I don't care. I just need to get the hell away from here as fast as I can.

I try to swallow back the sob at the back of my throat. Hot tears crowd my eyes until I can't hold them back any longer. I blink, and it's like a dam breaking.

It's not like there's anyone watching me. I'm alone in the car, speeding to nowhere in particular, and now there's a rock in my stomach. It's regret and sadness balled into one. And it's all my fault.

A million what-ifs fly through my mind.

What if I hadn't been so stubborn?

What if I hadn't been so closed off?

What if I had just let my guard down and taken a risk?

I wipe my runny nose with the back of my hand. It's not like poring over these doubts does any good now.

I stare at the road ahead through my blurry vision. Crying won't solve anything, I know that. But somehow I need to leach out this pain, this frustration, this sorrow. The rock in my stomach is now a boulder. Inside, I scold myself for not consuming anything this morning except for some crappy French herbal tea I found at the back of the pantry.

A minute later the boulder burns. Grief and regret have a funny effect on my GI system, because I'm suddenly nauseous. Christ on a stick, I'm going to be sick. Great. That's just what I need after watching the man I love pair up with someone new from fifteen feet away.

When the acid in my stomach curdles, I have to swallow back a heave. I've got seconds before vomiting. Yanking on the steering wheel, I pull to the side of the road and open my car door just in time to puke that French herbal tea onto the concrete.

# Chapter 23

"Are we good, Nikki?" Penelope asks from the back of the food truck.

It's the end of another busy day at Makena Road, and both Penelope and I are ready to head home.

"I think so," I say.

We step out of the food truck, and I hand her the keys. "Thank you again for helping out today. You have no idea how much I appreciate it."

Penelope scrunches her face and waves her hand. "Oh, please. It was my pleasure. All those times I begged you to let me work the truck and you finally caved. I had a great time."

She smiles, not an ounce of fatigue apparent in her cheery expression or sparkling blue eyes even though we just pulled a ten-hour shift. I pull her in for a bear hug. She saved my skin today when Mrs. Tokushige's nephew called in sick. It was Mom's day off, and I dreaded asking her to fill in at the last minute, even though I know she happily would have.

Penelope and I break apart, but she keeps hold of my arms. "Anytime you need an extra hand, call me. My schedule is flexible, and I love working here."

I chuckle. "You've only done it once so far."

"I know, but it was amazing. Seriously. I thrive in fast-paced environments."

It's true. Penelope was a natural, balancing orders, helping me with the food prep, and cleaning up like she's been doing it for years. I don't know if I've ever worked with anyone who caught on that quickly.

It's been two days since upchucking my tea on the open road, and I'm on the path back to normal. No more annoying vloggers asking me invasive personal questions. They still show up, but to order the food and film themselves chowing down for their websites like they used to do.

"You were amazing on the live video," Penelope says as we make our way to the front of the truck. "I know I've said that a million times, but I mean it. You were so bold to do it."

"Yeah, but it didn't really work out." I wince at what a sad sack I sound like.

She stops in front of the driver's side door. "Don't say that. You put yourself out there. That took major balls."

I smile softly at her phrasing.

"You ready to head home?" She opens the door.

I reach for the bag I packed under the front seat. "Actually, I think I want to go for a swim at Little Beach tonight."

It's been ages since I've seriously entertained the thought of swimming there. It used to be my go-to place to decompress when life and work got to be too much. But ever since the falling-out with Callum, I haven't dared to set foot there. The thought of running into him sends me into near hives, even more so now that he has someone new and I could possibly see them together.

But it's eight thirty on a weeknight in the middle of the summer, meaning the beach will be crowded. He probably won't be there since he prefers early-morning swims. But if he is, it's unlikely he would see me through the crowd.

"You sure?" Penelope asks.

"Positive."

"But what if you run into . . . you know . . ." She frowns, her worry radiating all the way from her furrowed brow to her scrunched lips.

Since becoming friends, I've filled her in on why Little Beach is such a hot-button topic for me: how early-morning swims there used to be my lifeblood and that first off-the-charts awkward run-in with a naked Callum.

I grab her hand in a gentle squeeze. "It's okay, Penelope. You can say his name."

"I just don't want to bring up sad memories."

"I know," I say softly. I'm lucky to have a friend like Penelope who cares about how I feel, who goes out of her way to make sure I'm doing well.

"It's just . . ." Her perfectly shaped eyebrows furrow in concern. "I know things are still raw, and I don't want to make it worse by saying the wrong thing."

"That means so much. But I'm moving on. And part of moving on is normalizing things that used to set me off. So you can say his name. I'm totally fine with it. You don't have to walk on eggshells around me, okay?"

"Totally fine?" She raises an eyebrow.

I purse my lips at how easily she calls my bluff. I am light-years away from "totally fine." Every day I still think of Callum. Because every day something happens to remind me of him. All it takes is a flash of golden hair in my peripheral vision or someone with an English accent ordering from the truck. I think of him cradling me into his chest when we slept, his perfect smile, his sandalwood cologne that always gave me goose bumps every time I took a breath. Of how I always, always felt at home in his presence.

In these moments, it's a battle to get myself back on track. I try everything and anything. I breathe extra deep, take an extra long pause if I'm speaking, or close my eyes to collect myself for a moment.

But every day I do it because I have to. It's the only way to move on.

One day I won't have to silently tell myself to breathe until the pain passes. One day I'll just instinctively do it. One day my chest won't tighten, my eyes won't water, my breath won't catch. One day it won't hurt anymore.

"Okay, not one hundred percent fine," I say with a sigh. "But I'm managing. Every day is easier. Callum is a hell of a guy to get over, but I'll get there. Eventually."

She gives me another hug. "I'm so proud of you for how you're moving on. Want me to wait here in the truck until you're finished swimming so I can give you a ride home?"

I shake my head. "No, it's okay. I'll get an Uber. You should go home and rest. You worked so hard."

I head to the back of the food truck to change, taking in the new look of the exterior. Penelope even helped me apply a fresh coat of paint on the food truck the other day, then touched up the images and lettering.

I pop out and pull her into a hug. "Thank you. For everything. I'm beyond lucky to have you as a friend."

I slip her an envelope with her pay for the day, plus a little extra for her help with painting. I try and fail to keep my mouth from stretching into a grin that would give away the surprise. I can't help it though. Just a few months ago I was struggling to break even, but now, I'm thriving and can afford a surprise like this. It's a game-changing feeling of accomplishment.

I wave to Penelope as she drives away, then make my way to Big Beach. The walk across Big Beach to Little Beach is long, but it's what I need after hours of nonstop cooking and serving. I weave around the haphazard array of locals and tourists lying on the beach. Gazing at the crystal-blue waves crashing against the sand is the reset I ache for after being on my feet all day.

I cross the rocky mound that separates Big Beach and Little Beach without tripping or scrambling. My legs and feet remember the path perfectly, even though it's been months.

Just then my phone buzzes with a text from Madeline.

Hey!! SO good chatting with you the other night! I absolutely cannot wait to come see you next month ☺

I type back that I'm equally psyched. We've chatted a couple of times on the phone, and it's like no time has passed at all. There are no pleasantries to power through before we feel comfortable. We simply dive back into chatting about our day, our rants, our raves. It feels so good to have my friend back. When I asked her to come visit, I wasn't even nervous. And when she said yes, I bolted up from my bed, bursting with excitement.

I'm itching to show her around the island I now call home, to take her to my favorite eateries and beaches. Comfort sets in. Before I know it, I'm beaming. Finally, after all the struggle and uncertainty, it feels like I earned my spot here on this island, like I belong. Like I'm home.

I'm nowhere near Baldwin Beach, but I whisper assurances to my dad, certain he's listening.

"It's all going to be good, Dad. Just like I promised."

Before, I always had to be home or at Baldwin to feel connected to him. But right now, I feel closer to him than I ever have since he's been gone. Because I know now that no matter where I am or where I go, he's always with me.

I peer at the scene around me. Little Beach is exactly what I expected. Crazy crowded, a mix of clothed and naked beachgoers in the sand and water. I walk a few feet, staying at the edge of the beach, and drop my towel in the sand. Shedding my flip-flops, shorts, and tank top, I head for the shoreline. Instead of diving in, I curl my toes into the wet sand, the water lapping at my feet. I scan the waves ahead of me. A few dozen people swim and splash. I'll need to take extra care not to run into anyone if I want to do proper laps today.

When I take a step forward, a large shadow appears next to me in the water. I twist to my right to acknowledge the person and make room. And then I promptly forget how to breathe, how to walk, how to talk.

Bare-chested Callum stands exactly one foot away from me. "Nikki."

I open my mouth to say hello, but no words form. Only stuttered air. Clamping my mouth shut, I take a moment to swallow.

*Breathe first, then talk.*

"Callum," I finally say.

"It's so good to see you." His words are a contrast to the indecipherable expression on his face. I can't tell if he's glad or upset that I'm here.

"I'm so happy to see you." A breathy chuckle follows my words. It's that laugh of disbelief that always comes when I'm overwhelmed or shocked. "How . . . What . . . How have you been?"

I bite my tongue, riding out the wave of embarrassment coursing through me. I guess my mouth didn't hang onto the memo my brain just sent. My eyes do a measured once-over of his body. It probably looks like I'm ogling him, but I don't care. My gaze moves slowly, like I'm surveying a swath of land I'm about to excavate. He looks good. Happy, even. In his shirtless state, I see that leanly muscled build I miss so much. His golden hair is cropped close to his scalp. He must have gotten a haircut recently. There's about a week's worth of blond stubble on his face too. He looks absolutely delicious.

His smile fades, the edge of it turning sad. "I've been all right. How have you been?"

"Um, okay." Instinctively, I cross my arms. My eyes drop to my feet, which are now covered in wet sand. I jerk my gaze back up at him. "Work's been busy."

"I heard."

One corner of his mouth curves up into the sweetest, most endearing half smile ever. I could cry, it's so damn beautiful. And after tonight, I'll probably never see it again.

"I took your advice," I blurt, just to keep from bursting into tears.

His faces turns curious. "Oh?"

"I reached out to one of my friends in Oregon. Madeline. She's coming to visit me." I swallow, commanding the tears not to fall. "You were right. She understood everything, just like you said she would."

This time when he smiles, it's with his eyes. His entire face is warmth and softness. It makes my heart thud so hard, I'm scared it will fly out of my chest.

"I'm so happy to hear that."

"Are you really? Happy, I mean." The words fall out before I realize what I've said. But I want to know. I *have* to know. Even after all we've been through, after how things ended between us, Callum deserves to be happy. Everything in me hopes that he truly is.

There's a slight twist to his expression that makes him look mildly pained. My heart lands in the pit of my stomach. He's still hurt, still reeling. Because of me.

He sighs, eyes still on me "It's been a bit rough since we . . . well, you know." Clearing his throat, he drops his eyes to my sand-covered feet, then lifts them back up to my face. "Lemon and the kittens miss you."

"I'm dying to see them and give them a cuddle." I smile at the thought of them. "How are they?"

"Playful and curious. And always hungry. Lemon's been a great mum, though, always keeping them in check." Callum lets out a chuckle, his face turning joyful when he talks about them.

"Finn told me there are two boys and a girl."

He nods. "You still have to help name them."

I wonder how exactly we'll figure out cat custody now that we're over and he's paired up with someone else. I'm about to bring it up when he speaks again.

"Congratulations by the way," he says. "I know I left a comment on Instagram, but I never knew if you saw it, and I wanted to say it in person too."

"Thank you. I did. You were so sweet to do that."

His eyebrows wrinkle, concern painting his face. "I'm sorry for what I said to you at the festival, how dismissive I was. I was out of line. I know how much your work means to you, what it means for your mum. I always have. I just didn't . . . I just wasn't thinking straight in the moment. I was so caught up in my feelings at the time."

*At the time.*

Of course. Because now everything has changed between us. He doesn't feel the same way about me anymore.

I pause, biting my lip. I still owe him an apology. Now's my chance, to finally say what I've been aching to say to him for weeks, even if it won't change a thing. "I'm so, so sorry, Callum. For how I lashed out at you, for how I didn't even give us a fighting chance."

My voice trembles. I can't help the sadness coursing through me. It's been lying dormant inside me for weeks, but now that he's in front of me, it explodes, like lava bursting through a crack in the earth.

"I know I messed up big-time," I say. "And I just want you to know that I regret what I said to you." Despite the way my voice quivers, I hope he can hear just how much I mean it.

Tears fall, but this time I don't bother to wipe them away.

His face twists, then softens. "Nikki—"

"Wait, just let me finish." My voice trips on a sob. "My mom pointed out to me not so long ago that I've been pushing people away ever since I lost my dad. And just like you said, I was afraid of getting hurt—because I didn't want to lose another person like I lost my dad. I was just too scared to admit it."

I stop to take a breath. Callum's chest heaves up and down in unison with me.

"I know it's too late to fix things between us, but I just wanted to tell you how sorry I am. You deserve an apology."

The words "I love you" spark on the edge of my tongue. I even open my mouth, but I don't say it. Because what good would that do, to tell him I love him when he's with someone else now? It would just add to the stockpile of pain.

With a swallow, I erase the words. The pause between us stretches. All I hear are crashing waves and the sound of chatter around us.

I wipe both palms of my hands against my soaked cheeks, sniffling. "I've wanted to tell you that for a while now. I even . . ."

I contemplate explaining my romantic grand gesture, but I stop myself. What would be the point of that? I bend down to rinse the snot and tears from my hands in the warm ocean water. Callum watches, still saying nothing.

"I should have found you sooner so I could apologize in person, but I don't even know where you're working now," I say.

"Kahului. By the airport."

"Oh. That's good. Really good. You probably get a steady funnel of tourists who arrive from their flights starving."

"Nikki—"

A sound like a joyless laugh spurts from me. "That's actually genius. Why didn't I think of that when I first moved here?"

"The only reason we managed to land that spot in Kahului is because another food truck had just closed. It was all luck and timing. Everything in that area is so full already." He sighs. "We drove around the island right after the festival to find a decent spot. It was bloody awful. I can't believe Finn did that for months before I came here. And I can't believe you did it, too, before you found that spot on Makena. Now I know why you were so territorial when I first parked next to you."

He takes a step toward me. We're inches apart now. His body is so close, I can feel the heat radiating from him, skimming my skin. Like a soft kiss, a whisper. I'd give anything to hug him, to touch my hand to his skin. But I can't. He's not mine. He almost was though.

I will the thought away. At least I can talk to him, at least I could apologize to him face-to-face. And now I can move on.

When I blink this time, no tears fall. "I'm really happy for you and Finn, Callum. I'm glad business is going well for you. It was really good seeing you."

I turn to walk back to my towel, but then he grabs my hand and I'm on fire. Even though it's just our palms touching, I feel the flames over every inch of my skin. That delicious warmth I've missed so much, that I've ached for every single day. Nothing feels as good. Not sunlight, not my favorite fuzzy blanket, not a warm ocean breeze. Nothing can compete with Callum's simmering warmth. It is bliss on my skin.

When I look up at Callum, my gaze latches on to those perfect hazel eyes. I couldn't break this stare if my life depended on it.

"I finally watched your video on Penelope's Instagram," Callum says. A swallow moves down his throat. "You love me?"

My breath catches, but I steady myself. "I do. So much. I'm sorry." I stop before my voice can break.

He looks at me like I've started barking instead of speaking. "Sorry for what?"

Pulling my hand out of his is the single hardest physical act I've had to complete in recent memory. But I have to. Because Callum isn't mine. He's someone else's. And if he were with me and some other woman confessed her feelings to him, I'd rage. It's not right what I'm doing, going on like this. I have to stop.

"I'm sorry that I'm doing this, that I'm saying this to you. It's not right."

"What do you mean it's not right?"

I clasp my hands behind my back to ensure I won't touch him again. "You're with someone else, Callum. That means I shouldn't be saying any of this to you."

When my head droops to the ground, he guides me back to his gaze with his thumb under my chin. "What are you talking about? I'm not with anyone."

I'm frowning so hard, the muscles in my forehead ache. "But the redhead. I saw you two together."

"The redhead? What redhead?"

"*Your* redhead, Callum. Or ginger—whatever you call redheads.

I—okay, listen. This is going to sound so creepy and crazy, but I drove to your condo the other day to try to work things out with you. I ran into Finn at the farmer's market, and he told me I should go see you and tell you how I feel. So I drove to your condo, but before I could even get out of my car, I saw you walk out the door with that gorgeous woman . . ."

I stop to catch my breath. Callum's hand falls from my face to rub his own. I can't tell if he's smiling or grimacing. "Oh. Her."

"Yeah." My reply is barely audible over the crashing waves. They're picking up in intensity now that it's evening.

When he lets out his next breath, he looks relieved. "Nikki, that was Rose. Our cousin. She was visiting us from Scotland."

"Oh." The word falls from my lips like a hiccup. "So . . . you're not with anyone?"

"I've not been with anyone since you, Nikki. I don't want anyone but you."

"But . . . but I thought you were so hurt . . . I thought you didn't want me—"

He grabs my hands in his again. Warmth simmers all over me. *Home.*

"I still wanted you, Nikki. I was just hurt. I needed time. But that didn't mean I ever stopped loving you."

"You still love me?"

He nods, pulling me closer by the hands. We're nearly chest to chest now. I have to tilt my head up just to keep looking at him.

"I've been miserable without you. Just ask Finn." Callum's chest heaves with a breath. "Last night he got back from a day trip with Grace, sat me down, and asked if I finally watched Penelope's video. I hadn't, of course, since I had been working, volunteering, and entertaining our cousin. So he pulled out his phone and played it for me. I was speechless. He said he was sick of me being an insufferable lump and I had no reason to be sad knowing you felt the same way about me, and that I needed to find you and make things right."

I tear up once more, but this time it's okay because I'm smiling. "Finn said that?"

"He did."

He wraps his arms around my waist. "So let's do this the right way. I want a proper relationship with you out in the open, for everyone to know and see. No more hiding."

"I want that too. I love you, Callum."

"I love you, Nikki."

He leans down to kiss me, and it's an explosion. Our tongues tangle and tease until we absolutely have to come up for air. I collapse into him, and he hugs me tight against his body.

Whistles and claps follow our very public display of affection. I tuck my face into Callum's chest, smiling.

"Half the people on this beach are naked, and this is what they stop and stare at?" Callum growls into my neck.

I lean back to look at him. "Maybe they're staring because we're the odd ones out."

He squints.

"You promised we'd go skinny-dipping together some day, remember? Today could be the day."

He leans his head back in a groan.

"Oh, don't tell me you're shy all of a sudden. You swim in your birthday suit regularly, Mr. James."

He raises an eyebrow. "So I'm Mr. James now?"

"Anything to get you naked as soon as possible."

He lets loose that melodic laugh, and I almost can't breathe. That sound. Good Lord, I missed it.

He tugs at the waistband of his maroon swim trunks. I catch his wrist, chuckling. "Wait, I was kidding. You don't actually have to get naked in front of all these people."

He doesn't even flinch at the prospect of being in his birthday suit on the beach in front of a hundred strangers. "I honestly don't care if there are zero or a million people around. I do this all the time. It doesn't bother me." He loosens the drawstring of his shorts.

A second later the fabric drops to the sand, and I indulge in a seconds-long ogle. Just as glorious as the first time I saw him dripping wet and completely nude on this exact beach months ago.

I can't help the wide smile that splits my face. I look up at him. His unflappable expression and tone have me hooked. Normally, I'd balk at the idea of being naked in front of strangers. But with Callum next to me, I'm at ease. Clothed or naked, I'm comfortable, as long as I'm with him.

I reach for the tie of my bikini top, but he stops me with a hand on my wrist. "You don't have to just because I'm doing it."

"I want to. Really. And look."

I point to the people around us, none of whom are paying attention to us anymore. Half of the people running into and out of the waves are naked. Half of the people lying on the beach are naked too.

"No one's even looking at us. Nudity isn't a novelty on this beach," I say. "But even if they do look, I don't care. No more hiding. I'm with you now, and I want everyone to see."

A wide smile stretches across Callum's face.

I toss my bikini top onto his rumpled shorts, then hook my thumbs through the waist of my bottoms, but then stop. "But I do have one condition."

"What's that?"

"You agree to cook with me at Travaasa Hana."

"Seriously?"

"Absolutely. I got that opportunity because of you. And I want to share it with you."

He grins, his hands falling to his hips. I can't help but run my gaze along the most flawlessly cut Adonis belt I've ever seen.

"Ah, so this is a pity request," he teases.

I grab the meaty part of his forearm. "Hardly. You forget I've cooked with you. I know how amazing you are in the kitchen. I loved working with you for that one service we had together. I don't want it to be our last."

He beams and says he accepts.

My hand falls from his body to the string of my bikini bottom. I tug it loose, and the fabric on one side falls away. "Besides, now that we're not working close to each other anymore, I want every opportunity to see you. Cooking together at Travaasa meets that requirement."

Callum takes the other string in his hand and pulls, freeing my lower half of all fabric. "So what will we whip up, Chef Nikki? Some British-Filipino fusion dish that will blow everyone away?"

"Maybe." Sliding my arms around his neck, I wag my eyebrows at him.

We stand completely naked, but I've never felt warmer. It's the heat of Callum's body, the reassurance of his words, the look in his eyes.

With his hands cupping my face, he leans in for another kiss. It's softer this time, but still teasing, still tantalizing, still full of feeling.

"What do you have in mind?" he says, his whisper skimming across my lips.

"Hmm. Let's see. We could do a mash-up of blood sausage and *dinuguan*, this really yummy dish made with pork blood."

Callum hugs me tight against him. "Sounds interesting."

"Or we could have a fry fest. Throw in a few *lumpia* or *turon* with a basket of fish-and-chips. Voilà. Fusion food like you've never tasted before."

Chuckling, he takes me by the hand and leads me to the water. He twists his head at me. "I don't care what we cook. I'll do anything as long as it's with you."

"Really? Even let me name all of Lemon's kittens ridiculously cute names?"

He mock frowns. "How ridiculously cute?"

"Like, so cute it hurts. I want to name the gray one Lulu, the white one Chowder, and the gray-and-white one Sushi."

His head falls back as he laughs. "Almost all food names. Brilliant." He tucks my hair behind my ear. "Yes to all of them."

Inside my chest swells. I wait until we're in waist-deep water, then press my body against his. His hands fall to my waist, and I wrap my legs around his lower half, letting the salt water current make me practically weightless.

A wave hits us, and we tumble under. But Callum's got me, his hold tight, secure. The biggest wave could hit us and I wouldn't budge. I'm in his arms, the safest place I could ever be. As I grip onto him, he pushes us above the surface and we take identical gasps of air. We open our eyes, sputtering and laughing at once.

I cough on a gulp of salt water that managed to seep into my mouth. With the back of my hand, I wipe my mouth, then kiss Callum once more.

"You taste salty," I say.

He laughs. "You do too."

"I love salt."

He squints down at me, the eager look in his eyes as bright as the sun against the horizon. "Do you?"

I nod. "I didn't used to."

In my head and in my heart, everything is different, and I'm overcome at the joy of it all. I press my shaky hands against Callum's warm, wet skin. I still. Instant calm. Instant home.

I lick my lips. Salt in the air, in the water, on me, on Callum. It dances on our tongues. As I breathe in, the delicious burn sets in. Still I want more.

Leaning up, I lick his lips.

"Funny how things change," he says.

He captures me in a kiss. Still so much salt. Still so good.

"It really is."

# Epilogue

*One Year Later*

What did I tell you about the walk-in?" Callum hovers over me, his toned chest lifting slightly with the gentle breath he takes.

"I don't remember." I take a step forward until we're chest to chest and squint up at him.

For a second all he does is frown, but then the corner of his mouth lifts up in the naughtiest smirk. "Liar."

I shrug, biting my lip to keep from cracking. We've played this game before so many times—in person, on the phone, over text. He always, always knows when I'm full of it. And I love it.

It's hell trying to keep a straight face when he calls me out. This little game we play is my favorite thing about the crazy early mornings we pull nowadays. I absolutely loathe the 6 a.m. daily wake-up time of this past month, but I love this part.

Even though we're standing in this restaurant walk-in refrigerator and the temperature is just a few degrees above freezing, the heat radiating from Callum's body warms mine. He wags his eyebrow, slides his arms around my waist, and I break. My face splits into the most obnoxious grin before I press a kiss to his mouth. He trails his luscious lips down the side of my neck.

"Okay, okay." The words fall from me in a breathy whimper. "Of course I remember you saying how important it is to label all of the produce in the walk-in. I just forgot."

Closing my eyes, I dig my hands into his thickly muscled shoulders. It's the only way I can keep myself steady against his mouth.

He runs his hands up my back, and underneath my tank top, leaving me with a gentle bite on the collarbone before leaning back to look at me.

"It's all right, petal. We all make mistakes."

I smack his shoulder in response to his playful admonition. And then he pulls me in for a kiss that's even filthier and sloppier than before.

Seconds later, the door flies open.

"Fucking hell," Finn groans.

Callum and I pull apart and turn to him, dual flustered grins on our faces.

Finn flashes an exasperated frown at us and rests his hands on his hips. His stance reminds me of a disappointed chaperone. It's like we're horny teenagers who got busted at the school dance by the principal.

"In the walk-in? Really? Do you know how unsanitary that is?"

Callum shakes his head. "Give us a bit more credit than that, Finn. All we did was kiss. We didn't touch a thing."

Finn holds his hand up. "I don't want to hear another word."

He grabs a tray of chopped veggies from the walk-in. Callum grabs a tray of sliced fish chunks and follows him out to the main prep area of the restaurant kitchen. I follow with containers of homemade tartar sauce and malt vinegar in hand.

"That's the trade-off, Finn," Callum says as he follows his brother out the back entrance of the restaurant to the Hungry Chaps food truck parked outside.

Finn climbs into the back of the truck, sets the tray of veggies on a shelf, and turns to grab the tray of fish from Callum and the sauces from me.

"You get to store and prep your food in our kitchen for free in exchange for seeing us snog every once in a while," Callum says.

Finn lets out a disgusted moan, exaggerated in volume for dramatic effect.

"Sorry, Finn," I say, fighting back a chuckle. "We'll try not to make out in the walk-in from now on."

He rolls his eyes in that boyish, good-natured way I've come to love so much. Finn is big on giving Callum and me a hard time for how lovey-dovey we are as a couple.

"I'll get used to it. Eventually." He jumps down from the back of the truck and shuts the door. "You two are so cute and happy all the time. It's bloody disgusting."

I beam. Cute and happy are an understatement. I twist my head to catch a look at the brick exterior that makes up the back of the restaurant—*our* restaurant. Six months ago, Callum and I took the plunge: we opened a British-Filipino fusion restaurant in Kihei featuring mash-ups of our customers' favorite dishes from each of our food trucks. He manages the finances, Mom does most of the cooking, and I run the front of the house and help with cooking whenever it's slammed. We settled on calling it Lulu's, after one of Lemon's kittens. It's been a hit with customers and tourists who heard about our unconventional love story online before vacationing on the island.

I look back at Finn. "I appreciate that. Almost as much as I appreciate how well you've been managing the food trucks."

You'd never guess Finn ever had any trouble running a food truck by the way he operates now. He still runs Hungry Chaps at the spot by the airport with an old restaurant coworker of his, but he's taken on managing Tiva's Filipina Kusina too. His girlfriend, Grace, cooks the food while Kyle Tokushige takes the orders. When it's busy, Penelope alternates helping at both trucks.

As an added bonus, Finn and Callum's parents have finally come around to supporting their sons' choice of career. They visited Maui this winter and saw firsthand how well business is doing and how content their boys are. I'd never seen Finn so happy as when his mom and dad told them how proud they were of them.

Finn flashes a bashful smile before running a hand through his shaggy blond locks. "Well, I just appreciate that your mum was willing to trust Grace to take over cooking duties at Tiva's when she started working at the restaurant."

I shake my head, remembering the panicked look on Mom's face when I suggested she join us at the restaurant and let Grace take her place at the truck. But then I assured her that Grace had spent her whole life cooking with her Filipino *lola* and would do the recipes justice.

"Once she tasted Grace's *pansit*, she was sold," I say. "And it helps that she still cooks at the truck once a week."

That once-a-week shift at the food truck was a nonnegotiable for Mom.

"My name is on the truck, *anak*," she said when we hammered out a schedule for Lulu's. "I have to cook there at least once a week. Otherwise it won't technically be Tiva's anymore."

I couldn't argue with her on that.

Finn rounds the corner to the driver's side door of his truck. "Your mum is a force of nature. The rest of us are just trying to keep up."

Callum and I share a laugh at how true that statement is. We wave good-bye as Finn pulls out of the parking lot, then head back to the kitchen to prep for the day's lunch and dinner service.

When we walk into the kitchen, Mom is standing at the center table, hacking away at heads of cabbage with a cleaver. She beams up at us. "Good morning, you two!"

I stop to give her a hug and a kiss on the cheek. Callum does the same.

"You're here early, Tiva," he says.

She waves her hand. "I couldn't sleep. I was too excited about this new recipe I want to try today."

She chats about frying up pork chops and sunny-side up eggs over white rice with brown gravy.

"Sounds bloody delicious. That would make a great menu special for today," Callum says as he stands at the far end of the metal table to crack endless eggs into a giant metal bowl. When he's done, I'll scramble them in a huge wok along with some bacon, peas, carrots, and white rice to make our signature fried rice.

I pat Mom on the back after bringing out more produce to chop from the walk-in. "How are things at Mrs. Tokushige's house?"

"Oh, you know how moving goes. Empty boxes everywhere. I hope Nora and Nigel won't mind the mess when they come visit in a few weeks."

Three months ago, our families did a home shuffle for the record books. Callum moved out of his condo to live with me, and Grace moved in with Finn. Mom moved into the guest bedroom of Mrs. Tokushige's giant beach house in Wailea. Not only did we blend our work lives, but our home lives are intertwined now too.

Mom moving out was a hard sell for me at first, given my control freak tendencies when it comes to her. But she was so excited when Mrs. Tokushige suggested it to her. They're both widows and spend most of their free time together anyway. Mom said it would be like her younger years, when she roomed with her best girlfriends. But instead of spending their days clubbing and drinking and sleeping in, Mom and Mrs. Tokushige are models of the active senior lifestyle. They wake up early every morning for a three-mile power walk on the beach before Mom heads to work. When she comes home, they play cards or mahjong, go to book club, have movie nights, and cook together.

I couldn't help but support the idea when I saw how happy it made her. And seeing her almost every day at the restaurant helps. We're still connected and close as ever, even though we don't live together anymore.

"And how does Sushi like living at Mrs. Tokushige's?" Callum asks.

"Oh, he loves it." Mom laughs as she tells us that he spends his days napping in the sun, then extensively bathing himself in the evening before gorging on food and falling asleep.

"That sounds exactly like how Chowder spends his days at Grace and Finn's," Callum says.

Mom's pointed gaze passes between Callum and me. "How about you two? Enjoying the condo . . . all by yourselves?"

I fight off a cringe. Now I know how it must feel when Finn catches Callum and me making out, because I can barely handle her *subtle* hint for a grandbaby.

Callum's face burns red as he studies the eggs he's cracking.

I hold up my left hand at her. The shiny diamond on my ring finger glistens under the kitchen lights. "One step at a time, Mom. We've only been engaged for a month. We haven't even planned the wedding yet."

Mom shrugs, her gaze fixed on the cutting board while she

speaks to me. "An adorable baby would be the best wedding gift to yourselves, don't you think?"

Callum booms out a laugh while I roll my eyes. As annoying as Mom's good-natured prodding for a baby is, it doesn't come close to bursting my bliss bubble. I recall that perfect night when Callum proposed to me. He took me to dinner at Mama's Fish House in Paia, then asked if I'd be up for a stroll along Baldwin Beach at sunset. Hand in hand, he walked me all the way down to the end of the beach, away from the crowds, just as the sun was dipping below the ocean horizon. And then he stopped, dropped down to one knee, and pulled out a black velvet box from his pocket. Inside was the dazzling square diamond from my mom's engagement ring, set in a brand-new white gold band.

I couldn't speak when I saw him on one knee, his eyes glistening before he could even get out the words I knew he would say. All I could do was cover my mouth with my hands to keep my sobs of joy under control.

"I already asked your mum, and she gave me her blessing," he said, his voice shaky. "I wanted . . . I wanted to ask you to marry me here because this is where you dad is and I wanted him to be part of it too."

I nodded yes before he could even get out the words. Because it was the most perfect, most thoughtful moment Callum could ever dream up. And he did it for me. And I knew without a doubt I wanted to spend forever with him.

"I'm just saying, *anak*." Mom's voice pulls me back to the present. "You two would make the cutest babies. You're so beautiful." She nods at Callum. "And you're so handsome. They would be the best-looking little ones. And free babysitting from me and Mrs. Tokushige whenever you want."

I walk over and hug her from behind. "Promise we'll give you a grandbaby someday," I say. "But right now, we have to finish prepping so Callum and I can run back to the condo and film our latest episode for Chic TV today before we open."

She turns around excitedly to face me. "Oh, that's right!" She pats my hand. "You two go on home and do that. I've got everything under control here."

We thank her and promise to be back before eleven when we open. When we climb in the car, I check my watch. "It's just past seven right now, so that means we've got a little over three hours to film how to prep and cook chicken *adobo* wings for this episode."

The commercial Mom and I filmed for Chic TV was a hit. Viewers loved it so much that Chic offered us a contract to film a dozen cooking videos to feature on their website this year. The only catch is that we have to film them all this month so the network can edit them and release them according to their strict production schedule. It means we're waking up early every morning this month to prep and film before working our regular shifts at the restaurant. Last episode Mom and I cooked together, but with how busy the restaurant has been, I'm doing today's shoot on my own. Sometimes when Mom doesn't feel like being on camera, I'll make Callum film with me. It's a hectic schedule to keep, but the exposure is awesome. We get customers from all over raving about our webisodes.

But it's even better because it's one more thing Callum and I can do together.

He starts the engine and makes the quick drive back to the condo. "Don't forget, we've got to plan the menu for our next dinner service at Travaasa in a couple of weeks."

I set a reminder in my phone.

"Ted will have my head if we forget him in the midst of all this other stuff we've got going on," Callum says.

"No way would I ever forget Ted. He gave me my first big break, and I plan to cook for him until he gets sick of me."

"That won't be happening anytime soon, petal. The guests at the resort love the dinners we serve. There hasn't been an empty table on any of the nights we've hosted."

Callum parks the car and shuts the engine off. He unbuckles his seat belt and leans over to kiss me. "I can't believe I get to marry a famous chef."

I nibble his bottom lip. "Believe it."

He chuckles and we climb out of the car. Lulu scampers up to us and rubs against our legs the moment we walk into the condo. Lemon looks up from her sitting spot on the arm of the couch, then goes back to napping. Callum scoops Lulu up and greets her with scratches under the chin.

I turn around and nearly "aww" out loud at the adorable sight of sexy, muscular, masculine Callum cuddling our cat.

"You need to stop taunting me like that," I say, pressing myself into him.

"Taunting you? How?"

He looks genuinely confused, and it makes my heart squeeze. He still has no idea just how sexy he is on the inside and out. And it makes me crazy in the best way.

He sets Lulu back down on the floor and pulls me into his arms.

"You're just . . . I'm so lucky you're mine," I say.

We partake in another filthy, sloppy kiss, only this time nothing interrupts us. When we finally stop to breathe, he slowly peels his mouth from mine.

"No one on earth is luckier than me," he says.

Inside I'm burning, which translates to some hard-core blushing on the outside. He cups my cheek with his hand.

"Let's push pause on all this hot flattery talk and pick back up later," I say. "We've got a camera crew coming over."

Callum looks up from his laptop to me. "Naomi from Chic TV said our last cooking video was a hit. More than a thousand views the first morning it was up."

He sets the laptop on the coffee table, then swipes up the remote control and flips on the TV.

I plop down next to him while holding a pink champagne bottle. "I think we deserve something special to drink for that."

It's nine at night, which means with work and filming, we've been going nonstop for fifteen hours. Now it's time to unwind with our favorite pastime: sipping champagne while watching reruns of *The Office*.

I hand him the bottle. "So you're going with the American version tonight. Interesting."

He smiles at my teasing tone before tapping his bottle against mine. We take a sip at the same time.

"It's grown on me," he says.

We cuddle together, silent and content as we watch. Soon Lemon walks across the couch to his lap. He scratches under her chin.

"Just like old times," I say, thinking back to our first "pink champagne while watching *The Office*" date when we were hooking up in secret.

Callum twists his head to look at me and wraps his arm around me, pulling me closer. "This is better than old times," he says.

"Really?"

He nods before slinking his hand over mine, then thumbs the diamond of my ring. "It is. We're official now. You're my fiancée and

I can be affectionate with you whenever I want. We live together, which means we can do this whenever we want."

Lulu lets out a squeaky yawn from the other end of the couch.

"And we have double the number of cats we used to, so this is definitely a million times better," I say.

He lets out a laugh that spooks both Lemon and Lulu from the couch. They scurry down the hall.

Again he pulls me into a kiss that's so powerful and intoxicating, it leaves me dizzy. When his hazel-green eyes lock with mine, I feel like I'm free-falling into an abyss I never, ever want to climb out of.

"I love everything about this," he says, his voice that beautiful mix of a growl and a whisper.

"Me too," I whisper, gazing up at him.

I was wrong before when I said that our playful early mornings were my favorite. Everything I do with Callum is my favorite.

I burrow closer against his body, giddy that I get to call Callum James mine forever. "You. This. Everything. It's all I ever wanted. You make me the happiest."

My throat squeezes as I say the last word. But the ache is welcome. It's every emotion I feel for Callum pulsing inside of me.

He squeezes me tighter, and I sigh in satisfaction.

"Petal," he says, his own voice full of emotion. "You stole the words right out of my mouth."

# Acknowledgments

The tough part about writing acknowledgments is that words are never enough to express just how thankful I am to everyone who helped make this book possible. But words are all I have, so I'll give it a try!

Thank you, Lexi Banner. You are more than a beta reader; you are a superhuman alpha reader whose feedback helps take my early drafts from dumpster fire to readable manuscript. I heart you.

To Skye McDonald, a million thanks (and glasses of whiskey) are owed to you for trudging through that messy early draft. All the red lipstick kisses to you, lady.

Stefanie Simpson, thank you for your friendship and support. I was so unsure about this story, but your feedback gave me confidence. I can never thank you enough for that.

D. F. Bowstrong, thanks for helping Callum sound like a real person and not a caricature. I bloody owe you one.

Thank you, J. L. Peridot, for your insight and your lovely words. They motivated me so much.

Thank you to the best agent on the planet, Sarah Younger (and your amazing interns!), for your never-ending support.

Thank you to my editor, Sarah Blumenstock, for helping make

*Simmer Down* into the story it is today (and for thinking of that killer title).

To my husband, thank you for being my biggest cheerleader and believing in me always. I'm lucky to have you.

To my friends and family, thank you for loving me and being proud of me.

Thank you, Mom, for the memory of writing this book while I stayed with you. That time was a gift and I'll cherish it forever. I hope I did Maui justice for you.

And last but never, ever least, thanks to all of you who bought and read this book. It means everything to me that you enjoy reading my words.

Photo by Daniel Muller

**Sarah Smith** is a copywriter turned author who wants to make the world a lovelier place, one kissing story at a time. Her love of romance began when she was eight and she discovered her auntie's stash of romance novels. She's been hooked ever since. When she's not writing, you can find her hiking, eating chocolate, and perfecting her *lumpia* recipe. She lives in Bend, Oregon, with her husband and her adorable cat, Salem.

CONNECT ONLINE

---

SarahSmithBooks.com

AuthorSarahS

AuthorSarahS